Diva Diaries

Diva Diaries

Janine A. Morris

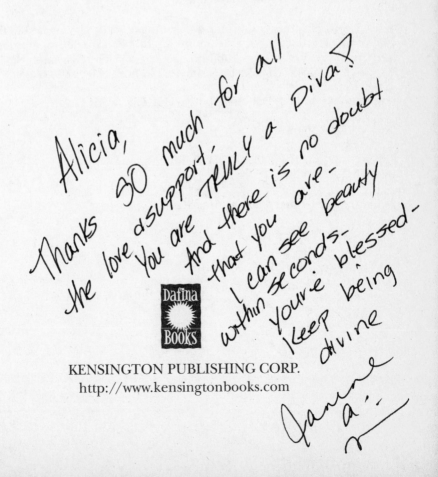

Alicia,
Thanks so much for all
the love & support.
You are TRULY a Diva!
And there is no doubt
that you are —
I can see beauty
within seconds —
you're blessed —
Keep being
divine
Janine A.

Dafina
Books

KENSINGTON PUBLISHING CORP.
http://www.kensingtonbooks.com

DAFINA BOOKS are published by

Kensington Publishing Corp.
850 Third Avenue
New York, NY 10022

All Kensington titles, imprints and distributed lines are available at special quantity discounts for bulk purchases for sales promotion, premiums, fund-raising, educational or institutional use.

Special book excerpts or customized printings can also be created to fit specific needs. For details, write or phone the office of the Kensington Special Sales Manager: Kensington Publishing Corp., 850 Third Avenue, New York, NY 10022. Attn. Special Sales Department. Phone: 1-800-221-2647.

Dafina Books and the Dafina logo Reg. U.S. Pat. & TM Off.

ISBN 0-7582-1304-2

First Kensington Trade Paperback Printing: July 2006
10 9 8 7 6 5 4 3 2 1

Printed in the United States of America

I dedicate this first and foremost to my parents!
Mom, the source of my strength—you are truly a phenomenal woman.
Dad, my backbone and inspiration, I will always be your little girl.
My brother, who is my protector and friend,
My sister, my other half—it's automatic!
My nieces and nephews, Tylah, Leila and Hamilton.
My twin brother who may have left me in the flesh,
but whose spirit keeps me striving every day.
You are my angel.

My girlfriends Sytieya, Derica, Nicole, Rene and Ebony—
thanks for all the listening . . .
And to Ahmad—my love and my best friend—"You Are My Air."
"Why can't your heart do what your mind tells it?"

ACKNOWLEDGMENTS

First and foremost, I want to thank God. I thank you for allowing me to obtain my dreams, and for all your blesisngs. I thank you for loving me regardless of anything. I am so greateful for all that you do in my life.

I want to start by thanking Dafina Books for helping me make a dream come true. Karen Thomas and Nicole Bruce, thanks for all the patience through my annoying and stressful journey. Barbara Bennett, thanks for all the advice and inspiration with my law school journey. You have been an angel to me through all of this.

I must thank Frank Iemmiti for believing in me and my possibilities from the very start. Although I was still a college kid, you stuck with me, and gave me opportunities and allowed me to learn and grow hands on. I have so much to be thankful to you for. You're still one of the best people I've ever worked for or with, and I love you for all that you've done. Andrew Mosko, you too were there from the start, when these ladies were just a thought—smile. Thanks for your skills that helped bring the story to life, which helped it be what it is today.

I also want to thank my radio family. Envy, the People's choice, my real buddy, I love ya, and I wish you nothing but blessings. Ebro, for being my big brother in the business. Tracy Cloherty, thanks for being my friend and a mentor. Barry "Big" Mayo, John Dimick, Angie Mar, the Voice of New York, I respect you for being such a strong talented female. Enuff, thanks for always supporting me. Kay Slay—holding you down always. Shaila, thanks for never doubting me. Miss Info, thanks "little bit." Fatman Scoop, love ya with your ignorant self. Funkmaster Flex, the Franchise, you're a big reason why I'm still in this game. Bugsy, all those hours of advice is more appreciated than you know. Mister Cee, Absolut, since Forest Hills '97. Jazzy, Dennis, Kulture, Bobby Konders, Jabba, Cocoa, La La, thanks Girl. Clue— "Queens run this, ask Russell Simmons." Mega, Cipha—don't get me gassed. Raqiyah, Ralph McDaniels, Jonesy, Tay, Rod, Camilo, Julie Gustines, Kesha Monk, Lenny Green, keeping the ladies of the tri-state feeling sexy. Michael Baisden, thanks for the advice. Toya Beasley, you're an inspiration for black females, keep me in your prayers. Alex Cameron, a fellow author and marketing guru, thanks. Tricia Clarke, I can't thank you enough, many blessings to you and your fiancé. Ruben, the Bronx, Donyshia Benjamin, Patricia Robinson—a real Scorpio diva at her best. Nikki Smith, you know what it is, and thanks for everything. Gwynet Cowan and Randi Hatchel—my girls; and everyone else at Emmis . . . thanks for everything and I love you.

I want to thank Alicia McFarlane and Lisa Grant, my friends and classmates. I don't know what I would do without you sometimes. We're going to get through this law school thing ladies—and well. Some people God put in your life for a reason, and I know you two are two of those people.

Ebony, thanks for being there all those years. "We got it going on . . ." Tenille, happy to know there are still some "good girls" left, smile. Nelcida, you have a blessed inside and out. My girls Suky, Sister, Rene, and Munchkin, our ladies nights out are the highlights of my post college years. You were the inspiration and strength for this book. The power of friendship is amazing. When we just can't take it anymore, any spot in the city that can handle six loud emotional women is all we need, because we already have each other. "Miami here we come."
Speedy Claxton, I love you, too, and thanks for everything, especially all the spontaneous nights out when I needed them most—just never forget—Cerebellum.

"Mommy" Meggett, thanks for the advice and input, and all the love you have showed me from day one.

Ahmad, saying thank you isn't enough. You already know that I love you and appreciate you for everything that you do. When I had to stay on my computer for days at a time, you made sure I had food and water . . . and Pina Coladas (smile). When times got rough you made them easy. When I was feeling overwhelmed you reminded me I could do it. You are truly my joy. I am blessed to have you in my life. There isn't a thing that I wouldn't do for you, and I know you are here for me as you always have been. "This is like something from a fairy tale."—"I'm in this for the long haul." Edwyn, I love you with all my heart. B.F.F.

Last but surely not least, thanks to my family for tolerating me. Mommy for holding me down, and setting an example for me of what a black woman should be. Tasha for being my other half and a shoulder that I can always count on. I couldn't love you enough TT, and thanks for the creative jumps when I was fried; JR for allowing me to grow up knowing I was safe from harm, and always being there. Dad for allowing me to know what to expect from a real man, I love you, Pop. No matter how old I get, I'll always be daddy's little girl. To my entire 100+ Morris/Young family—thanks for the support. I love you all.

1

Fool Me Twice,
Shame on Me

"I am such a fool—I am getting too old for this crap," Dakota said to herself as she sat on the edge of her king-size bed. Her bed was covered in peach silk sheets, with two scented candles burning on both nightstands. The lights were dim all throughout her condo, and her Bose stereo in the bedroom was quietly playing Avant's latest album. Right outside her building was the busy traffic and chaos of midtown Manhattan, but on the inside of 4D was a romantic getaway.

Dakota had already spent thirty years on this earth, but there were times she felt like she hadn't learned a thing. It still amazed her how, with all the street smarts she had from her years of growing up in Brooklyn, she was able to make her way through life and through corporate America, but she couldn't seem to prevent nights like these.

She had made her way from her bedroom into the living room, attempting not to focus on her rising anger. She hit PLAY on her TiVo box, and her television began playing back her recorded episode of *Judge Judy*. After about twenty minutes, she had stopped paying attention to what the evidence was from the plaintiff and her mind started to wander again. She began to analyze what was happening on yet another Friday night.

"I can't believe I am lying here alone in this expensive lingerie, freezing my butt off, and God knows where he is or who he is with," she murmured.

A dozen thoughts ran through her head as she slowly felt herself losing any bit of romantic or sexy vibes she had left in her body. The more emotional she got, the more she knew it was only minutes before she would completely lose it and leave Tony a nasty message on his answering machine. She would have told him to his face, but he was m.i.a. and wasn't answering his house or cell phone. He was supposed to be at her place at 9:00, and it was now 11:30, and not even a simple call was made to inform her of any change of plans.

Maybe he fell asleep, maybe he had a car accident, maybe something really urgent came up, maybe he is on his way and his cell battery is dead. Maybe, maybe, shmaybe. She knew he was just fine and he was just being a man. She was tired of making excuses for him, to herself, to her friends; she had to fill in his blanks constantly. It was just her way of delaying having to face the reality that he was up to no good. She couldn't give him the benefit of the doubt, because he didn't deserve it. She had done that early in the relationship, the first few times he pulled something like this, but at this point she knew from experience.

She sat there and envisioned just how the night was going to play out, how it would happen and what he would say and do. He would eventually call or show up and actually almost pretend like nothing was really wrong. He would just hope his sorry excuse would be enough, or at least his sorry attempt at apologizing and seduction. On nights when she just wanted not to waste her preparation for the night, she would just let it go, but on other nights, when her self-pride was shaking its head at her, she would make a big deal out of it.

Some nights she would call up her girls to vent, and try to get some sense talked into her head. But this relationship was becoming way too dysfunctional, and quite honestly, Dakota was not in the mood to face that. At least not tonight, not as she sat in her room in a teal-and-pink Fredericks of Hollywood negligee. Besides, she knew what they would say, or at least what they would think, even if they didn't tell her. She knew so well because she knew what she would think when she heard a story from one of her female counterparts getting played by her man. Even when the girl is in denial, it's not hard to tell when she is getting played. Dakota was a realist—she knew her man was up to no good.

Dakota didn't know if she was more frustrated with herself or with men, because before Tony, the last guy she let into her heart was her college sweetheart, Chris, who turned out to be a real barking dog.

She spent years trying to work through stuff with him and forgive him for his infidelities. Once she realized he was just taking advantage of her obvious fear to let go of him and be alone, she promised herself she would never be that way with any man again. She had convinced herself no man was worth losing her self-respect, and she wasn't taking any nonsense from any of them. She had decided she would much rather greet them, freak them, fuck them, then duck them. She preferred that over getting all caught up in fairy-tale land. In a sense, she adapted to the ways of men; she wasn't looking for a serious commitment and wasn't trying to make one. So, Tony was the first one to break through some of that wall in a long time. Still, she had made all of these rules for herself about things she wouldn't accept, but once again, love and emotions found her back in the same predicament. Dealing with the same excuses, different man . . . or, better yet . . . same shit, different dog.

Tony was probably the worst man that she could have let her guard down for, too. In no time, she allowed good sex to turn into feelings she had no business having. Tony wasn't just a professional athlete who was often traveling—he had another woman in his life. Dakota heard at some point they were engaged, but he told her differently. Either way, she was aware there was a woman out there whom he kept protected. He would tell Dakota he was only with this girl for the sake of their child and that he didn't love her. Of course, he loved Dakota and wanted to be with her—at least that's what he said. Whenever Dakota would complain or catch him in a lie, he would say *I just ask that you be patient with me and understand my lifestyle.*

Dakota was naive when she was in love—that's why she tried her best not to feel that way. It wasn't worth the headache or heartache. Even as naive as she could be, she could usually see through Tony's b.s. Unfortunately, she really wanted to believe him. He was just the kind of guy that Dakota felt was a match for her. Successful, handsome, charismatic, and he had great taste. If she settled down, she wanted it to be with him, if she could only get him to do it. So she sat here on nights like this, trying to show him what she had to offer. Except he was nowhere to be found.

It was now about midnight, and Dakota broke down and called her girlfriend Chrasey. Just sitting there watching television was not making her feel any better; she was leaving room for a variety of angry thoughts to fill her head. She needed some type of human contact.

"Dakota, leave his behind alone . . . stop putting yourself through this . . . I don't even know why you wait on him . . . You know how it goes—he fooled you once, it was shame on him. But now he *keeps* fooling you—shame on you," Chrasey rambled on as soon as she heard Tony was pulling one of his disappearing acts.

See, this is exactly what I didn't need right now, Dakota thought to herself. It wasn't that she wanted to be in denial, but she wanted to try to keep from getting upset, and letting negative opinions cloud her thoughts. Besides, every female knows we love our girls until they are talking junk or telling us to leave our man. Then it's a totally different situation. It was moments like these when she understood how some women say they don't have female friends. She could see how jealousy, envy, deceit, and all those things could make females distrust one another. She could see how a female telling you your man who deep down you're hoping you can share a white picket fence with, ain't worth a darn could make a chick choose the man over the friend. Lucky for Chrasey, that was not the case for Dakota. She and Chrasey, along with their third amigo, Jordan, had been friends since college and they were almost like sisters. Of course, most close friends say that, but these three came the closest to that bond. Most friends say that until they have some really big fight, and then they can't bring themselves to put it behind them. Or better yet, that's just the case until they grow apart, or jealousy and competition or another female trait gets the best of them and they decide they are too grown up for that play-sister crap. These three, though, had been through over a decade of real sisterhood, fights included. Not the little fights, either— big fights, fights most people don't make up from—but in the midst of those fights, if one was going through something like a true sister, the others would still be there for her. So, when Chrasey or Jordan told her something, she knew it was from the heart and one of the reasons she hated listening. The truth can hurt. So she sat there and listened to Chrasey, and she knew deep down that she was right; she was breaking all of her own rules and putting up with even more than she did from Chris.

"Chrasey, it's just that when things are good, they are so good. Then he goes and pulls something like this and messes it all up."

"I know, 'Kota . . . and if it was the first or second time, I would tell you you're overreacting. But he does this way too often—you can never depend on him. And let me guess—you got all sexy and ready for him, didn't you?"

"Girl . . . my favorite teal-and-pink teddy I had been waiting to wear," Dakota responded. They both giggled.

"Look, 'Kota . . . you just need to put your foot down. Any time you guys have plans, he feels no obligation to keep them or even call you to cancel. Each time he apologizes, and you step back out there and expect him not to do it again, there is disappointment after disappointment. It's just out of hand." As if she was more upset than Dakota, Chrasey rambled on. "Showing up hours late without even calling—you don't even do that to a hooker, let alone someone you care about. You need to let him go or get serious and let him know that this is the last time. If he does it again, you're through. I know you two don't have a commitment, and deep down you know there may be some side pieces somewhere, but he has to know he can't take you for a fool."

"Yeah, you're right. When he does show up, I am going to have a long talk with him."

After about another ten minutes, Dakota got off the phone and jumped under the covers. After ten seconds on her plush peach pillow, the tears began to roll down her cheeks. She didn't want to cry. What if he showed up right now? She would look terrible, with bloodshot eyes and a runny nose, and on top of that she was messing up her silk pillow covers. She realized, though, she wasn't crying because of what Tony was probably out there doing, but because of what Chrasey had said. Just hearing that made her feel really low.

When it came to Tony, she could barely understand herself. It wasn't like Dakota wasn't well put together. Dakota was in great shape for her age. She was five-feet-five, 125 pounds, with just enough titties and ass—not too much and not too little. She had a pretty, dark-chocolate complexion, with off-black long hair reaching about a quarter of the way down her back, and brown eyes. Her high cheekbones brought character to her face, but her full lips and slanted eyes were what actually made Dakota beautiful. However, Ms. Dakota Watkins wasn't all looks—she had brains, too. She was the top publicist at her PR firm, and the youngest female on her level. She had several high-profile clients, was making over $95,000 a year, had a nicely furnished loft in a chic area of Manhattan, drove a 2004 purple BMW, and had what would be considered a great life. Despite all that she had accomplished, her love life overall was still chaotic.

Here she was, letting Tony ruin another Friday night for her. Regardless of how many times she asked herself why, the only answer she could come up with was because she allowed it. Feeling disgusted with herself, for lying in an empty bed wearing lingerie, she finally got up and threw on an oversized night shirt. She took her stereo remote control and hit PLAY. Keisha Coles's single, "I Just Want It to Be Over," seeped from her Bose wave speakers as she wrapped her hair and got ready for bed. She had just put her Razac Perfect for Perms hair crème away and finished tying a scarf on her head when her phone rang. She wasn't sure if it was Chrasey calling back, or Tony finally calling.

"Hello." Dakota tried to use her sexy-yet-upset voice.

"Hey, miss," a male voice responded from the other end of the phone.

"Who is this?"

"It's David—you busy?"

David was this "guy friend" of hers. They had been cool for some time; they had worked together a few years ago and never broke contact. A few years back, they'd had a few "indiscretions" between them, but they now had one of those "mature friendships."

After a few minutes of conversation, he was able to hear in her voice that she wasn't at her best and offered to come over and cheer her up. She was hesitant at first, but then he offered to come make a late-night meal. Full of emotion, anger, and lust, she accepted his offer. Fully aware that she had no clue if Tony was going to just pop up eventually or not, she left her night shirt on, combed her hair back down, put on some lip gloss, and waited to see who would arrive first.

2

About That Time

The Burken antique clock on the wall read 6:30 P.M., and Jordan was sitting at her black marble desk trying to finish up a project that she had given a Monday morning deadline. She was quickly scanning over the forms and notes, highlighting and marking comments down as she went along. She usually took more time with her cases, but time had flown and she couldn't pull a late-nighter, not tonight.

It was Friday, and the day before her six-year wedding anniversary. Her husband had called about three hours earlier and informed her that he had a special night planned to start off their romantic weekend. He told her to make sure she was home no later than 9:30, which at that time was giving her more than enough time to finish up, so she'd promised she would.

It was still only 6:45, and she knew she had time, but she wanted to get home even earlier to take a shower and change clothes and still be ready by 9:30 instead of just stumbling through the door at 9:00 or so. With that in mind, she finished reviewing the documents and started packing up for the evening. She locked her office door and walked down the hall and placed the documents in her partner's in-box.

Already feeling a sense of relief about starting her weekend, and this was a special one that she had been looking forward to for weeks, she began to walk happily toward the elevator. Just as she went to press the DOWN button, she heard a voice call her name. She turned around to find her paralegal, Jackie, standing in the hallway with a file in her hand.

"Have a good evening, Mrs. Miller. I just wanted to make sure you remembered the Martinez case is first thing Monday morning."

Jordan's shoulders dropped, "Oh, my goodness. I forgot Jayon asked me to work on that for him. What time are we due in court?" she asked.

"At 9:30 A.M.," Jackie said in her sorry-to-be-the-one-to-break-it-to-you tone.

"Damn," Jordan blurted.

She had spent all that time with that other case, when she could have been working on this one and been finished. The other case's court date wasn't until Tuesday; she had marked the deadline for Monday so she would be ahead of the game. So to remember there was actually something on Monday that she was behind on, and that now she had to stay to do, just ruined her whole happy mood.

Jordan looked at her watch and realized she could afford to spend another hour or so at the office and still get home in time for Omar's plans.

"OK. Thanks so much. Are you staying late tonight?" Jordan said.

"I will be here for about another half an hour," Jackie replied.

"OK, great. Is that the Martinez file in your hand?"

"Yes, it is," Jackie said as she handed her the file.

"Thanks—can you pull the other miscellaneous file for the case from Jayon's office and bring it to me."

"Sure," Jackie replied in her chipper tone.

Jordan walked back down the hall to her office, unlocked the door, placed her briefcase and other belongings in the chair by the door, and plopped into her chair. She had already calculated that she would not stay past 8:00 P.M., regardless of what wasn't completed. Normally she would have just taken it home, but she knew she would be celebrating all weekend and probably wouldn't get to any work. Besides, all she had to do was type up an outline for their appearance on Monday. It wasn't the trial, it was just some pretrial procedures. The case was important, so they wanted to be prepared, but Jordan had other priorities as well. She was fully aware that her extensive workload was keeping her away from her happy home, and she had been struggling to balance the two. Omar had dropped their son off at his mother's, and Jordan really wanted the time alone with her husband; it wasn't often they had that. So, determined to get her work done quickly, she started scrambling through the file, sorting what she needed to type up her outline and notes for the case.

Next thing she knew, Jordan looked up at the clock; it was already 8:30. She had no idea the time had gone by so fast. She found herself deep into the case and must have gotten carried away. Once she realized the time, she immediately panicked. She had decided to bring it home with her and sneak some time away to tend to it, but she remembered her colleague Jayon would need the file.

She picked up the phone to call Omar, and as she went to dial the number, she heard a voice.

"Hello."

"Hello," she replied.

"Hi, it's me, Jayon."

"Oh, I was just trying to dial out to make a phone call to Omar."

"Oh, OK. I just got back into the office and wanted to see if you were still here. Do you want to go over some last-minute things on the Martinez case? We have court Monday morning."

"I know, Jayon—I just spent the last couple of hours reviewing all our notes and preparing. Where have you been?"

"I went out with some clients to have a few drinks," he responded.

"I am coming down to your office in a few seconds to wrap this up—just let me make this call," Jordan responded.

Jayon was Jordan's colleague and one of her closest friends since undergrad. Both of them ended up going back to graduate school at the same time—Jordan went to law school, and Jayon went for his MBA in accounting. A few years out of law school, Jordan and one of her classmates, Elizabeth, from Columbia University, decided to start a law firm together. At that same time, Jayon wanted to open a private accounting office, and was looking for office space. Jordan found an office building in midtown that was leasing a floor. It was in a great building, and at a fair price. It was too good to be true, so the three of them decided to lease the space together to make better use of it. It worked out pretty well, because they had all become a great help to each other. Elizabeth's specialty was tax and labor law, so she and Jayon were always able to assist each other with different clients and cases. Jordan specialized in entertainment law, but with some of the clients, Jayon would assist her as well and vice versa. This was also their way to have some teamwork despite their busy work schedules. After all, the door did say MILLER, MESSING, & MITCHELL.

Jordan gathered all that she had been working on and put it back in the file. She placed it in her briefcase, and picked up all of her things from the chair and headed down the hall to Jayon's office. She locked up her office, just figuring she would leave straight from his.

She suddenly remembered to call Omar. She ran back in her office and quickly dialed the number. She called the house and there was no answer. The answering machine picked up and she left a message.

"Hey, baby. It's 8:45, and I know I am supposed to be home by 9:30. I'm running a little late. I just have to work on some loose ends with Jayon for a case we have first thing Monday morning. I am so sorry . . . I love you . . . I won't be too late—I should be there by 10:00. Call me if you need me."

She hung up, locked the door, and walked down the hall to Jayon's office. She placed her briefcase on his couch and sat across from him.

"Is Jackie still here?" he asked.

"I don't think so."

"Oh, so it's just the two of us. Cool. Do you want to order some dinner?"

"Jayon, I can't stay. It's me and Omar's anniversary, and he is actually waiting on me at home now."

"Oh, OK. So, don't let me keep you. Maybe we can do this Monday morning."

"Showtime is 9:30 in the morning—we won't have much time. Real quickly, let's just take a few minutes to get on the same page for Monday."

Jordan felt slightly uncomfortable speaking of her and Omar's anniversary, because Jayon's fiancée had called their engagement off a couple of months earlier. He had been going through a lot, which was another one of the reasons he'd asked for Jordan's help on this case. He'd fallen behind on a lot of his work, and was kind of just getting himself back together.

Quickly getting on the same page took longer than expected, and about forty-five minutes later, Jordan was at the copy machine making a copy of her notes for Jayon. She glanced up at the clock over the water cooler—it said 10:00.

"Damn," she said out loud to herself. She knew Omar was at home waiting for her, probably pissed off.

She rushed back toward Jayon's office. "Here are my notes . . . I gotta go . . . I'll see you at 8:00 A.M. at the courthouse," Jordan said hastily as she scurried into the office and toward his desk.

As she leaned over to place the notes on his desk, he reached for her hand.

"Don't go yet, Jordan," he said, looking her straight in her eyes. "Can you stay and keep me company for a little while longer?"

As Jordan pulled her hand away, her heart started to beat so fast she thought even he could hear it.

"Jayon, I told you Omar has plans for us tonight. I'm sorry."

Jayon rose from his seat and began to walk around his desk toward Jordan. She backed away slightly from his desk, feeling a sense of shock at what she assumed was happening.

As he approached her, he reached for her hand once again. "Jordan, I really need you tonight. Can you just stay a little bit longer?"

Trying to pretend she did not pick up on the seductive vibe, Jordan kept her hands in his and said, "Is everything OK? Do you want to talk?" She thought this might defuse the situation—she always believed when in an awkward situation, you should act like you don't notice.

Her plan didn't work. Jayon pulled her closer. "I just want you to be here with me tonight."

Before Jordan could register her next thought, Jayon had leaned down and begun to kiss her lips. As the little voice inside of her screamed, Jordan jerked and tried to back away. Determined, his lips continued to attempt to connect with hers.

Jordan placed her hand on his chest to keep him at a distance. With a sense of control, she finally spoke. "Jayon. What are you doing?"

He covered her hand with his on his chest. "Jordan, I know this is our workplace, but what happens here doesn't have to interfere with anything."

She took her hand away and walked toward the chair that had her belongings in it. As she picked up her stuff, she turned back around and looked at him. Disappointed, she said, "I'm not sure what you mean by 'what happens here.' I thought we had a friendship—and a company."

He just looked at her.

"Jayon—what are you thinking? We're not in college, we are adults and I'm married. I know you have been drinking, and I don't know if this has to do with Dawn breaking up with you, but you can't do this. To be honest, I'm disappointed in you," she said as she stood by the door.

Despite her comment, he continued, "This has nothing to do with Dawn or how much I've had to drink—this has everything to do with me and you," he said.

"Well, Jayon, my *husband* is at home waiting for me and I must go," Jordan said and went to walk through the door.

"Can we talk about this later, Jordan?," he said, seeming worried that she was upset.

Without looking back at him, she said in an aggravated tone, "I guess we will talk later."

3

Friend or Foe?

She opened the back passenger door to her midnight black 2005 BMW X5 jeep to put her briefcase and jacket on the seat. She closed the back door, opened her driver's side door, stepped up inside of it, and sat down. As she checked to make sure her mirrors were straight, she took an extra minute to glance in the rearview mirror at what was left of her at the end of her crazy day. Her eyes looked tired and her makeup was completely gone. Jordan didn't wear much makeup—she didn't really need any, and she would wear just enough to accentuate her features. Jordan was five-feet-seven, 150 pounds, with a Coca-Cola-shape body; she was a 34D on top, and a size 8 on the bottom. She still hated her extra weight, and was desperately trying to start an aerobic class to tone up her stomach and thighs. She was brown-skinned, with shoulder-length, dark-brown hair with copper highlights. Her light brown eyes were almond-shaped, and sat above her button nose and petite lips. She had an oval-shaped face, with a slight pudge in her cheeks, giving her a baby-face look to contrast with her sexy shape.

She took about ten seconds before starting her car. Her mind was racing through a million thoughts; she couldn't believe what had just happened. She and Jayon had a thirteen-year friendship, and they had maintained a rare platonic opposite-sex friendship. He was the closest male in her life, excluding family, and she was the closest female in his, excluding family. They had always treasured their bond, and even when they weren't as close as usual, they had an under-standing that they were always there for each other when needed. After college, once while Jordan was in law school and Jayon was in grad school, they had a few weeks when they strayed from their pla-tonic friendship, maybe just to satisfy their curiosity. She and Omar had broken up, and after a few weeks she and Jayon were taking ad-vantage of the opportunity to spend more time together and go on a much-needed vacation.

They went on a cruise to the Caribbean, and while on the ship the romantic environment influenced them and they overstepped the line. Still, they never did sleep together. They had shared their first kisses during that cruise, but even with all the temptation, all they had done was made it to about second base. After they returned home, their time together increased and they discussed the possibility of a relationship. They both knew the history between Omar and Jordan, and they couldn't make a decision until more time had passed. Sure enough, after another month had passed, Omar decided to try to work it out, and as usual, Jordan agreed to try. She had discussed it with Jayon and he was supportive of it; she and Jayon both knew that was typical for her and Omar, and that's why they had decided not to go all the way in the first place.

For a while, immediately after, it was weird between Jayon and Jordan, but they both knew the decision to mend what she and Omar had was the right thing to do. She and Omar had been together for nine years at that point—a couple of weeks of lustful fun couldn't erase that. So, there were no hard feelings, and for the next six years, what they'd shared was just a moment in time, in the past. In less than a year, things were just as they had been before. The two of them were back to being friends, and other than an occasional joke about their time together here or there, it was in the past. There had been no temptation between the two of them since—well, nothing worth not-ing, at least. That's why Jayon's behavior in the office was so shocking to Jordan. What the hell was he doing?

Just as she went to change her gear shift to DRIVE, her cell phone rang. She glanced in the Caller ID and it read home.

"Where are you?" Omar said as soon as she answered the phone.

"I am leaving the office now—I'm on my way," she explained.

"I called you at the office and there was no answer."

"I was working out of Jayon's office, but I am on my way now . . . I will be there in about fifteen minutes, so I will see ya when I get there."

Jordan heard Omar sigh, and then he hung up the phone.

Jordan's brain was racing—she had a million thoughts running through her head. She just wanted to get off the phone before her guilt became obvious. In her work, Jordan was damn good at hiding the truth and keeping her emotions hidden, but in her home life with her husband she couldn't lie to save her life. She knew she hadn't done anything wrong, but Omar would feel justified for his occasional complaints that he thought her friendship with Jayon was inappropriate. She would always disagree and defend herself and Jayon, on the grounds that their friendship was respectful of her marriage. She knew what had just happened would change that entire theory. Trying to fathom the changes that Omar would probably request was just too much for Jordan. It wasn't just their business relationship— since college she and Jayon had been the best of friends, and she wanted to continue that. Still, what Jayon had just done was so disrespectful—something like that can be so damaging.

As she pulled out of the parking lot, onto Sixth Avenue in midtown Manhattan, she turned her radio to Hot 97, wanting to hear some hiphop to clear her mind. Funkmaster Flex was spinning, and he was in the middle of a throwback set. Just what Jordan needed—some of her favorite old school hits. She started rapping along to Slick Rick's "Mona Lisa," and within minutes her mind was completely off of Jayon and Omar's anger. As she mumbled the words, *Excuse me, dear, my god you look nice, put away your money, I'll buy that slice,* Jordan was in her own club, Club X5. She made her way through midtown and through the midtown tunnel on Thirty-fourth Street. By the time the next song by Jay-Z came on, she had got onto the Long Island Expressway, and as soon as she reached the first exit she hit traffic.

Why in the world would there be traffic this time of night, Jordan thought to herself. "Just to make my night worse than it already is," Jordan said, answering her own thought out loud. She knew now it was going to take forever to get home to Elmont. She decided to try not to let the delay upset her, and let Funkmaster Flex keep her entertained. He had switched up and started playing some current songs, and she just kept grooving. For the next fifteen minutes or so, she moved her foot on and off the brakes, trying to get from exit to exit. After she realized this was going to take quite some time, she decided to call

Omar to let him know. She turned down the volume just as the commercials were about to come on. After the fourth ring, the answering machine answered at her house. She hung up and put her cell phone back down in her lap.

Jordan started to look for ways to maneuver through the traffic, but after a few lane changes it seemed like she would just have to wait for it to break. With the silence and traffic, her mind wandered back to what had just happened with Jayon. As she thought of it, she shook her head, still kind of in shock. For years everything had been on a platonic level, with no hint of anything like this. Of course, the inevitable attraction between man and woman had made itself known at times, but it was something these two always had control over. They had always kept their friendship, and then business relationship, a priority, so it was always natural not to feel any temptation. Another reason they had always refrained from that behavior was that Jordan had been with Omar since she and Jayon first met thirteen years ago. There were breaks and issues between Omar and Jordan, but even when spending time together during those times, Jayon had always respected her and Omar's relationship, sometimes more than Omar deserved. It was bugging Jordan out how Jayon had just gone against everything the two of them stood for and made that attempt.

In some way, she was flattered that he was still attracted to her in that way. She wasn't unaware of that attraction; she always found Jayon to be fine his damn self. He was five-eleven, about 190 pounds. He definitely had some meat on his bones, but with his height he appeared stocky. He was just Jordan's type. He wasn't fat nor was he skinny; just like the bowl of porridge, he was just right. He had a caramel complexion, with a low ceasar and two slight dimples in both of his cheeks. His brown eyes were round and distinct, almost as if he was wearing eye makeup; he even had long black eyelashes that were fit for a female. Although he had the prettiest eyes she'd ever seen on a man, they didn't subtract from his masculinity, they only added to his good looks. He had bushy, untamed eyebrows, a thin moustache, and a peach-fuzz beard. He had a very handsome face, but Jordan's favorite feature had always been his lips. Got damn, his lips were sexy. They were perfectly defined with a plumpness that just invited sucking. If there was one thing Jordan always had to resist, it had been his lips.

Jordan had to snap out of her daydream about Jayon. She didn't know what to think about what just happened at the office, but by that time the traffic broke and she was too busy swerving through traffic to come to a conclusion.

It was about a quarter to eleven when Jordan finally arrived home. She hurried in the house, dropped her tan leather briefcase by the door, and kicked off her tan Gucci pumps. She went through the front porch and family room—there was no sign of Omar. She walked into the dining room and found that the table was set for two, including two glasses of champagne and two lit candles. She studied the room for a minute, at the carefully decorated details, before she continued to search for Omar. He had managed to make the dining room feel like a restaurant with a romantic ambiance, right in their own home.

She headed back out of the dining room and was about to walk upstairs when she heard the TV in the living room. She walked into the living room, and there was Omar lying on the couch, fast asleep. He still had the remote in his hand and was fully dressed, with the exception of his shoes. She just stood there looking at him for about two minutes, feeling absolutely horrible and momentarily hating her career. He had done so much to make tonight special, and here he was, knocked out on the couch, because he was here all alone waiting. Instead of harping on the guilt, she headed upstairs, planning on trying to still have a romantic night the best they could.

Jordan prepared herself for the night, hoping that she hadn't ruined it completely. She took about ten minutes to freshen up and change, and then she headed back downstairs. Omar was still fast asleep on the couch, unaware that Jordan had even come home. She quietly walked up close to him, knelt down, and gently kissed his lips. At first there was no reaction, and then she gently kissed them again. He jumped up, and after shaking off his confusion, he looked directly at the time on the satellite cable. He then looked back at Jordan, frustration all over his face.

Once she saw that he was obviously upset with her late arrival, she quickly explained, "Baby, I'm so sorry . . . I hit traffic . . . I tried to call you, but you didn't answer the phone."

Omar didn't respond—he just got up off the couch and walked upstairs. She knew that she couldn't get upset; she hated waiting on Omar more than anything in the world, so she would be a hypocrite not to understand. Not to mention, he had given her advance notice of his special plans for the evening. This was just one incident where her demanding job caused a problem at home.

Jordan figured she'd better try to salvage what was left of the evening. She went into the kitchen and started heating up the meal that Omar had cooked at least two hours earlier. Once it was heated, she served the food and the champagne. She made sure the table was all ready before she went upstairs to get Omar. She just hoped he hadn't gone back to sleep or had already decided to assume his stubborn mode.

When she reached the bedroom, he was just changing out of his clothes to get ready for bed. She took a few moments before she said anything, and he didn't say anything to her, either, although he noticed her in the doorway. She watched him slip out of his pants and shirt, and was admiring him walking around in his blue-and-gray boxers and wifebeater. Omar was five-eleven, 185 pounds, and had a nice chisel to his body. He wasn't stocky or cut up, but he had a full frame, just how Jordan liked it. He was light-skinned, with a bald head, and piercing, dark-brown eyes that always had a slight puffiness under them. He had lots of facial hair, which he kept manicured, just leaving a slight goatee. After she finished admiring her husband's physique, she realized if she didn't speak soon he would be under the covers.

"Sweetie . . ." she called out in a light, apologetic, sweet tone. "Will you please join me at the dinner table?"

At first he just continued with what he was doing, removing his watch and bracelet. After he was done, he glanced over in Jordan's direction, and then did a double take. He realized that Jordan was dressed in a little sheer black teddy. As much as he probably wanted to stay mad, his manhood overcame him. His facial expression changed almost instantly, but after a few seconds he still turned away, trying to keep his cool. Jordan knew the teddy would do something, if not everything, to get him back in the mood.

Making a delayed response, he said, "I will be right down."

Without saying anything, Jordan turned away from the door and went back downstairs. She went into the living room and turned on the stereo to 98.7 Kiss FM and tuned into *Kissing After Dark with Lenny Green*. He was playing hits by Barry White and Luther Vandross—just the perfect music for the evening. She turned the volume to a soothing level and headed back into the dining room and waited for Omar.

She sat at the table, taking some sips of her white zinfandel champagne, and less than five minutes later he joined her at the table. She bowed her head to say a little prayer and then started digging into her meal. After the first bite, she remarked "This tastes delicious."

Omar was a chef and had prepared the meal from scratch himself. He had made one of Jordan's favorite dishes, his special seasoned grilled chicken breast with yellow rice and broccoli. He had done this a few times before for her birthday and Valentines Day—he liked to prepare this meal as a treat to Jordan on special occasions. This time, just like the other times, it tasted great.

"Thanks," he replied.

After she realized that wasn't enough to break the ice, she just went for it. She didn't do all of this to have an argumentative night.

"Oh, I am so sorry about tonight. It was crazy at the office. I have been backed up with work, and Jayon has been going through a lot and he really needed my help preparing for a very important case Monday morning."

Omar gave no reply. Jordan continued, "And listen, I don't want you to be mad but . . ."

Omar interrupted, "Honestly, Jordan, I don't want to hear it. Let's just enjoy what's left of the night."

With just that sentence, Omar made Jordan feel guilty again. Feeling terrible, she just started back eating her meal. He had actually spoken up just in time—she was just about to confide in him about what had happened at the office with Jayon. Luckily, not knowing what she was about to say, he stopped her, because it definitely was not the time or the place for that. Jordan had just gotten so caught up in her ramble, she didn't evaluate the circumstances correctly. She was happy that she hadn't, though. There was enough tension in the room without adding that to the equation. She decided her confession could wait.

They ate the rest of their meal in silence, other than a comment or two. As their plates started to empty, they started to chat a little bit more. Omar decided to share a story about when he picked their son Jason up earlier in the day. They were finally at ease and the tension had cleared by the time they had finished their food. With full stomachs, and finally engaging in conversation, they sat around the table for a while, talking and sipping champagne.

After discussing Jason at school, a couple of news events, and the latest gossip about Omar's cousin, Omar remembered, "Lexia called."

"Oh, really? What did she say?" Jordan replied.

"She will be in town on Monday. She wants to hook up with you, Chrasey, and Dakota."

"That's cool. It would be nice to see her. Is that all she said?"

"Pretty much . . . I think she wants to stay here."

"You think? . . . Did she ask you that?"

"Not directly, but in so many words."

"Well, what did you tell her, in so many words?"

"Nothing, really."

Lexia was a friend of Jordan's, but not a friend she loved and trusted enough to let her stay with her and her husband.

"Well, let me call her before she pops up over here. I will suggest to her that she stay with Dakota—she has more space at her place."

"Whatever," Omar said as he excused himself from the table.

"So, what's for dessert?" Jordan asked as Omar headed in the kitchen with his plate.

After a few moments with no response, Omar walked out of the kitchen with a can of whipped cream and some strawberries, "I don't know what you're having, but I know what I am having for dessert!"

Jordan smiled, and gave a dirty grin. From the outside it appeared as if that was just what she had in mind. On the inside, though, Jordan was kind of hoping somehow it would have gotten too late for sex. She simply just wasn't up for kinky, all-out performance sex. She knew her outfit said, "come get me," so there was no way she could back out at this point. Between what had happened with Jayon, and the overall frustration from the whole night, she would have preferred a quickie. However, Omar had so much more in mind. So Jordan attended to her wifely duties and since it was their anniversary, she quickly adjusted her attitude and enjoyed every minute of dessert.

4

Here We Go Again . . .

"He was supposed to be here thirty-five minutes ago. I just can't stand it when he does this."

Chrasey was standing outside of her workplace at 5:35 P.M., waiting for her husband Keith to pick her up. Frustrated and downright livid, Chrasey walked down the street to the bus stop on the corner of Stewart Avenue and Mason Street, in Long Island. As she approached the stop, she reached in her bag to check her cell phone for missed calls, just to see if he had called. As she pulled it out, her wallet fell to the floor along with a piece of paper. As she kneeled down to pick it up, so did a gentleman who was standing beside her who she had been too pissed to even notice. He got to it first and picked up the wallet and piece of paper and handed it to her.

"Thanks," she said, hardly looking at him.

Looking at her cell phone, there were no calls, just as she expected. There was no sense in calling him, because she had already done that five times since she first stood in front of the building. The last time she spoke to him was at about 4:00 P.M., and he'd said he would be there at exactly 5:00.

For the past month, Chrasey hadn't had a car and Keith had been picking her up from work. A drunk driver had hit Chrasey's car and practically totaled it. It would be at least another month before all the insurance stuff was handled and she could get another car. A month more seemed too long, because by then she would probably have killed Keith. His running late to pick her up, just like his coming home late, had become normal behavior for him. It wasn't worth discussing or arguing over because he would act like she was crazy, so most days she didn't even mention it.

Keith and Chrasey had been married for eight years, and the past three had not been so good. They fought at least three times a week, and their communication was minimal and unhealthy. Keith was usually distant—she couldn't even get him to have a full-fledged conversation with her. The only time he was sweet was when he wanted some from her. Chrasey tried to go along with the way things had become instead of fighting every day, but all the while she was feeling more resentment toward him and their marriage. Still, on days when she was going through things like this, she could just explode.

"You are too beautiful to be at bus stop—where is your chariot or limo?" said the gentleman behind her.

"Don't even ask," she responded.

"Well, I assume you must not have a man or he must not be handling his business."

"A little bit of both," she replied.

At first, Chrasey thought, *what a bad pick up line—millions of New Yorkers take public transportation home every day. Why does my man have to be slacking for not picking me up?* However, she did understand that most people on Long Island got a ride or drove home. Either way, he was right that Keith wasn't handling his business.

"May I ask your name?" he said.

Chrasey had been too busy looking toward the driveway in front of her job, checking to see if Keith would pull up from another direction. To make eye contact with the young man keeping her company at the bus stop, she turned around to finally get a real look at the guy and noticed he looked at least ten years younger than she. Chrasey knew she wasn't an old fogey, but she wasn't a young teeny-bopper, either. Chrasey was five-seven, and had a weight problem. She weighed 210 pounds, but as her mom always told her, her face made up for it. She had the most beautiful brown eyes with long lashes and perfectly arched eyebrows. Her skin had a caramel tone, and she had high cheekbones, a button nose, and full, perfectly shaped lips, all making up a pretty, round face. Even though her body had some extra pounds on it, she still had most of it in the right places. She was a 38D, and had junk in the trunk that most men drooled over. She was always receiving compliments on her rear end, but Chrasey always felt self-conscious because she had a gut with her butt. Dakota and Jordan hated this about Chrasey—she rarely saw how beautiful she truly was, and she always focused on her flaws.

Her frustration with her husband had her feeling a lot more spunky than normal, though.

So, she answered, "My name is Chrasey, and I'm not sure how old you think I am, but I am 34 years old, and I am really not into children."

The young man, not even looking offended or fazed by her response, said in return, "Well, my name is Trevor and I'm not sure how old you think I am, but I'm 27 years old and I am far from a child, so it looks like me and you may have a bright future."

Not being able to help but smile, Chrasey reached over and shook Trevor's hand.

"My apologies, Trevor. It's just that I am waiting on my *husband* to pick me up from work and he is forty minutes late, and I am really in a bad mood."

"He is picking you up at the bus stop? That's kind of weird," Trevor said jokingly.

"No, he picks me up in front of my job, but I don't feel like waiting anymore so I am going to take the bus if it comes before he gets here."

"You have so little faith in him, you must not think he is coming at all . . . or he has done this before, because you seem to have no patience," Trevor said.

Chrasey just gave him a look, like *don't get me started.*

"Maybe something happened, and he got held up," Trevor continued.

It's like some man thing, like the police's blue code of silence. All men, regardless of how little they know a man, must defend other men. It's like the dogs' secret bark.

"He *has* done this before. I have heard every excuse in the book, trust me."

Just as Trevor started to respond, after scrambling for a clever comeback, she saw Keith's black Jetta pull up at her workplace.

"There he goes . . . nice talking to you," Chrasey said as she gave Trevor a slight wave and hurried down the street.

Halfway back down Stewart Avenue, her cell phone rang. Of course it was Keith calling because he didn't see her standing in front. She didn't even bother to answer—she was only steps away from the back of the car. By the third ring she was walking around the side opening the door and getting in.

"Where were you?" he said as soon as she sat down in the car.

"Keith, don't you dare. Where were *you* is the question." She looked him right in the face.

"I was caught late in a meeting at work," he replied with his already prepared excuse.

"You couldn't call, Keith? You knew I would be out here waiting."

"By the time I got out of the meeting, I just rushed here."

"Whatever, Keith, let's just go," she said, frustrated by his lame excuse.

As Keith made his U-turn to go down the block, Chrasey noticed Trevor was still standing at the bus stop down by the corner. As Keith proceeded down the block, Chrasey glanced over at the bus stop in Trevor's direction. He was already looking at Chrasey when she turned her face, and as soon as she made eye contact he smiled and winked. Feeling like the moment seemed to be in slow motion, she gave him a sweet smile and turned away.

It was then that Chrasey took in just how fine Trevor really was. He stood about six-two, 205 pounds. He was brown-skinned, with a round face. He had a slight dimple in his left cheek, and a narrow nose with a few dark-brown freckles. He had pretty, light-brown eyes, with perfectly trimmed eyebrows. He was a good-looking young man, surprisingly handsome. If she had just seen him walking by on the street, she would think he was out of her league—not that she was looking. As she realized that this fine young man had showed interest in her, and thinking she looked a hot mess as usual, she thought to herself maybe she needed to give herself a little more credit.

Fifteen minutes after her moment with Trevor, Keith and Chrasey were just making it out of Long Island and back into Queens, heading home. First they had to stop off of Rockaway Boulevard to pick up the kids from Keith's mother's house. Once they reached home, it was business as usual.

By day Chrasey was the director of TMHS Human Services Corporation. She ran the quality assurance department for the agency's facilities for the developmentally disabled. She had been in this field since high school, and she had been promoted enough times to make her one of the field's experts. By night she was supermom for her two kids, Kelsey and Quinton.

Starting her normal routine, she began cooking dinner for the kids, helping them with their homework, and got them washed up and ready for bed. Kelsey was 5 and Quinton was 6, and between the two of them, Chrasey had her hands full at all times. With two small kids, she barely found time for herself, which made it hard to keep herself up as she would like. She was usually not dressed to impress and sometimes it was weeks before she made it to the hair or nail salon. Her normal outfit for a day was a pair of black Lycra work pants and a sweater or button-up with the same pair of black shoes. On weekends, she was a complete mess. She would wear sweatsuits that sometimes had a bleach stain or a hole or two, with an old pair of sneakers. She would pull her hair back in an unbrushed ponytail, and wear no makeup except maybe some lip gloss. Chrasey wore a lot of different-styled weaves, always halfway down her back. That was the one thing Chrasey didn't play with—her weaves were always tight. The rest of her needed maintenance on a regular basis. Her kids, though, they were fresh from head to toe. They had taken all of her self-admiration and style away the day they were born.

Her inability to put time into her looks only lowered her self-esteem and made it easier for her to tolerate Keith's neglect. He barely needed to help with the kids because Chrasey did so much. It wasn't as if he even tried to split the parental duties in the evening. The only time he would help is if Chrasey wasn't home from work early enough to do it. He usually crawled onto the couch with his Heineken beer and started watching television. It didn't dawn on him that she could use a break from time to time, even when she was home.

Most nights Chrasey would just bite her tongue and feel a bit disturbed about her situation. At other times she would end up asking Keith a provocative question or just flat-out start an argument because he barely helped out. More times than most, she went the quiet route, just trying to keep peace in her house. However, on this specific evening, she was feeling a little better than usual about her situation. That young man at the bus stop made her feel attractive for the night.

5

Prince Charming

The next day was Friday, Chrasey's day had ended, and as usual she was ready for part two of her life's work, her kids and her home. She came outside of the building to wait for Keith, and when she didn't see him she walked to the snack shop a few feet away from her building's front door. She ordered an iced tea, and as she waited for her change she glanced to make sure Keith wasn't there yet. Once she was done with her purchase, she proceeded back to her waiting post, sipping on her drink. She heard a horn, looked around, and all she saw was a black BMW parked in front of her. Thinking it was intended for someone else, she paid it no mind and continued to wait.

Then she heard someone call out, "Chrasey!"

She turned and looked closer into the car. After she was able to make him out, she realized it was the young man from the bus stop yesterday.

"Oh, hello there . . . Trevor, right?" she said, faintly showing her excitement at seeing him again.

"Yes, how was your day, Chrasey?" he said, trying to show he hadn't forgotten her name, either.

"I'm good, just got off work. I am waiting for my husband again . . . what are you doing out here?"

"Just waiting to pick someone up," he replied with a serious face.

"Oh, you know someone who works here?"

"Yeah, this gorgeous lady I met yesterday. I wanted to be out here just in case she ran out of patience again waiting for her ride."

Now, Chrasey was a 34-year-old woman who had seen her share of chivalry and heard all types of game, and, she thought, almost every line in the book. Still, Trevor managed to impress her with his charm and pickup lines. For some reason there was something about Trevor and his smoothness that was getting to her.

"Stop playing, Trevor. You are waiting for your girlfriend or some- thing, out here trying to make me blush. You better get on your way before you get in trouble," she said quickly, trying to disguise her thoughts.

"No, I'm not. I really came back to check on you . . . *and* I don't have a girlfriend, to answer your question. If I did, I wouldn't be here regardless of how beautiful you are . . ."

Chrasey didn't say anything—she just looked at him and gave him an expression that read, *you're good.*

"Honestly, I'm here because I got off work early today to get my car out the shop, and I couldn't help but try my luck and see if you were left out here again," he continued.

"Oh, so my pain—your gain!" she said, smiling.

"Well, I was hoping it could be both of our gain."

Chrasey just laughed. "Good one," she said.

After fifteen more minutes of waiting and chatting, Trevor con- vinced Chrasey to tell her husband she got tired of waiting and took the bus. He promised to take her straight home—he just wanted a few moments to talk to her without her looking over her shoulder the whole time.

Chrasey knew better than to get in the car with strangers and all those rules every woman is to follow. But something about Trevor's angelic baby face made her feel like she was safe with him. She told him he would have to drop her off at the bus stop by her house in case her husband was already home, and she didn't want him to know where she lived. He agreed, and at 5:25 off they went.

"So, do you do this knight in shining armor skit for all the girls you meet?" said Chrasey.

Laughing, Trevor replied, "No, just the ones who look like they need my help."

"I am not in need of any help, especially not from another male. All of you are problems waiting to happen."

"So, are you saying you are about to switch to the other side?"

"No, I'm just saying I can do badly by myself."

"So, you are doing badly? That means you can use some help."

"Listen, I am happily married. Like all couples, we have our issues . . . he works a lot."

"So your relationship has issues because he works a lot? I find that hard to believe."

"No, it's a lot of things. But we are fine. Is that why you picked me up from work? You wanted to help me out because my husband was a few minutes late yesterday. You figured I was your good deed for the week."

"Not at all, Chrasey. Just something about you really stuck with me for the rest of the day, and I had to see if I could get the chance to get to know you."

"So, what's with the whole husband interrogation?"

"We don't have to discuss anything you don't want to discuss. I just found it odd that you said you were happily married, because you're sitting here with me."

He must have made a strong point, because Chrasey had no reply, just silence.

6

Rise and Shine

As Dakota slowly opened her eyes, she looked over to the other side of her queen-size bed and noticed David, fast asleep.

She immediately jumped up and eased further away from the side of the bed he was lying on. She must have had too many glasses of wine, because she couldn't believe she'd allowed him to sleep over. Lucky for her, Tony hadn't called or come over.

After about ten seconds of thought, Dakota got out of the bed and went to the bathroom. After she brushed her teeth, she looked in the mirror and noticed her hair was a mess. She hadn't wanted to wrap it the night before because it would have ruined her sex appeal. Her hair was evidence of a wild night with David; she picked up a brush and began to fix it. One thing Dakota never felt comfortable with was letting a man see her first thing in the morning. She wasn't insecure, but she wasn't quite as secure with just the raw Dakota . . . stank breath, ruffled hair, crusty eyes, hoarse-voiced Dakota Watkins. The "morning" Dakota didn't have quite as much sex appeal. So, it became her ritual that any time a guy slept over, when she woke up she would slightly fix herself before engaging in any type of interaction with him. Not too much fixing up, but just enough to look like she even woke up beautiful.

After she finished flattening her hair back down, wiping her face with a wet washcloth, and brushing her teeth, Dakota started back toward the bedroom. As she reached the doorway, David had just finished his morning stretch.

"Hey, beautiful," he slurred.

"Good morning."

She lay back down beside him and gently kissed him on his cheek.

"Did you sleep well?" he asked.

"Yes, how about you?"

"Well, I must say you put me to sleep quite nicely."

She smiled, and rolled over toward him. "Well, how about I wake you up just as nicely?" she said in a seductive tone.

"Mmm, that sounds good to me."

Just as Dakota begin to guide her hand under the sheets, her cute little Sony cordless phone rang. "Hold that thought," she said. She reached over and checked the Caller ID. It was Chrasey. Calling at 10:00 A.M. on a Saturday morning, it had to be something either real important or real juicy. Tempted not to interrupt David, but curious to know what Chrasey wanted, she answered the phone.

"Yes, my dear. You better be calling me for a good reason this early in the morning," Dakota said.

"I don't need a good reason to call you. Besides, 10:00 A.M. is far from early on a Saturday morning for a woman with kids. Just because you have no one to wake *you* up at the crack of dawn . . ."

"Don't assume," Dakota said with a hint of bad girl in her voice.

"What . . . you have company over there? Tony finally showed his sorry behind up?"

"Yes and no."

"Yes, and no? What, someone else is there?"

"Yeah. I was a little busy—can I call you back in about—"

David interrupted Dakota. "Go ahead and talk. I will go and cook breakfast."

After a moment's hesitation, she responded, "OK, I will be in the kitchen soon."

"Mmm-hmm. And who is that?" Chrasey said.

"Girl, you all messing up my groove."

"I will let you go, you little freak."

"No, he is going in the kitchen to make breakfast."

"Who is he?"

"Remember that guy David I told you about a while ago?"

"The cutie you used to work with?"

"Yeah, him. Well, he came by to cook dinner last night and—"

"Cooking dinner and breakfast—he sounds like a keeper."

Dakota couldn't help but laugh. "Tell me about it, girl. And he put it on me last night . . ."

"Don't even tell me—it's been way too long for me, and I am tired of living vicariously through you," Chrasey said.

Dakota loved being the single one sometimes, getting to still be a black Carrie from *Sex in the City*, while her two close girlfriends were married with kids. These were the times it didn't depress her. She knew these were the times that being married was a bore compared to her life.

She called Jordan on three-way, so she could have her moment. Dakota described pretty much blow for blow how David showed up, cutting short her night of depression. How he cooked dinner, served dessert with champagne, kicked back and watched a Lifetime movie with her, and waited for Dakota to make the first move. It was perfect. As soon as the move was made, though, he took over like a champ.

About twenty minutes into the phone call, Dakota, Chrasey, and Jordan had all shared their juice from their previous nights of drama. Dakota told them all about David's skills in bed, and how bad she felt at first because he was just some rebound sex because of Tony's no-show. She felt bad until Chrasey reminded her how Tony still hadn't shown up or called, so she did what she had to. Chrasey told them both about her new friend Trevor, and how she gave him her number.

After Jordan reprimanded her for being a married woman giving her number out, Chrasey explained, "It's just something about him."

Jordan took the exchange of gossip as her opportunity to get what happened with Jayon off her chest.

"Are you serious?" Dakota yelped.

"I wish I wasn't," Jordan said.

"I knew he never stopped wanting you. He was probably pissed you and Omar had gotten back together when you guys were in grad school," Dakota said.

"Well, I don't know what to do now. I don't even think I can face him. I haven't even told Omar yet," Jordan said.

"Don't tell him that, Jordan. You are just going to start something for nothing. Keep this one to yourself," Dakota advised.

After Chrasey agreed, Jordan explained, "I can't do that. I wouldn't want Omar to keep something like that from me. Besides, what if something big comes from this—how can I explain it to Omar after the fact."

Chrasey said, "You are right. Do what you feel is best. But I ain't telling Keith a damn thing about Trevor."

They all laughed.

"So, what are you going to do about Jayon? That's if Omar doesn't get to him first," Dakota said.

"Omar isn't like that. Besides, I'm not telling him during our anniversary weekend. First, I will talk with Jayon on Monday, and tell Omar after it is all handled."

"Well, good luck with that. I personally think a hot affair will loosen you up some, Ms. Esquire," Dakota said.

"Ha ha. I'm going to ignore that comment. Only Omar knows just how loose I really am," Jordan said jokingly. "Speaking of loose, Lexia is coming in town Monday, and she wants to stay with one of us, I think—and it ain't gonna be me."

"Why not?" Chrasey said.

"Because I am having a hard enough time giving Omar the time he needs without having another woman in my house to give it to him. Besides, Chrasey, let me see you let her stay with you and Keith."

"Oh no, she isn't. I guess that just leaves Dakota—she is the only one who doesn't have a husband to be stolen," Chrasey said.

"That's not right. Why you guys treat her like that?" Dakota said.

"Please, Dakota. Have you forgotten about how she had sex with Tim when he was with Tasha? And she boinked Edgar, Tammy's boyfriend Chris, and Alicia's man. The girl just doesn't care. I know she claims to have changed, but I'm just being on the safe side," Chrasey replied.

"Well, she can stay with me. Besides I have my men whipped, so I am not worried about it," Dakota giggled.

"M-hmm. Well, she should be in town on Monday—I will tell her to call you when I speak to her," Jordan said.

"Well, I have to go, you guys. Breakfast is ready," Dakota said.

"OK. I will call you guys later," Chrasey said.

They all hung up.

Once Dakota leaned over and placed her cordless phone on the cradle, she swung her legs out of the bed and put on her lavender monogrammed robe. She walked down the hall and stood in the kitchen doorway. She was just in time to watch David set the table.

As she watched him carefully place the forks and knives on top of the napkins, in her mind she was thinking to herself, *This is husband material all the way.*

Right during that very delightful thought, the doorbell rang. Without thinking twice, too far in "la la land," Dakota glided toward the door. She looked through the peephole and didn't see anybody.

"Who is it," she called? When she didn't hear a reply, she opened the door to see if someone was in the hall.

Maybe worst case she thought it could have been her landlord, maybe a Jehovah's Witness, maybe the paper boy coming to collect money, a FedEx package, something . . . but she damn sure wasn't prepared for it to be Tony. After waiting for him to ring her doorbell all night, when he finally arrived he wasn't even on her mind. There Tony was, standing at her doorstep, bright and early, dressed in a dark gray Sean John sweatsuit and a baseball cap. All six-four of his frame filled her doorway, and the wifebeater underneath his sweat jacket clung to his six-pack.

Too in shock, mesmerized, and panicked to remember she had every right to just slam the door in his face and have a great excuse, she just stood there, looking dumbfounded.

As he mistook the open door and the lack of words for a welcome, he began to step in. Just as he took his second step in the door, reality hit her and she realized what was happening.

"Where do you think you are going? You think you are just going to waltz in here like everything is OK?" she said.

"Damn, Dakota. You're not even going to ask if I am OK? You are just going to start your drama as soon as I walk in the door . . . I was in jail all night."

"For what?" she said, clearly seeing through his well-planned excuse.

"I got pulled over, and they said I had too much alcohol in my system."

"Well, why didn't you call me? And why were you driving around drunk?"

"I wasn't drunk at all—it was more to do with me being a black man driving a nice car. And I called my brother to come bail me out."

"Well, I don't know what to tell you, Tony—you always have a million excuses. You do this all the time. Quite frankly, it all seems hard to believe."

"You're calling me a liar?"

"No, I'm just saying I knew you would . . ."

Just then, a loud noise came from the kitchen. Either David dropped something by accident or he made the noise on purpose as a friendly reminder that he was waiting.

"Who is here?" Tony asked.

"I was just about to mention that. I have a friend over, a friend from work. We were about to have breakfast and do some work."

"It's Saturday. And isn't it a little personal to be doing work at your house?"

Dakota knew that there was no way she was going to fool Tony into believing it was all innocent—she was in her damn robe, for Christ's sake. But she figured she'd play his own game on him—that was her story and she was sticking to it.

"Oh, no. We worked on some projects here last night. I was waiting on you to show up—you never showed so we just worked for hours and hours. Before we knew it, it was so late I just let him stay over. He lives way out on the Island. So, he slept in the guest room, and now he is up, cooking breakfast."

"Mmm-hmm, Dakota. That sounds like bullshit to me."

"You're calling me a liar?"

Tony knew right then what Dakota was trying to do, what game she was playing. It was way too familiar for him not to notice.

"Not even. Well, since I am here why don't I join you two for some breakfast," he said.

"Tony, we really have a lot of work to get done. You will just be a distraction for me."

After what looked like an *I can't believe this chick* look, Tony replied,

"OK, 'Kota. Well, I am going to let you get back to your business breakfast. I guess you can give me a call when you're done."

"OK. I definitely will."

She waited as he walked back out the door, gave him a peck good-bye, and closed the door after him.

Proud of her "playa point" she just earned, she walked to her terrace and waited for him to come into sight. She watched him get in and pull away in his black Cadillac Escalade truck. Once she was sure the coast was clear, she returned to the kitchen. Tony was sitting at the table, sipping on a cup of orange juice, reading Dakota's *Essence* magazine.

"Is everything OK in here?"

David looked up. "Yes, other than the food getting cold."

"I'm sorry. Let's eat."

David was so tempted to ask who the guy was belonging to the male voice he'd just heard in the living room, but he figured it wasn't his place. He hadn't earned that right, and if she wanted him to know, she would tell him.

So, they sat there and ate breakfast like nothing had happened.

7

What a Celebration

About three hours after Jordan had hung up with Chrasey and Dakota, she was all dressed and ready for her and Omar's anniversary lunch at Jezebel's. As she slipped her foot into her dark-brown Italian leather pumps, Omar yelled down the hall.

"Jordan, phone."

"Who is it?"

"Jayon," Omar yelled back with a little attitude in his voice.

Jordan took a deep breath before picking up the receiver that was lying on the table.

"Hello," she said.

"Hi, Jordan. I'm sorry to call you at home on a Saturday but I couldn't sleep last night, " Jayon said, all in one breath.

With Omar in the room getting some things together, Jordan felt under pressure.

"It's OK, Jayon. We can handle this on Monday."

"I just want you to know that I am very sorry. I have been going through a lot since the whole thing with Dawn and me. I had no right to do what I did, though, Jordan. I had too much to drink yesterday when I stepped out of the office—I know that was dumb of me. I don't know if I told you, but yesterday I found out Dawn called our engagement off because of some guy she was cheating on me with and I was really feeling it. I guess I just wasn't thinking straight—I just wanted someone—"

"Jayon, I understand. Truly, it's OK."

"You promise, Jordan? Can we put this behind us?" Jayon asked.

"Yes, we will."

"Are you going to say something to Omar?"

"Jayon, I will see you in court Monday morning."

"All right, Jordan," he said, quickly catching the hint.

"And don't forget all the files," she said. "And Jayon, don't be so hard on yourself. I understand—we all do things without thinking first sometimes."

Jordan threw that last comment in to ensure it would sound like they were discussing business. It must have worked, because Omar left the room moments later instead of waiting to hear the whole conversation out.

"Thanks for being so understanding."

"OK, I'm on my way out with Omar, so I have to go."

After Jayon apologized once again for calling her on a Saturday, they both hung up.

Jordan walked down the hall and grabbed her dark-brown leather purse and headed toward the living room. As she sat down and began to place the belongings from the bag from the day before into the brown leather bag, which matched her outfit for the day, Omar walked in.

"Can I at least have you to myself on weekends?" Omar said in a sarcastic tone.

"Omar, don't go there. It was a two-minute call."

"OK, but I'm just saying, you're with him every day, all day. What he had to say couldn't wait? I mean, damn, when we do have our time, Jayon and your work is going to start invading that, too."

"Omar, let's not ruin our day. He just wanted to make sure I was clear on some things before we met on Monday, that's all. Now can we go?"

As she finished her sentence, Omar was already walking out of the room.

About ten minutes later, no words had yet been exchanged, and they headed out for their lunch date.

Once they were seated at Jezebel's, they were both pros at making the waiter think things were just fine, smiling and saying thank-you through the whole ordering session. However, the moment he turned away, back to complete silence. Jordan and Omar were pros at this. They had mastered the art of going out, even when they were mad at each other. Quite pathetic but true—it came with being in a relationship for fourteen years. Fights and attitudes were a given, so like most aspects of it, you just learn how to live with it. But this was their anniversary—a line had to be crossed.

"C'mon, Omar, are we gonna sit here and not talk through the whole lunch?" she said, finally deciding to be the bigger person.

"Talk," he said, obviously deciding not to join her. How typical of him, she thought to herself. She wanted to strangle him.

"Talk? Fine," she said. "Jason has his exam for kindergarten next week. I wanted to plan a trip to take him to Disney World when he passes."

"And what if he doesn't pass?" he replied.

"How dare you say that. Of course he will pass," she said.

"I'm just realistic. Just because you think you're the smartest woman on the planet doesn't mean your son can't fail some silly test," he said.

"What is all of that for, Omar? Is there something you want to talk about?"

"Nope, nothing at all," he replied, clearly hiding his real thoughts.

The waiter approached the table. "Salmon?"

"Right here," Jordan said.

The food was a good reason to be quiet for a while, but after the first few bites she started back up. "Omar, are you upset about last night or about me getting that phone call earlier?"

"I am upset because you put our relationship second to your career and I'm tired of it."

"Omar, that is far from the truth. Everything I do is to produce money. I am not at all the industry parties or social events. Every time I'm not at home, I'm producing a dollar. And I don't see you complaining when I have to pay your half of the bills."

It just slipped out. She knew once the words were leaving her mouth it wasn't the thing to say. At the same time, she was tired of having this conversation with Omar.

I would love not to have to work and be able to stay home and take care of my son, but he doesn't have it like that. So I do my part—and I do it quite well, I might add, Jordan was thinking to herself.

Before she could try to fix it, he put his fork down and gave her a look of death.

"Well, maybe if you did stay your ass home, I could work more and I could handle things. But you want to be the damn man in the relationship—you wouldn't know what it's like to stay home. You wouldn't even know how to be a kept woman—you're too damned 'educated.'"

Wanting to defuse the situation, since they were at their anniversary lunch, she just remained calm. Besides, she knew not to mess with a man and his pride, and practically saying he couldn't head his household was pretty damn risky.

"Whatever, Omar. Let's just eat. I promise you I will do whatever I can to be home as much as I can. And if you want, I will give up my whole career to take care of you, your child, and your home. You just let me know." Her slight sarcasm was evident, but she took a bite of her food and thought that was the end of it.

"I want you to give up Jayon," he said.

She almost choked. "What?" she said.

"You heard me," he replied.

"Where did that come from?"

"I'm tired of sharing you with him. You guys have been best friends for all these years and he gets to spend more time with you than me. You guys work together, you're on the phone all the time. When you and I fight, you go out with him—I feel like he is my fill-in."

"Omar. I only see him when we are at work—and then we are working. We may be friends, but I rarely see him unless it's work-related. The whole best-friend thing kind of went out the window when we grew up. We are not nearly as close as we used to be," Jordan explained.

"You guys are still a lot closer than we are."

Hearing him say that almost broke her heart. But deep down she knew it was true. Still, she made an attempt. "Baby, don't say that. You have been my best friend for fourteen years and still are."

He didn't say anything. She took that as a sign, so she said nothing more. They just sat there and finished their meals.

8

Surprise Visit

"Wait up, guys . . ." Chrasey said through her gasps of breath. She was walking fast down the street, trying to keep up with her kids—her son Quinton and daughter Kelsey. Chrasey was just returning home from taking her kids to the park. Her inability to keep up with them was just a reminder of how badly she had to lose some weight. She hated that feeling of gasping for air.

As she rattled through her keys for the key to get into her house, she heard a car coming down the street. When she looked over her shoulder, she noticed a black BMW. She thought nothing of it, but as she unlocked the door, she noticed it slowed down a few houses away. She opened the door, and the kids took off running. She stepped in after them, leaving the door open. Kelsey ran into the living room and turned the television on, and Quinton ran to the refrigerator to grab a Capri Sun. Once Chrasey saw they were jumping right into things, she stepped back and took a peek out of the door. The car gradually pulled up in front of her house. Her heart was beating fast. Through the tinted windows she couldn't see who it was. Of course, her mind had already taken in the possibility that it could be Trevor, thus the fast heartbeat. Keith was out taking his mother to run her errands and shouldn't be back anytime soon. Still, Chrasey was afraid that he could pull up any minute. She was even more nervous thinking to herself that Trevor could be so bold—she was worried she had started something with a crazy man.

To act as if there was a reason for being outside other than to see who was in the car, she pulled her mail out of the mailbox. As she shuffled through the envelopes, the window on the driver's side started to lower. As she looked up, Trevor's face appeared with a sweet and sexy smile.

"Trevor? What are you doing at my house?" Chrasey asked as she approached the car.

"I was just in the neighborhood. I had to come by here on my way home," Trevor said. After Chrasey gave him a look of doubt, he continued, "And I saw you out here. I wouldn't just pop up like this, Chrasey—I am not crazy."

"Well, you are here in front of my house . . . and you did drop me off yesterday. It could almost look as though you were looking for my house."

"Chrasey, I have been driving through this neighborhood for years. It just so happens that I am driving through and you were outside. Besides, how would I even know what block you lived on—you had me drop you off around the corner. You could have lived on any one of these streets."

After Chrasey took a moment to realize the logic of what Trevor said, she said, "So what is in this neighborhood that brings you through it so much?"

"My daughter. She and her mom live on Brinkerhoff Road."

"I didn't know you had kids."

"Not kids, just a daughter. She is 3."

"Oh, that's nice. Look, I am sorry I accused you of stalking me," Chrasey said with a giggle.

"That's OK. I can completely understand how it seemed."

"So I guess we both spent our Saturdays doing parenting stuff—I just came back from the park with my kids."

"How many do you have?"

"Just two. One boy, one girl."

"That's cool. Aren't you lucky! I hope my next one is a boy."

"Hey, you never know."

"Yeah, well, after I dropped you off yesterday, I went by to see my daughter. I realized as I was on my way that there's a lot of great things for me in this neighborhood."

"Oh, really . . ." she said with a smile, knowing exactly what he was hinting at. "Well, listen, my husband will be home any minute, and I was going to start dinner."

"Oh, so I see you're just going to ignore my flirtatious comments . . . so am I at least invited to dinner?" Trevor said, obviously playing around.

"Yeah, right. Speaking of, I better not see you back by my house again . . . coincidence or not. My husband is the very jealous type."

Chrasey said this, but the sad truth is she knew Keith wouldn't care one bit. He was too busy doing his dirt to even notice Chrasey.

"OK. I'm not trying to start nothing. But maybe I can have you for dinner one night . . . I mean *take* you to dinner one night," Trevor said with a smirk.

"We can talk about that later . . . maybe we can go to a *friendly* dinner," Chrasey said, returning a smirk to let him know she recognized his devilish slipup.

"OK, I will call you later," Trevor said.

Trevor watched as Chrasey walked toward the house. As every woman does when she knows a man is watching her walk away, she added a little bit to her strut. She put a little extra swivel in her sway and made sure her posture and pace was sexy to go with it—you know, just to give him something nice to look at. Once she reached her doorway, she turned around and waved good-bye, and then she stepped inside. As he pulled off, she watched him through her window. Even though she was nervous about the risk of seeing Trevor, she had to admit to herself she liked the thrill . . . and something about him.

9

Mixing Business
with Personal

It was Monday afternoon, and Dakota was in the middle of a business call when her assistant's voice came over the intercom, announcing, "There is a Tony here to see you."

Dakota had called Tony twice that Saturday night and once on Sunday, to no avail. She wasn't sure if it was revenge or he was just simply up to his regular tricks, but she did know her heart was almost jumping out of her chest, knowing he was standing right in the lobby about ten feet from her office door.

"Send him in," she responded.

As she hurried to conclude her phone call, she quickly applied some Mac Lip Gloss, fluffed her hair, sat up straight, and prepared for his knock on her door.

Tony stepped inside her office without saying a word. He closed the door behind him and his sexy six-four frame was in Dakota's direct line of sight for her to admire.

"Hey there, stranger," she said.

"Hey, 'Kota."

"What brings you up here? I thought maybe you were locked up again."

"Aren't we funny, little Miss Business Breakfasts at Home . . ." he said, giving her an mmm-hmm look. "I was in the neighborhood and decided to stop by."

Always ready for toe-to-toe combat, Dakota struck right back.

"Maybe if you would make yourself more available, I would put pleasure before business."

"Yeah, well, looks like you do a good job of that without me."

"Tony, let's not turn the tables. You were the one missing all weekend—where were you?"

"When? After your business meeting at home in your robe?"

"Tony! . . ." Dakota said, losing her cool for a minute. "I have been calling you since Saturday night."

"The nerve of you, D. So, after you were done with your 'business,' you didn't like that I had 'business' to attend to."

"Oh, you think you're funny, don't you, Tony? Let's not forget you were m.i.a. Friday night when I was waiting on you, then you were m.i.a Saturday night and Sunday when I was looking for you . . . but I guess that's not my business."

"I was hanging out with some friends at Justin's on Saturday night, and last night I went to a club," Tony said, seeming to just want to get back to business, at least the business he had came to Dakota's office to tend to.

By this time Dakota had made her way from behind her desk to lean on the front of her desk, positioned directly in front of Tony.

"Sounds like you had yourself a bunch of fun this weekend," she said.

"Well, we can't all work so hard until we have sleepovers."

Dakota knew Tony. He wasn't mad at her, he was jealous. He wasn't comfortable with what happened on Saturday. He would never be the type to admit jealousy of no man or over no woman, but he sure wasn't good at hiding it, either. His jealousy was turning her on, since she was usually the one feeling that way and she was loving one of the few times she'd gotten the best of him. At that point she no longer wanted to talk about it; she was ready to move on to something else.

"Tony, are you going to let that go?" she said as she reached out to hold his hand.

"There is nothing to hold on to. Business is business, right?" Tony said in a semi-sarcastic tone.

"Exactly, and pleasure is pleasure."

Familiar with Dakota's "I want some" voice, he decided to let bygones be bygones and see what she had in mind. "Let's say you make it up to me," he said.

Now he was talking something Dakota wanted to hear. Feeling her hormones go wild, she said, "And how would you like for me to do that?"

"Well, let's mix a little business with pleasure," he replied as he moved closer to her.

Not being able to resist it anymore, she didn't bother to respond, Dakota just leaned in toward Tony and kissed his lips. Tony, not hesitating to indulge, took his hand and placed it on her neck and kissed her back deeply enough to awaken every sense in her body.

Five seconds later, before either of them thought twice, Dakota reached over and locked her office door. Tony was grabbing at her dress straps, trying to pull them down, and Dakota was grabbing at his zipper trying to pull it down. Eventually they slowed down enough to get some of their clothes off. Tony was rock hard, and his eleven-and-a-half inch tool was looking to get to work. Dakota always grew with excitement at the sight of it. It was the best she had ever had—it had a great track record at keeping her satisfied.

After she pushed some things off her desk to make room, she sat back on it and pulled up her dress eagerly, waiting for Tony to plant his feet and align himself with her area of entry. After a few seconds of repositioning himself right, Dakota felt his head poking her in her pleasure zone. She dropped her head back in anticipation. Then she felt the thrust. She let out a loud moan, almost forgetting she was at work. Tony covered her mouth and began to drive in and out of her. As Dakota took the pleasurable pain, she tried to keep from making too much noise. She felt her wet walls welcoming his every movement inside of her. She felt his penis pulsating with excitement, which only made her more animated. She felt herself beginning to climax, and she grabbed on to his waist for dear life. After her body convulsed and she let out a silent moan, her body began to relax. Still, Tony wasn't done yet. He was, as usual, impressed with himself for pleasing her, but he was just as eager to bust his nut. He lifted Dakota up with one arm, and bent her body over her desk. Excited about what was to come, Dakota spread her legs with anticipation. She waited for the feeling of its head to rub up against her lower lips in search of entry. That was one of the best feelings in the world to Dakota, that feeling of expectation. Then, as she grabbed the edge of her desk for support, she felt him enter from behind slowly. Another amazing feeling went through her body. She could feel every inch slowly enter her from behind. He pulled back out just as slow as he had entered, and then back in. After about the third thrust, he started to pound harder and faster. She could feel his balls banging up against her. Just as he started to speed up with excitement, she felt his grip getting tighter on her hips. The fast pumps turned into one long one. He pushed inside of her real hard as if he was trying to reach her ovaries, as his body slightly shook with pleasure. The shaking stopped and Tony just leaned over onto Dakota's back.

Their hot and sweaty bodies were sprawled over Dakota's oak-wood desk. For a few moments they stayed like that in silence, breathing heavily. They eventually got up, and started to regain their composure after their kinky office quickie. Dakota started to giggle, realizing that it was quite humorous that they had just treated her office like it was a short-stay motel room. They got straight to business, with no foreplay whatsoever. Dakota looked at the mess she had just made—the guest chairs were out of place, and the top of her desk was cleared. The floor was covered with everything from papers and books to a stapler and paper clips. They spent a few more seconds reveling in their joy before they spoke to each other, officially ending the moment.

As Dakota fixed her dress and undergarments, she said "Mmm, mmm, mmm. That's what keeps me here, dealing with your ass."

"Yeah, and that's what keeps me coming."

Both humored by their compliments, they knew it was the sex that they shared that kept them entwined in their drama-filled relationship.

"I see you're no joke at work, because you wasted no time getting down to business."

"Please, you were putting down the pipe. I was just trying to hang."

"Later on, when you get home, I'll stop by for some more. I know how you hate having to keep quiet."

Laughing, she said, "Just don't keep me waiting again like the other night."

"I'll be there. I couldn't really get at you the way I wanted to just now, but that was a great appetizer to the main course."

Just as equally satisfied, Dakota said, "Well, I'm happy to hear that. Anytime."

As they both laughed and got themselves back together, they both had a happy glow about them. It could have been the good sex, or it could have been that they were both relieved that they were out of the hot water they had gotten themselves into over the weekend. But regardless of what it was, they were feeling good, and neither of them was thinking about all the drama from the weekend.

10

Guess Who?

At around 6:00 o'clock, Jordan had called Omar and told him she would be late getting home again, approximately 10:00 P.M. She could sense the frustration in his voice. He didn't say much, but she could tell his lack of response meant he had more to say. All he really said was, "Well, try to get home as early as possible, because you know Jason is going to want to wait up for you."

Jordan hadn't spent much time with her son lately, and he had started this phase of whining and crying if she wasn't there at night. Even though Jordan hated not always being there for Jason at night, she knew that Omar felt the same way but just couldn't express it quite as immaturely as Jason did. It was rough for Jordan. Her family and career had put her between a rock and a hard place, and she was constantly trying to squeeze them both in.

As soon as Jordan hung up with Omar, she started to feel guilty. She was always working late, and although she knew it was a problem, she didn't know what to do about it. She decided, at least for the moment, she would resolve it. She decided to wrap up and head home early after all. She figured for once her work could wait, and she would surprise Omar. Besides, she was feeling real good; she'd had a smooth day in court with no real drama. She and Jayon were very professional, and there was no real awkwardness between them. Jordan and Jayon had been friends long enough to shake off just about everything, and once again they had.

After their terrible lunch on Saturday, Jordan and Omar managed to have a wonderful weekend. Omar finally put the negativity behind them and allowed them to have an enjoyable evening. They got a couple-massage at the Peninsula, and spent the evening at home watching movies and making love. They continued the fun on Sunday with breakfast in bed, and going to the science museum, one of Omar's favorite places. Then they went to dinner at The View in Manhattan, which happened to be a beautiful place. The rest of their weekend was just pure bliss. So when she heard Omar sounding upset, it gave her the urge to get home and keep their good thing going.

She pulled up in the driveway and noticed another car was parked there as well. She didn't think much of it until she walked by the car and noticed an open makeup kit in the passenger seat. Immediately, Jordan's inner spy surfaced. Her mind started wondering as she walked toward her doorway.

Oh, he thought I was working late so he thought he was slick, trying to put on that deprived-husband act . . . I can't believe him . . . I know he does not have some woman in the house with my child . . . she thought to herself.

Her mind couldn't complete her thoughts quickly enough to even know what was what. All she knew was she had a lot more pep in her step as she fumbled to get her house key in the keyhole.

Immediately en route to find Omar, Jordan walked straight toward the living room, where she heard the TV on. The room was empty. As she went to walk out, she noticed a purple blazer and a pink-and-purple purse sitting on the couch. She picked up the remote to turn the television off, and immediately heard a female giggling. She threw the remote down and began to walk toward the back of the house where she heard the voices. By this time her blood pressure was sky-high and butterflies were taking over her stomach.

She hot-stepped through the dining room, and as she approached the kitchen door she saw Omar standing across the kitchen table from some woman. The woman had blond hair and was dressed like she was one of those stank girls in the new Juvenile Video. The two of them must have been real deep into their conversation because neither of them noticed Jordan standing in the doorway. Omar was standing with his back to her, so Jordan couldn't get a clear look at the woman's face. All she was able to get a glimpse of was the blond weave halfway down her back.

Jordan just stood there waiting to see their reaction, when they saw her. The two of them continued talking and laughing when, a few seconds later, Omar walked toward the refrigerator, and then Jordan and this woman were looking directly at one another.

"Jordan—oh my God," the girl screamed.

"Hey. What are you doing home so early?" Omar said in a calm voice as he closed the refrigerator door.

Jordan could have been on *America's Funniest Home Videos*, for all she knew—she had no clue what was going on. Omar's sense of calmness threw her off, and the woman's response surely wasn't what she expected, but she was way too riled up to be able to compute anything quickly enough.

"Wasn't expecting me, huh?" Jordan said, giving him a look that could kill. Before Jordan could register his response—or anything else, for that matter—the girl jumped up and ran toward her, opening her arms to hug Jordan.

"Lexia?" Jordan said.

"Yes—look at you, looking like Mrs. Cochran," Lexia replied as she grabbed Jordan in her arms.

The two of them hugged for about a minute as they rambled all sorts of silly jokes to each other. Lexia definitely hadn't changed a bit. She was a grown-ass woman, still looking like she was auditioning for the sequel to the Players Club. She was only five-four, 115 pounds soaking wet—she was borderline skinny. She still wore a bleached-blond weave, with the bleached eyebrows to match. She was light brown, with hazel contacts. She had on a short miniskirt with a pink tank top and pink pumps. Her makeup was actually well applied, but was still more than the average female would wear on a regular day.

Omar had noticed Jordan's initial reaction and knew exactly where her mind had been. "I will leave you two to catch up," he said as he walked out of the kitchen.

Full of shame for what she was thinking, but yet full of relief, Jordan said, "Where is Jason?"

"Upstairs in his room," Omar said as he continued on his way out of the kitchen.

"Lexia, come take a seat in the living room. I will call Dakota to let her know you're here, but I want to run upstairs and see my baby first," Jordan said.

Lexia followed Jordan back into the living room and took a seat on the couch. Omar had already gone upstairs, and Jordan was a few moments behind him. When she reached the top of the stairs, she noticed Omar in the bedroom. She walked in and immediately put her arms around him.

"I'm home so early because I wanted to continue where we left off last night," she said.

"Yeah, or was it to catch me doing something?"

"Of course not, baby. Why would I even think that?" she said. Once she realized he wasn't responding to her nonsense, she continued, "I'm not going to lie—when I did get home and saw a woman was here, I didn't know what was going on. But that has nothing to do with why I am home. I'm sure you understand . . . I didn't even know she was coming in today."

"Yeah, yeah," Omar said as he walked away from Jordan's embrace.

"Omar, let's be serious. I'm sorry I acted that way when I came in, but I'm home early because I wanted to spend some time with you and Jason."

"Well, go tend to your company and we will be waiting for you."

At that moment, Jason came to the doorway. "Mommyyyy . . ." he shouted as he ran toward her.

Jordan picked him up. "Hey, baby. How's my little man?"

Like most kids, he answered that question with the details about what happened in school, how he scored eight points in basketball, and how he finished his homework. And after she gave him that "Mommy's so proud of you" line, she placed him back on the floor and told him, "Mommy has company downstairs—one of my old college friends is in town. So go play your PlayStation and I will be up before you're ready for bed."

"OK, Mommy," he said as he ran out of the room, back to his own.

Jordan sat next to Omar on the bed and kissed his cheek. "Baby, I am going to let her follow me to 'Kota's house, and I won't be gone long. When I get back, it's going to be me, you, and that massage oil," Jordan said.

"OK, that sounds like a deal," Omar said in a fake-excited voice.

Jordan could tell Omar was holding back what he really wanted to say. He just said that to get her out of the room. She knew that trick when she saw it, but not wanting to increase the negative aura that seemed to surround their marriage, she just went with it and headed downstairs.

11

Why Try?

Chrasey had spent the whole day thinking about Trevor. She didn't know what it was, but he was on her mind all day. She called him and left a message but he hadn't called her back yet. When Keith came to pick her up from work, she made an excuse to run back inside and get something she left, hoping that when she came back downstairs Trevor would be waiting across the street. The whole ride home she had a little attitude with Keith because he was on time, not allowing her Prince Charming to come and rescue her.

It was about 7:00 when she took a ride through Brinkerhoff Road, where Trevor said his daughter's mother lived. When she didn't see his car, she realized just how crazy the whole thing was. What would she have done if she had, knocked on the door?

"I am a married woman with two wonderful kids. What in the hell am I doing even thinking about this little 27-year-old kid? I need to be home with my husband," she murmured, trying to convince herself as she drove back home.

Her own thoughts were making her feel dumb and guilty. She remembered that Jordan warned her not to entertain him. It just seemed for some reason, Trevor had said something that struck a nerve with her, and although she knew it was crazy, she wanted to entertain him some. Even if it was just for fun—she was just a tad bit curious.

When she walked back in her house, Keith was in the living room as usual, watching television. At first she was tempted to go sit next to him and try to spark a conversation. The temptation left when she saw that he didn't even acknowledge her presence. Instead she walked upstairs to her bedroom and started to change into something more comfortable. As she slowly switched from her work clothes into some sweats, she realized that she wasn't giving much of an effort with Keith, either. She had settled for the relationship he was giving her and she hadn't fought for what she wanted. She found herself trying to avoid the rejection; it had just become easier to allow him to treat her like she wasn't there than to beg him for attention.

She convinced herself that she should make an attempt. Who knows, maybe he was waiting for her to make a move. He had probably gotten so caught up in his ways, he couldn't just change his behavior without some help. With this in mind, she went back downstairs and he was still watching ESPN as he was when Chrasey walked in. She sat next to him on the couch, and as soon as she sat down he looked over at her with a look of surprise, confusion, and annoyance, all in one. Once she confirmed with her eyes that she meant to sit there and interrupt his alone time, he turned away.

"Hey there, mister," she said.

"What's up, Chrasey?" he replied without looking over at her.

"How's everything going at work?"

"Fine, Chrasey, why?" he said with frustration.

"Just asking. I'm wondering why you come home these days and you barely speak. I thought something was going on at work, and you had it on your mind."

"No, work is just fine. I'm barely speaking because I'm watching television."

"Every night, and you find time to talk on your cell phone."

"Chrasey, can we talk about this later? I really want to see this."

Chrasey sat there in silence for a few more minutes. Then she figured now that she had started to try to break through the wall, she didn't want to give up that easy.

"Keith, that's the thing—everything gets more attention than I do around here."

"What are you talking about, Chrasey?" Keith said with a tone and facial expression of disgust and aggravation.

"TV, your phone conversations . . . but when I want to talk or sit with you, that's when you have no time."

"Because you always wait till I am in the middle of something to want to talk to me—besides, there is nothing to talk about anyway . . . now really, can we please do this later. I want to see this," he said as he pointed the remote at the television and turned the volume up.

By turning up the volume, he made it clear that she had no choice—he was about to tune her out anyway. So after a few seconds of just looking at him with sympathy, hoping he would notice her cry for attention, she stood up and walked away, once again feeling worse than if she had just left the issue alone. Keith had a way of making her feel small even when she was right. She walked back upstairs. Keith didn't budge from what he was doing. He didn't even bother to notice the sad look in Chrasey's eyes as she walked away.

She glanced in the bedrooms at Kelsey and Quinton. They were still coloring in their homework books, oblivious to the silent war that was being fought right outside their door. When it came to the kids, Keith was magnificent at his fatherly duties. On nights that Chrasey had to work late, he even cooked for them sometimes, he helped with homework, bathed them, everything. He had no problem leaving his television set for them—it was just Chrasey that was not worthy. It was like he just didn't want to interact with her, because the nights she was home he barely spoke to the kids, as if it would leave the door open for interaction with his wife.

Before things got so bad, most nights when the kids were having their own fun and she was tired of watching television, she would find herself in the bedroom or living room trying to get some attention from the man who vowed to give it to her. Of course, like tonight, trying to spark a conversation with him was useless. He never had much to say about anything. When he was home, the most he would do was watch TV or talk on the phone. She found herself throwing sex at him just to get his attention, and that didn't always work. Deep down, her intuition told her that he was cheating with another woman, but she had no hard-core proof of that. Her proof was in her gut, so unless she had something concrete he wouldn't even try to console her to make her feel more secure. It was as if he knew she knew, but didn't care because he felt that he wouldn't get caught. He also knew without proof she wouldn't threaten to leave—she had put too much into the family. Keith was the only man Chrasey had slept with, and they had dated since they were teenagers and been married for years. Chrasey wasn't trying to walk away and he knew that.

Trying to keep her spirits from hitting a new low, she turned on the television in her bedroom and started to flip through for some sitcom characters to keep her company. Moments later, her phone rang and it was Dakota.

"Lexia is in New York, and Jordan is about to bring her by my house. I was thinking you should come meet us so we can hang for a bit."

"Come out to the city, 'Kota?" Chrasey asked as if her idea was crazy.

"You are such an old lady—it's only twenty minutes. Bring your butt on . . . unless the warden won't let you out."

That's all she had to do was bring up Keith, and Chrasey realized she needed to go out 'cause there was nothing there for her.

"I'll leave in about ten minutes," Chrasey said.

She changed her clothes, pulled her hair back into a neat ponytail, and headed down the stairs. She gave the kids kisses, asked Keith to watch them, and without waiting for his reply, was on her way.

12

Girls' Night

About a half an hour after Dakota hung up from telling Chrasey to come over so they could all give Lexia a big old college welcome, her doorbell rang.

Rushing to the door, thinking it was Jordan and Lexia or maybe Chrasey already, she opened it. Once again, there stood the sexiest brother she'd ever seen. Again, his six-four frame was a sight to be envied. He stood there, towering in her doorway.

She forgot that he said he was coming over.

"What are you doing here?" she said.

"I'm just stopping by. I felt bad about how I haven't been spending that much time with you. So, I just came to make it up to you," Tony said with a smirk.

It was just something about him that got her every time. Feeling the juices beginning to flow, she knew he couldn't have had worst timing with this one.

"Sweetie, my friends are on their way over."

"So."

"Tony, they will be here any minute."

"OK. That's all I need."

Both laughing, Tony moved toward Dakota and held her in his arms.

"Baby, that's not all I came by here for. How about I go lay down in the bedroom. You guys can have your little girls' night and when you're done, we will be waiting for you."

"We?"

"Yeah, we," Tony said as he looked down at his manhood.

Before she could bust Tony's bubble and let him know that one of her "girls" would be staying with her, the doorbell rang.

Dakota backed away from Tony with a smile and opened the door. It was Jordan, Chrasey, and Lexia. Chrasey arrived at about the same time that Jordan and Lexia did and they all met up in the downstairs lobby. The next twenty seconds was an exchange of big hugs and "hey, girl"s and little jokes.

Jordan said hello to Tony in one of her obligatory tones, and Chrasey followed with another not-so-sincere hello. Tony returned the greeting in a similar tone. He was aware of what Dakota's friends thought of him, and he had never really bothered to care.

Brushing off her friends' obvious disgust for the man she would love to spend the rest of her life with, she turned away from the two of them. She began to introduce Lexia, and as she did, she kept her eyes on his to make sure they didn't wander over her half-naked body.

"This is our home girl from college, Lexia. She is in town for a while and she will be staying with me."

"Hello, " Tony said.

"Hello," Lexia replied.

"I will be in the bedroom watching TV," Tony said to Dakota as he walked out of the living room, giving her a look.

"Where did you find that one?" Lexia asked Dakota as soon as Tony was out of hearing range.

"You don't want to know," Jordan assured her.

"Yes, I do," Lexia confirmed.

Dakota began to tell Lexia the story like a proud mom bragging about her son. As she started telling Dakota, they all had made themselves comfortable on Dakota's custom-made sofa.

"Well, he used to play football for the Atlanta Falcons, and the NFL is one of my clients. We were at a season-opener party and we were introduced by a mutual friend. He was there with a girl, but by the end of the night we were back at his place getting to know each other."

"Damn girl, it's like that," Lexia said.

"Well, he was fine and I had some drinks in me . . ." Dakota jumped to her own defense.

"Yeah, yeah. He was fine and you were horny," Chrasey corrected.

"That, too," Dakota said.

"So, what happened from there? Looking for rings yet?" Lexia asked.

"No, nothing like that. I flew back to New York and we spoke for two months on and off. And then one day he showed up at my office, telling me he was moving to New York. His contract with the Falcons was up, and he was retiring from the NFL and wanted to start his own record label. He owns Touchdown Records, now another one of my clients," Dakota said matter-of-factly.

"Really? That's with that new R&B girl . . ."

"Yeah, Shidaya."

"Oh, well, that's good. He is fine and got money—ain't nothing wrong with that."

As the three of them laughed and sipped on their drinks, they talked about their current situations with their men. The delivery man brought the food Dakota ordered, because she wasn't bothering to cook, guests or not, and after everyone was settled with their food and drinks, Chrasey figured she would be a daredevil and get into Lexia's updated business.

"So, what brings you here to New York, Lexia?" Chrasey blurted out.

"Business and personal. I am looking for a job here, so I set up some interviews for this week. And also, I wanted to come check my girls," Lexia said.

"Are you still doing accounting?" Dakota asked.

"Yes, but I am willing to try another area of the business world. As you know, I have also worked in marketing and management."

"Well, that's cool. Good luck with the whole thing. I can talk to some of my contacts and see what I can do for you before you leave," Dakota replied.

"Thanks so much, Dakota. I really appreciate it."

Jordan broke the sentimental moment with a loud, "Sooo—how is Maurice?"

"I am done with men. They all get me sick. They are just headaches to deal with, and I'm through with them," Lexia responded with true disgust in her voice.

"Preach on, sister," Chrasey agreed.

"I feel ya," Jordan said.

"You ain't never lied," Dakota laughed.

Now one thing was for sure—these four women had a lot of different perspectives on a lot of different things, but they all seemed to be in agreement about at least one thing: men were headaches. Maybe not that they were through with them . . . but they were headaches.

13

Boy Toy

Trevor had called almost every day that week, and he had met Chrasey for lunch once. Every morning she put a little extra effort into her clothes and makeup, never knowing when she might see him.

The last time he called her at work, when she answered her phone, the first thing he said was, "I'm downstairs with lunch and I am waiting for you."

After Chrasey was sure he wasn't pulling her leg, she went downstairs to find Trevor parked in his car. When she walked around to the passenger side to get inside, she noticed a picnic basket in the backseat. Trevor had packed some sandwiches and snacks. Chrasey couldn't believe it, but she tried not to act too excited. She had been married to Keith for eight years and he had never done something so sweet.

They pulled over and parked by a pond close to Chrasey's job. They unpacked the picnic basket and ate their lunch and talked. They talked about Chrasey's marriage, Trevor's daughter's mother, work, life, and ambitions. By the time Chrasey had to head back to work, they had talked about almost everything they needed for a detailed introductory class about one another. All the while they talked, Chrasey was enjoying the lunch that was so well put together. Trevor had sliced some fruit in little Tupperware containers, he had all the condiments in the cute mini Heinz jars, and he even had rolled-up napkins with the utensils inside. It wasn't just a basket thrown together; Trevor really put time into their lunch together. Chrasey couldn't recall the last time Keith put effort into anything pertaining to her.

Trevor drove Chrasey back to work and assured her he would be in touch. Ten minutes later, Chrasey was sitting at her computer when her cell phone rang. It was Trevor. "Just checking on you," he said.

Chrasey was floating on cloud nine. She wasn't that easy to take there, but at a time like this when her marriage was depressing her daily, Trevor was just what the psychologist ordered.

Through their talks she could tell he wasn't just trying to be a player. He rarely made flirtatious or sexual comments, and he really seemed to want to get to know her. He let her talk about Keith, never putting him down or comparing him. He actually advised Chrasey not to read too much into his actions and explained that it's hard for men to open up. Most men would try to say how bad a husband Keith had been to win points and make it seem as if they were so much better at tending to a woman's needs. Not Trevor—he made it clear that all men had issues just like women do, but men aren't trained to express themselves. He advised that it's best to just be patient to make things work. So even though Trevor didn't seem to be trying to disrespect Keith's wife, he was closer to her than any other man had gotten in a long time.

Chrasey walked in the house and Keith was sitting on the couch watching TV as usual. She walked in, gave a brief hello, and headed toward the dining room. She didn't bother to bend over and give Keith a kiss, because she knew he wouldn't acknowledge it or care either way. She was fed up with giving so much effort to the marriage and getting nothing back, so she had decided that until he could at least hold a decent conversation with her, she wouldn't keep trying to be a perfect, perky wife.

She walked upstairs to see what her children were doing. When she got to their bedroom door, they were both in their room playing a video game. She stood in the doorway.

"What are you two doing? Your homework better be done," she said.

"Not yet—Daddy said we could play a game first," Quinton said.

"It is almost 8:00—get your butts up right now and start your homework," Chrasey said as she went to turn the TV off.

Ignoring their whiny complaints, Chrasey walked straight downstairs to Keith. "Why didn't you have them start their homework when you brought them home from school?"

"I told them they could play a game first," Keith defended.

"So not only in addition to cooking dinner and giving them a bath and getting them ready for bed, I also have to get their homework done? You couldn't at least do that?"

"Chrasey, please. I don't want to hear all of this. If you don't want to bathe them, don't, and if you don't want to help with their home-work, don't."

"Keith, they're kids—one of us has to do it."

"Well, go do it instead of wasting more time."

"I can't believe you, Keith. What is happening to you?"

"What's happening to me is my wife keeps nagging me—I'm trying to watch the game."

"I'm surprised you still call me your wife—you damn sure don't treat me that way," she said as she went to walk away.

"What's that supposed to mean?"

Shocked that he even responded or was bothered by the comment, she quickly replied, "You don't. You treat me like the maid for your kids."

"Chrasey, please. They're your kids, too, and you're their mom—that's a part of your role."

"There are no roles, Keith. I have to work just like you, so you can help with the kids just like me."

"All right, Chrasey. Whatever. Next time I won't let them play a game."

She just walked away. He didn't even get it. This was far from about a game. Chrasey knew that on most nights he was great with the kids, and when she wasn't there he did a great job of getting things done before she got home. It wasn't that she wanted to make a big deal about this one night that he didn't get them ready for bed. It was just that his teamwork in their marriage overall was terrible, and what made it harder to deal with was she knew the old Keith and she hadn't yet adjusted to the new one. He used to be so sweet, bringing home flowers every payday, attentive, helping with any and everything. These days, it's like he couldn't care less. She couldn't even remem-ber the last time he brought flowers home.

14

Sexy Sisters Night

Every Thursday the Mirage Club on Fifty-sixth and Third hosts Sexy Sisters Night, and rumor had it that it was always jumping. Dakota, Jordan, and Chrasey had been planning to get together and go for months. They all had separate reasons for wanting to go. Jordan and Chrasey weren't the club type, but Mirage was known for being an entertainment industry hot spot, and Jordan was slacking in her networking. Dakota also had a few clients that told her she should stop by and she wanted to make it so she could at least say she'd been, and Chrasey just desperately needed a night out. Their busy schedules always got in the way, but since they promised to take Lexia for a night on the town, it was a perfect opportunity.

Once inside, they all figured out just why the night was called Sexy Sisters—the ladies walking around were absolutely gorgeous. It looked as if the promoters had paid every supermodel in the tri-state area to attend. Of course, there were your average-looking and normal good-looking females walking around as well, but the majority of these girls were flawless; and of course that meant that there were enough men to start another million-man march. The spot was definitely hot, and the place was filled to capacity, especially crowded for a work night. There were model chicks dancing on some of the tabletops in skimpy outfits, and the waiters and waitresses were dressed in similar skimpy outfits. It wasn't hard to tell that the club was selling and promoting sex, and the women were four new consumers.

After about three minutes of standing back admiring the crowd and soaking up the vibe, Dakota suggested a trip to the bar. Once Lexia's low-cut shirt gained the bartender's attention, Dakota ordered an apple martini for her and a hypnotiq for Lexia. Chrasey then ordered her favorite, a Mudslide, and Jordan an Amaretto Sour. Feeling that successful, independent feeling from knowing that they didn't have to wait for no man to buy their drinks, they went along about their business. As they sipped on their drinks, they glided along, looking for a place to settle. Other than Lexia's completely "come get me" outfit, the ladies looked stylish, classy, and sexy themselves, giving fair competition for all of the sexy singles.

As they turned to walk away from one dimly lit area of the club, they peeked inside one cornered section. As they realized there were no seats, they turned to walk away when Chrasey felt a hand on her arm. As she turned around, standing behind her was Trevor.

"Hey there, stranger," he said.

"Hi, Trevor," she replied with almost too much obvious excitement.

"It looks like I'm going to have to become a stalker just to get your attention," Trevor said playfully.

"No, I was meaning to call you. It's just that I have been so busy."

"Yeah, yeah, I bet. You found time to come here."

Right about then, Jordan nudged Chrasey to get her attention.

"Oh, I'm sorry. Trevor, these are my girlfriends Jordan, Dakota, and Lexia. Ladies, this is my friend Trevor."

After a round of handshakes and "nice to meet you"s, Chrasey gave Trevor a little hug good-bye, the normal call-me routine, and walked away.

After walking to a few more of the seated areas, they finally found a table and sat down to finish their drinks and talk. As soon as everyone was situated, Dakota yelled out over the music, "You didn't mention that Trevor guy was fine."

"He's OK," Chrasey said. "Besides, it's nothing like that."

"It didn't look like nothing," said Jordan.

"Well, I hope it's something, as young and fine as he is," said Dakota.

By the time everyone's opinion had been stated in regards to what Chrasey should be doing with Trevor, drinks were low and the special music guest was due to come out in another twenty minutes or so. Jordan had agreed she would stay until the performance was over, so she was excited to hear that announcement. She was enjoying herself, but she had to get home to her family; she was feeling guilty that she found time to do this and she hadn't had a spontaneous night of fun with Omar in months. But hearing the special guest was New Edition made her feel like it was that much more worth it—she loved them.

Lexia volunteered to go get seconds on the drinks. Everyone except Jordan asked that Lexia bring them a second round. No more than ten seconds after she walked away, Dakota began to vent.

"I am so frustrated—I want my place back," Dakota said.

"'Kota, you said she was welcome," Chrasey said, jumping to her defense.

"I know, but things are going so well with me and Tony and we can't even be free with her around. She is always walking around in skimpy clothes, and she is always on the phone with some friend of hers from back home. This girl calls at least every day, if not twice a day. It is driving me crazy," Dakota replied.

"That's what you get, Miss. She can stay with me—I don't mind," Jordan teased.

"It's not that I don't want her there, but I have like two or three more weeks to go. And to be honest, I just want a break. You know how I am. I moved out from our suite in college because I needed my privacy, and I love you guys."

"Well, it's not that much longer . . . besides, you need to be watching her around Tony and not her phone calls," Chrasey warned.

Before Dakota could put her drink down and respond, Trevor was approaching the table.

"Sorry to interrupt you ladies," he said to all the eyes that were on him. "I came to see if I could possibly have this dance," he said, looking at Chrasey.

Feeling the pressure from the six eyes watching to see her next move, she thought fast and quick.

"Actually, I don't like rap that much," she responded. As if she was being given a moral test by Jordan and some other force, before Trevor could reply, the song changed to Sean Paul's "Give Me the Light."

"Well, that's your jam," shouted Dakota as she pulled her up toward Trevor.

Wishing she could kill Dakota and the DJ behind the turntables, she stood up. Trevor smiled and took her hand in his and started toward the dance floor. She followed close behind Trevor, and took advantage of the opportunity to tastefully take a glimpse of his firm butt.

As soon as they hit the dance floor, Chrasey realized she did really want to be out there. It was probably her guilty conscience by the name of Jordan making her feel like it was a naughty thing to do. She knew she felt deprived of the opportunity to be up close and desired by a man, and she was more than happy to be up close and up against this young and sexy, fine specimen. She noticed a few younger and sexier girls checking him out on the way to the floor, and that made her feel that much more special. As soon as they were positioned on the dance floor, he started winding and grinding up against her. Refusing to let him down, she winded and grinded right back, showing him what she was working with. As she rose to the occasion, so did he.

As the next song came on, Lexia was just returning to her seat.

"What took you so long?" Jordan asked.

"The bar was busy," she responded.

"Who was that girl you were talking to?"

"Just someone I was chatting with while I waited," she replied. Without waiting for a response, she continued, "And I see Chrasey is out there getting her groove back."

As they all watched Chrasey and Trevor tear up the dance floor like they were teenagers, they couldn't believe it was Chrasey. Chrasey couldn't believe it was Chrasey. She was so into the moment, it was as if it was just the two of them in the room. She had no fears about what if one of Keith's friends saw her, what was Jordan thinking of her, nothing. All that mattered during their dirty dancing was the two of them, and she was feeling damn good. She knew she was feeling him when she answered yes when he whispered in her ear,

"Will you come home with me tonight?"

15

Unfamiliar Territory

Chrasey stepped inside of his house, and instantly she felt awkward. She knew that this was not a good idea; even through the disoriented judgment caused by her alcohol intake, she still could sense the wrong in her actions. If she was to go through with this, it would be the end of all that she knew—her fidelity, her vows to Keith, and her innocence. Keith was the only man Chrasey had ever been with; he was all she knew sexually, and lately she didn't know much of that. She knew she had no business being there, and she knew she should be ashamed of herself for even coming to his house. She also knew that she wouldn't have been there if Keith had been a better husband to her, and catered to her needs and wants more. She knew that Keith never paid her a bit of attention, and took advantage of his belief that Chrasey would never stray. She also felt that Keith, too, was getting pleasure from outside of the marriage, while he just let her suffer in silence. With mixed emotions about her presence in Trevor's house, for some reason she just went with the flow.

He took her by her hand and walked her around his house. He had a nice home, especially for a bachelor pad. The living room was painted dark gray with black leather furniture. His carpet was both gray and black, with a beautiful silver coffee table right in the middle of the floor. Of course hanging from his plasma television were the wires to his PlayStation 2, like most men. He had expensive-looking paintings on his living room walls and professional pictures in frames on the mantel of himself, his parents, and his daughter. His dining room was spotless with a nice dining set. Displayed in his china cabinet, along with wedding souvenirs, were his daughter's memorabilia. The kitchen was also well kept, excluding some dishes in the sink.

The kitchen seemed to be his temporary destination—once inside, he pulled a bottle of champagne from the minibar that he had well stocked and took two flute glasses from the cabinet. As he set the glasses down and opened the champagne, no words were exchanged. Chrasey's discomfort must have been obvious, because he asked, "Are you OK?"

"I'm fine," she replied.

"Listen, Chrasey, I understand if you aren't. If you want to stay and just sit and talk, I promise you we can do just that, and if you want to go, I will take you home right now. I am perfectly fine with whatever you want to do."

It was clear all over Chrasey's face how comforting she found Trevor's words.

"Thank you, Trevor, but I'm fine . . . this is a little fast for me, and I'm not one hundred percent cool, but I can hang for a bit. Besides, I'm not rushing home to someone."

He handed Chrasey her glass of champagne. "Well, there is no pressure and no expectations on my part. As much as I would love to make sweet love to you tonight, we can take this whole thing as slow as possible."

Chrasey just sipped on her Moët.

Trevor walked out of the kitchen and toward upstairs, with Chrasey behind him, to continue the rest of the house tour. There were two guest bedrooms furnished and decorated. The bathroom was a typical man's bathroom with nothing in it but a shaver and some toiletries. That was the one room with no scheme or interior design. Along the tour, Chrasey made comments and gave compliments on his well-kept house. She was also sure to tell him, "You forgot about the bathroom."

"That's the guest bathroom—my bathroom is a little better-looking."

"Well, why you have your stuff all over the guest bathroom?"

"So that I don't mess up mine as fast," he replied.

They both laughed as they walked down the hall to the room that he had strategically waited for last.

"Here it is, my master bedroom."

Chrasey looked around the room and was pleased to see that it was also just as clean and maintained. He had a king-size bed, and two nightstands, one on each side. A 42-inch television, with another game system sitting below it along with a DVD player. On the wall was a huge portrait of him and his daughter.

"She is a beautiful little girl," Chrasey said.

"Thanks—that's Daddy's angel face."

"It really sucks you and her mom couldn't work it out for her sake."

"Yeah, I guess . . . but we were young and we just outgrew one another. Trust me, we tried—sometimes it's just nothing you can do."

Chrasey didn't comment, because she knew exactly what he meant. She felt that way from time to time with Keith—they also had outgrown each other. The difference was she was married with two kids, and it wasn't that easy to just walk away.

He picked up the remote and started to flick through channels. Chrasey sat on the foot of the bed looking at the television as well, both pretending that they were eagerly anticipating a good program to watch. It was damn near 3:00 in the morning, and they both knew what they were there in his bedroom for. Still, they wanted the motions to get everybody a little more comfortable.

He eventually landed on HBO, where *Four Brothers* was playing.

"You saw this before?" he asked.

"No."

"Good, me neither, and it just started like ten minutes ago . . ."

Trevor kicked off his shoes and pushed back to the middle of his king-size bed. He patted the area beside him, telling Chrasey to do the same, and she did. She lay next to him with her head resting on his chest, propped up to see the television. About five minutes into the show, way before either of them could have possibly grasped what was going on with the movie so far, Trevor started to caress Chrasey's thigh. He slowly made circles up and down her thigh as far he could reach. It was sending chills through Chrasey's body, and it wasn't long before her slight squirming made it obvious that he was making her hot. Trevor knew that Chrasey's body was yearning for him. Just with that slight touch, she was ready for more. He began to raise his hand further up underneath her shirt until he felt her breasts. He began to slowly touch them as well; all the while they both pretended to still be focused on Andre Benjamin and Tyrese Gibson's attempt to find their mother's killer in the movie.

After a few strokes, Chrasey placed her hand beneath his shirt and started to rub his stomach. The more turned on she got, the lower her hand went. In less than three minutes, her hand was inside his pants and his hands were all over her body. Once she placed her hand on his manhood, he turned her over and began to kiss her. He moved too fast for her to even see what size tool he was working with, but she knew she would probably find out sooner than later. His kiss wasn't as slow and soft anymore—he kissed her with passion and aggression. It was obvious that his hormones were raging, and although he wanted to let Chrasey go at her pace, he was ready to take over.

While he kissed her mouth, her neck, and made his way down to her breast, he started to remove her skirt. He kept his mouth on her nipples as he took off her skirt with his hand down below. She helped him as she was trying to remove his pants. At this point both of their hormones were raging, and poor old Andre Benjamin wasn't getting an ounce of attention.

Both of them had taken off their clothes, all except Trevor's boxers and Chrasey's panties. Upon the sight of their half-naked bodies, Trevor decided to slow down to make the night more memorable for Chrasey, keeping in mind this was emotional for her, even though she had gotten caught up in the moment. He slowly kissed her stomach and continued all the way, going very slow until he made it to her place of privacy. As he pulled her beige panties out of the way, he looked up at her and saw that her eyes were closed and she was enjoying every minute. He continued below, and slowly began moving his tongue back and forth on her clitoral area.

Chrasey was squirming and moaning like she had never been eaten out before. This turned Trevor on even more—he felt like he was outdoing any sex she had ever had with Keith, and he wanted to make it that much better. He began to do all types of tricks with his tongue to heighten the sensation for Chrasey, and once he realized it was working, he grew more excited at her moans. He couldn't take any more. He climbed on top of her and started to kiss her neck as he put on the condom he pulled out of the nightstand drawer and positioned himself. He found where he needed to be and with one slow, gentle movement, entered her. Chrasey could feel what felt to be about ten inches full, inside of her. He completely engulfed her walls, and her body welcomed him.

For the next ten minutes he slowly made love to her, making sure he watched her body movements to prolong her pleasure. When she didn't seem obviously pleasured, he asked, "Are you all right, baby?"

"I'm fine," she replied with a tone assuring him.

Once he knew that she was still into it, and hadn't drifted into guilty land, he continued trying to own her body. He slowly but vigorously stroked her, and simultaneously kissed her neck, and caressed her breasts and as much of her ass as he could reach. About ten minutes later, Chrasey let out a moan that if decoded said, "job well done."

After her body stopped convulsing, Trevor lay down beside her and held her in his arms. She rested her head on his shoulder and they lay in silence. He just rubbed her arms and they both waited to regain control of their breathing.

"Are you OK, Chrase?" he asked, once a few minutes of silence had gone by.

"I'm feeling fine—thanks for asking."

"My pleasure."

"How are *you?*" Chrasey asked.

"I'm fine as well, just happy that you're good."

That was Trevor's way of saying, *I know I didn't finish off but I just want tonight to be all for you.* As long as she was sexually satisfied, he was happy. That was the sweetest thing, which was just what Chrasey needed. Had they continued, she would have had too much time to think while she waited for him to come. Then she wasn't sure if she liked the idea of him walking away unsatisfied.

"You sure you don't want to continue? I don't want to be selfish."

"Trust me, I'm just fine. I would have come any second if you didn't finish—then I would have felt bad. You can make it up to me next time."

Next time? she thought to herself. Wow, he already has plans for the next time. What does he think, that I am going to be his mistress? After she thought about it, after that sex session, she would be a fool not to. They lay there cuddling for a bit longer, until they were both fast asleep.

About an hour later she woke up, and saw the time. She knew that she should have been home long ago and she must have completely lost her mind. She had to be on her way to work in a few hours. She looked for her shirt that was somewhere on the side of the bed, and she picked it up. As she pulled it over her head, she still couldn't believe that she was sitting on the edge of Trevor's bed, half-naked. All the thoughts racing through her head weren't even making sense to her. All she knew was she had changed her life forever.

Just as she pulled her skirt on, she felt Trevor moving in the bed. He had still been asleep as she was getting herself dressed.

"Where are you sneaking off to?" he groaned as he looked at the clock.

He sat up and she felt his arms embrace her from behind and his lips touched her neck.

"Trevor, I have to get home."

"I was hoping you would stay the night with me."

"I can't. I have to get home. And the night is gone—it's the morning time."

"OK, I will take you. I don't want you to take a cab this time of night."

It was 4:45 A.M. on a weeknight, and Chrasey felt a guilt she had never felt before in her life. It wasn't just her husband who was probably pissed off and possibly worried sick, but her children, who she hadn't prepared for school the next day. Here she was in some guy's bedroom—a man she hardly knew.

Her friends didn't even know she was there. At around 1:30 A.M., while they were all still at the club, Chrasey had walked over to the table that she and her girlfriends were stationed at and told them that she was going to get something to eat with Trevor. Of course, Jordan advised her otherwise, and once Chrasey made it clear that it was too late, she had already said she would go, Jordan warned her and told her she'd better be careful with this guy. Dakota told her to be careful and have fun, and Lexia cheered her on, telling her at least she was lucky to leave with a man instead of, and unlike, the three women she came in with. She knew when she walked out that she and Trevor may end up having something to eat, but they weren't going to a restaurant.

She had two missed calls on her cell phone, one from Jordan's house at 2:30 A.M., and one from Dakota's cell phone at about 2:00 A.M. She wasn't trying to call anyone back this time of morning; besides, she knew she couldn't face anyone. On the car ride home, Trevor and Chrasey shared the most uncomfortable silence. He knew that because she was heading home, what she had done was probably making her feel guilty. He reached over and touched Chrasey's leg, and just lightly caressed it as if to say, it's going to be OK. The touch made the emotions surface even more, and her eyes began to tear. The rest of the ride, Chrasey cried silently to herself and Trevor didn't even notice.

16

The Morning After

Chrasey came in the house, and all the lights were out except the one in the living room. She didn't hear a peep, except the noise from the refrigerator in the kitchen. As she tippy-toed through the house she noticed that the living room light was on. She stopped in her tracks, and realized there was no noise coming from in there, so she figured someone just left the light on. She went ahead and continued to walk lightly toward the living room to turn the light out. As soon as she reached out to hit the switch, she saw Keith sitting on the couch watching television in complete silence. When she looked at the screen, he was watching an old *Martin* episode, and the television was muted. It was obvious that he was listening to Chrasey creeping in the house. It was 5:00 in the morning, and on any other night Keith would have been asleep. She knew that he was waiting up for her, and even though he said nothing, the look he gave when he looked up at her made it clear that he was pissed off that she was walking in at that time of morning.

The nerve of him, she thought at first—he does this all the time. He was unable to take his own medicine, and he wanted her to feel bad. She refused to feel bad, so she held her head high and walked out of the living room. She went upstairs to the bedroom and started to take her clothes off. She knew Keith would probably spend the rest of the night on the couch, refusing to come upstairs and sleep in the bed with her.

Once she was done putting on her nightgown, she got in the bed and lay down under the covers. Even with it being way past her usual bedtime, she couldn't go to sleep. She couldn't get the thoughts of her and Trevor's evening out of her mind. She replayed the whole act in her mind. She was remembering the touches, the sweet sayings, the caresses, the kisses, and his hard body.

After she finished envisioning the memory from only an hour ago, her mind started to race with a mixture of regretful feelings and satisfying thoughts. She knew she had started something she wasn't sure she was ready for. She hoped she wouldn't start feeling like some young schoolgirl with a crush. She questioned if he would soon fade away, now that he got what he wanted. Her only solace was that Trevor wasn't the only one who got what he wanted—so did she. She not only wanted that, she needed that. Keith had neglected her for so long, she yearned for the attention. Physically and mentally she had needed someone for a long time, even if only for one night.

Only two hours had passed when Chrasey heard the voices of her children less than two feet away. They had come into her bedroom to request their breakfast. It was way past the time she usually gets them up for school. And of course Keith didn't bother to wake her—she figured he just didn't want her to ask him to drive the kids to school for her. Kelsey was rubbing her face up against Chrasey's like a little kitten.

"Mommy," she whined . . . "I'm hungry."

"Go tell your father," she whined back.

"He said to come tell you," Quinton interjected.

Chrasey hated it when Keith would do this type of stuff. She was so tempted to send a not-so-nice message back to him, but she didn't want to put her kids in between their nonsense.

With resistance, she rose from the bed and dragged her feet out of the bedroom and down the stairs into the kitchen. As she passed the living room, she saw Keith sitting there watching sports highlights on Fox 5. He didn't even look up at her, even though he knew it was her because the kids didn't make that much noise when they walked. She just wanted to slap him in the back of the head with her slipper.

She decided to go the lazy route and make the kids a bowl of cereal because cooking was just out of the question. She reached into the cabinet to pull out the box of Fruity Pebbles and a bunch of other food items fell out behind it. Chrasey knelt down to try to pick them up while still holding the box of cereal in her hand.

"Daddy, come help Mommy . . . she can't pick it all up," Kelsey yelled to Keith.

Keith ignored Kelsey, just as he had the noise from when the food fell in the first place.

Now Chrasey was mad. She picked up all the contents from the floor, with the help of Kelsey and Quinton, and continued making their breakfast. Once she was done and the kids were at the kitchen table eating, she walked to the doorway of the living room to where Keith was.

"Why didn't you answer Kelsey?"

At first he didn't say anything.

"Keith!" she said louder.

"What?" he snapped.

"Why didn't you answer Kelsey?" she repeated.

"You were fine—you could handle it," he said with an attitude.

"You could have come to check, and even if you were so sure, you still could have answered your daughter."

"Yeah, whatever."

"Whatever nothing—you need to stop involving them in your issues."

"I don't have any issues," he quickly snapped back.

"This morning they asked you to make them breakfast, and you sent them to me?"

"Yeah, so?"

"Well, you knew I was still sleep—why couldn't you just do it?"

"Because your ass shouldn't have been out so late, and you would have been up just fine."

Chrasey knew that him sending the kids to wake her was just a small opportunity to punish her for her late night out.

"Well, as you see, I got up. That's not a problem for my kids, no matter what time I came in. The principle is sending them to me—you should have done it if they asked you."

"You do things your way, and I'll do mine. Now if you don't mind, I'm watching something."

Once again, she wanted to just smack him in the back of his neck.

She walked back to the kitchen where the kids were finishing up their cereal. Once she saw they were oblivious to her and Keith's conversation, she turned to go back upstairs .

"Put your bowls in the sink when you're done, and come upstairs," she said to them.

Chrasey sat on the edge of the bed trying to gather all of her thoughts and reflections from last night. After about a minute or so, she noticed her cell phone blinking. She reached over and read that it was Trevor who had called her. Eager to see what he had to say, she called her voice mail to retrieve the message.

"Hey, Chrasey, it's me, Trevor. Just wanted to call and see how you were doing . . . I had fun last night, and I hope you did, too. I woke up this morning feeling like a new me. I hope you're OK, and I hope you'll call me when you get a chance."

She was happy to hear that Trevor cared enough to call, although she was surprised that he wasn't afraid to call her cell phone, even when he knew she was at home. Chrasey's decision to go through with it last night was a milestone moment—it was so unlike her and everything she stood for. After hearing the message, it made her feel a little bit better. At least Trevor was a sweetheart. The whole time during sex, he did everything a man could do to make a woman feel good. Including calling early the next morning just to check up on her.

Chrasey had closed her cell phone to hang it up and place it back on the table. Inside and out, she was a new Chrasey as well. The old Chrasey had walked out the door last night to go hang out with her girls, but the new one came home at 5:00 this morning after cheating on her husband. Although Chrasey knew that she had changed overnight, and she was starting to feel good about it, she knew that she had to keep Keith from noticing that she had swapped his wife.

17

Let Me Work It

The next morning Jordan arrived at work and noticed a card on her table with a single rose.

"Thanks for overlooking my stupidity. Maybe I should listen to you more, need to take it easy with my drinking. You don't know how much your friendship means to me. Love ya, Jayon."

Jordan was flattered yet upset because all she wanted was to put what happened that day behind her. Besides, why was he even still bringing it up—it was the past. She knew that Jayon was upset with himself because of what happened, and that he truly didn't mean to be disrespectful to her or Omar. He had already admitted he had too much to drink that night, and told her how apologetic he was. She couldn't really be mad at him—she knew what a caring person Jay was, and he probably was beating himself up for his slipup. Jordan was still feeling bad, because she hadn't even told Omar yet. She had every intention of telling him as soon as she found a way to make him more comfortable about it.

She started her usual morning office routine, checking her e-mail and voice mail and sorting her desk for all the work for the day. Just as her paralegal brought her a cup of coffee, inquiring about the gossip behind the rose and card she received, her phone rang. She could see in the Caller ID it was Dakota, so she answered it.

"Have you heard from Chrasey?" Dakota said as soon as Jordan answered.

"No," Jordan replied. "And I really don't want to right now. I called her that Saturday night and there was no answer."

"Me, too—she may have been in bed by then. I didn't get around to calling her again until late last night, and she didn't answer again—she was probably asleep. I didn't want to call the house."

"Well, I just hope she made it home that night and not back to that boy's place."

"Oh, ease up on her, J. She is a grown woman and she needs the attention. God knows she ain't getting it at home."

"Well, then, she should go to counseling with Keith, not go to see Trevor."

"Jordan, not everyone is as righteous and perfect as you," Dakota said mockingly. "She is our best friend—let's just try to understand she is going through a lot."

"Whatever. I have nothing more to say about it then," Jordan said.

"Well, I am getting a little worried. I called and checked up on her last night like she knew one of us would, and she didn't answer. I didn't hear from her all day yesterday, and now I just called her at work and she is not picking up her phone. I hope Keith didn't murder her," Dakota said.

"Don't say that," Jordan replied.

"I'm just joking. I am just saying, I'm surprised Chrasey didn't call us right away to share what happened with us."

"Call you maybe—you know she wouldn't call me right away because she probably don't want to hear my mouth . . . and you know she made it home because Keith would have called one of us by now."

"Well, neither one of us has heard from her—I'm about to keep calling her until I get a hold of her."

"Call me if and when you get her," Jordan said, and they hung up.

Jordan reflected on what Dakota had said, about Chrasey not getting attention at home and having to get it somewhere. In Jordan's home, that was probably the way Omar felt, and she started to wonder if she could be causing him to stray. She had these thoughts before, that he might feel neglected and seek some attention outside of the marriage. Usually she would just shrug those thoughts off because she had no time to worry about Omar cheating. However, after hearing Dakota justify Chrasey's actions with that logic, she began to really think about how Omar's was handling her busy schedule.

As she tried to continue her work, her mind was being consumed with a variety of thoughts. She wasn't really worried about Chrasey—she figured she was fine and just needed some time to herself. Jordan was worried about Omar, though. She picked up the phone and called him at work.

"Hey, baby," she said.

"Hey."

"Let's play hooky today," she said, almost matter-of-factly.

"What?" he replied.

"I will finish up some work and you can meet me at home by noon."

"Baby, I can't. It's busy today."

"Omar, come on. We haven't had much time together. It will mean a lot to me."

After a few seconds, he agreed.

Now *she* had work to do. Her heart was pounding. She was like a teenager who was just asked to the prom by the football captain. She was all flustered, trying to take care of all the things that had to be done before she left.

When Dakota called to tell her Chrasey was OK and was at home, Jordan quickly ended the phone call with "spare me the details right now. As long as she's OK, we will talk later."

She told Jackie to take messages for the day and to inform clients she was at a meeting. Once she was done with work, she jumped in her X5 and headed straight for the kinky sex stores in the village. She was going to make sure Omar was getting it at home, and getting it good.

Ever since Jason was born, Jordan felt like her marriage was at a standstill. Once she went back to work, her biggest task was trying to juggle being a mother, wife, and a lawyer. All three being big jobs, she felt incapable of doing them all. She cried so many days and nights because the stress was overwhelming. One day when she figured in order to keep her sanity she had to focus on one thing at a time, somehow her career became that one thing. She never quite got around to her home life.

With no intention of neglecting her husband, somehow that's what was happening. Omar built his career as a restaurateur and because he was the owner he made his own hours. Due to this he was the one who picked up their son, fed him, and did a lot of the typical motherly duties. Sometimes when Jordan would come home on time, he would head to his restaurant to check up on it and do more work, but for the most part he worked 9:00 to 5:00. Most nights she had so much work to do at the office she would get home about 9:00 or 10:00. By then he was tired and would go to bed, or he would leave to go help close up his restaurant while she spent what was left of Jason's evening with him. She did make it a priority to try to have some time with her son every night, most nights just reading him to sleep or helping him with homework. This routine of hers resulted in her and Omar barely having sex and they had very little quality time together. With all the issues her career was causing, there was a lot of unspoken resentment from Omar.

That's why, right then and right there, she decided she was going to give it to him like he'd never had it before. When she hung up from Dakota, she started to think about all of what Omar had been through with her. While driving to and from the village to visit the sex stores, she thought about the changes she wanted to try to make at home. She wanted him and Jason to come first at all times. She would try to be home every night in time for dinner with her husband and son. She was definitely going to make it a point to keep Omar happy, and try to let him know that he comes before her career.

So as she stood there in her sexy construction worker outfit that she got from the sex store, she had plans to put in some hard work. It was daylight, so there was no room for candles and all the romantic sounds. There is nothing like some loving in the middle of the afternoon, and she wanted to cut the romance and make it straight sex, no chaser. Omar walked in the bedroom to find Jordan in an orange-and-gray construction hat, some blue booty shorts with a work belt hanging, and a ripped white wifebeater. On the stereo she was playing Missy Elliot's perfect-for-the-occasion "Let Me Work It." He stood at the door watching her practice how she was going to work it, admiring her every move. She turned around to bend over and found him watching her. Embarrassed as all hell, she fell to the floor, laughing. Without saying a word, he walked over to the bed and lay down, ready for his action. He had never seen Jordan wear anything like this before, and it caused him and his manhood to pay full attention to what she had in store.

As she got herself together and began her little dance routine, whipping her whip and twirling her handcuffs, Omar was mesmerized. She undressed him aggressively and began to caress and search him. After he was fully undressed and handcuffed, she made her way down to his penis and placed it inside of her mouth. While simultaneously working it with her hand, she slipped his manhood in and out of her mouth with aggression and speed. She could tell she was driving him wild just by his body movements. He had his handcuffed hands on the back of her head as she moved it up and down his shaft. She massaged his balls with one hand and jerked the other hand up and down the shaft of his penis while she sucked and licked around the head. Once she felt him pulsate, she knew what that meant and she licked one last time and got up. The frustration from her stopping was clear in his face, but he just watched as she removed her shorts and work belt and straddled him. She sat down on his moist, erect penis and started to ride him like a wild woman. Rapidly and with full strokes, letting her rise just to the top of his penis and back down. She was trying to give him the ride of his life, like the one Simore was talking about in *Queens of Comedy* where he can hardly close his mouth. Less than five minutes later, she felt his penis pulsating again, but this time she kept riding until the pulsating turned into one expansion of his penis inside of her. His face tightened up, and his body jerked with pleasure. Although Jordan had just begun, she was happy with the job.

They lay in the bed with clothes lying everywhere around them, sweaty and breathing heavy.

"Let me find out—it's been years, and now you're deciding to let out the freak in you," Omar laughed.

"Please. You have met her before, she just gets too busy to visit sometimes."

"Yeah, I know . . . I get stuck with the busy lawyer . . . why can't I at least get the busy *freaky* lawyer?"

"Oh, OK. So you like her better than the one who is usually here with you?"

"Definitely. Tell her to visit more often . . . forget visiting—ask her can she move on in."

"OK, I will speak with her about it."

They both just laughed, as they lay worn out across their king-size bed.

Jordan was unsure it would last, but for the moment she felt an understanding between the two of them that she hadn't felt in quite some time. Omar seemed content with her attempt to make up for some of her absence in the bedroom, and he seemed sexually satisfied with her performance. Jordan was happy, too; she had worked it all right. She knew she still had it.

18

Storytelling

It was 7:15 P.M., and Dakota was just leaving her office, heading out to Queens to go see Chrasey. There was traffic on the Grand Central Parkway, and Dakota was starting to regret that she had decided to take this trip. She had a million things to do at home, her own man problems, and a house guest she liked to be home to monitor. At this point, though, it didn't make sense to go back. She was already halfway there, and Chrasey did ask her to come over because she needed a friend. What type of friend would she be if she changed her mind? Besides, Dakota did want to get all the juicy details from Chrasey's night at Trevor's house. So, she sat eight exits away, waiting for traffic to break.

Once she reached the 188th Street exit, she drove straight down to Hillside Avenue, she made her right toward Chrasey's when she noticed a couple standing at a bus stop arguing. The guy looked like he was being such a prick toward the female—you could tell just from their body language. The girl was crying and looked like she was pleading for him to do something or other. As Dakota passed by the pathetic scene, she thought to herself, *why are we females always the ones asking for something? Why are we always the ones crying? We give so much of ourselves, but we have to almost literally beg to get just a little bit back in return.*

As Dakota was making her right and left turns to get closer to Chrasey's house, she thought about this female stereotype. This was one of the reasons Dakota believed in multiple partners, because just one man isn't enough to keep you happy. Men are barely trying to keep you happy. They want you to be content with what they give you, and they always feel like you should appreciate whatever you get. Not Dakota—she was convinced that where one man was slacking, another would pick it up. There wouldn't be no crying at bus stops for her. If home boy was handling his business, he shouldn't have her at the bus stop to begin with—they should be in a car. By the time Dakota had pulled up in front of Chrasey's house, she thought she understood where females went wrong in their relationships. Men go outside their relationships when they aren't happy, and women need to do the same thing. At least with us, they're usually really not doing their job; when men do it they are just being greedy. It's time women realize they deserve better. By the time the female Dr. Phil was exiting the car, she had focused on Chrasey's situation. Chrasey was a prime example of Dakota's philosophy—Keith did unto her and now she did unto Keith. She took her happiness into her own hands, because Keith wasn't handling his business. Dakota was proud of her girl.

The grass was cut and the front of the house looked neat and presentable. Keith was doing something right—at least he was still putting some TLC into his house and yard. Now all he had to do was put that same TLC *inside* his home. Dakota walked around to the side door and knocked. Chrasey had mentioned she would be starting dinner, so since this entrance was in the kitchen she was hoping she would get Chrasey's attention without disturbing Keith or the kids.

She was right—after a few seconds, Chrasey came to the door with a large spoon in her hand dripping with Jiffy batter.

"Hey, girl," Chrasey said, clearly happy to see that Dakota made it.

"Hey, miss," Dakota said as she stepped inside.

Chrasey just made a face, a "signal face," as they called it. This signal was a "girl, you know who is in hearing distance" face. Dakota just smiled back, as if to say "I got you." She sat down and picked up one of the magazines on the table. She tried to peek discreetly into the living room to see where Keith was, and she saw him sitting on the couch, on the phone. She instantly felt the tension in the air. This was a typical scene in their house—Keith sitting in the living room talking on the telephone and Chrasey standing in the kitchen thawing out dinner. Their disconnection was visible, and Dakota could see it as well—she knew she was in the middle of an uncomfortable situation.

Dakota was happy that she had decided to come in through the side door, directly into the kitchen. She didn't have to walk through the living room and converse with Keith just yet, and have that ice-breaker conversation. He wasn't talking to Chrasey, so she knew he didn't want to talk to Chrasey's close friend. Dakota and Keith were cool—she'd been the maid of honor in their wedding, and for all these years they'd had a friendly relationship, but Dakota still always tried to fly under his radar at times like these. So she chose not to say hello just yet. She just sat down at the kitchen table and kept looking through her magazine.

"Where are my godchildren?" Dakota asked.

"Upstairs, supposed to be doing their homework. Go say hi."

"I'm not passing your pit bull in there on the couch, especially after you pissed him off this weekend."

"He isn't going to say anything to you. He hasn't said two words to me all day—it's like he knows or something," Chrasey said in a low tone.

"You're just being paranoid. What did you tell him?"

"That I was with you guys."

"Well, you were . . . kinda. Look, maybe he will realize he can't just treat you like you ain't there. Let him think something."

"Yeah, but I feel terrible."

"Don't . . . now, how was it?"

Not being able to help but smile, Chrasey and Dakota started laughing.

"Girl, maybe that's why I feel so bad, because I liked it so much."

"What? He put it on you?"

After a slight hesitation, Chrasey blurted out, "Did he! That young stuff was right—I tell ya."

As they were both laughing hysterically, Keith walked in the kitchen, probably trying to be nosy.

After greeting Dakota, he asked Chrasey, "What are you making for dinner?"

"Fried chicken, rice, broccoli, and butter rolls."

"Oh, OK. I'm going upstairs—let me know when it's ready."

When he walked out of the kitchen, they started to giggle again.

They sat at the kitchen table and continued talking. After Dakota got all of the juicy details, from how Chrasey and Trevor ended up in his bed to his various sex tricks, she assured Chrasey she wasn't wrong and Trevor was what she needed.

After about an hour or so, Dakota left to go home. The whole way home, she was anticipating calling Tony over to calm down her hormones.

19

Something New

It had been weeks, and Keith seemed more distant than usual. His neglect had been difficult for Chrasey the past few months, but having a new friend made it a little easier to deal with. Trevor was just somebody to keep her mind off all the painful thoughts caused by Keith. Keith's behavior had become more obvious. He would come home, change clothes, and hang in the living room all night, even sleep there a lot of nights. He would keep his cell phone in his pocket, and when he used it he would often speak in a low voice. Those were actually the good nights, because most nights he wouldn't even come straight home from work—he would just call and say he wasn't coming home until later. Some of these nights, Chrasey would end up hanging out with Trevor to keep from crying herself to sleep at home alone. She would go somewhere to eat or just talk in the car with Trevor, and then she would have Trevor drop her off. She would get her car and go pick up her kids from their grandparents' house and take them home and put them in the bed. The sad part was some of these nights she would still cry herself to sleep, because she would still beat Keith home and she just felt deep down he was cheating, and even if he wasn't, he definitely wasn't interested in her. Other nights she would feel just fine, because she knew she, too, had someone else to keep her company.

Trevor was supposed to help Chrasey, but he didn't fill the void completely. He didn't erase the pain. There were days that Chrasey would call Keith at work and he wouldn't be there when he should have been. It was like he was leaving blatant clues that he was up to no good, but it was like he knew she had no proof and couldn't just flat-out accuse him. There were a few occasions when she would make comments or ask questions, but he would just brush it off. He would try to make her feel insecure and convince her she was nagging. Eventually it would work, or she would start to feel her own guilt. She didn't know if it was just mind games or a great cover-up for his dirt. Either way, he was spending his mystery time somewhere, and he was on his cell phone with somebody and she wanted to know who.

She hadn't slept with Trevor since that first time—she had explained to him about a week later that she felt guilty about sleeping with him and just wanted to be friends. He was very respectful. He believed Keith's behavior meant he was cheating, but he tried not to take advantage of her vulnerability. He would suggest another night of intimacy here and there, but he was giving Chrasey time. They ended up getting together maybe once every two weeks at minimum. Other times, Keith was coming home, Trevor was busy, or neither Chrasey nor Keith's parents could watch the kids; so her time with Trevor was short compared to Keith's time with whoever he was with.

She didn't know what to do. She didn't know if she should just stop seeing Trevor and focus on fixing her marriage or continue coping with their dysfunction in her own way. She knew what she was doing was no better than what he was doing, even though she wasn't still sexually active with Trevor. Then there was her fear that she was wrong, that he wasn't being unfaithful and she was the one sinning and ruining their relationship. If that was the case, Keith was still a lousy husband and didn't seem to care either way. She didn't know what would hurt her more, knowing it was another woman or that he just didn't care about her. He barely spoke to her, he wouldn't eat what she cooked most nights, he never held her in bed, and she couldn't remember the last time he said "I love you." He would barely have sex with her, and when he did, it was obviously out of convenience. It was like he was disgusted by her. She thought it may have been her weight gain, but she wasn't sure because he would always deny being displeased by it. Those were his words, but he made her feel repulsive sometimes, and she was clueless as to what he was thinking anymore.

20

Jordan's Jayon

"He says the craziest things sometimes," Jordan said to Jackie, sharing with her a story about Jason.

"I know, kids today are absolutely too grown," she responded. "My niece be talking to me like she is 20 years old—she bugs me out with some of the things she says."

"I know, she and Jason need to hang out."

They were talking for a few more minutes when the elevator doors opened on their floor. Jayon stepped off, and he was with a young lady, engaging in conversation with her. Jordan and Jackie slowed their conversation and watched as they came closer.

"Hey, ladies," he said.

"Hey there, Jay," Jordan said, and Jackie said something similar.

"Jordan and Jackie, this is Michelle."

"Hi, Michelle," Jordan and Jackie replied.

Jordan looked at Jayon, hoping that he would have more information than that, but he just subtly changed the topic.

"What are you two over here gossiping about?"

"Just kids, and how crazy they are," Jackie replied, seeing clearly that Jordan was focused on something much more important.

How dare he bring some woman in our workplace and not tell me who she is. We are supposed to be best friends, for crying out loud, and I've never heard of any Michelle, Jordan was thinking to herself.

He didn't introduce her as a client, and it was clear she wasn't one.

He's trying to be slick by not giving titles. Jordan wanted to show her ass and ask who she was, but she didn't want to play herself. That's something she would have done with the quickness back in college; now that they were adults, she needed to handle this professionally.

Completely disregarding the children comment, she said, "What brings you two through here?"

"I just had to grab some stuff from my office—we will be right on our way," Jayon said.

"On your way where?"

Jayon knew exactly what was on her mind and what she was trying to do, and Michelle was smart enough to stay out of the line of fire.

"Going to eat at the Olive Garden down on Thirty-fourth. Want me to bring you something back?"

She had considered going all the way with this, but Jackie and Michelle would think that she was crazy, so she just said, "Oh, that's nice. Bring me back some fettucine alfredo."

"Not a problem," Jay said, giving her that look telling her that he was reading her every thought.

Jordan hoped he was able to read, *I'm going to kick your behind when no one's around, too. Have your little fun now, but when I get the chance it's going to be on and popping.*

Jordan didn't know why she was so protective over Jay. He was just her friend and she was a very married woman, but she had just always been possessive over him. In a caring way, but it still sometimes was strange. She couldn't even explain it, because she knew that he was free to do what he wanted and she was married and had no intention of being with him. Part of it was out of concern—she didn't want any woman to come into his life and hurt him. Another part of it was just the principle—as his female best friend, she was supposed to be privy to all the details of his life, especially his love life, so when she was missing a detail she became very unpleasant. He knew this, and from time to time he would do things to purposely bother her. Like this, for instance—bringing this woman to their job without her having a clue who she was. Damn, she was tempted to pull him to the side, but she decided to grow the hell up and interrogate him later.

After he walked back out, with Michelle in tow, Jackie said to Jordan, "Mmm, who is that, his new girlfriend?"

Not even wanting to admit it, she replied, "I have no idea, so it better not be."

Jackie laughed—she had been around long enough to know Jordan and Jayon's madness. She thought they were the cutest thing, the way their friendship was so special, and they fought like brother and sister sometimes. Jackie had said that she and her guy friend had nothing on them, and she tried to get him to be as cooperative as Jayon was to her madness. If she only knew—Jordan and Jayon had their drama, too.

Jordan spent the next few hours working on a recording contract for Ozfather, this new rapper out of the Bronx. He just got signed to Atlantic Records and she had to get his contract up to par by the end of the week. She sipped on pineapple juice and snacked on cashews while she looked over and marked up the draft she received from the record label. Jackie came in and out with different calls on her line, and she told her repeatedly to just take a message. She wanted to get this contract done—this guy had done a lot of work to get his deal, and she didn't want to hold him up any longer than necessary.

Then Jackie walked in and said, "Jayon is back . . . by himself."

She loved that Jackie—how did she know that in the back of her mind, while she was diligently working on that contract, she was anticipating the moment Jay stepped back in the office so she could get his butt for his little uninformative conversation earlier?

"Thanks," Jordan said as she got up from her desk and walked out of the office behind her and down the hall to Jayon's office. He was just signing on to his computer when she walked in.

"Hello there, mister funny man," she said.

He looked up at her and started to laugh. "Hey, nosy."

"Nosy? Oh, I'm nosy now. What happened to *concerned?*"

"Yeah, OK. Concerned about what . . . my business and . . . ?"

"Knock off the bullshit, Jay. Who is Michelle?"

"My friend—why?"

"Why? How dare you ask me why?" She felt herself getting upset.

"I'm just saying you ran in here like I did something wrong, and you were rude to her like I was cheating on you with her."

"Jay, don't play stupid with me. You know what I want to know and why, so just get to it so I can go."

"I know what you want to know, but I don't know why," he said.

"You know—forget it," she said as she went to walk out. Jordan wasn't in the mood for him to make her feel like she cared too much. Maybe she did, but they had been down this road so many times she hated when he felt the need to suddenly try to figure it out.

"She is just my friend from grad school," he said as she was walking out.

Jordan stopped in her tracks and turned back around.

"And you guys have been friends all this time or you just got reacquainted?"

"We have been cool since then. We used to have a lot of the same classes—we became very cool and we kept in touch since school."

"You two ever did anything?"

"Why?" he asked.

"Jay, don't make me take my shoe off and throw it at you."

"No, we didn't."

"Why haven't I ever heard of her before today if you go back like that?" she asked.

"I don't know—I don't talk about her much, we ain't cool like that. Nothing like me and you are, we are just cool."

"So why were you hanging with her today?"

Clearly becoming tired of her curiosity, he still cooperated with the questioning. "There was an accounting seminar one of my professors was having, and we both attended and decided to grab some lunch after."

Jordan wasn't one hundred percent pleased with what she had heard, but it did ease her curiosity some.

"OK," she said, "but you know the rules—no female is allowed into your life that I don't know about. Don't mess up again."

"That's *your* rule," he said.

"You made that rule up."

"Yeah, to satisfy your crazy questions," he replied.

"Whatever the reason, don't catch a beat down in here," she said.

"Can I step off the witness stand now, counselor?"

"Ha, ha, ha," she said as she walked out of the office.

Jordan never quite knew why she cared so much about Jayon's escapades. It was like that since undergrad. Back then, though, she tried to be more discreet, and he didn't have as much tolerance. It was like she had a man, but yet still wanted full approval rights of his love life. He was her buddy, and she needed to make sure that any girl he was with was able to deal with her role in his life. Fortunately, he understood that, and he would tell them up front about Jordan and how their relationship was so that they wouldn't cause any problems. As they came, they went, and Jordan was still there before and after each saga so it became an understatement to make it clear that his chicks better respect her. Still, she hated the reality that in a way her concern for Jayon was inappropriate in her marriage. It was what Omar hated about Jordan and him. Still, it had to be understood that just as she was there with Jay when his girlfriends came and went, he was there with her when Omar came and went. When they would fight and he would pull a disappearing act, it was Jay who kept her strong. Jordan understood why Omar had a slight problem with it—she probably couldn't handle it for a week, let alone thirteen years. Still, he had to understand he had nothing to worry about—Jay could only be a threat if Omar and she weren't together, just like any other man would be at that point. Even then, Jayon wouldn't be an option because the last thing they would want to do is ruin their friendship.

21

Femme Fatale

Roosevelt Field mall was packed, and the girls had spent almost two hours there already. Dakota, Jordan, and Chrasey had met up to have lunch and decided to go to the mall. Dakota was the shopaholic of the group, and had picked up a new Movado watch, three pairs of shoes from Steve Madden, and three shirts and some jeans from Armani Exchange. Jordan had bought Omar two polo shirts from Macy's, Jason a cute Gap outfit, and herself an outfit from Ann Taylor. Chrasey was ready to wrap it up and go home. She was always the one who hated shopping, because she always complained she couldn't find her size, and although she was a size or two smaller on occasion, she had never become addicted to the thrill of splurging yet. So, all she had picked up was clothes for her kids, and one pair of shoes for herself.

They walked out of Coach, where Jordan purchased a new briefcase, and headed straight toward Bloomingdale's. After reaching the women's department, Dakota sifted through a clothes rack. After a few moments a handsome young gentleman approached her.

"Do you need help with anything?"

Tempted to say *you can help me with everything*, she controlled herself and replied, "I'm just looking to see what you have."

Realizing she was still being an obvious flirt, she looked over at Jordan, who had already recognized Dakota's mischief and was shaking her head.

"Well, all of our cashmere sweaters are twenty percent off today," the sales guy replied.

"OK, thanks. What if what I want in the store isn't for sale?" she asked. He instantly picked up on her discreet pickup line.

"As you know, everything is for sale—it's all about the price."

"Well, can you give me your number so I can discuss this transaction further with you?"

As the gentleman walked off to write his number down, Jordan and Chrasey just watched in awe as their girlfriend worked her magic. A few moments later, he returned with his number on a piece of paper and handed it to her with a smile. She assured him he would be hearing from her, waved good-bye, and walked out of the department with Chrasey and Jordan behind her.

"You are terrible. I thought you would get better with age. Picking up men in clothing stores—you just don't stop," Jordan said to Dakota.

"I was just having fun. It's OK to have a little fun . . . right, Chrasey?"

"Don't put me in this," Chrasey replied quickly, not wanting Jordan to shift the guilt trip to her.

"Yeah, well I guess not. You're not married," Jordan said in a sarcastic tone.

For some reason, Chrasey wasn't in the mood for criticism, and before Jordan could get the last word out of her mouth, Chrasey shouted, "Why are you always judging me? Your honesty-best-policy theory doesn't work for everyone!"

Dakota and Jordan, both stunned at Chrasey's outburst, just looked at each other.

"Chrasey, I'm not judging you. As your friend, I'm just telling you my advice. You're going to be asking me for it when you need my services as your divorce attorney," Jordan said with a little giggle.

Dakota's laugh broke the tension.

"Jordan, I'm going through a lot right now. I just need you to be my friend and not make me feel worse for every mistake I make."

Jordan stopped, crossed in front of Dakota, and gave Chrasey a hug. "OK, I'm sorry, Chrase. I won't say anything. All I will say is you are married, and marriages go through problems. Don't throw it away chasing some young guy and listening to this scandalous heifer," Jordan said, giving Dakota a nudge. "If it's that bad at home, at least try counseling," she continued.

"Yeah, we are going to have to do something because God knows *problems* don't even begin to describe . . ." As Chrasey was mid-sentence, she felt a nudge in her side.

"Look, there goes Lexia," Dakota said.

"Who is that she is with?" Jordan asked in a low tone.

Coming straight toward them was Lexia, walking with someone who appeared to be a girl but it was hard to tell. Lexia had her arm around the girl, but when she saw the girls she removed it, or at least that's what it looked like to Dakota.

"Hey there, ladies," Lexia said as she approached.

Noticing how uncomfortable their presence had made Lexia, they all hesitated before they spoke with a phony "hello."

After a moment of silence, Jordan finally said, "What're you doing out here?"

"Oh, just picking up some things. I have my last few interviews this week."

"Oh, OK," Jordan replied.

"Will you be coming to my house tonight?" Dakota finally said.

"Ummm, I'm not sure. I may be staying out again. But I will surely call and let you know."

Noticing an apparent attitude from Lexia's little girlfriend, the girls couldn't tell if it was because she hadn't been introduced or some other reason. It did seem to escalate when Dakota asked if Lexia was coming back to her house. The girl had been looking away most of the time that the girls were conversing, making it very obvious that she wasn't attempting to be social. When the comment about Dakota's house was made, she sucked her teeth some and turned away even further. Once she did that, Dakota gave her a look as if to say, *what the hell is your problem?*

"This is my friend Monique—Monique, these are my home girls from college, and this is the one I'm staying with," Lexia finally said.

After an exchange of phony "hellos," with lingering attitude, Lexia ended the little gathering before it became any more uncomfortable.

"OK, ladies, I will see you guys later."

Dakota, Jordan, and Chrasey headed off to their original destination, and Lexia and Monique went in another direction. After they had all walked far enough away and the coast was clear, of course all three of them looked at each other.

"What in the hell is that about?" Chrasey asked.

"I have no idea," Dakota replied.

"That girl looked like a man," Chrasey said.

"Yeah, or she is definitely trying to be one," Jordan said, looking at Dakota as if she had some answers.

"Look, she is only at my house like maybe three nights a week. Other nights she says she stays out with friends or stays in hotels. I ask no questions."

"We were worried about her with our men—we need to watch ourselves," Jordan said, laughing.

They all joined in the laughter, before Chrasey said, "I would find that hard to believe—that girl loved herself some penis in her bed regardless of whose it was. I would have thought she would be strictly dickly."

"Yeah, me, too, but you never know," Jordan replied.

22

This Can't Be Wife

"**A**m I too tired and lazy, too nice, or just too stupid to get my butt up?"

It was a Saturday night, and Dakota was sitting in Tony's house waiting for him to come back home from a night at the club.

She had wanted to go out in the first place, and not be sitting home like a lame duck while he went out spending time with a bunch of dressed-to-undress women. She would have felt much better if he knew that she was out on the scene, too, so he would also have something to worry about. Why is it that women have to feel the need to go out when the person they are dealing with is out? It's like a game played in almost every relationship. It doesn't matter how old the relationship is, how serious it is or it isn't, how good, how much trust is in it, or how happy they are. When one person goes out, the other person feels almost obligated to go out as well. Dakota wasn't in the mood this night, though. She'd much rather stay in and chill, and as submissive as it may be, wait for Tony to arrive.

It was all good until she started to get tired and was afraid that she couldn't wait up for him. Then she started realizing that he could at least have the decency to come home at a decent time. She started trying to convince herself to remain calm by looking at the bright side of her being there, there were a couple of reasons that she was able to come up with. One of the bright sides was that if she remained calm, she would be the cool, understanding chick, and every girl wants to be that cool, understanding, secure girl. Another is that he will get all wound up from bumping and grinding, dancing at the club and drinking, just to work it all off with her. She figured that's her job, that's what she was there for, and she was happy to be of service.

It was her pleasure until she glanced over at his alarm clock and it said it was already three-something in the morning and there was still no sign of Tony. She called his cell phone and there was no answer—that's what pissed her off the most. She was so tempted to put her clothes on and leave. If she wasn't so tired, and if it wasn't raining, she really would have. She kept thinking to herself, *let's try not to make a big deal out of this.*

Dakota had to wonder if she was playing herself, and it was too late in the morning to call any of her friends to ask. She wanted to know what did she look like, just sitting there waiting on him? He told her that he wouldn't stay out too late. At first she stayed because it felt like a wifey privilege to be at his house while he was away. It wasn't like she was staying at his house because she couldn't be at her own. Initially, they were supposed to be spending time together. She understood enough to let him go out with his friends on her time; it was one of his old teammate's birthdays, and they wanted to go out and celebrate. She didn't get upset that he didn't invite her, because she would've been the only female coming along. As much sense as it made when he was leaving, now she was wondering if she was being naive and if he was just taking advantage of her.

Out of anger and spite, she wanted to call David. In her mind it meant she was still in the game. Whenever she started to give a guy too much of herself or she thought she was getting played, it was a remedy to call or go out with another guy so that she could be clear from feeling or getting played. As long as she was doing her thing as well, it was all fair in love and war. So, the more minutes that went by, the more stupid and slutty she began to feel by sitting in Tony's bed all alone, and the more she decided what she was going to do. Minutes were feeling like forever, just watching the time go by. She was going to call David and she could only hope that Tony came home and found her on the phone, so she could be just as rude as he had been.

She didn't care that it was damn near 4:00 in the morning. She reached for Tony's cordless phone, dialed *67 to make Tony's number private, and then dialed David's number. He didn't answer the phone and his voice mail picked up.

"Hey, Dave. It's Dakota—just wanted to say hello and see how you were doing. I missed your last few calls, but I have been so busy with work and I haven't had a moment. I know it's late, but I'm up and I can't sleep, so I was seeing if you were up to keep me company. Call me when you get this so we can make a plan to hook up."

She knew damn well she wasn't going to hook up with David any time soon. Not unless Tony messed up again. She tried not to get David too open while she was on a run with Tony, because it just became too much work to balance. It was much easier dealing with David when Tony was on time-out, which felt like too often. Still, she didn't like not reaching out at all, because she wanted him to know he was still on her "to-do list." This time, though, it was also her way not to make herself feel so stupid for sitting in Tony's house. As long as she was still keeping her player status on point, she couldn't be too upset with Tony. She wouldn't feel like one of his dumb girls he was keeping. Although being left in his apartment made her feel like she was at the top of his list, she knew this was just his condo that he was staying in for the summer. It wasn't his real home—he had two beautiful homes, one in Atlanta and one in New Jersey. She thought he had the mother of his son living in the one in New Jersey; he wouldn't admit that, but that's what she heard. She was waiting in his plush condo that he kept in the city, which served the purpose of easy stays there, entertaining guests and fancying his female counterparts. Still, to leave a woman access to any of your stuff stands for something.

She almost knew in detail what she could and couldn't expect from Tony. He was an ex-professional athlete who was currently the head of an up-and-coming record label, for crying out loud. She knew that when she met him he was enjoying being a rich, handsome black male that most women would plot to trap. If she didn't have some class, *about herself,* she would have poked a condom or two herself. She would've settled down with Tony if she could, but she had become used to just being a side chick and a piece of sexual fun for most men she dated. So, even when she did catch feelings for someone she was seeing, she tried to accept whatever it was for the moment. It was no different with Tony. She didn't know if it would ever be different between them, but she decided to just take what she was getting and be happy. Life is too short.

Within the next half an hour, she was sleeping like a baby. She did imagine as she dozed off, how sweet it would be when he did come home to her in his bed asleep. Maybe he would like it, and get some ideas about making that a more regular thing.

Tony didn't get home until 5:34 in the morning. Dakota was still asleep, didn't even hear him crawl in the bed.

23

Go, Shorty—It's Your Birthday

The very next night Dakota was all dressed up in an outfit she had imagined in her mind since her last shopping trip. It was the weekend before her birthday, and she was turning thirty-one years old on Tuesday. The funny thing was, although she was turning thirty-one, Dakota looked and dressed like she was still twenty-five years old or even younger. On her feet were the metallic pink pumps she had bought from Steve Madden that day at Roosevelt Field, Armani Exchange jeans, and a Shiny pink shirt. She was looking hot to death, and she knew it. Dakota had her mind made up that she was going to have herself a good old time tonight. She was tired of being caught up on Tony when she knew deep down that he wasn't as caught up on her.

Dakota was positioned in front of the Mirage club, standing in her extra-sexy stance. She was waiting on Chrasey, Jordan, and Lexia, and since Chrasey picked up Lexia from a friend's house, they were arriving together. Jordan was getting there a little later because she got a late start after running her errands.

After they had called to say they were looking for parking, they finally walked up to the club at about 11:00 o'clock, also looking sexy and inviting. Lexia wore a slinky brown dress with brown shoes, and her gold makeup and body glitter was just the right touch. Chrasey wore a low-cut red top, jeans, and red-and-black sandals. She hadn't done too much to her hair or makeup, but Chrasey had such a pretty face that most men didn't usually pay attention to detail with her.

Jordan had called and said to go on in, she would be there shortly and meet them inside. Once inside, the dance floor was packed. Women grinding on men's pelvic areas with their backsides. Men holding on to the ladies' waistlines for dear life. Hair was being sweated out, and shirts were getting damp with sweat. It was a very mixed crowd, predominantly black people with some Spanish and white people sprinkled here and there. The club was twenty-one and over, so it looked like the ages ranged from about twenty to thirty-five years old. Everyone was having a good time, though, just the right party scene for Dakota to celebrate in. She had been invited to a bunch of celebrity affairs, and had many other ways to celebrate. She had decided she wanted to just spend time with her girls.

Twenty minutes later they had already purchased their drinks, scanned the club, and found a place to sit. It wasn't much later that Lexia was on the dance floor with some Asian-looking guy, and she was holding on to him like she was ready to take him home with her. Dakota and Chrasey were sitting at a table against a wall, sipping on their drinks, Dakota her Apple Martini and Chrasey a Sex On the Beach. Chrasey engaged in conversation with Dakota, but kept her eyes on scan mode, as she hoped to see Trevor walk by at any moment. Dakota talked and bobbed her head to the music as she watched Lexia, along with some other girls, grind to the bass line. Jordan was going to stay home—she was busy working on cases, and she was really trying to make extra time for Omar and her son. But at the last minute she decided to come on out for an hour or two, because her girls' birthdays only come once a year. Jordan's temporary absence from their girls' night out had seemed to make Dakota think of how stable Jordan was. How she was at a point in her life where she had things to prioritize. Dakota thought about it, and she realized that despite her love of freedom, she herself wanted priorities and stability. The liquor didn't help, but it was only moments before Dakota started to have depressing thoughts. She looked over at Chrasey and blurted out, "Do you think I will ever get married?"

Not knowing where that idea came from, Chrasey replied in a confused tone, "I guess."

"What you mean, *you guess*?" Dakota said sternly.

"I mean, I'm sure you will. Why, you trying to have my problems? I wish we could switch places."

"No, you don't, girl. Trust me. Don't get me wrong—I don't want a dog leaving his shit all throughout my house, but at least you have stability."

"How do you figure?"

"You know who you're going to wake up with each morning. Like Jordan, it didn't mean anything for her not to come here, because she knew that she had to finish working on that case and tend to her husband. So, this was a small priority for her. But see, me, this is one of my priorities because I constantly have to be looking for who I may have to replace my current boyfriend with."

"'Kota, are you serious? How am I any more stable than you? And how is Jordan any more stable? Just like you, our men can get up and leave us any day. Husbands can get up and go, too, and that's even scarier for us because we have some serious attachments to our kids."

"Yeah, I know. But I'm getting old and I'm not even engaged and my biological clock is ticking," Dakota said with a giggle.

"Girl, like I said, I wish we could change places. No kids, no pain in the neck husband to worry about, good career, and fine men in the Rolodex . . . " Chrasey laughed.

"Yeah, well. This is getting played out. I'm tired of that life—I've had it for ten years already."

"That guy David is husband material, and he has been trying to get with you all this time, but you won't give him a chance."

"You know I like a challenge—he is too easy."

"That's your problem—you always want what don't want you. Not me—I don't like rejection. I don't want to work for nothing—if you want me, then you're the type of guy I want," Chrasey replied, giggling.

"Yeah, I see Trevor didn't have to work too hard," Dakota said, throwing a friendly stab.

"That's right. Keith's neglect ain't gonna turn me on and make me want to fight for him—I'm gonna go where the loving is easy to get," Chrasey said, laughing.

"Well, when Tony acts up, David is my easy call."

"Why can't you make it vice versa? You'd probably have to make fewer easy calls."

"What do you mean?"

"You should give David a chance, and make Tony your easy call when David acts up . . . And since David is a good guy, you will probably have fewer easy calls to make."

"Yeah, I'll think about it."

"Look at it this way—you don't have to share David. Tony is only partly yours—why do you want him to have all of you?"

"He doesn't have all of me—you know that I do my thing, too."

"Yeah, but he has all of your heart, because if he didn't you would let David in. You shouldn't let a player have your heart, but let the good men only have your body. What sense does that make? It should be the other way around."

Before Dakota could think of a logical response to Chrasey's question, they noticed someone approach the table who gained their attention very quickly.

Standing about six-three, 200 pounds, was this fine, brown-skinned, nice-built, neatly dressed brother. Both Chrasey and Dakota fell speechless as he stood there over their table. Noticing his effect on them, he gave a devilish grin and said, "What are you ladies doing sitting down in the corner? Why aren't you out on the dance floor?"

"I was waiting for you to come over here and ask me to dance," Dakota said, hitting him with some of her charm.

"Well, all you had to do was say something," he replied devilishly as he reached for Dakota's hand. She put her hand in his, asked Chrasey to excuse her, and headed out to the dance floor with her new potential husband.

As she walked off, Chrasey mouthed to her, *it ain't that played, huh?*

Dakota laughed as she made her way to the crowded dance floor to shake what her momma gave her. She felt bad leaving Chrasey alone, but she knew that she understood . . . he was fine as hell and you don't pass these rare commodities up.

Jordan finally arrived—it was about 12:15 when she walked up to their table. She ordered a Cosmo, sat down, and joined the festivities. Dakota and Lexia were back and forth between the dance floor and the table all night. Chrasey stayed at the table for the most part, keeping her eye out for Trevor. A few guys asked her to dance, and she would satisfy them with a quick two-step to a song or two, but she didn't want to give any guy too much attention just in case Trevor spotted her before she noticed him. She knew this was his spot, and he had mentioned when she spoke to him that he may go out, and he may go to Mirage. So most of the evening she spent patiently waiting for Trevor. Of course, she denied that to the girls, but deep in her heart her night was ruined because Trevor hadn't showed up. Jordan spent most of the evening nursing her drink, replying to business e-mails on her BlackBerry, and talking to the girls when they made their way back to the table. She danced one time the whole night, and that was because Alicia Keys' latest single came on, and that was her jam.

It was about a quarter to two when Jordan headed out. The rest of the ladies left shortly thereafter.

24

The Night is Young

Dakota pulled up in the parking lot on Sixteenth and Union Square. She got out, handed the keys to the valet, and got her ticket.

She walked out onto the sidewalk and started walking toward the W Hotel. It was about 3:15 in the morning, and she was on her way to meet her dance partner from the club, *Darryl*. There was a lot of bumping and grinding on the dance floor and they had decided to finish the experience in a more private location.

Once she stepped in the lobby, he was sitting there waiting. He had already checked in. They appeared to feel a little awkward, but it was obvious it wasn't either of their first time doing something like that.

They went up in the elevator to the tenth floor, and made small talk about the club.

"Where did your friends go?" he asked.

"They went home—they are both married."

"That's cool. You ever been?"

"No, you?"

"I'm actually married now. We are separated, though."

Dakota tried to see if she wanted to back out or be a homewrecker. She never believed a married man when he said he was separated. That was their excuse for their disgraceful behavior.

"I hope that doesn't make you feel uncomfortable about accompanying me here."

"I like to live in the moment, but I don't want to be part of any marital issues."

"Trust me, this isn't the issue. I'm not a dog like that. We haven't been together for almost a year now. I'm just living in the moment as well."

By this time, they had arrived at the hotel room, room 1012. It seemed as if Dakota had been convinced to go through with their plan. To hell with it, she figured—it's my birthday weekend.

Darryl sat on the bed and reached for the remote; he began flicking through channels. Dakota knew that he just didn't want to seem too eager and jump right into it. So she took this time as an opportunity to go to the bathroom to freshen up.

She came out of the bathroom and noticed he had turned off the lights; all she could see was the flicker from the television. She made her way toward the bed, and noticed that the television was turned to an xxx-rated movie. This was actually a turnoff for Dakota—she hated when guys tried to play a porno to drop a hint or make her horny. She always felt that was an easy way out. She ignored it and continued on her way to the bed. She noticed he was in his boxers and his undershirt. She eased out of her Armani Exchange jeans and top. She left her bra and panties on and crawled into the bed.

Once she aligned herself next to him, he leaned in and started kissing her neck. She could feel herself becoming aroused; she had always enjoyed the feeling of a tongue twirling on her neck. She reached down and put her hands in his boxers and felt for his manhood, and she could see he, too, was aroused. He was an average size, not too big and not too small—he was a good size. As she massaged his erection, he began to start to explore her body as well, rubbing her breasts and back and wherever else he could reach. As he exchanged the hands on her breasts for his mouth and tongue, he began to slip his hand between her legs. She allowed her body to surrender to the pleasure and enjoy Darryl's birthday present.

She had forgotten her questions, and her doubts. The club or marriage factor, which was all a blur. The fact that this Darryl fellow had skills was the only thing quite clear for Dakota.

Dakota knew that being in some hotel room with a strange man was a little slutty. She knew Tony played a subconscious role in her decision. When she woke up in the morning, he told her she had to go because his daughter's mother was coming over in a little while. Trying to be understanding, she agreed without a fuss, until he asked for oral sex first. Dakota then told him he had some nerve to ask that as he was kicking her out, but he sweet-talked her into understanding it was just out of respect for his child's mother. It wasn't until after Dakota got up off her knees and into her car that she felt bad about herself and pissed at Tony. She hadn't heard from him the rest of the day. So a piece of her letting loose tonight was to prove to herself she didn't care about Tony and not getting closer to settling down.

However, the reality was she wasn't proving anything, because about an hour later when she was in her car leaving the hotel, she felt bad about herself again, and more pissed at Tony and herself.

25

Bedtime

"It amazes me how you find time for your girls, but you can't seem to spend any time with your family," Omar said a few moments after Jordan walked in the bedroom. He hadn't said hello, or anything else. Jordan thought he was sleeping, until he turned around with that comment.

"How could you say that? she said.

She was just getting home from the Mirage with the girls. It was about 2:30 in the morning and she had been the first one to leave the club. She was trying to get home as early as possible, although she was the last one to get there. She could never please Omar, though.

"It's true. What did you get married and have a kid for if you didn't want this?"

"Omar? Why are you tripping right now . . . It was Dakota's birthday . . . and when is the last time I went out?"

"When is the last time *we* went out?" he asked.

"Whose fault is that? Half the time you don't want to go. The other times we are fighting about something," she said as she kicked off her black Gucci pumps.

"Whatever, Jordan—you have excuses for everything."

"And you don't? You know what amazes me? You will be angry for days, barely speak to me, but you will break your silence to have another argument. You won't pass up that opportunity. You don't even see yourself."

"I'm too busy having to watch you."

"Don't watch me . . ." she said, feeling herself get more upset. "And if you were looking good you could see all I do is work to try to keep us in this beautiful house and Jason in that expensive school," she continued.

"The house you're barely in, and the school where the teachers barely know your name. Not to mention if going to a club comes before us on your list of things to fit in your life, what does that say?" Before she could answer, he continued, "And I'm happy you take credit for all of this—last I checked, I paid the bills around this damn house, too."

"Yeah, maybe going to the club is not a priority, but hanging with my friends is on the list. Not that they come before my family—that's not it—but sometimes I need a break from my stressful life."

"Sorry that we are so stressful for you—we didn't mean to cause any problems in your chaotic life."

"I'm not arguing with you, Omar. I'm going to bed. Most men would be happy to have me as a wife."

"Yeah, I'm sure your male friends feed you that bullshit every time we have a fight, don't they?" he said sarcastically.

"Maybe if you stopped dwelling on the things that's wrong, you would make sure our home was happier."

"That's your job."

"No, my job is to practice law, and yours is to cook."

She stormed out of the room before he could reply. She had finished changing out of her club clothes and into a wifebeater and some lounge pajamas. She went straight across the hall to Jason's room. He was sound asleep; she pulled the covers back and crawled in the bed with him.

A few seconds later, Omar walked in the room and started back up. "That's your problem, Jordan. You think because you're a lawyer that your career says it all for you. You act like Jason and I are just the background props in the Jordan movie."

Jordan was not in the mood to argue, which was unusual for her. Her life was hectic enough trying to balance her career and her personal life. A law career with very expectant clients, a husband, a son, close friends that try to help her enjoy life more, and then just time for herself; it was a lot of pressure. Jordan felt that Omar just didn't understand that, he didn't appreciate her and what she brought to the table in their family. He damn sure wasn't supportive. She felt if she was home more, he wouldn't be half as concerned with their quality time. It's just something to complain about. When men have a woman who has no life of her own and is home all the time, they try to get them to go out more or give them some space. *Can't make these freaking men happy*, she thought to herself.

After he realized that she was ignoring him, he walked away. She wasn't in the mood to go back and forth—she was tired. Omar would never see it her way, and she didn't want to wake Jason. So, he just had to deal with his issues by himself tonight.

Jordan was sleeping with her son tonight. She missed him, she did admit. Just being there for all his stories that excited him so much when he first got done with school, and just seeing him progress at certain things. She missed out on a lot—she did realize that. This isn't the mother she wanted to be, or the wife she wanted to be. She just hadn't found a way yet to be everything, but she was working on it. Jordan got out of the bed and knelt down by her son's bedside.

"Now I lay down me to sleep, I pray the lord my soul to keep, if I should die before I wake, I pray the lord my soul to take. God, please pour blessings on my family and household. Please give me the insight to know what I should and should not do . . ." Jordan spoke to her savior. She was a grown woman still saying the prayer her son said. Jordan never outgrew her childhood prayer, and even when she learned the other one she felt more comfortable with the kiddie one. She would say it's God, he doesn't have a preference, he just needs to hear from you. So she continued asking for blessings for her family and friends, one of her clients, and the less fortunate.

When Jordan got back in his bed after saying her prayers, her mind went back to the argument she just had with Omar. As she started getting upset, she realized that Omar was making her knock herself for what she did. She had to realize that she couldn't let Omar put a guilt trip on her for earning success and wanting the best for her family. Jason was able to be privileged to those exciting experiences and able to progress so well because she could afford to send him to a top school. As she thought about how proud she was of her little guy, she held him close and listened to his breathing. His little chest rose and lowered in a silent, vibrating motion. As she held him in her arms, she knew that this was the one man who loved her most, and it was for him she would continue to be a mother he'd be proud of no matter who had a problem with it.

26

On the Scene

Dakota was sitting in the dentist's office, impatiently waiting to be called in to get her teeth cleaned. She had been there twenty-five minutes already, and she was on time for her appointment, so she wasn't feeling how they were keeping her waiting. What was the point of the appointment, she thought to herself; she could have just walked in if she wanted to wait and waste time.

She was supposed to be meeting Tony later for lunch, and she wanted to take care of some errands before she had to leave to meet him. So, just sitting there wasting time was making her irritable. To pass the time, she picked up an issue of *People* from the magazine rack. Surprisingly, it was an issue she hadn't seen that came out a few weeks ago. In her field it was her job to be on top of all media and press reporting—she was slipping.

She flipped through the pages, seeing makeup tips and stories about today's stars. She skimmed through, with no intention of having enough time to read a whole article by any of the writers. As she made it to the *On the Scene* section, she started to look at the pictures from different parties and red-carpet events. There were pictures of 50 Cent with his new love interest, Toni Braxton and her husband at an album-release party for Jadakiss, Lamar Odom with his daughter at a charity football game, and a few people that she didn't know. She turned to page two of the section, and standing there in a picture with some girl at an album-release party was Tony. He was wearing a chocolate-brown suit, with brown-and-tan gators with a brown base-ball cap. She almost choked. She grabbed the magazine tighter and brought it close to her eyes to carefully examine every inch of the picture. She was about five-eight, a lot thicker than she was, with wide eyes, and a round nose. She wore a tan slip dress with matching tan Dolce and Gabana shoes and bag. Her hair was hanging, with some curls in her face.

She is pretty, but she doesn't have shit on me, Dakota thought to herself.

Dakota was tempted to call him and ask him who the hell she was, or how could he embarrass her like this by taking pictures and things for the press with some other woman. She had brought Tony to too many of her celebrity affairs—how stupid did she look that he is taking some other woman? He obviously didn't care about that, because there he was with his arm around another woman, right smack in the middle of the magazine. She tried her damnedest to see how expensive her jewelry was, or anything else she may have had on to let her know just how well he was keeping her. She knew it was her, the *her* that he claimed was nothing more than his child's mother. It was clear from the picture that it was much more than that. The caption below it read, *Ex- Oakland Raider/CEO of Touchdown Records Tony Taylor with his date at the Ludacris album-release party.*

She wanted to talk to him about it face-to-face, but she couldn't stand it anymore. She had forgotten all about her extended wait in the dentist's waiting room—she was actually happy he kept her waiting. She picked up her phone and dialed his number.

He answered on the third ring. "What's up, 'Kota?"

"What's up, Mr. Taylor?" she said with a very sarcastic and sinister tone.

"Chilling—I'm at Rick's house. What's good?"

"I'm at the dentist's office, and I'm looking through one of last month's issues of *People*, and guess who made a guest appearance?"

Tony didn't reply right away. Then he said, "What? You see that picture of me and my daughter's mother in there?" He never liked to say her name—it was like he didn't want to make her count or something. It was too late for that, though; now Dakota had a face, and to her that made her more real than ever.

"Yes, I do see it. You didn't tell me anything about this party, and how could you go with her?"

"That night, me and her had some business to discuss, so to kill two birds with one stone, we went there and talked at dinner after."

"Tony, the girl is dressed up—that wasn't last-minute planning. Not to mention that her outfit complements yours. Please don't tell me that was coincidence, too."

"Me and you never ended up wearing the same color somewhere, Dakota?" he asked, really trying to sell his story.

"Whatever, Tony—just perfect press opportunity, right? She just happened to have that outfit laying out when you came over, right?"

"'Kota, why are you tripping? That's my baby's mother—she is not just some chick."

"What, and I am?"

"No, Dakota. But you are acting like one right now."

"Fuck you, Tony. It's enough that I have to put up with our terms and conditions, but you can at least keep it real with me. Don't tell me some bull that you had to discuss business with her that night and ended up at some big party and in *People* magazine. Give me more credit than that."

The guests in the waiting area were starting to stare, and one lady was trying to see who was on the page in the magazine so she could see who Dakota was talking to. She tried to calm down before she embarrassed herself even more.

"Dakota, me and her go places from time to time—we aren't enemies or anything. We have a relationship and that entails a lot of things, not things that I have to tell you about, either."

"Fine, Tony—you can keep everything you do to yourself, because I'm tired of this."

"You are really overreacting about some picture," Tony continued.

Dakota remembered her thought from earlier. "I bring you to several parties with me—most of the music business and movie industry has seen me with you. How do I explain you in the magazines with other chicks?"

"You explain that is his daughter's mother," he said.

"So what? She needs to be home mothering your daughter, then . . ."

Before he or she could say anything else, the dental assistant had walked up and said, "Dakota Watkins?"

She stood up. "Tony, I will call you later—the dentist called me in."

"Later, " he said, relieved to get off the phone.

She made her way into the back room and sat in the dentist's chair waiting to get her teeth cleaned. As she sat there, she knew there wasn't much she could say—it was his daughter's mother. Tony never did promise more than he was giving Dakota—her desires from him just slowly expanded from when they first started. She could admit he tried not to hurt her feelings, because she knew what she had gotten into. She knew he wanted to tell her to remember her place at times, but as long as he didn't she knew he was more caught up in their relationship than they planned, just like she was. She couldn't be too upset with him for being in public with his baby's mother. Besides, Dakota was sure she was upset when she saw us in a few other magazines over the past year or so. Her mission was to make her obsolete so that Dakota would be in all the pictures, and in all the houses, and in all the jewelry and clothes. She just had to figure out what she wasn't doing right and get on the job.

27

Small World

Trevor and Chrasey had just finished their second game and it was tied—he won the first one and she won the second one. Of course, they couldn't leave without someone having bragging rights, so they decided to get a third game and play one more time. He gave her the money and she went up to the counter to tell the man they wanted a new game on their lane.

While she was standing there waiting for the clerk to wait on her among all the people returning and getting their bowling shoes, she looked off and watched Trevor. He was just so cute, and so sweet, and so much fun. Whenever they hung out, it was like a day off from her stressful life. She was able to forget about her dysfunctional marriage, and be happy for the time being. Her kids were the only thing that brought her joy, and unless she was able to get out with her girls they were all she had. So when she was able to spend time with Trevor, it was like she was able to get her mind off everything wrong in her life.

Chrasey was feeling a lot better about herself this past month—she had lost sixteen pounds and was feeling more confident. Trevor would tell her she didn't need to lose weight and that she looked good at her original size, but he was also very supportive of her goal to lose twenty more pounds. He had become her motivation for looking better; she knew he was out there seeing all these young, sexy ladies and she wanted to be a little more competition for them. She used to wonder what Trevor saw in her, being that she was older than him and he could get younger, skinnier girls, but he always said he never met anyone like her. He said the younger girls were immature and had their priorities all screwed up, and he didn't like skinny girls, so Chrasey was perfect for him. He also knew that since she was married, what they shared was just for the moments in time that they shared it; it could never be much more than that. They were both content with that.

The man finally came over and took her money and set their game up. It was only 9:00, and she was sure Keith wasn't home yet. It was a Friday night—he usually didn't get home until about 1:00 in the morning. She went to walk back toward their lane. Trevor was patiently sitting down, observing other bowlers' games. She approached him while he was still focused on the game next to their lane.

"You ready for your butt beating?" she said.

He looked her way as he snapped out of his trance, and started to laugh. "Yeah, I am ready. I just hope you are," he replied.

Just as he started to enter the information on the screen for their new game, she heard someone say "Chrasey?"

She and Trevor both turned and looked in the direction of the voice.

Oh, man, it was Denise, Keith's niece. Why, of all people, did it have to be her? She thought she was trying to act normal, but she knew it was clear all over her face that she wasn't happy to see her.

As she approached their lane, she asked, "What are you doing here?" without any hesitation.

Everybody who knew Chrasey knew she didn't go out much, barely at all. Whenever she went out, it was usually with the kids, maybe Keith, and from time to time Jordan and Dakota. So, if people saw her out under different circumstances, they usually would react that way, but she was asking even more so because she was curious as to who this man was here with her.

"I'm bowling—what are you doing here?" Chrasey couldn't think quickly enough. She guessed her answer made her look even more suspicious, but it was all she could spit out. She was completely caught off guard, and she had no experience at getting caught and lying.

She figured she was afraid to ask too many more questions, because she could tell by the look on her face she was in an awkward position.

"I'm hanging out with my friends—we just finished our game and we are about to go get something to eat."

"That's good. Well, you be careful and I will see you this weekend, probably," she said, trying to wrap up the small talk as quickly as possible. Besides, it was obvious that since Chrasey wasn't introducing Trevor, who was sitting right beside her, that there was probably a reason for that. A reason she or Chrasey didn't want to acknowledge.

"OK, I will catch you later," she said as she gave Chrasey a kiss and ran off.

Chrasey was thankful she didn't do what she could have done, which was either flat-out ask her who he was or mention her uncle just to see her reaction. She almost silently gave her a pass. She was a twenty-year-old college student; Chrasey was hoping she was too distracted to care or would get wasted tonight and forget what she saw.

When she finally walked away, she looked at Trevor, who looked back at her and she said, "I'm sorry for that."

"For what?" he said, acting as if he had no idea what she was referring to.

"It was rude not to introduce you or acknowledge that you were with me."

"Don't worry—it comes with the territory."

"What does that mean—are you a professional at being the other man?" she asked.

"No, but I do know that when you're married, it's really hard to go around introducing me to people as a friend that you're out on a date with. That's not always accepted in marriages."

"Yeah, and that was his niece, so that really was uncomfortable."

"What if she tells him?" he asked, seeming really concerned.

"She probably won't, and if she does I will tell him what he has told me when I have heard of him out with females . . . it was some of my co-workers hanging out."

Trevor had already finished putting in their information and was picking his ball for the game when he looked back at her and said, "You get a kick out of this, don't you? Is all of this just to show your husband you can do it, too?"

She was shocked that he asked such a question; she and Trevor tried not to discuss what they did outside of each other too often. Especially not the moral issue behind what they were doing.

"No," she said clearly, unhappy with his question.

"So, then what is it?"

"This was about me being in the company of someone I enjoy and who enjoys me. The fact that Keith has been a terrible husband is not justification or cause for revenge. It just means to me that what I do is acceptable because it's nothing he hasn't done to me."

"You're not even sure if he is cheating on you—you're just assuming from his actions, and you know what they say about assumptions," he said.

That fast, Chrasey's whole happy night had just turned left. First Denise popping up, and then Trevor wanting to become righteous on her as if he wasn't a participant in her wrongdoings. He wasn't talking all this shit the night he asked her to come to his house so he could make her feel better.

Chrasey just got up, picked up her pink-and-purple bowling ball, stepped up to the red line, and threw it at the little white-and-red pins, imagining that they were Keith, her extra weight, her boss who pissed her off, the skinny girl at Lane Bryant, and one was even Trevor. She threw that pin with all her might, and it was clearly heart-felt because she bowled a strike.

28

Decisions

"I am going through the most confusing time of my life. I wanted to be a lawyer for as long as I could remember, but then I also always wanted to be a mother and wife," Jordan complained to Dakota.

"Girl, I love you, but I'm getting tired of you with this same issue, and you aren't doing anything about it," Dakota said.

"Forget you," Jordan said with a slight giggle, knowing she was right. "It's just that every day I live through it and I still don't know what to do," she continued anyway.

"Aww, poor baby. Go ahead, what's wrong now?" Dakota asked.

"It's just that even the career path I chose is becoming questionable," Jordan complained to Dakota.

"Why do you say that? Your career is fine," Dakota replied.

"I worked in law and in entertainment, and I never explored any other options. Now, all of a sudden, I am finding myself unsure of my life choices. I just wonder if I should have chosen a career more conducive to home life. I feel like maybe I was being an overachiever, and was really hurting myself overall," Jordan said, sounding completely depressed.

"Girl, there is no such thing as an overachiever. There is nothing wrong with shooting for the stars. You should be proud of yourself, not unhappy," Dakota told her.

"I know, but it's just that at some point I feel like as a woman we have to choose career or family. You can't overachieve at both."

"You can be successful at both, though, and I think you do a damn good job at both. I know for me, I don't know if I can handle my job, a man, and some snotty-nose kids. There is not enough time in a day," Dakota said with a slight giggle.

"I never had the mentality of a woman being kept by my man—I liked the feeling of being independent. I liked knowing that I didn't need anybody to sustain my lifestyle, and no man could feel me needing him was the reason I stayed. So, it's like, even when I consider lowering my standards of success, my gut never lets me settle. Yet, here I am, now that I have obtained most of all that I desired, and I am realizing that I may not have had my priorities straight," Jordan said.

"I think you're just PMSing, because there isn't anything wrong with you. I never wanted to need no man, either, but we all want one deep down inside. I think it's true you have to sacrifice certain things to save your marriage, but I don't think your career has to be one of them. You saw *Waiting to Exhale*—if your man walks out the door, you need to have taken care of you."

"Yeah, but what if he walks out because you're taking better care of you than him and your family?"

Dakota laughed. "You asking me? I'm a single bitch. I don't know." They both started laughing.

"I am really considering either giving up law or maybe becoming a teacher or something."

"After all you went through with law school?"

"I know. Law always seemed to be the most rewarding career I thought I could have. I would be proud of myself, have a lucrative income, and I could work for myself, which were all of my requirements. But it has become so stressful trying to balance my business and personal life, I am starting to lose some of my passion," Jordan said. After Dakota didn't reply right away, she continued, "Now my mornings are dreadful, and I hate getting up every day, dragging myself in to the office. My colleagues and staff are getting on my nerves—I am not being the fierce attorney I was known to be with some of my clients."

"Jordan, go to bed. You need sleep 'cause you are bugging out."

"I mean it. I know I am failing at motherhood and being a wife, and I hate to admit that to myself. I have no time to spend with Omar and Jason, and the little time I do have just isn't enough. Omar is doing all that he can as a husband, and Jason is the best son I could ask for. I just have to face the fact that sacrifice is needed to succeed at this point. My career isn't fulfilling anymore, especially when I come home to a house that's missing my nurturing."

"I want to see you home every night cooking and cleaning—that would be a sight. You have never been a domestic chick, so don't try now."

"I know I'm not the housewife type, either. Shoot . . . I'll be making microwave dinners every night," Jordan said, laughing at herself.

"Jordan, you will be just fine. I am not always happy in my field. It's competitive and cutthroat—sometimes I have to deal with some real egos, but at the end of the day there aren't too many other things I'd rather do."

"I've considered going back into some of my niches before law— entertainment, freelance writing, or maybe something new. I want to be able to keep my freedom as well as my income, but being an attorney is hard to beat. I am willing to sacrifice the prestige and money, but only if it is something that fulfills me in a different way."

"Girl, you're just burnt out, and you need a break."

"It's not that easy to take a break when you're in the middle of major deals," Jordan replied.

"What does Omar say?"

"I try to discuss it with Omar, but he has a tendency to make me feel even worse about these 'simple problems.' As usual, he thinks my dilemma is ridiculous and is no help at all. It just leads to arguments because I feel like he is not being sympathetic to my needs. I don't need the added stress. At times he can be so inconsiderate and insensitive. He makes me feel like my issues are trivial and I am just making a big deal out of them."

"Well, they're not trivial, but you do need to count your blessings."

"I know in the scheme of life they aren't serious issues, but in the scheme of my life, they matter."

"Listen, drama queen, you getting all poetic on me and shit . . . go to bed," Dakota said, laughing.

"Good night . . . love ya," Jordan said, laughing as well.

"Love you, too, girl," Dakota said, and she hung up.

29

Perfect Timing

It was Monday morning, and it was Jayon's first day back in the office. He was out all last week on the annual cruise that he went on with his family. Ten A.M. rolled around, and he still wasn't in yet.

Jordan made some calls and started typing one of her case briefs. At about 10:30 A.M. she finally saw his name sign in the computer. She felt a bit of excitement go through her. *Jayon's back*, she thought to herself. She didn't know why she got excited. She was used to Jayon, talking to him about work and home. When he wasn't around, she felt his absence more than she cared to admit sometimes. She had her girls to talk to, of course, but Jayon also knew a side of her most people didn't. Like her thing to be honest with Omar—he didn't make fun of her for it like her girls did. He knew how she took pride in being faithful in her relationship, and he was the same way when he was in a relationship. He was the friend that she could talk to for hours, and he would listen. He never judged her, and he always had a way of looking on the bright side. Jayon was the type of man that was going to make some lady very happy one day. For some reason they just hadn't found him yet.

After about fifteen minutes, he walked into her office and when he approached her desk, he placed a bag down in front of her. The plastic bag advertised Royal Caribbean Cruises.

"Those are your souvenirs," he said.

"For me?" she asked jokingly.

Jordan peeked in the bag at her treats. There was a bottle of Gucci Rush perfume, a key chain, a handmade jewelry box from Puerto Rico, a picture frame from Jamaica, and some other trinkets from the boat.

"Thank you, Jay," she said as she gestured with her face to come get a kiss.

"You're welcome," he said as he leaned over and kissed her forehead.

"My mom asked about you. She said you should come on the cruise again."

"I know, it's been a while. I would love to go again," she replied.

"Well, you're welcome to come anytime."

She started to fiddle with some of her souvenirs.

"Make sure you tell your mother I said hello. I have to go by there and see her."

"So, how is everything going?" he asked, changing the topic.

"Cool, I guess," she said. "Work was busy last week. Two new clients."

"That's great."

"Yeah—great, I guess. Two new clients, two hours less spent at home every week."

Jayon looked at her with disbelief.

"Jordan, you're not allowing yourself to be thankful for your blessings. Every good thing that happens for you is counteracted by something negative in your mind."

"I know, Jayon, but that is how it seems these days . . . the more successful I get at work, the more unsuccessful my marriage is becoming, and I truly don't know what to do."

"I can imagine that it's not easy. Still, if you're going to dread each accomplishment, you might as well just stop practicing now or stop trying to build your practice. It makes no sense to strive for something and then when you get it, regret it," he said.

"I know—I just wish he would give me this time to get where I want to be and then in time I will balance it all out."

"Why don't you try to include him more?" he asked.

"I have—he usually doesn't want to get involved. He doesn't want to hear it, he doesn't want to go anywhere with me—he'd rather complain. He says he just wants a regular marriage—he doesn't want to have to be out at all the Hollywood parties just to spend time with me."

"I can feel him on that, but . . ." Before he could finish his thought, Jordan's phone rang, and before she could read the Caller ID, her assistant answered. Seconds later, she walked in and said Omar was on the phone.

"Give me a second," she said to Jay.

"Don't worry, I need to get caught up in my office anyway. I will come back in a few." He walked out.

She answered the phone. "Hey, sweetie."

"What's up?"

"Nothing much."

"Listen, can you bring home some of those cookies you brought home last night with you tonight?"

Laughing, she said "Damn greedy . . . you called me to ask me that?"

Realizing how greedy he sounded, he replied "Shut up. Those cookies were good as hell. I was thinking about them all morning."

"Yes, sweetie. I will bring some home."

They hung up the phone, and she continued back with her work that she was doing before Jayon came in. She started to think about what Jayon said, and things she was doing wrong and the things she did right. She thought about the people she affected with her decisions and the people that she let affect her decisions. She wondered how women all across the world dealt with these issues. She also realized that successful women like Oprah didn't have children or a husband, which allowed them to be such impressive career women. Oprah was Jordan's idol, but she knew that it was too late for her to follow in her footsteps. She always envied her for what she stood for, and being an African-American woman with power and dignity. Even Oprah, who seemed like she could do and had done it all, probably had to sacrifice somewhere. If she had kids and a husband, maybe she would have given up some of her success.

Jordan remembered her old boss when she worked in radio was also a very successful, powerful woman. She told Jordan it was hard to be a mother and wife and be successful, that in this business you had to give up something. She had a chance then to change her goal, but Jordan was already years into love with Omar and wanted nothing more than to pop out a baby. So although she wanted success, she thought she could do it all. Now here she was, trying to figure out most successful women with kids greatest challenge. Another woman she used to work with who had a very high title stepped down in position, accepting less money and power. She told Jordan that she made the decision because on her tombstone it would never read her salary or title at work, but it would read loving mother and wife. In life every woman has to find her own way down this path, and Jordan just had to take some time to find hers.

30

Two Birds with
One Stone

DJ Envy was having a private party to celebrate his new television show. Jordan had to attend—he was a good friend of hers and a very important person in the music industry. In Jordan's field you just didn't miss these affairs unless you had to. Besides, she had known Envy and his wife since she worked in radio years ago.

It took a lot, but she convinced Omar to attend with her. She knew bringing your spouse to events like this was always risky, but she figured she had more to lose by leaving him home. Any opportunity to get in quality time with the husband and still get some work done was a great thing for her. Once they got there, she could tell that it was going to be an interesting evening. Her plan was to stay for a short while in hopes of avoiding any drama, and then be on her way back home with her husband in tow.

DJ Clue was spinning and Fabolous was hosting. The guests ranged from music artists and Hollywood actors, MTV hosts and radio personalities to music business executives. It was a who's who affair. Jordan visually searched for Envy and his wife—she had decided not to walk through the crowd to try to avoid any uncomfortable moments. In the business, there was a lot of innocent flirtation and other things that could easily be taken the wrong way. They were all used to it, but their spouses weren't. It was very likely that someone wouldn't notice a spouse, and say something that would make someone and their spouse uncomfortable. By the end of the night, the couple's arguing, or they're thinking in the back of their minds that you must be some type of whore at work. This was usually the reason people didn't bring their spouses with them, and when they did, it was a task to introduce them before you greeted anyone. For Jordan, it was just easier to play the background so that Omar wouldn't feel out of place. So she didn't work the room; at most parties she just stayed in one place and conversed with Omar. Even Omar could tell she wasn't herself. People came up to her and said hello, and she would introduce them to Omar and make very little small talk.

Finally, Envy walked in with his wife, and she was happy because she knew that she didn't have to stay much longer after he arrived. She had been there about an hour already and she wanted to stay about a half an hour more, but she knew she couldn't leave until she at least saw the guest of honor. He walked in with all his icy jewelry on, of course, having to make a grand entrance. His wife, Gilda, looked absolutely beautiful. She, too, was blinding people with her dazzling jewels. Envy had been working hard in this business since he was in college. He had done well for himself, and he was finally at the top of his game. He was happy and he deserved every minute of it.

They made their way through the crowd, giving out hugs, kisses and handshakes. Everyone who was there to congratulate them waited for them to stop by. In the meantime, everyone continued in conversation, periodically glancing to see how far through the crowd they had made it. One of Jordan's clients, Black Jewlz, a new artist from Queens, was there and he came over and had started talking with her and Omar. He was with his manager and one of his boys. He had just released his first single on Virgin Records. The video was out, and it was receiving a lot of airplay throughout the country. So, although he was new, he had a buzz already, and a career with potential. They discussed what was going on with him, and his new fame. He seemed excited and said so far it had been nothing but great.

Finally, Envy and Gilda approached.

"What's up, J," he said as he gave her a hug.

"Hey, Env," Jordan replied. "Congratulations." She introduced them to Omar, and as he and Omar did the handshake-pound thing, she gave Gilda a hug.

"You look amazing, miss," Jordan said to her.

"You do, too," she said.

"How are the kids?" she asked.

"Both of them are doing great—Kahmel just started the second grade," Gilda replied.

"Damn, time flies," she replied, laughing.

They talked a bit more, about the kids, and Envy's new show. After a few more minutes they went on to finish greeting the rest of their guests and Omar and Jordan went back to their conversation. They sipped on their drinks and talked about different upcoming artists and some of the new ventures of the old artists. It was real cool for Jordan to talk to Omar and let him know about things she was working on and get his feedback. When they first got married, he used to be real interested in her line of work. He would tell her about songs he thought would be cool for airplay when she was working in radio. When she was fresh out of law school, he would tell her about street artists that he heard of who were looking for representation. He was into it—Jordan figured that was until he felt it took her from him. Then one day he decided that it was the last thing he wanted to talk with her about. So, she was actually enjoying sharing her updates about her work with him again.

By the time they left the party they had been there about two and a half hours. She had introduced him to a lot of the celebrities and executives, and a lot of people told him how nice it was to finally meet him since they had heard so much about him. She felt the whole evening helped let Omar feel better about what she was doing. She thought he was able to see that he was just as much a part of her work life as she was. She brought him with her even when he wasn't there.

On the way home, they decided to let Jason stay at his grandmother's—she would take him to school in the morning. As soon as they got home, before they even had a chance to change clothes, Omar backed her up against their bed and started kissing her neck and grabbing on her breast. Maybe it was the liquor, maybe it was seeing his successful wife in her world, or maybe it was just that he was finally trying to remember that they were in this life together. Whatever it was, Omar hadn't been so passionate with her in what felt like a year or two. She had no complaints whatsoever—she gave him just what he was asking for, all of her, right back.

31

The Freaks Come Out at Night

Ten, nine, eight, seven, six, five, four, three, two, one . . . Happy New Year! The New Year was here, and the crowd in Dakota's house was jumping all over the place. She threw a little party to bring in the New Year and it was getting a little wild . . . even Jordan was a little tipsy. She was happy because she was just hired by one of Elektra's new artists and she had wanted him as a client for months. Omar was there with her—Keith even came with Chrasey. The party was real nice and even better than Dakota was expecting. It was just supposed to be a little gathering, but the word had spread and people brought other people and before she knew it she had a house full. Lexia had invited a few friends, male and female, including the girl from the mall, Monique.

Dakota had hired a professional waitress as she usually did for her affairs. The woman just walks around serving the hors d'oeuvres and drinks. Dakota damn sure wasn't doing that. She always felt that hiring help was just the diva thing to do. She barely decorated, but she had a banner hanging, and had some noisemakers and party hats for the guests. In one room she had holiday music playing and in the other she had Hot 97's Top 97 songs of the year on the radio. So the romantics and more mature folk were able to cuddle and smooth-talk to TLC's happy new year song, and Kenny G and the others were able to jam to Kanye and Jamie Foxx's Gold Digger song, Mary J. Blige, Papoose, Keisha Coles, Busta Rhymes, and G-Unit. The key ingredient for the party was the liquor and she had more than enough of that. All the guests were having a good time, and Dakota was off in the corner somewhere talking to a client.

By one o'clock in the morning everybody had their buzz on and was involved in conversation or in a corner hugged up with somebody. Dakota was trying to play hostess, but she was having too much fun testing her player skills by having Tony, David, and the guy she met at the club all there mingling. After her fourth drink she was scared she would be too out of it to keep the game up, and she would blow herself up. It was going pretty well, because Tony had his own friends there, so he was preoccupied; David was sitting and talking with another co-worker of hers; and the new guy came with a friend as well. So since no one wanted her undivided attention, she was able to handle the situation quite well. She also knew none of them really knew of each other or what each other looked like, except that one time, David showed up at her door unexpectedly when she was expecting Tony. She asked if he could stop by at another time because she was waiting on someone to be there any minute. He seemed to understand and left right away, but it just so happened that Tony was walking up the hallway as David was leaving. She was sure they both saw each other in the hall, and being that Dakota's the only black person on her floor, they had to have some funny thoughts about each other's purpose there. When Tony came in with his detective hat on, she 'fessed up and told Tony that her co-worker David had just stopped by to drop off some work. Well, she *kind* of 'fessed up. Tony was no fool, though—all he had replied was, "Mmm. You have some very accommodating co-workers."

So during the party she figured they might recognize each other, but she wasn't worried, because she was sticking to her story either way. Besides, between the two of them, she was only really involved with and having sex with Tony. She hadn't messed with David since that time a few months ago, so there was not much to hide. The guy from the club she hadn't even slept with since that night, either. They had spoken on a few occasions since that night, and she had every intention on giving him some the first time Tony pulled another missing-in-action routine; and even though Tony was the only one who had some rights to say anything, even he knew his rights were limited because they weren't officially committed. It was cool, though, because the boys and girls were playing nicely, and Dakota had nothing to worry about so far. Although Chrasey and Jordan couldn't believe she had all of them at the same party, Dakota's rebuttal was that there was more where they came from, and she actually left most of her black book off the guest list.

It was late and the bottles were getting empty. People were slowly starting to leave. Jordan and Omar left the earliest so they could pick up their son and get home in time for Jordan's freaky side to visit Omar for the New Year. Both David and Dakota's new friend left soon after, leaving Dakota at ease and with a feeling of victory. After a great deal of the crowd left, Chrasey decided to drag Keith's drunken butt home. Then it was only a few more inebriated people sitting around who seemed to have no intention of leaving anytime soon. Dakota was walking around, straightening up some. Lexia helped, until she went to lie down in the guest room. Dakota was in no rush to make the rest of the guests leave until Tony smacked her butt, hinting what she was in store for, and she began kindly getting everyone's coats and helping them on their way out.

Once the house was clear, other than Lexia in the guest room, it took only a few minutes before Dakota and Tony were rolling around in her bed. Their hormones had been raging all night and they were being released with every heavy breath they took. Once they managed to undress each other, Tony wasted no time pleasuring Dakota, making sure to moisten her body before he took her for a ride. He licked, kissed, and touched her all over. Once she started squirming and practically begging, he rose on top of her and gave her what she was asking for. Both high with lust and drunk from Hennessy, the moment seemed to be as intense as it could get.

He thrust in and out of her as if he was trying to cause her pain, but pleasurable pain it was. The bed was banging up against the wall and Dakota's petite body was jerking back and forth with each bang. Tony was trying to bring the new year in right, making sure Dakota remained sprung off his pipe game. They were both breathing so heavy and banging up against each other so hard, they didn't even notice Lexia in the doorway.

As she took a step inside, her footsteps made a slight noise and Tony was the first one to notice. When he looked over his shoulder, he saw Lexia coming into the room. She was in only her bra and panties and was approaching the bed. Lexia could hear Dakota's moans and groans all the way in her bedroom, and the sounds of their sex were turning her on. She couldn't take it anymore—she had to at least try to join in the fun. This wasn't the first night—there were many nights when she had overheard Tony and Dakota's sex sessions. Usually, she would turn the TV up to drown it out, or try to cover her head with a pillow; some nights she would just give in to the urge and listen and pleasure herself. But tonight, alcohol was in her system, she was excited, and she just couldn't resist anymore. Once she entered the room and saw Tony's sexy body with sweat all over it and Dakota's naked body spread on the bed, she was even more excited. She wasn't invited, but she felt confident that they would both be happy she came.

Tony and Dakota had both noticed her slowly walking toward the bed, and neither of them stopped what they were doing. Lexia was looking very sexy, her perfectly shaped body covered in nothing but a sexy lace bra and panty. The sight of her just heightened their sexual senses. Tony was looking at Dakota, then glancing at Lexia as she made her way to the bedside, never stopping his strokes in and out of Dakota. He grew more excited as he realized what was taking place.

Once Lexia noticed that neither of them was jumping to cover themselves, she knew that she was going to join the party. Dakota wasn't sober, but her mind had a million thoughts running through it, most of them saying, *Girl, get up and curse this chick out.* She was also waiting for Tony's reaction, but everyone seemed to just be silent, almost ignoring what was happening. Of course, it's every man's fantasy, so Tony wasn't going to speak first. Dakota knew that when she saw it on porno films it turned her on, but she wasn't trying to experience it. Her mind was thinking to stop her, but it was like her mouth was on mute. Before Dakota could even sort her thoughts to react Lexia's lips were on hers!

After Tony realized that the fun was just about to begin, he removed himself from on top of Dakota and allowed Lexia to continue pleasuring Dakota as he watched. With Tony out of the way, Lexia immediately made her way down south. Once Tony was sure that Dakota was enjoying herself, he began to give Lexia what he was sure lured her in the room to begin with. Dakota was being brought to orgasm by Lexia, while Tony was banging Lexia from the back. Dakota couldn't believe she was participating in this, but it all felt so good she didn't want to stop. Her emotions were feeling all crazy inside, but her body was screaming for more. She wasn't taking the time to evaluate the situation—she was living in the moment, but all she knew was that she was going to have regrets in the morning time.

32

Loose Lips

Jordan had just walked in the office, but before she could even sit down, her cell phone rang. Hands full with her briefcase, purse, and a cup of coffee, she decided to let it go to voice mail and tend to it after she set down her belongings. She put everything down, hung up her coat, and fixed her "hat hair" with her fingers. As soon as she settled at her desk and signed on to her computer, she looked in her phone and saw it was Omar who had called her and that he had left a message. Omar usually didn't leave messages, so out of curiosity she dialed her voice mail first before calling him back. The first few calls were clients and colleagues who called the previous night; she listened as she jotted down some of their information. Then the last call was from 9:10 A.M. and it was Omar's message.

"As I was on my to work this morning I remembered a conversation that I had with Jayon at Dakota's house. I guess I was too out of it to register it all then, but I would love for you to explain it to me. Give me a call when you get this."

She could tell by the tone in his voice that he was perturbed. He remained calm on his message, but she knew that was the prelude to what he really wanted to say. That was the preparation message.

Jordan's mouth dropped. She had never found the right time to explain to Omar what had happened between her and Jayon; she knew that he would flip, knowing that she still had to work with him every day. *Damn, what did Jayon say?* she thought to herself. She sat there panicking—she knew that nothing had happened between her and Jayon, but she also knew Omar was going to be more upset that she never told him and was going to feel like she had been hiding something. She didn't want to call Omar back unprepared. By leaving her a message he had given her a fair opportunity to come correct in her response. She couldn't call back without knowing what she was and wasn't going to say about the matter. As her brain ran through everything, she realized it was about 9:30 and Jayon may be in already—she could just ask him. She jumped up and went straight into Jayon's office. She passed by Jackie, barely registering that she had just walked in a half-hour late. She reached Jayon's office and he was also just getting in.

"Morning, J," he said as soon as he saw her walk in.

"Morning, Jayon—sorry to bust in here first thing in the morning but . . . what did you say to my husband the other night at the party?"

Jayon's expression changed completely. "What are you talking about?" he asked.

"Don't tell me you were too drunk to remember, Jayon."

"Remember what?"

"Omar left me a message this morning asking me to explain a conversation that you had with him, and he didn't sound very happy about whatever it was."

After a few moments of thinking, he replied, "Oh, yeah."

"Oh yeah *what*, Jayon?"

"I just apologized for my actions."

"What actions, Jayon?" Jordan said in a panicked tone. "What did you say, exactly?"

"I said 'sorry about that situation with me and J. I was going through a lot and didn't mean to disrespect you or her.'"

Jordan just wanted to reach down, grab her shoe, and throw it right at his head. Trying to remain calm, she asked, "And what did he say, Jayon?"

Jayon knew Jordan was annoyed, because she kept saying his name in all of her questions. She always did that when she was trying not to get upset with him; it was like she was reminding herself who he was and not to go crazy on him like he was a witness on the stand or something.

"He just said that it was OK, no problem . . . what, did you not tell him about it?"

"No, Jayon, I didn't! But thanks for telling him for me. Now he is going to think it was even more than it was because I never told him."

"Well, why didn't . . ."

"Don't even ask me why I didn't tell him, Jayon. The question is, why did you? Or for that matter, why did you ever have to take it there in the first place?" She stormed out of the office, leaving the door open behind her. Jackie and the file clerk had happened to be standing close by the door, and it was obvious they had both caught the early-morning closing arguments.

"Good morning," they both said as she walked by them.

She muttered "Good morning" back to them and continued down the hall. *Dammit,* she thought to herself. *Great way to add more drama to the situation.* She knew they would be gossiping about it with everyone all day.

Once she got to her office, she noticed Jayon was not following her. She bravely picked up her phone and dialed Omar's number. She thought perhaps she should wait, but she didn't want him wondering what she was doing at work that she couldn't call him back. While it was dialing, she intercomed to Jackie to hold all her calls until she got off the phone. After a few rings and sweat beads on her forehead, his voice mail picked up.

"Baby, it's me. I just got your message. I think I know what you're speaking of, and if I'm right, I can explain. Please give me a call back when you get this so we can talk. 'Bye."

33

It Hits the Fan

"He is just your friend, right? All that bullshit you be kicking and the nigga tried to push up on you and you still trying to front like shit was all good . . ." Omar yelled.

They were sitting in her bedroom, arguing for the past fifteen minutes about what had happened months ago when Jayon made that move on Jordan in the office. She had planned to tell him, she swore she had. The right time just never came around, and now he thought the worst.

"Omar, he was drunk, and he apologized several times. He didn't mean anything by it and I knew that. I was going to tell you, but I wanted to tell you at a time when me and you weren't arguing over him or my job, or when me and you were stable enough to handle another issue," she explained.

"What issue? You claim it was nothing."

"It was, but I knew like now you would make a bigger deal out of it than it was."

"Oh, I'm making a big deal out of this? This dude that you claim has just been your friend for all of these years, and that you work with and spend more time with in a week than you do with me and your son, tries to fuck you and you say that I'm making a big deal out of it?" he said in a sarcastic tone.

By this time, tears were streaming down her face. She couldn't take it anymore. Omar yelling, her confusion and guilt. She had lost control and she knew that if she was in Omar's shoes she would feel the same way.

"He didn't try to fuck me," she said through her tears.

"So, what you think that was, he just wanted to try and see if you would do something with him, but he wouldn't have if you let him? Please, Jordan, you sound retarded."

"No, I'm just saying it didn't go that far. It was just a conversation—he was drunk. The very next day when he was sober he apologized," she said.

"Yeah, because you didn't give him none," he replied.

"Well, where is my credit then? I didn't do it—does that mean anything?"

"First of all, this isn't about you—this is about him and his pretending to be just your friend and he knows that he is just waiting in the wings . . ." he said. She opened her mouth to reply, and he shouted over her, "And as for you, NO, it doesn't mean anything . . . you might as well have fucked him. You been with him day and night since like the shit was all right what he did, and you kept it from me and let me smile in his face like everything was sweet . . . and you claim to be all honest . . . yeah, OK, honest about everything except the stuff about your good ol' best friend," he said.

Still crying, she couldn't believe what she was hearing. She was just as guilty as if she had given in to Jayon, is what Omar was saying.

"I was going to tell you, I swear—it was just never a good time," she said.

"I bet, never a good time to say, 'hey, babe, Jay asked me to have sex with him, but I said sorry. Now, see you later tonight around eleven—I'll be with him all night,'" he said mockingly.

"So what was I supposed to do, make him close his business over a mistake?" she asked.

"So you chose to risk losing your marriage over his mistake?"

"Why would I lose my marriage? Nothing happened . . ."

"Jordan, that nigga shouldn't even still be an issue. Ever since you guys' little month together when we broke up that time, I told you I wasn't feeling him and you being friends, but you refused. Then you go and share an office with him, and I just sat here to see how far you would let things go," he said.

"We haven't been anything more than friends since me and you got back together. You sat and watched, you say, but then you saw that nothing happened . . . it's been strictly business and nothing more," she replied.

"Until one day, he comes in the office drunk and tries to push up on you?" he said.

"Drunk . . . drunk, Omar. Don't act like you have never been drunk and misbehaved since we have been married."

"Whatever, Jordan—keep defending him. You can't even help yourself. You're so busy trying to keep him up on a pedestal, you don't even hear the stupid shit you say," he said.

"Omar, I understand your point. I just want you to understand you're imagining the worst."

"No, you think the worst would be that you did fuck—that's not the worst, because at least you could see then that you are just as wrong and that that nigga is no better than the rest of them . . . He wants the same thing they all want. The worst is having you stand here thinking he is some kind of angel, and you look me in my face knowing that you think he is better than me," he said.

"Omar, I don't think that. You are my husband. He is just my friend. He can never take your place in my life or in my heart," she said, sincerely meaning every word.

"Prove it, then—it's either him or me," Omar said.

She was speechless at his sudden ultimatum.

He continued, "I'm done with this shit. You have a choice—if you don't let that dude go, I'm done."

"Are you saying you are going to leave me if I don't end my friendship with Jay?" she asked.

"That's exactly what I'm saying."

"I can't kick him out of the building—he is on the lease," she said.

"Well, then you leave, I don't care what you have to do, but you have a choice," he said as a matter of fact.

"So, close up my office and start all over because you can't have a little more faith in me?" she asked.

"I have faith in you, but I don't have faith in him."

"Well, Omar, that's a lot to ask. You can't expect me to choose between you and my career that I have worked for so hard. That's selfish," Jordan said desperately.

"Is it really? Was it selfish when you agreed to work on the same floor as him? Was it selfish when you started to work day and night and were never home, so he got to see you more than I did? Was it selfish when half of your colleagues thought he was your husband because you attended all of those parties with him? And *I'm* selfish?" Omar said.

"He comes because he is doing business like I am, and you were welcome to come as well. And I can't help having to work late hours—you think I don't want to be home?" Jordan asked.

"Why would I come? I don't want to be his backup. You go with him usually, and you can't help working late hours. There is just no rush to get out of there, because you're there with your homeboy."

"If that's what you think, then fine. I can't change your opinion—think what you want. I'm tired of arguing. I don't know what I can do to make you see the truth."

"I don't know what to do to make *you* see the truth, but I know I refuse to let this nigga have my wife while I sit home with our son," he said as he walked out of the room.

It's funny how men and women can perceive the same thing totally differently. Here Omar had made up his mind that Jayon was after his wife and that she was being totally selfish by having another man around. On the other hand, she saw Jayon as a remedy for her and Omar's unhappiness. If it wasn't for Jayon keeping her sane half the time, her and Omar's marriage would be terrible. Not to mention that Jayon was enjoying his single life—he wasn't plotting on how to get Omar's wife. There was no way Omar would ever believe that, though. He thought everything Jordan said, was because she was defending Jay's throne, when in reality she was defending theirs.

34

Jekyll and Hyde

"Quinton, get in here and finish this math problem," Chrasey yelled toward the living room.

She was in the dining room helping the kids with their homework, and somehow Quinton got slick and walked away while she was focusing on a problem with Kelsey.

"One," Chrasey yelled. When she started counting, they knew that she wasn't playing. He came running back to his seat.

"Now, finish these math problems." She didn't have time to sit there all night with these two. Homework was always the worst time—they always wanted to start playing or talking with each other. Getting them to concentrate was the hardest part. She tried separating them, but it made it harder for her to help both of them with their work.

"Is it four, Mommy?" Quinton asked after he did some scribbling on the paper.

She looked over at what he had done. "Yes, baby. You see, it's not hard. You just have to try."

A few moments later, the door opened and closed. She could hear Keith coming in the house. He came in to the dining room, and of course the kids took advantage of the opportunity to break their concentration. At first she wanted to tell them to sit back down and do their work, but she didn't want to prevent Keith from getting a loving greeting after his long drive home to Queens.

"Hey, Daddy" they both yelled.

"Hey," he replied as he walked toward them. He patted Quinton on the head, gave Kelsey a kiss on the forehead, and then leaned over to Chrasey and gave her a kiss.

She almost didn't know what to think. Keith never greeted her anymore—maybe with words, but hugs and kisses? Not for quite some time.

As the kids finished their work, he sat down and began to talk to them. He seemed to be in such a good mood. He was telling them that after they finished their homework he wanted them to draw three cool places they wanted to go or things they wanted to do, because he had a surprise for them. His exact words were, *Me and Mommy have a surprise for you.*

Where was this coming from? He had been home for over five minutes and he wasn't in the living room with his beer—something was wrong. While he finished answering all of their questions about the surprise, Chrasey decided to get up and make his plate. She poured him a glass of juice and walked into the dining room with it.

"Where do you want your plate? In here or in the living room?"

"I'll take it right here," he said.

She walked around the table and put the plate down in front of him.

"Thank you, baby," he said as she placed the glass down.

"You're welcome, " she replied. She was completely confused. She tried to act normal but her mind was racing. Baby? Thank you? A kiss? Was it her birthday or an anniversary she forgot about? It felt like some sort of prank. She wanted to ask what was going on but she didn't want to start any problems, and the kids were there. Still, she wasn't sure what to do.

"So how are things at work?" he asked once she sat back in her chair.

"They are going well. I may be getting a new title and more money real soon," she replied.

"Really? That is great. What's that about?"

"Well, they were going to hire someone else to work with me to handle this new program we started, but my manager asked me if I wanted a promotion instead and I would just pick up the extra work, and I said yes. I know it's just because it saves them money, but it also earns me more so, hey."

"That is really good, baby. I'm proud of you."

She couldn't believe that Keith was having this conversation with her. Not just because he was showing concern about her job, but he was being so sweet.

"What about you? How is work?" she asked.

"Work is fine. Just doing some major projects and there are a lot of changes going on. It's been a little stressful but nothing I can't handle."

"That's good. At least you have new challenges that keep you from becoming bored at work."

She was amazed that Keith was showing an interest in what she was up to. He continued asking her questions about what she was doing and what she wanted to do; she actually began to enjoy the conversation. He told her what was going on at his job, and what he wanted to do next in his career. He even asked her about Dakota and Jordan, and what they were up to. She was amazed, but after a while she wasn't thinking about it. She was enjoying the rare moment that they were sharing.

When they finished dinner, he went up to the bedroom to get comfortable. When she walked into the bedroom to get a scrunchy to pull her hair back with, Keith walked up close to her. She tensed up some, and she could tell that Keith noticed it.

He looked in her eyes, and said in a sexy tone, "You look very nice."

"Thank you," she replied. It was weird that she felt so strange standing so close to her own husband.

"After you put the kids to bed, can you meet me back here in the bedroom?"

She tried to laugh it off. "OK—I'll see you then."

As she was putting the kids to bed, she heard Keith taking his shower and getting ready for bed, or for her to meet him in the bed. When she was finally done, she came into the bedroom and Keith was already in the bed. It appeared as if he came home with this on his mind. They hadn't done it in a while, and she wasn't looking forward to the awkward situation awaiting them. For her it was even more uncomfortable, because her last few sexual encounters were with Trevor and she wasn't emotionally prepared for the change. The sad part was she was sexually more comfortable with Trevor than she was with her own husband.

When she first felt his tongue in her mouth, she tried to just pretend that it was years ago when they were still a happy couple. It worked for a while—she just let herself go and tried to enjoy it for what it was. She tried to keep all the random thoughts from going through her head as he leaned over her, making love to her. She was feeling guilty that she no longer belonged to just him. She wondered if he noticed, she wondered if he cared to notice. Was he just horny, or was he trying to fix things between them?

She couldn't stop thinking. The more excited she saw him get, the more emotional she became. Before she knew it, tears began to roll down her face. Keith stopped for a quick moment, and asked was she all right. She told him she was just fine and to continue. He hesitated, but then he did go on until he was done. When he finished he held her in his arms and cuddled with her. It felt good to Chrasey for Keith to hold her. He probably thought she was crying because she was emotional about sleeping with him after so long. That did play a role, but even more so, it was guilt. Guilt from letting herself go so far with another man that her husband had become a stranger to her.

35

Support Group

Jordan had spent the week dealing with Omar's guilt trip and could barely take any more. She had beat Omar home every night that week, just to lessen the issue of the late nights working with Jay. Still it served no purpose, because once he got home he had this attitude, as if he didn't notice or care about her efforts. So, on this particular day she didn't even bother. Instead she asked Chrasey and Dakota to accompany her to an after-work dinner in an attempt to cheer herself up.

When she spoke to them on the phone, though, they both seemed to be in a bad mood themselves, possibly even worse off than her. It seemed ironic that they were all in the midst of some drama, but this wasn't the first time that all three of them were dealing with something serious simultaneously. After all these years of being friends, they had experienced a lot of their ups and downs at the same time. The worst part about when this happened was that it was hard for them to split the time up fairly to listen to and advise each other.

"It's been a while since Jordan had any drama for us, so let her go first," Chrasey said.

The usual unspoken rule was they would take turns, starting with the person who had the least drama before, and so forth. So according to the rule, it was Jordan's turn to go first.

"No, you go first, Chrasey—you have a lot more serious things going on with Keith. Besides, just getting out of my routine is healing enough for me," Jordan said.

They sat around the plush cushioned booth in Justin's restaurant, in deep thought. Chrasey updated the ladies on her current state of depression, and how Keith had been back and forth with his behavior. One night he was the extra-sweet husband, and the next back to normal. She was confused and didn't know if this was their gradual road back to happiness or something worse.

"I can't tell if his actions are because he is feeling guilty over something or if he is just actually ready to do right."

"You can't figure these men out, girl—they work on their own clock," Jordan replied.

As Chrasey talked, Jordan listened and commented and Dakota was quieter than they had seen her in all the years they'd known her. Well, other than the time she slept with that basketball player twenty minutes after meeting him and waited two days to tell anyone because she was too embarrassed, but that was in college.

"It's just . . . I never thought I would be at this point in my life," Chrasey said. "I thought I'd be making more money by now, I thought I would be happy in my marriage. I'm just disappointed in myself, that's all."

"You're being too hard on yourself, Chrasey," Jordan said.

"Yeah, you say that now. But if you knew how I've practically fallen in love with a boy, you would be just as disappointed."

"I'm not condoning that Trevor thing, but you're still being too hard on yourself."

"Jordan, I have snuck out to meet him almost once every week for the past two months. I have bought him things I had no business buying, and I think about him all the time. I'm pathetic."

"No, girl, you're just sprung," Jordan said as she burst out laughing. Chrasey joined in and when they both looked at Dakota, they noticed she was giving one of her phony laughs. Now, that was something Dakota would say and she didn't even find it funny.

"And what is wrong with you?" Jordan asked.

"Nothing, just so much on my plate," 'Kota replied.

"Look, I called you girls so you could hear my issues, but you two are depressing me even more. Got damn, you two are useless."

"Tell us—what's wrong?" Dakota said, trying to perk up.

"Nothing, just Jayon. He opened his big mouth on New Year's Eve, apologizing for trying to come on to me, and Omar never knew."

"Oh, my goodness," Chrasey said.

"I know—he claims he is more upset that I didn't tell him all this time, that I claim to be so honest and yet I kept such a big secret. Of course, the fact that I work with him every day, and I see Jayon more than I do him, entered the conversation."

"See, the first time you don't tell him something, look what happens. I guess I see why you try to follow that honesty-best-policy rule," Chrasey replied.

"It just takes too much effort for me to try to keep a lie up—besides, once you're caught in a lie, nothing you say is believable. But with this I was going to tell him. I was just waiting for a good time. I tried to explain that to him, but he is not really trying to hear me . . ." Jordan said. After a quick pause, she continued, "I guess I understand why that sounds so naive, but it's still frustrating because he knows how I am but still he is treating me like I've been lying to him all through our relationship."

"Well, girl, he should know you wouldn't intentionally keep anything from him, as much as you tell him," Chrasey said.

"You would think. I guess because it's Jayon, he thinks I am protecting him"

Once again, Dakota hadn't commented at all.

"'Kota, what is wrong?" Chrasey suddenly shouted.

Brought out of a state of trance, she responded, "Just tired."

"Don't even try it," Jordan said. "Is it Lexia? She driving you crazy?"

The mention of her name made Dakota uncomfortable, and she quickly said, "No, nothing to do with her."

That's what she said, but her tone and instant attitude read just the opposite and Chrasey and Jordan picked right up on it.

"Mm-hmm, you're probably stressed out thinking that she is about to steal your man," Jordan laughed.

Dakota really didn't find a damn thing funny about that. She knew they were just trying to break the ice for her, but she'd spent the past couple of weeks trying to face reality and tell herself what happened; she definitely wasn't trying to tell them. She had barely had a full conversation with Tony or Lexia, and she went straight to bed almost every night and made sure her bedroom door was locked. The part that was making it so hard for Dakota was how nonchalant Lexia was about the whole thing. Once or twice she asked Dakota if Tony was coming over, she gave Dakota compliments every chance she got, and she was watching a porno one day when 'Kota came home, and suggested she watch it with her. 'Kota was starting to feel like a prisoner in her own house—she made her bed and now she was lying in it. Tony was quite nonchalant, too. He would walk around the house freely when he was there, wearing no shirt. He also made comments and asked about Lexia. The funny thing was, none of them had ever directly spoken about it.

Dakota's reluctance to talk about what was really going on gave the girls the hint. She would spill when she was ready—they had been friends long enough to know when one of them just needed to hear someone else's drama for a change, sometimes just to feel like they weren't alone in their mess. So, as they finished their dinner, Dakota remained somewhat quiet and Chrasey and Jordan vented. Chrasey explained how she found a matchbook from a hotel in Keith's pockets, and that she was ready to just run away with Trevor. Jordan recommended that Chrasey and Keith take a trip where they leave their kids at home and get away together. Perhaps all they needed was a change of environment, and maybe he would open up and talk to her.

They all came to the restaurant feeling a little down, but they all left feeling a little better than when they came. Jordan was feeling better because she was reminded that she wasn't the only one with problems. That helped, but what really elevated her mood was good old Chrasey reminding her "this too shall pass." That cliché always did the trick; whenever Jordan was getting depressed, that phrase would change her whole attitude toward life. Chrasey was feeling better because she really liked Jordan's idea and was looking forward to going home and trying to spark Keith up. She knew that Trevor wasn't her real answer, and she wanted to try to save her marriage before it got any worse. There wasn't a better time to work on it than when she had someone on the side, so any hurtful or discouraging thing wouldn't feel so magnified. So, Chrasey left feeling like she had work to do. Dakota didn't really get much off her chest, or really get to enjoy the therapeutic evening like Chrasey and Jordan, but she felt better because she knew in her heart when she was ready to tell her friends the drama she had gotten herself into, they would be there for her. They would listen to and attempt to mend her life just like they did for each other tonight.

36

Boiling Point

Dakota walked in her house and as usual, quietly walked directly toward her bedroom, hoping to avoid Lexia. As she got closer, she heard that her television was on, and she slowed down some. It could have been Tony but she thought he told her he had something to do, and in her mind she was hoping it wasn't Lexia. As she approached her bedroom door, she could see Tony's Timberlands kicked off at the foot of the bed. As she got closer, she saw him lying on the bed in a white t-shirt and sweatsuit. Confused but relieved, she took a few more steps. That's when she noticed Lexia lying there beside him.

It wasn't like she even took a second to let the situation register. Her emotions just took over and before she knew it, she was reacting. All those nights of frustration and feeling like a prisoner came to a boil. The first word out of her mouth was "bitch." The rest kind of got mixed up but the gist of what she was saying, "Get the hell out, you nasty whore!"

"You don't understand, 'Kota. We were just talking," Tony said, jumping to their defense.

"Don't even say anything to me, Tony. I can't believe you would disrespect me in my own bed like this," Dakota replied, not even looking him in the face, keeping her eyes on Lexia.

"Dakota, we weren't doing anything, if that's what you're thinking."

"No, what I'm thinking doesn't matter. It's what I know—and I know you were lying in my bed with her. It doesn't matter to me what you were doing—you shouldn't even be in here with her."

At this point, Tony was looking out for himself. "'Kota, I was in here watching TV and she just came in. I'm not even sure how she ended up lying down, but I was just talking to her and I didn't touch her yet."

Now, Dakota's attention was directed to Tony. It all came flying out like one elongated sentence. "*Yet?* What the hell you mean, *yet?* . . . So you didn't touch her yet, but if I had gotten here two minutes later, you would have had sex with her, right? Not to mention what the hell are you doing here, anyway? I took my key from you, and this was why. I didn't want you around this trifling ho."

Before Tony could reply, Lexia interrupted. "Why are you acting like this, Dakota? Ever since that night, you have been bugging out. I thought we were all cool with everything."

"We are not cool, Lexia. I don't rock like that, OK?"

"What was that, your new year's resolution? Because you rocked like that on New Year's Eve," Lexia replied.

Why did she say that? As if Dakota hadn't been struggling with that terrible decision "to just let it happen," she had to go and throw it in her face. Before Dakota even thought twice, she lunged at Lexia. She was swinging, punching, pulling weave tracks out, and kicking. Lexia didn't have a chance; she had no idea the attack was even coming. Lexia had managed to pull the ghettoness out of petite, high-maintenance Dakota. Tony was finally able to pull Dakota off of Lexia, who staggered to her feet and was standing there in a ripped shirt, and a piece of weave track on her shoulder.

Gaining her composure, Lexia quickly walked out of the room into the guest room. Right before she entered, she heard Dakota yell at her, "Pack your stuff and get out of my house."

Scared to death, Tony sat silently as Dakota fixed her clothes and stood catching her breath. She tried to remain as calm as possible as she gathered her thoughts, but she couldn't stop the tears from rolling down her cheeks. Tony was too afraid to reach out and try to console her. She picked up the phone and dialed Chrasey's number. This was the time when she needed her girls. As she sat on the bed, she realized Tony was looking bewildered.

She put her hand over the phone, and said, "I don't know what the hell you're still doing here—you need to get out, too."

There was no answer on Chrasey's phone—she may have still been on her way home. She tried her other phone, and by then Tony had put on his boots and started to walk out. No answer on Chrasey's other phone, either. She was getting ready to call Jordan when she broke down in tears at the sound of Tony's exit.

"This has been going on for too long. I feel like I am still a wild college girl trying to have some fun," Dakota said aloud to herself. She stood there looking in the mirror, and she didn't like what she saw looking back at her. It's a horrible feeling not to be able to face the world, but an even worse feeling not to be able to face yourself.

"I am thirty-one years old and a grown-behind woman. There is no reason for me to be having threesomes and catfights, there just isn't. I haven't done this stuff since I was in college, and I should be ashamed of myself not to be past that," Dakota spoke out loud to herself as tears streamed down her face. "I should be settled down with one man by now, and I shouldn't feel the need to have to do this stuff to keep him. What is wrong with me?"

The guilt and shame had gotten the best of her. She stood leaning on the bathroom sink with buckets of tears rolling down her face. Her soul was crying out—she knew she had some major things in her life to change. She was in a world of make-believe. A world of anything goes. She was constantly pretending that her life was just what she wanted. She equated her loneliness to freedom, and her promiscuity to sexual expression; but she knew deep down she was leading an empty life, one where she had to share the man she was most committed to, and she never knew when her turn was. Dakota was starting to feel that her sexy single life was becoming stale, and if she didn't have something more to live for, she would just die inside. This incident just reinforced that for her. She was aware that she thought and lived outside the box, but even she knew that having a fistfight with one of your friends from college at the age of thirty-one was just downright ghetto. Besides, every woman knows the rule: you don't fight no woman over no man, and if you ever have to lose your cool, the man is the one you go after. Dakota came off as that insecure female who was always blaming the woman instead of her man.

"Lexia, she's no real loss as a friend—she was definitely on a different level than I am, and that girl is nothing but trouble. We are not in Iraq—I can't tolerate my man having free access to two women and I'm supposed to be comfortable with that," she murmured, trying to justify her reaction to herself.

As for Tony, she knew she had given up so much of herself for him. She put her pride aside and accepted things she knew she shouldn't have. She just couldn't believe that he would do something like that to her—he should've known better. All these thoughts ran through Dakota's head, until she realized she couldn't really blame them solely. Especially Tony—he was just being a man. He did what she allowed him to do. Still, the fact remained that they would never get married or have a real future. Tony said time and time again he wasn't even sure if he ever wanted to get married. Why she had chosen to settle for that, she didn't know. Why had she allowed him to crush her desire for more? She knew she should have kicked him to the curb.

Dakota had made her way to her bedroom and was lying on her bed. She had allowed her depressing thoughts to take over her small frame, and she just lay sprawled out on the bed with teary eyes and a wet face.

The crazy part was, David tried to be so good to her, but she treated him like Tony had been treating her—second hand. She was well aware that David was a good man—he would make a great husband and father, but she wanted the one who didn't really want her.

So typical of us dumb-woman types—then we wonder why we get dogged, she thought to herself. *We always want what we can't have.*

She guessed David was just too easy. Getting Tony to settle down would feel more like an accomplishment—he was more of a catch. David was easy—no bait was even needed. She thought the other part was that she was afraid that if he knew the side of her that most men would not want to make their wife, he would probably run, too. Still, she owed herself more.

I am a good person—maybe I have been a little promiscuous in my time, but I am not a whore, she said to herself.

After about ten more minutes of talking to herself, Dakota dozed off. The exhaustion from her boxing match, her tears, and her depression had finally worn her down. The next day would be when she really had to face the world, with shame, guilt, and no Tony.

37

Make Me Over

One more lap to go.

Chrasey was on her third lap around the track at Elmont High School. This was her second time here in the past week, and she was determined to complete the mile, unlike last time. She couldn't even remember the last time she went running before this week; and even with the walk one lap, run one lap trick, she was half dead.

The last couple of weeks Keith had been real back and forth at home. One night he was the sweetest husband, the man she married, and then other nights it was like he was back in his zone. At first she was excited about the change—she thought she was getting her husband back, but then she started to become frustrated. She never knew what she was coming home to. She wouldn't know if she should be prepared for nice Keith or mean Keith.

She had been trying really hard, too. Days that he would want to eat his dinner in the living room, she would sit with him. Even when he didn't acknowledge her, she wouldn't give up so easy; she would sit with him until they were done anyway. She would bring him a beer if she saw he was done with the one he had. She was just trying to be accommodating, even in his world that excluded her. It was either that or nothing, because most of the time he wouldn't watch TV or a movie with her, he wouldn't play games with her or share anything that they could call quality time. So she had to get what she could. There were some days when he would pay her some attention. They played card games once or twice, and he would come upstairs in the bedroom and watch sitcoms with her. She didn't know what went through his head on the different nights, what caused nice Keith and what caused mean Keith.

She started to wonder again if it was her. If she turned him off with her weight, body, and maintenance. She had decided to try to work on herself, just so she didn't have to feel that way. She also knew that even if it didn't make a difference with Keith, she still had Trevor and herself to impress. Ever since Trevor came in to the picture, she had felt more motivated to look good. It just felt nice, knowing that somebody would actually notice the difference. The last few times she was on a diet and lost a few pounds, Keith didn't even notice and if he did, he didn't care. More than likely he didn't pay her enough attention to notice a few pounds here and there. She had to lose a substantial amount before he would comment. With the hard work it takes to drop each pound, she wanted encouragement along the way, and Keith was not the source. This time, she was looking forward to getting compliments from Trevor. She knew she could count on him for that because he would notice everything different about her every time she saw him. Her hair, her nails, weight loss, jewelry, anything. It was amazing how good it felt to be noticed.

She was on Operation Chrasey. She even went out and bought herself some new clothes and shoes. She had been wearing a weave for a year, and had wanted to get the new fusion weave. It was really expensive, but last week she finally went ahead and got it. So with her new clothes, hairdo, and attitude, she was feeling like a whole new woman. People at her job noticed, the staff at her kids' school, too. A little effort for yourself goes a long way—she didn't have to feel like a stepchild when she went out with Dakota and Jordan now.

She had been considering getting that stomach-staple surgery, but she had agreed to give the natural route just one more try. Besides, Jordan, Dakota, and Keith were adamantly against her getting the surgery. They were all caught up on the possible side effects and risks. Chrasey's thing was she would give it one last try the "right" way, but if her behind didn't lose at least twenty more pounds, under the knife she went. It's not like it was plastic surgery or anything. It was just a procedure that made the size of your stomach smaller so you couldn't eat as much. That was all she needed, because she had no self-control on her own. When she was on a serious diet, she could sometimes lose the weight, but it was having the self-control to keep it off. Although she had already lost about twenty pounds, the loss had slowed down and she hadn't lost one pound since. That is why she figured it was time to include exercise. So since she made the promise to try, she was back at it.

She wasn't really up for all the work and deprivation anymore that comes with being on a diet and exercising, but she really wanted to feel better about herself. Trevor had been really good at making her see her worth. Sometimes she thought Keith wanted her big so she could keep her low self-esteem and accept his crap—it might be his way of keeping control. This time, though, it didn't matter—it was more about her than anyone else.

When she was at work and she would hear a fat joke, she would always just assume it was about her. She was so self-conscious it was becoming awful to be around people. She always felt like they were thinking about how fat and nasty she looked, even if they weren't. Her arms were like sausages and in Chrasey's eyes, her stomach was literally disgusting. She didn't like looking in the mirror in the morning because she was never happy with what she saw. She didn't mind looking in the bathroom mirror or in her car mirror, where she could only see her face, because that was all she could bear half the time.

She was tired of feeling like the odd one out, the big one, the pathetic one. Before these past few weeks, she had started to feel defeated by her circumstances. Especially after being able to enjoy her initial weight loss, she was getting frustrated that she couldn't lose any more and was gaining some of those pounds back. Her career and her great kids were the only stability she had in her life. Her weight and her marriage were a complete disaster, and were both things that she felt she had no control over. For some reason she woke up one morning, determined not to give up. That was the same day that she went shopping and started back on her diet.

No more low-self-esteem Chrasey—it's all about me from now on, she thought to herself as she finished her laps.

38

Rebound

This was Dakota's third date in the past few weeks. Not booty calls but dates, and this was a lot of effort for her. She had to find a Mr. Right to fill Tony's shoes, though. Of course, for him to fill his shoes, he had to be successful and fine, so she had a scarce crop to choose from. Lucky for her, most of her colleagues were at least successful. There was this one real good-looking record-label executive, and an all right-looking VP of marketing for a major music television channel who had asked her out once or twice. Those were her first two dates—she had called them up and told them she would take them up on their offers. The date with the VP of marketing turned out to be more of a business dinner. That was fine with her, because he wasn't her type anyway. He was more of the professional guy who seemed like he had no real fun side. The record-label executive was more up her alley, but she didn't get the feelings that she was *his* type. He was cute and all, but he wanted a girl and not a woman. At lunch, just from the things he said, it was clear he only had game for a chick that didn't have much of her own stuff going on. Just because he wasn't her type didn't mean that she didn't sleep with him, though. She was still horny—they didn't have to get married but they could at least have one good night. He wasn't all that good in bed, though, so she could have done without. She had also met up with Darryl, the married man from the Mirage Club. They had a good time, but she was not in the mood to share another man.

This date tonight was with David. It had been a while since she and David had been anywhere other than her bedroom. They were on their way to catch a movie and get some dinner. He picked her up in his silver Acura, and when she came outside he opened her passenger door for her. She wasn't used to that with Tony, but she knew David was that type of guy, so she wasn't all that impressed. What David didn't know was that part of him was a turn-off. She didn't want chivalry. It came off as a weakness to Dakota. Her thing was let us just be ourselves at all times. She didn't need a man constantly trying to impress her. She liked being the center of attention, but she wanted to feel like she had the better end of the deal. When a man was constantly trying to flatter her, she felt like he was not worthy of her because he appreciated her too much. She knew it was kind of sick, but it's the way she thought sometimes.

They caught a movie, and then ate at a really nice restaurant. They had a lot of interesting conversation. It was like the perfect date, just not for her. She was able to see all of David's great qualities and what terrific husband material he was. He just wasn't her cup of tea. She liked the guys with a little edge, with a little bad boy in them, and David was the gentleman of the year. It's not that she wanted a roughneck—she just wanted a challenge, and David wasn't one.

With Tony, the excitement was knowing that when she got him it was like an award. He was something to be proud of—she had to work for him. Also, although David made good money, he couldn't compare to Tony. She wasn't being a gold digger, but she wanted a man with some money and power. That was one of the reasons she'd dealt with Tony so long, even if only for a little while, it was an honor to be with him. Being seen in public with him was a high. Just because he had a name and he had money, and most of the time they drew attention. The women would be jealous of her and the men envious of him. When he was playing ball, he was big, so he would get people telling him they miss him in the game, and all types of compliments. She couldn't just get with a regular guy after being with Tony.

By the end of her date with David, she realized there was no replacing Tony. Tony was Tony. If she wanted that kind of relationship, it would have to be him. Who is to say she would get a chance with somebody like him again? Tony was not the type of man to settle down before, like, forty, so she wondered what made her think another man like him would. Although Tony wasn't settling down with her, either, she had already invested time and effort into him so she had a better chance of cashing in with him than she did someone new. She realized that she hadn't been thinking straight, and she needed to get him back on the roster.

39

Can't Fool a Friend

Jayon felt uncomfortable being the root cause of Jordan and Omar's fights these days. He asked if he could call Omar and smooth things out, but she told him that would just make things worse. When he asked if he should work from home for some weeks or months until the whole thing died down, she told him that wasn't necessary. Her and Omar's issues weren't related to Jayon—it was everything to do with her and Omar. Jordan felt that if he just trusted her, and understood that she was married to the man she planned to be with forever, then none of this would matter.

This was an ego issue for Omar, and Jordan refused to involve Jayon or anyone else in this. Jayon had been nothing but a friend to her for the past thirteen years, and just because of an incident when he was drunk, Omar wanted to act as if he had been disrespectful to their marriage. The fact that years ago she and Jay were more than friends for that short period of time was irrelevant. That was in the past, and they were grown up now, and if Omar couldn't see that, she didn't know what he wanted from her.

"I can see why a male-female relationship like mine and Jayon's, where we are so close, could be uncomfortable, but we are both respectful and have brains. We both know that as long as I am in a relationship, there is no experimenting," Jordan said to Chrasey and Dakota.

"Please, if he was hip, he would realize he needs to be worried about your female friends, too," Dakota said, trying to make fun of herself and Lexia. The three of them laughed, realizing the truth in that.

They were on a three-way call. Dakota was at home in her Manhattan apartment, Chrasey was home in Queens, and Jordan was home in Elmont. None of them was up for meeting up to go anywhere, so the good old three-way call was going to have to be enough therapy for Jordan today.

"Maybe that's the thing, Jordan. You and Jay are only being respectful of your relationship. It's not like Jayon is butt ugly. Omar knows that it's just not impossible for something to happen," Chrasey said.

"But it's not going to. I just pray that Omar can understand that. Omar's gripe used to be that he felt I enjoyed being with Jayon more than him, or that I praised Jayon. Most friendships, male or female, were always a little more pleasant than a romantic relationship or marriage. That's just because there is no shared stress between friends. At the end of the day, Jayon and I go separate ways—we don't pay bills together or raise a child together. To compare the two relationships is ridiculous. Instead, what Omar does by being so unpleasant with me is make me need my friends that much more," Jordan said.

"Jordan, I must admit I am the one who is always about doing what floats your boat, but you're wrong on this one. If the situation was reversed, you would never stand for it," Dakota insisted.

"Men aren't as strong as we are when it comes to that, and females are trifling," Jordan replied.

"Omar probably thinks the same way, so you're being unfair," Dakota said.

"On one end, I hear it is unacceptable to have a friend of the opposite sex when you're in a relationship or married, but then it seems like Omar is being insecure and unfair. If he trusted me and our marriage, this shouldn't be an issue . . . and Dakota, you have to remember that the fact that he works with me changes the dynamics drastically. I don't hang out with him by choice—we are colleagues," Jordan rambled.

"To me that makes it worse," Chrasey said. "It would make me even angrier to know my husband spent the whole day with some woman five days a week."

"I see both angles, and I do understand Omar's issue. I just wish that life could be simpler. I wish that I could get credit for being a faithful and loving wife. There are women out there cheating on their husbands . . . not being funny, Chrasey . . ."

"Whatever—my situation is entirely different," Chrasey defended.

"I know, that's what I'm saying. Everybody's situation is different. There are women staying with their men because of their money. I am faithful to my husband, and I love him. I receive offers from many rich, successful, and delightful men, and not once did I ever indulge in any of the offers."

"Yeah, and you're stupid for that, too. I don't know what's wrong with you. Tell them to call me up," Dakota said, causing the girls to laugh.

"I know, Dakota. You still never let me live down giving that guy back that pink and yellow diamond ring," Jordan said, laughing.

"You damn right. Wouldn't be me," Dakota said.

"I won't *even* lie, that was the hardest thing to do . . . I felt like asking Omar if I could keep it, but I could tell by his reaction he wasn't even hearing that," Jordan said, laughing. "I'm just saying, I have had a client with fame and money practically beg me to leave my husband and marry him. Offering me expensive gifts and tickets for trips and things, and I wouldn't accept any of his gifts. Here I am with my husband, out of love and not for material reasons, and my only crime is having a male friend that I am 'too close' to. I'm just asking, where is my appreciation for what I do? It just seems unfair."

"Life ain't fair, heifer. Stop with your complaining," Chrasey said. "You're driving me and Dakota crazy about this damn job and that damn Jayon."

"If you want, send that fine-ass Jayon over to me. I'll bang him for you and you can live through me," Dakota said.

After they all laughed, Jordan said, "You get me sick, you dirty whore. I wouldn't let Jayon no where near your butt."

"You sure won't because whether you ever use it or not, deep down you know that's your emergency dick in a glass," Chrasey said.

"You two are bugging—I'm not paying y'all any mind. This is about Omar and me. I'm not checking for Jayon—less than a year ago I was getting sized for a dress to be in his wedding," Jordan said.

"Yeah, y'all both play the role so well. I'm not Omar—you don't have to *front* for me," Dakota said.

"I'm human—several people have caught my eye or made me wonder, but I haven't done anything," Jordan said.

"Jordan, I get it. Forget miss Dakota Diva over there. Don't worry. You have been faithful to Omar and that's all that counts. That's hard to do in a marriage these days, so you don't worry yourself," Chrasey added.

"Thank you, Chrasey. I might as well have cheated, as much as he accuses me of it," Jordan replied.

40

Done in the Dark, Comes to Light

Trevor was waiting at Red Lobster on Queens Boulevard, and Chrasey was trying to find a way to escape from home. She had already put the kids to bed and Keith was downstairs watching television.

She knew if she walked by and said nothing that she would give Keith an excuse to misbehave. She tried to always keep a certain image for Keith because any time Chrasey went out or did one thing that Keith didn't like, he would do something twice as bad, like stay out twice as late. Although Chrasey cared less about Keith's activities, she still hated wondering what he was up to when he was out for hours at a time.

Chrasey had been living on the edge with Trevor for about six months. Other than a guilty conscience from time to time, she was enjoying her Trevor extravaganza just fine. They had been to the movies twice, and out to dinner at least six times. They had been on more romantic dates in the past six months than she and Keith had been on in three years. They went to a comedy club, a boat ride around New York, and enjoyed a few romantic nights at the motel. Chrasey had begun to really like her secret life. There were times it depressed her, because she was ashamed of her actions. However, she knew she deserved the type of treatment she was getting from Trevor, and if she couldn't get it from Keith because he didn't want to do it, she had to do what she had to do.

As Chrasey's relationship with Trevor became more intense, she had grown more afraid of the consequences of Keith finding out. Then she would realize just how little attention Keith paid her or what she was doing, and she realized he wouldn't find out and he probably wouldn't care if he did.

Even when she was being careless, and knew she could get caught, she felt justified and deep down wanted him to know. A piece of her felt like if he ever did find out, and he realized that his behavior pushed her to that point, he would feel guilty and try to win her back. She never really analyzed what would happen if he didn't react that way.

She had spent so much time firmly believing that he was cheating, she never bothered to realize she had no proof whatsoever. Although she had strong suspicions, suspicions were no justification for infidelity in her marriage. Her vows said for better or worse, but yet when things got bad she was the first one sleeping around. Here she was tearing down Keith for being so unaffectionate and just plain rude over the past months, but who was she to point fingers when she was cheating? Although her time spent with Trevor often had no sexual activity, it had still become quite a romantic relationship. They had only slept together about six or seven times, but Chrasey knew that was more than enough.

Since Keith's drastic change toward Chrasey, he had never given a heartfelt explanation. He was always short or just denied that he noticed a change. Chrasey was certain about her conclusion, but she had not yet found proof that he was cheating on her. Although there was no other logical explanation for his behavior, she had no real usable clues or concrete evidence, just signs and suspicions—definitely not enough. To make matters worse, over the past month or two, with her sneaking around with Trevor so much, Keith had become quite the family man, staying home with the kids, cooking, picking up where Chrasey was leaving off while she was creeping. All this time she was too confused to sit back and analyze the situation. She had fallen for Trevor, or at least for his attentions. Trevor made her feel like a woman again. He courted her, he gave her compliments and really listened to her when she talked. She could have a bad day at work, and Trevor would really listen and even give his advice. When it came to Keith, if she ever attempted to talk to him, if he wasn't asking her to tell him later, he would just nod his head and it would be very obvious he wasn't listening to a word she said. Any woman in her situation would have fallen for Trevor. She was just a mother at home, but Trevor made her feel like more.

The thing was, she never stopped to put things in perspective. If she had, she would have realized the risk that she was taking, that she was risking her whole family situation for a younger man who had nothing to offer her but some of his time and good sex. Not to mention that if she allowed herself to focus more on her marriage, maybe she could have received those things at home. The last attempt she made was when she suggested a trip for the two of them. She took care of travel arrangements, child-care plans and everything, and all Keith said was, "I can't take time off work right now." Chrasey pleaded for a few moments, but Keith made it obvious that her idea was not exciting to him at all; in fact, it was the last thing he wanted to do, to go away with his wife. Keith felt no need to even pretend they were happy. He never even tried to pretend they were like the Cosby family. He was there for the kids, but he wanted out or he wanted a different wife. At least that's what Chrasey felt every time she was with him.

Chrasey had blamed Keith long enough, but now she really had to face the music. Here she was, sitting on Dakota's couch hysterically crying because Keith had found out about Trevor and didn't take it too well. He had walked in the bedroom with the downstairs cordless phone in his hand, and as Chrasey hastily got off the phone, her guilty look made it even more obvious. He had picked up the phone to make a call and instead overheard Chrasey talking to Trevor. She didn't know how much or what he heard, but she knew he heard something from the look on his face. As he entered the room and dropped the phone on the bed, he simply said, "I'll get out of the way so you can have your boyfriend over."

She started making excuses and defending herself; she tried to make him think he was interpreting whatever he heard wrong. "He is just a friend of mine from work. We talk and hang out sometimes but that's it."

All the while, he just continued to gather some things and pack a little bag. Chrasey felt the pain of what they mean when they say silence is the strongest response you can give. He said nothing more, other than "I will see you guys soon" as he kissed his little ones before exiting the house.

As he walked out the door, tears ran down her face. She managed to leave him with the words, "I just needed someone there for me."

Keith got in his car, threw his bag in the backseat, and drove off. As he pulled out into the street, he didn't even look back—there was not an ounce of emotion on his face. Chrasey went back in the house and called Trevor back to tell him what happened.

"Aw, damn. I am so sorry if I caused any trouble. Is there anything I can do right now?"

"No, Trev—I just need to handle this on my own. You have done enough."

That's when she headed to Dakota's.

41

In Retrospect

It had been almost a month since Omar found out about the incident with her and Jayon. Jordan was working on an important case with her new client she'd retained at the end of the year, so she had been real busy at the office for a couple of weeks. This didn't make the situation better between her and Omar. He had said verbally that he was cool and believed Jordan, but his actions said something different. When she came home at night, he would barely talk to her and hardly ever wanted to have sex anymore. Most nights he would eat his dinner in the living room alone, and if she tried to join him he would just watch the TV like she wasn't even there.

"It's starting to take a toll on me," Jordan told Chrasey and Dakota on a three-way call. "I am in bad moods all the time and I am depressed many nights, eating dinner by myself. It's like I can't get to Omar—he is in a totally different place and doesn't care how much it bothers me."

"Have you tried to have a sit-down talk with him?" Chrasey asked.

"I tried everything and he won't give in, I even suggested counseling. I have popped up home in a trench coat with nothing underneath, candlelight dinners, arrived at his restaurant at closing time with a sexy chef's outfit on . . ."

"Look at you, you freak. I taught you well," Dakota interrupted.

"Shut up, girl . . . well, not *that* well, because it isn't working. It may have been cool for the moment between us, but as soon as those moments were over, so was the happiness. We have been going through the motions and it is just making me miserable at home," Jordan said.

"You may just have to give it time, J. You always want things to be perfect in your life at all times. That's unrealistic. Marriages have problems . . ." Chrasey said. "Hell, I just got caught cheating . . . life can be a trip sometimes."

"Yeah, I know. It's just that it's getting to the point where my only happiness is at work where I can try to ignore and forget how bad things are at home," Jordan said.

"Who you think you fooling?" Dakota asked. "You're at work so much because that's where Mister Jayon is."

"Don't even go there. Not now, when that is what all this drama is about," Jordan responded.

"Please, just like back in college—you're running to Jayon to be your strength to get through it," Dakota said.

Jordan couldn't deny that Dakota had a point. Jayon would come into her office and talk to her about everything, just like in college. He would let her get all of her complaints off her chest. He would never knock Omar; in fact, he would even defend Omar, trying to help Jordan see things from his point of view. Not that it helped, but even when Jordan would understand and go home and try to explain to Omar that she did, Omar still behaved the same way.

"I know y'all are going to have jokes . . . but I will admit Jayon does make my days brighter," Jordan admitted.

"I'm sure he does," Chrasey teased.

"No, I mean it. Not in that way. He brings me my favorite ice cream to the office, he accompanies me to places so I won't feel alone . . . he fills my void to make the situation less painful," Jordan said.

"That could be because he feels somewhat responsible for your drama, or Jayon's smooth ass is trying to take advantage of the situation to snatch up Omar's wife," Dakota said, laughing.

"No, I know better than that. This is just Jayon's nature. Y'all know he has always tried to be that kind of friend to me. Regardless of what else is in the picture, even when he has a girlfriend or he is with a slew of girls and enjoying his single life, Jayon always tended to our friendship . . . Friendship! Instigators," Jordan said.

"I know Jay isn't a conniving guy," Chrasey said.

"Besides, he is not desperate like that. He isn't the type to plot to steal someone's woman," Jordan said, truly believing that in her heart.

"Yeah, but he is still a man, Jordan—he ain't above that shit," Dakota said.

Jordan heard Dakota's point, but to Jordan, Jayon's actions during this time were out of concern and nothing more. She and Jayon would talk about girls he was seeing, the ones he did like and the ones he didn't. He had really been on the scene since his engagement was off. He gave her advice about what to do at home to work things out with Omar. Jordan knew that Omar knew he was only a small part of the problem; to Jordan, the bigger issue was Omar feeling neglected overall and Jayon understood that. He tried to explain to Jordan how men are. "It wasn't his self-esteem, it was his pride. Every man wants to be king of his castle," Jayon told her. No matter what they discussed, Jayon would never say one negative thing about Omar. It's like he knew that was crossing the line, Omar was still Jordan's husband, and regardless of how stupid he was acting, she loved him.

The reality of the situation was that Omar had felt like he was at the bottom of Jordan's priorities. She worked too much, she found time for her friends and her son, but when it came to Omar, he got what was left. Jordan didn't agree with that but that was what was bothering him. It was never directly said, but it was always insinuated. Omar felt like she thought she was better than him because she had a Juri's Doctorate and a more "prestigious" career. He would always make sarcastic comments about her degrees, her being so smart, or just her successful career. It was rare when he mentioned any of those things without a hint of sarcasm in his voice.

Jordan knew that it didn't help that she was around other men who had also earned the same accolades, accolades that he had not. All the celebrities and big-shot people she dealt with day to day never sat well with him. She always thought he took it better than she would, though; she would have had a fit if he were working with Janet Jackson or Oprah every day. So she could understand her working around all these rich, successful, famous, and handsome men was intimidating to him. Especially because he knew he could never give her what they could. What he never understood was they could never give her what he could. However, he allowed a wedge to come between them, which allowed her to see more than she would have been too blind to see otherwise.

One night, Jordan had a business dinner with Morris Chestnut and his agent. It was common knowledge that ever since Jordan was in college she'd loved Morris Chestnut. She knew when she told Omar, deep down he was probably a little uncomfortable and jealous. However, Omar was never one to admit jealousy of no man—he found other ways and words to express his disapproval. With these situations, though, it was business, and he knew she always kept business separate from personal things. It's all about the check. For some reason, though, on that particular night, when he saw her leaving in her black suit with the pink pinstripes, he almost lost his mind. Her hair was laid just right, makeup looking like it had been professionally done, and her breasts were peeking out of her pink shirt just enough to get the imagination running. As she walked through the bedroom, he said, "What are you wearing?"

"A suit," she replied.

"You look like you're going on a date, not to a business dinner."

"Just want to make sure he knows I'm the type he can bring home to Mama, too," she said playfully, before noticing that he really wasn't in a playful mood.

Once she noticed it, she immediately went over to him in the bed, moving slightly on top of him, and said, "Baby, please—if you're worried he is my fantasy man, just remember he is only the dream. I'm coming back home to you."

Hands down, she thought she had said the line of the year. Until he said, "Oh, I apologize for ruining that dream for you," and rose from the bed, forcing her to get off of him.

She didn't mean it that way, but it was just the way he took things—for the worst. It was just Omar's perception of his role in her life. He felt like a disappointment in her world of glitz and glamour. Like she was out in the world happy, and living the life, but then had to come home to reality, just Omar. It was almost like he felt out of place in her life. That really crushed Jordan's heart, but she didn't know what to do. She had no idea how to prove to him that he meant more than anybody or anything in her career. After his comment, he had sat on the edge of the bed watching the television screen intensely as if he hoped he could forget she was still in the bedroom.

"Do you want me to just quit my career and stay home? Would that prove to you what my priorities are?" she asked him.

"No, Jordan, and I am watching TV. I don't want to talk about it."

Of course he would say no. What man wants to be telling his woman to stay home and be barefoot and pregnant? Besides, whether he wanted to admit it or not, he got to enjoy the benefits of her career more than she did half the time. She was able to refresh his wardrobe every season from all the hot designers she knew and artists who had their own clothing lines. He never had to stress over how much money his restaurant was making, because he knew her income could cover all the bills. Without her income they couldn't afford to live in their nice house with four bedrooms, two bathrooms, a family room, a living room, a pool and Jacuzzi, and his custom-made kitchen any chef would die to have. He could complain all he wanted, but if Jordan didn't do what she did for a living, he would have had more stress on him. You can never make these Negroes happy.

It wasn't just the money with her career—it was the life that she wanted for herself. She worked hard at this career—she'd made it on her own, and she wanted to make her parents proud. Besides, she always said she wanted to be self-sufficient for her and her children in case her husband was to wild out one day and walk out, she would be independently solvent. She could pay all her bills, plus some, without Omar's help. That made Jordan feel secure, and that's how she liked it. The problem was if she started to put her career second and be a better wife, that could change very quickly. *Damn, what's a girl to do?* Jordan thought to herself before she was snapped out of her train of thought.

"Well, not to downplay your issues, girl, but we all have issues so you're not alone. I'm half lesbian now, had a fight as a grown-ass woman, and lost my man in the process," Dakota said.

"Bitch, that wasn't your man," Chrasey interrupted humorously.

They all laughed. As sensitive as Dakota was about that, she was able to laugh along.

"Shut up. You about to lose yours, too . . ." Dakota stabbed back.

"I know, we all about to be single whores . . . we may need to call Lexia back here and the four of us get this popping . . ." Chrasey replied.

"For real, Dakota. You kicked her out. She may be able to teach us a thing or two," Jordan added.

They all laughed.

The three of them always had the power to laugh at their pain together. On the inside they were hurting, but together they were healed.

42

On the Table

Chrasey had called Jordan and asked her if she would mind keeping her kids while she and Keith went out to talk. When she arrived to drop the kids off, she had about forty-five minutes before she had to meet Keith at Applebee's in Valley Stream. As the kids got settled in Jason's room, playing and bragging about who had what, Chrasey and Jordan sat down in the kitchen to some hot cocoa.

"Now listen, Chrasey. I'm not telling you what to do, but if you want your marriage to have a shot you should be honest. You can't live with that guilt forever," Jordan advised.

Chrasey's biggest regret was how stupid she had been for talking to Trevor from her house. It was obvious she was no real player—she was nothing but sloppy.

"Chrasey. It's OK. This may be the best thing for you guys—it will force you to actually talk now. Now you can get everything you have been feeling off of your chest, even if he is not receptive," Jordan added.

"I'm scared now. I think I've ruined my marriage completely," Chrasey replied.

"Chrase, you knew all along that this was risky. You have to man up to this—it was part of the gamble. Just let him know how you feel and pray for the best."

Chrasey knew Jordan was right—it was a little late to chicken out now. She was far from right, but she had to hope that Keith would understand what caused her infidelity and pray that it didn't cause her to lose her marriage. She left Jordan's home preparing in her mind everything she wanted to tell Keith.

She arrived at the restaurant in twenty minutes, and when she got there, Keith was surprisingly already sitting at a table. As she approached, he barely looked up at her. He was dressed in a black-and-tan, long-sleeved rugby shirt with tan khakis. Chrasey wore a low-cut purple top with dark blue jeans, and purple-and-black pumps. This was one of Chrasey's new and improved outfits. She knew she was there to talk things over with Keith, but she was going to at least try to throw some sex appeal at him. Hopefully make him see what he had at home. With that in mind, making sure her cleavage was well exposed, she sat down across from him without saying a word. He didn't speak and neither did she—it was definitely an awkward moment. They both just looked at the menus for the next few minutes, still not saying anything to each other. After a few moments of silence, the waiter came and took their order, and they sat there sipping on their water.

After she had sat across from him for ten minutes, practically in silence, she decided to speak, because it didn't look like he would. She kind of wished he would show some emotion and tell her off or something. Instead he let her suffer, not letting her know what he was thinking. So, she spoke first.

"Sorry," Chrasey said. It was all that came to mind.

He took another sip of his water, and in a very calm manner said, "Chrasey, it's a little too late for that."

Realizing that beating around the bush wasn't going to do anything, she just went for it and put it on Front Street.

"Keith, I slept with him. His name is Trevor—I met him one day at the bus stop. We have been seeing each other on and off for about seven months. We had sex a few times and we went on a few dates."

He didn't react at first. When he heard her admit that she had sex with him, he gave her a look as if he was surprised that she admitted it. He had finally made eye contact with her; she had his undivided attention for the first time in a long time but was unsure she wanted it.

"You fucked him, Chrasey?"

Hearing him say it, her eyes began to well up. "Yes, I did. I am so sorry."

"Sorry? You had sex with somebody a few times and you're sorry now?"

"Keith, he was all I had. I was lonely and he was there." She began to explain the situation and how empty she had felt inside for so long. She told him how he ignored her feelings, how she thought he was cheating on her, and how she didn't mean to hurt their marriage. After all her courage was built up, she finished off by saying that all of this led to her being intimate with another man. Through the whole confession, Keith didn't say anything—he just poked around at his appetizer and took a few sips of his beverage. Chrasey continued on, telling him about the nights that all she wanted was a little attention from him, and he would treat her like she didn't exist. She admitted she knew she was wrong for being unfaithful, but it wasn't for the sex—it was for the companionship.

Keith appeared to be devastated by the truth for a moment, and then he retreated back to his nonchalant mode. Once Chrasey was done, a moment of silence went by before he replied, "I could never trust you again . . . I want a divorce."

Her heart dropped. "Please don't do this, Keith. I'm sorry."

"Well, I'm sorry, too. Your excuse is you thought I was cheating on you. Well, did it ever occur to you that I was just overwhelmed with taking care of *our* household and all the new changes at my job? I can't help that you felt that way, and it was no excuse to go out fucking the first thing that gave you some attention," he said. "No wonder I couldn't get any." He stood up from the table, dropped some money for his bill, and left.

He hadn't even waited for his food to come—now Chrasey was sitting at the table all alone, looking like a fool. She called the waiter over, cancelled her order, gave him a tip, and left as well. She was embarrassed when Keith walked out—some people at other tables were looking, so she damn sure wasn't staying.

Once she got outside, she didn't see Keith anywhere in sight. She called his phone and he didn't answer. She hung up and tried again, still no answer. When the voice mail answered, she left a message.

Keith, I understand that you're upset. Walking away from this isn't going to help anything. I will do everything I can to make this up to you and make this work. I was wrong for what I have done, but more than anything in the world, I want to make our marriage work. Please call me when you get this so we can work this out.

It's funny how when you're about to lose something you suddenly realize its value.

43

It's Been Fun

This was one of those days Chrasey's staff wished they had stayed home sick instead of coming in to work. She was in such a bad mood and was taking it out on anyone who didn't get the hint in time.

She didn't mean to snap like that at her client coordinator, Ella—she just wanted to be left alone today. She woke up that way; she hadn't been too cool since she and Keith had their talk. Her guilt had eaten at her so heavy she couldn't even eat for the past day or two. She had made a decision on her way to work that she would officially cut things off with Trevor. Even though now she had no reason to because she and Keith would be over, she knew she could never have a relationship with Trevor. All that keeping the door open with him was doing was bringing her more confusion and pain. It was about noon, and she knew Trevor should be on his lunch hour.

After practicing over and over what she was going to say, she got herself ready to call him. Her feelings for him had grown very strong the past few months, but since Keith found out, her feelings had subdued and she snapped back to reality. She still cared for him, though, and she knew that he was practically in love with her as well. However, it didn't change the fact that she was a married woman, and although it was too late to change things, she should never have thought it was OK to have her cake and eat it, too.

After a long breath, she picked up the phone to dial his number. "Trevor?"

"Yeah—hey, babe. You OK?" He could hear in her voice that she wasn't in the best state of mind.

"I've been better. Listen, I really need to talk to you."

"I don't like how that sounds," he said.

"I know—I don't like how it feels, either."

"I already know, Chrasey—you think me and you should stop seeing each other."

"How did you guess that?" she asked.

"I can tell. Ever since Keith heard me on the phone, you have been real distant. You never really told me what happened with you two, and you have barely returned my calls. It's not hard to tell that something is wrong."

"Trevor, this is harder for me than I care to admit. It's embarrassing, actually. "

"What's embarrassing?" he asked.

"I'm a married woman with two kids, and I have fallen for a man seven years younger than me," Chrasey said.

"So, as you see, age doesn't mean a thing."

"I know, but you have years to meet someone and still have a healthy marriage. I just practically threw mine away."

"Is Keith threatening to leave?" he asked.

"He hasn't been home since that night."

"Really? I'm sorry, Chrase."

"It's not your fault. I just need time to try to get my life back together, and as soon as I get a grip on everything, I will call you," Chrasey said.

"Is it OK if I check up on you?"

"I'd prefer if you didn't, but I wouldn't hate you if you did."

"Fair enough," he said, trying not to make the situation harder.

"OK, talk to you later."

"You take care of yourself," he said.

Just as she went to hang up, he added, "Chrasey, for what it's worth, Keith owed you more than he was giving you. Don't be too hard on yourself. You are a beautiful person inside and out, and I would take you away from him and make you happy 24/7 if I could. Just please for me, keep that smile on your face, and don't let this get you down."

Her eyes teared up, listening to his kind words. She was more than just some side piece to Trevor—he cared about her well-being. That made her feel better, that her actions were at least somewhat worth it. If nothing else, she had gained a friend.

"Thanks, Trevor. I will remember that. I will be in touch."

They hung up. Damn, just when you think God has finished your story, he adds another chapter. Who would think that this late in life Chrasey would meet someone so special who would make her question her whole life? Most women think it's all over once they are married—they think that God has delivered them their soul mate and that the rest is building their family and vacationing and retirement. They are never quite prepared to meet another man who was possibly better for them to begin with. After Chrasey hung up with Trevor, she had to question why it was that God had her marry Keith when there were men like Trevor who seemed to be so much better at making her feel special than Keith ever had.

44

Déjà Vu

This was definitely a scene that Dakota felt she had seen before, but it wasn't her imagination—it was more of a pathetic reality. Here Dakota was, waiting in bed, looking all sexy and waiting on Tony. He was probably trying to make her suffer for throwing him out that night. It had been over a month since the fight with him and Lexia. He tried to act nonchalant when Dakota called him to come over, but he said he would be there at like 3:00 P.M.

She didn't go all out this time, because she wanted to just discuss what happened and try to work things out. Even though she had already decided to move past the incident, she had to be clear that him lying up in the bedroom with Lexia that night was unacceptable. So, she had to put up a front for a little bit—she couldn't have candles burning and wear lingerie saying "come get me." So instead, she was wearing a pair of nicely fitted sweatpants and low-cut tank top. She looked casual, but she was showing off all of her assets. Her place was spotless, and she had prepared a little afternoon meal. She had made a special pasta dish that he loved, made with three different types of meat, three cheeses, and tomato sauce.

Dakota had mulled over and over in her mind whether she should mend things with Tony, or should she just get him out of her system while she had a head start. It just seemed when she analyzed her life, he was one of the best and most enjoyable parts of it. Her job was great but it kept her on edge and stressed out. Chrasey and Jordan were good friends but they were both married, and when push came to shove, they had someone at home to kick back and enjoy life with. Her condo was perfect but cost her way too much money, and it was no fun being in it alone. With Tony, though, she could just enjoy him. Of course, sharing him hadn't been the best situation, but for some reason what he gave always seemed to be enough. They had fun together, and they had good sex, and she didn't ask for much more.

Dakota wanted a companion, and maybe marriage wasn't an option, but at least he was a substitute. David was probably the best man she had ever dealt with, with the most quality and most respect. There was just something inside of her that wouldn't let her let go of Tony, even though she knew better.

Dakota had been thinking that she wanted to ask Tony if he was willing to be in a committed relationship with her. He had tried to convince her time and time again that she was the only female that mattered that much to him. His daughter's mother was just in his life because he had no choice for his daughter, but that he didn't love her. So if this was remotely true, he should be open to Dakota's idea. Although she wasn't sure how he would react to her question, she wanted to ask him and see what he would say.

Another hour had gone by, and Dakota was starting to wonder if she had given Tony too much credit too soon. It was a Saturday afternoon and she was waiting in her bed, getting more upset as the moments went by. As she waited on him, she watched one of her favorite television programs, *Bridezilla,* on the Woman Network. She was aggravated, upset, and horny. She paged him two times and he hadn't replied yet; as usual when he was pulling this, he didn't answer his phone. She didn't want to think of all the possible things he could be doing or why he was ignoring her call. She didn't want to face the fact that he could have already chalked her up to past ass and wasn't going to show up or call.

Just as she was getting into Jaheim's new video, her phone rang. She jumped up and grabbed her cordless phone. She checked the Caller ID first and it was Tony.

"Hello?" she said.

"Hey, I'm downstairs parking—open up the door."

"OK," she said.

She knew that she had a few minutes before he actually reached the door so she went in the bathroom and freshened up a bit. She cleared her face, put on some lip gloss, and fluffed her hair back. Then she went and unlocked the door and sat down on the couch.

A few moments later he was at the door. As soon as Dakota looked up at him, it was obvious that she was impressed with what she saw. Maybe it was just that Dakota hadn't seen him in a long time, or maybe he really was that sexy. He was wearing a pair of green-and-white sweatpants, a white polo shirt, white Air Force One sneakers, and a green-and-white baseball cap. He had a fresh shave and was wearing a cologne that she'd never smelled before but liked. He was also wearing a whole lot of diamonds, including about three karats in his ear, and about sixty karats hanging around his neck on a chain and a diamond-encrusted cross pendant.

She stood up to greet him as soon as he stepped inside. He gave her a kiss on the cheek and proceeded to the couch as well. She sat back where she was, and for a few moments they watched the television screen as if they cared. It was very awkward for those first few moments, and then Dakota spoke.

"Did you eat?"

"I had a little something earlier, but I can eat again. Why?"

"I cooked. I made my pasta meat lovers dish."

"Uh-oh, you really trying to make a statement, huh?"

Dakota just giggled—there was no need to deny that it was no coincidence she'd prepared his special dish. She got up and went into the kitchen to make him a plate. As soon as she stepped away, he picked up the remote and changed the channel. Shortly after, she returned with his full plate and a glass of iced tea on a tray. She put it down in front of him at the coffee table and sat beside him. He took about a minute before he began to chow down.

"Now, this I don't want to miss," he said with a mouth full of food.

"Oh, is that all you missed?" she replied devilishly.

"No, I missed you, too, but I didn't miss your craziness."

"My craziness? Why am I the crazy one?"

Tony must have come over for business—he got straight to the point and didn't hesitate to explain himself.

"Because, Dakota, at times it was like you forgot what this was."

"And what was that?" Dakota said, already getting defensive.

He hesitated, trying to find the right words. "It was supposed to be fun. It was supposed to be something that wasn't serious. You knew my situation and I knew yours."

"How do you figure that it wasn't just fun for me?"

"For starters, you threw me out of your house one night in a jealous rage . . ."

Before he could finish, she interrupted. "Don't even bring that up, Tone . . . that was nothing to do with fun. That was disrespectful."

"OK, I can see how you saw things that night. I wasn't doing anything with her, and you didn't even calm down enough to hear my side."

"It shouldn't even have happened—besides, that had nothing to do with what this was supposed to be."

"That was small, because I kind of understood that one. But you were constantly wanting me to come over, and be here with you. You know that I have a busy life, and you know that most of those nights I was with my daughter's mother."

"Constantly, Tony? You used to come over on your own—I would only ask you once or twice a week, if that, and when you said no I didn't complain."

"Not all the time—most of the time you would get upset."

"Whatever," Dakota said.

"I'm not trying to play you—I just want to make sure you know what this is. We aren't committed to each other, we are just seeing each other."

"Let me ask you—is this the way it will always be?"

"I don't know, Dakota," Tony replied, clearly frustrated by the question.

"What don't you know? Do you ever plan on settling down with me?"

"I can't answer that right now."

"Why? You claim that you want to be with me. You're not with your daughter's mother, so do you plan on being uncommitted forever?"

"I'll let you know."

"See, Tony, this is why we have these issues. Sometimes you act like I'm one of your groupies from your football days."

"Dakota, I still have groupies now. I don't treat you like I treat them."

"Excuse me. I guess I should be flattered."

"I enjoy our relationship, and I want to continue it for as long as possible. We do some business together here and there, but if I didn't want to deal with you, I wouldn't. Hopefully I can spend more time with you and we can have our relationship—I just can't promise marriage or anything."

"What makes you so against it?"

"Listen, me and my daughter's mother have a weird relationship. She knows that I do me, but I owe her a certain respect because she was with me from day one . . . therefore I won't be committing to anyone anytime soon."

"So, then why don't you just commit to her and stop playing games?"

"I'm not, because you know the deal. If it's all of a sudden a problem for you, then let's discuss it."

"You know what I have a problem with. Why don't you ever say her name? All this time we have been dealing, you won't refer to her by name."

"Out of respect. I don't like people knowing her name because that's usually when games begin. People want to start asking questions, or making phone calls. I like it to be where she is a private part of my life."

"You keep her pretty guarded for you not to be with her."

"She is my daughter's mother, that's all. It's just my way of respecting her and my daughter."

"OK, Tony."

Dakota was tired of hearing about how she was woman #2, and that would probably be her role in his life forever. She got up and took his plate in the kitchen. He noticed her attitude, but like most men he figured if she was going to let it go, he'd better take advantage of it and let it go, too. So when she returned from the kitchen, they watched TV for a while in silence. He eventually broke the silence with talk about some business deals and what he needed her to do to help out. Then eventually they had sex, and not too long after that he left. Dakota was back in her bedroom sitting there watching TiVo shows, feeling alone and confused, just like she was before he came.

45

Breath of Fresh Air

The rest of the week went by and Chrasey still hadn't heard a word from Keith. She was home every night alone, keeping herself occupied with the kids. For some ironic reason she had no desire to even hear Trevor's voice. Now that she could speak to him or see him without sneaking, she didn't even want to.

She had called Keith at his job a few times through the week, but of course he wasn't taking her calls; the receptionist kept saying he wasn't in or he was in a meeting. She considered going to his job and popping up to force him to talk, but she also wanted him to come around at his own pace. Also, deep down she wasn't sure if she was ready to see him face-to-face, and she was sure the job wasn't the correct place to handle it, either way.

She knew Keith was probably staying at his mother's when he left work, either that or he was with the mistress he claimed he didn't have. There were a few nights Chrasey couldn't sleep, thinking about what Keith could be out there doing. She knew that her actions were all he needed to justify anything that he did. Most nights, though, she lay awake fearing the possibility that he really meant it when he said he wanted a divorce.

One evening after work, Chrasey grew tired of being home alone. She hadn't asked for any support from her friends—she had been really trying to stay strong and not let the situation get to her. She knew there wasn't much she could say, and that she didn't deserve much sympathy. She supposed this was a typical possible result from cheating in a relationship.

This evening, though, she dropped the kids off at her mother's and went over to Dakota's house. She hadn't told Jordan that Keith hadn't been back home yet—the one time Jordan called she missed her call. She wasn't ready to call her back, because she didn't want to have to tell Jordan just yet. It's not that Jordan would say anything negative, but she knew that she would say "I told you so." Jordan had been saying all along, what you're doing is a temporary fix for a lifelong matter. You and Keith could get through this lull and come out on top, but with what you're doing, if he ever finds out, that is increasing the risk that you two won't make it."

It was just easier for Chrasey to confide in Dakota for now, because she wasn't trying to claim the moral high ground like Jordan. So Chrasey sat in Dakota's living room, pouring her little heart out. She regretted what she had done—it took Keith finding out for her to actually feel bad. It was her guilt, knowing he felt betrayed. For some reason she didn't think he cared, but men are funny. They may not want you or treat you right but they don't want another man to have you or treat you right, either. So although Chrasey was upset over Keith leaving, she was also upset that he didn't take any responsibility for her actions. More than anything, she was afraid. Afraid of the possibility that it may lead to their divorce.

Dakota just listened for the most part, repeating, "it will be all right" to almost everything Chrasey said. The problem was, Dakota didn't know what to tell her. Truth was, she felt sort of guilty for Chrasey's situation. Dakota wondered if she had been a bad friend to advise her the way she did. All along she had encouraged Chrasey to have fun with Trevor and told her she was doing the right thing. Dakota did mean that at the time, and Keith wasn't treating her right. Now it just seemed like she was the type friend they are talking about when they say misery loves company.

So Dakota remained fairly quiet while Chrasey vented. That's all Chrasey really needed, anyway, was a good friend she could trust to listen.

"I don't know how I go from being faithful for eighteen years, only sleeping with my husband to possibly losing my husband because I have been sleeping with another man that's younger than me."

"It's gonna be all right," Dakota replied.

"How? Even if we work this out, I probably set us back years. Everyone kept saying this was a phase in our marriage, a normal, natural thing where one of us is going to be unpleasant and the marriage will feel like a living hell . . . But no, not me. I had to do a self-remedy—marriages don't always recover from infidelity."

"No, but a lot do. Keith will understand that neglect is a powerful thing. We all want some attention and love."

"Yeah, but I didn't have the right to break our vows."

Dakota still believed in her heart that Keith was up to no good, and just because he didn't get caught first doesn't mean he is innocent. She didn't want to say that and further upset Chrasey.

"It's gonna be all right," Dakota said.

"I guess if I end up single, at least I know there is a bright side—I can get to be free and glamorous like you. Like you have been saying, no man should control your happiness."

"Please, girl, don't let the image fool you," Dakota replied.

That's all she would say—she wouldn't dare tell Chrasey that she had been feeling down lately, wanting a stable relationship. Not after she spent the past few months saying that you only live once, and you can't let no man control your happiness. Chrasey might have killed her.

"Who am I fooling? I'm not ready to do this all by myself. I didn't get married to do it alone," Chrasey said.

It seemed like the thought brought back all the pain. As soon as she finished that thought, her eyes welled up with tears.

"It's going to be all right," Dakota replied, trying to console her friend before the floods came. Dakota couldn't stand to see Chrasey crying.

"I didn't start this family to do it by myself . . . I don't want to be a single mom. It's not fair, it's just not fair," she mumbled through her sobs.

All those times Dakota had told Chrasey to ignore Jordan's conscious talk, and now when stuff hit the fan, Dakota was at a loss for words. She held Chrasey in her arms, truly feeling her pain. Every woman can relate to that pain, where you know that your behavior may have caused you to lose a good thing and you didn't take the time to stop to notice that despite all the bad, it was a good thing. It's a pain that burns so deep, you feel like you can cry out your soul.

Dakota wiped a tear away, wishing she could make her friend feel better.

Why is it that after over thirty years on this planet, we women can't get our game together? Dakota thought to herself. *Why are we always in some messed-up situation with our men? We are either doing too much or too little. Why can't we figure out a happy medium? When do we learn, or do we ever? Do we just forever live on the borderline between happiness and turmoil?* Her mind went on as she rubbed Chrasey's leg to calm her. Out of three women, none of them had it right. She began to wonder if any woman had it just right, and if so, we need that sister's secret.

46

Dear Jordan

To Jordan it was starting to look like Omar had just been using the Jayon situation to broaden his and Jordan's issues, or at least that's how it seemed, because Jordan couldn't seem to understand why Omar was still so upset over the incident. She even joked around and asked Omar if he wanted to have a web cam on her at work so he could watch her. Omar didn't find it funny at all, but she was under the impression that this type of stuff is the kind of thing that successful, happy marriages just move past. They deal with it and move on. Not Omar—he was carrying around this chip on his shoulder for weeks as if she had slept with somebody else or something.

Jordan was beginning to think he just wanted her to feel responsible for all the problems in their marriage and all of his issues with himself. She did feel bad about their current state, and she also understood his jealousy of Jayon, but she also knew she had been the best wife to Omar and that she'd never cheated on him. She was actually getting tired of feeling guilty for something she didn't even do. It had gotten to the point where she was just mentally and physically drained. She hadn't been on a vacation in forever—just to get some time with her loved ones was a mission; her clients were calling her at all hours of the night, and yet Omar seemed to have no sympathy for what she was dealing with.

The only time Omar had shown her some real concern these past few weeks is when her mom called to tell her that her dad wasn't feeling too well. He had been diagnosed with Parkinson's disease years ago and had been holding up very well. These past few weeks he had been back and forth to the doctors with new symptoms, and Omar came with her to see him. Before and after that, he was barely paying Jordan any mind. She just wished that he could be a husband to her, and for once see things through her eyes. She wanted him to see that all she was trying to do was do the best that she could. She wanted to have him be proud of his wife, Jason of his mother, her parents of their daughter, and Jordan of herself. She wasn't trying to be the pro black sister—she had no problem letting her man be the king of the castle. She couldn't help it if her role as queen outshined him, though. That wasn't her plan—it's just the way it turned out, and he should be supportive of her regardless of the way he felt.

That's why she couldn't believe that when she came home there was a note on her dresser from Omar. She was exhausted and ready to jump in the bed. It was a Friday night and she had made it home by 8:00 P.M. She wasn't expecting Omar to be there waiting, because he had told her in his own way it was too late to try now. She just wanted to lie down and relax for about an hour. Instead she found this note:

> *Jason's at your parents' house—go pick him up when you get home. I don't know when I'll be back.*
> *—O*

That was all the note read. OK. What the hell was that?

There went her relaxing. She changed into something more comfortable and went back out to pick up her son. As she drove back into Queens to her parents' house, she called Omar's phone and he didn't answer. She left him a message asking him what the hell was with his note. He was really starting to piss her off. When she got to her parents' house, she asked her mom what Omar told her when he dropped Jason off. She said all he said was that he had something to do, and that Jordan would be by to pick him up. Usually if he was going to do something like that, he would call her to discuss it to make sure she was going to be home at a decent time. Jordan didn't know what Omar was thinking, but she couldn't wait until he brought his butt home to find out.

When she got back home, she was kind of happy that she got to spend some time with Jason. They played one of his video games, did his flash cards, and watched *The Incredibles*. They had a ball, and it felt good to just sit home with him. Once it hit one in the morning, she made him go to bed, and then she went to her bedroom wondering when Omar was going to get home. As it got later and later, and she still couldn't reach Omar and he hadn't called or showed up, she started to get more and more worried and pissed.

That morning Jordan woke up at about ten o'clock in the morning and Omar still wasn't home. She called his mother; she said she hadn't heard from him. She called everyone she could think of, from his family to his friends; everyone claimed to be clueless. She was somewhat worried, but because his note mentioned that he didn't know when he was getting home, she figured he was aware that he would be pulling something like this. She spent the whole day in her house with Jason, pissed off because Omar still hadn't come home.

Almost a whole week went by and Omar still hadn't called or come home. On Monday, she went by his job, but he wasn't there. The sous chef said he had told him he was taking a vacation and that Omar wanted him and the restaurant manager to hold things down until he got back. He told them, too, that he didn't know when he would be back. It really felt like Omar was nowhere to be found. Even his mother still didn't know where he was, or she was lying for him. She couldn't believe it was six days and he still hadn't even called.

By the end of the week she was through. She remembered being mad on Wednesday and Thursday, but once an entire week went by, she was ready to truly fight him. The nerve of him. She had left him messages, and he didn't reply to one, he didn't call, nothing. She had started to really wonder if he had lost his mind, but not once did she consider that he had left her—at least, not yet.

On Sunday afternoon, Jordan and Jason had just gotten back from church. They were in the living room watching television when she heard the door close. Jason went running, shouting, "Daddy, is that you?"

She could hear Jason and Omar's muffled voices from the porch. A few moments later Omar was in the living room doorway with Jason in his arms. He didn't even react to her presence right away when he saw her sitting there, nor did she react to his. He was obviously being nonchalant about his sudden arrival at home, and her facial expression had an obvious message, too: *I hope you don't think you got my at-tention—all you did was piss me off.*

After he put Jason back down, he made his way over to Jordan and gave her a kiss on the forehead. As he stood back up, he said, "Hey."

"HEY?" Jordan damn near yelled. Trying to keep her composure, she calmly said, "Jason, go upstairs—please, baby—I need to talk to your father."

"Jason, you can stay right here," he said to him just as calmly. Then he looked at Jordan and said, "I am going upstairs to take a shower and do some stuff. If you want to come talk to me, you can do so when I'm done."

She wanted to say, *Who in the hell do you think you're talking to? Did I become a white woman in the past week? Talking to me like you can say what-ever you want.* Instead, she remained calm, and not wanting to involve Jason, she said, "Jason, you finish watching television—Daddy and I are gonna go upstairs, OK?"

Before she could even finish what she was saying to Jason, Omar had already headed upstairs, never really hearing what she was going to say in response to him. She was too mad to be prideful and not fol-low him. *This nigga has disappeared for a whole week. Forget pride and sav-ing face—I have to hear what's on his mind,* Jordan said to herself as she followed behind him. When she got upstairs and came into the bed-room, Omar had already started to pull off his shoes and socks. He was walking around like nothing had happened; he didn't even ac-knowledge her standing there. She was in shock at how nonchalant he was behaving.

"Omar, are you serious right now?" she asked him.

"Jordan, I'm really not in the mood to talk right now."

Her mouth dropped. Her face had a look of shock. *This* was the at-titude he was coming home with after he had been gone a whole week?

After she absorbed it for a few seconds, she blurted out "You're not in the mood? You're not in the mood? Omar, do you think that I was in the mood to come home to a note? . . . Do you think I was in the mood to hunt you down? You are my husband. Who in the hell just goes off without telling his WIFE where he is going? You have to be joking." She said all of that in one fast breath. She was in read him, write him, and spit him out mode, and he was in trouble now.

Omar didn't stop what he was doing for even one second. He just took his precious time undressing and getting ready to get in the shower. After a few seconds of letting her response set in, he replied in a calm manner.

"No, there is nothing funny. When I'm done with my shower, I'm packing some things and I'm staying with a friend for a while."

"What?" Jordan said.

"I know you heard me, but if you would like me to repeat it, you will have to wait until I get out of the shower." He said this as he stepped inside and closed the bathroom door.

She stood there in shock. She couldn't say anything. So much for read, write, and spit him out mode. Omar wasn't even the least bit responsive to her mode. He was really telling her that he was only back for a little bit, and he was heading right back out. She sat on the bed thinking, trying to figure how she should go about things. Try to put her anger aside and see if they could sit down and talk this out? Or tell him the hell off for bugging out? She started to wonder if the situation had really gotten this bad and she was just ignorant of it or taking it for granted—or was Omar just overreacting? Her mind was going through 100 thoughts per minute. She couldn't even calm down long enough to come to a conclusion before he came out of the bathroom.

He walked right by her and reached into the nightstand to get something. It was like he wasn't even acknowledging her presence. Her anger had started to subside; she started to wonder what he was feeling inside. Why was he acting like this? Then she realized, he should have been able to communicate with her either way. There was no justifiable reason to act like this.

"Omar, are we going to talk or are you going to just go about your business like we don't exist?"

"Jordan, it makes no sense to talk to you because you don't listen. I'm tired of talking."

"What are you talking about, Omar? My career, Jayon, what?"

"I'm not talking about anything—that's my point. I just said I'm tired of talking."

She was getting frustrated again. Omar had started to put more things on the bed—clothes, chef suits, and stuff.

"What are you tired of talking about?"

"Everything, Jordan."

"Omar! . . . You can't just behave this way—we are married. You have to talk to me."

"Fine, Jordan—talk."

"So you're just going to leave?"

"Yup . . . I can't deal with you right now."

"So where are you going and how long are you staying?"

"I don't know yet."

"Where have you been all this week?"

"I went away—I took a flight to visit my father."

"You went to Georgia?"

"Yup."

"So where are you going right now—you have to know where you're headed."

"Staying with a friend."

"What friend?" she asked.

"You don't know this friend," he replied.

He was clearly trying to be difficult and piss her off by not giving her any real information. He knew this would just annoy Jordan. He finished gathering his stuff and put it in a bag. He was headed downstairs, and she didn't want Jason to see him leaving.

"Omar, don't let Jason see you walk out with a bag."

"I'll tell him I'm going on a business trip. Don't worry, I know what to say to MY son."

For some reason the anger just suddenly hit her. She had spent the past few minutes letting him rationalize his behavior and tell her what the hell was going on. "Let me just tell you something—you leave here, I can't guarantee you will be welcome when you feel like coming back."

"I'm willing to take that chance." He stopped and had a conversation with Jason, gave him a hug, and walked to the door. Once he got onto the porch, he turned toward Jordan. She was just standing there with her arms folded, looking at him with disbelief. He looked back at her with an emotionless face. A face that said this was all well thought out, and he had no hesitation about walking out that door, and he did. With a simple "See ya later," he opened the door and walked out. Just like that.

47

While Supplies Last

She didn't quite know how she got there, but Dakota was right back in her routine with Tony. Him coming by when he could, them speaking on the phone at least every other day. Whatever he could give her, is what she had to take. Her hope of having him all to herself seemed more and more unlikely. Tony's label was getting bigger, and so was he—right before her eyes. He signed two new acts; his first act, Shadiya, had two hit singles on the radio and BET and MTV, and she was nominated for best new artist at the BET awards. It was really good for Tony, and for Dakota, too, since Touchdown Records was a client of hers. It was just that the more he dealt with that, the less he dealt with Dakota. It was enough to share him with his daughter's mother, but she knew he was getting friendly with more and more girls.

They went to a party earlier in the week, and there was a woman there that she knew he'd had sex with. Dakota could just tell by the way they were dealing with each other, and the way she was looking at her. She didn't care, though; Dakota's look back at her said, You see who he is here with, right? This type of stuff was common when you were hanging out with Tony, but a lot of these women were from his all-star pro-football days. Dakota knew the woman wanted him and wanted to be her, so she didn't mind.

There were things, though, about their situation that she just couldn't take. Last night Tony came by to spend the night with her. After having a few drinks and watching a porno, they got into some real good, kinky sex. He was flipping her around the bedroom, she had some toys out, and they were both hot and sweaty. By the time they were done, she'd had two orgasms, and he'd had three. Once they were finished, they just lay in the bed butt-naked and relaxed. After about ten minutes, his phone rang. He took the call, had about a two-minute conversation, and ended it with, *I'll be there in a bit.* Dakota immediately got upset. When he hung up the phone, he explained that his old teammate was stuck on the side of the road and he needed Tony to come get him. She tried to remain calm and said OK, but it was hard. She knew that she'd heard a female voice through his phone.

She wasn't sure how much longer she and Tony would last. She wanted him as her husband if possible; she just didn't know how long she could tolerate this little of him. On nights like these, she wondered what was in it for her anymore, other than the good sex.

48

All Alike

"I just can't believe this is happening to me," Chrasey said. She still wasn't used to waking up in her bed without Keith next to her. Every morning was a harsh reminder of what was going wrong in her life. Her marriage was in a terrible state to begin with, but she didn't imagine it getting worse. She definitely didn't imagine getting a divorce. Since they had lived together in such turmoil all this time, she just thought they would stay that way, for better or worse.

"Girl, this will work itself out. He is just mad right now," Dakota consoled to Chrasey on the phone.

"I don't know. It wasn't like we were happy to begin with—this just confirms for him that our marriage isn't going to work. Besides, he already said he wants a divorce, and it really did sound like he meant it."

"I don't know what is wrong with these men," Jordan interjected.

Dakota, Chrasey, and Jordan were sitting at home on a three-way call. They were making plans to meet up for dinner later and got caught up in their conversation.

"They just need time to calm down, and eventually . . . hopefully they will come to their senses. With Keith, maybe he will finally realize the things he did and didn't do that caused you to step outside the marriage," Dakota declared.

"I know it's too late to say this, but there really is no excuse for stepping out . . ." Chrasey started to say.

"Yeah, you're right. It's too late for that now, because you wasn't saying that when Mr. Trevor was doing you right . . . and don't even front like you don't miss him, because he had you open," Dakota said quite frankly.

After a moment's hesitation, Chrasey replied, "I do. That's the crazy part. I don't know who I miss more."

"Well, maybe that's what you need to do. Maybe you need to realize what you really want. Figure out whether you really want your marriage and if it's the right reason, because maybe Keith is right then, and maybe it is time to let go."

Jordan hadn't said much the whole conversation. She was in a weird place and didn't really know what to say about anything. It wasn't like Jordan to be at a loss for words, but her feelings toward everything had her mind racing, and it was too many thoughts to share. So she just remained quiet, trying to figure out her own thoughts. She was paying only slight attention to the conversation.

"Jordan, what do you think? You think Keith and Omar ran away together?" Chrasey asked, trying to find some humor in the situation.

"I wish I knew, Chrase. At least you know Keith's exact issue. Omar just up and left—I don't know what is on his mind."

"Yeah, but at least you know Omar just needs some time to get over it. Keith has every right to walk away."

"According to Omar, so does he."

"Look, fuck them both, and my part-time boyfriend Tony. It can just be the three of us—we don't need their asses," Dakota blurted out.

They all laughed.

"That's right—what do they do for us, anyway, but cause us heartache and insecurity," Chrasey said.

"Yeah, I know. Mine can't even appreciate a good, strong black woman—wants to make everything an issue. He acts like a girl, with the little fits he throws," Jordan said.

"Well, let them walk out, disappear, threaten divorce, all of that. We will just have our time, too," Dakota said.

It sounded good, but all three of them knew they wanted their men back. Dakota was trying to convince herself that she didn't need Tony, and she wasn't even married nor did she have a kid. Jordan and Chrasey had a lot more to consider—they didn't spend all that money on those weddings, share their lives with and have kids with their husbands just to let them go that easy. So although it was a cool thought to talk some sister strength and how we can do without them, they all knew they didn't want to.

"Look on the bright side—we all have reserves if we need them. I have a phonebook full, Chrasey, you got Trevor, and Jordan, I know you may not really have anyone, but Jayon always fits the bill quite nicely," Dakota offered. She laughed at her own comment, and Chrasey joined her. Even Jordan started to laugh at that one.

"Shut up, 'Kota, I will be just fine. I know that Omar better have his butt home before I need any of that."

"Just don't forget, in case of emergency, break the glass."

A few minutes later they got off the phone. They had managed to make each other laugh and feel a little bit better about their situations. That's what they were there for, to be that shoulder to cry on.

When they were in college, they used to have a sisters' soiree Saturday once a month. It was with their friends from school, but they were the three organizers. They would share their stories about guys on campus, their boyfriends and whatever else was going on. The rest of the group would give advice, and make jokes and whatever else. The purpose of this meeting was to keep each other cheered up and looking on the bright side. It used to really do wonders for all the girls that came, because even if it didn't solve their problems it gave them a chance to laugh and see that they weren't the only ones with issues. That was in college, but even as grownups, it still helped to have their sisters' soiree, even with just the three of them.

49

Friends That Pray
Together, Stay Together

It had been a rough week. Today would make a full week since
Omar packed up his stuff and left. It hadn't quite hit me yet that
this could be something permanent, and it hadn't been easy, either.
This was typical of Omar, though. When we were dating he would just
not call or come by for weeks until he got over his anger. He would
hang up the phone in the middle of arguments and just not be heard
from for days. He had this habit of running and hiding—and he just
thought when he was over it everything would be cool. Jordan used to
tell him back then that it was the most selfish behavior. He had a partner, and that wasn't acceptable. He would apologize, they would get
back together, but when the going got tough he would do it again.

So this didn't surprise her, but it still had her very pissed off. Not to
mention their child, who was being affected. He spent most of the
evenings with her mother until she came to pick him up. It was a different routine for him, and he was used to having Omar around.

It was Sunday, and Jason and Jordan sat in church like most Sundays.
This morning she was really praying that the pastor would give her
some words of encouragement to get through this. She was clapping
and praising, and trying just to become one with the Spirit. In church
she always got the message that everything was going to be just fine,
and she was trying to engrave it in her brain. She had got so engrossed
listening for the message that she didn't even see Jayon excusing himself down the pew until he reached her and sat beside her.

"Hey, Jayon," she said. She was beyond happy to see him.

"Hey, J," he said as he patted Jason on the head.

Jordan had no idea Jayon was coming here—they hadn't talked since Friday at work. He knew that she usually went to church on Sundays, and what church she went to; it seemed that he just decided to pop up and look for her.

"What are you doing here?" she asked.

"I'm coming to praise the lord," he said sarcastically. "How you holding up?" he whispered as he patted Jason on the head again.

"I'm hanging in there," she whispered back, trying not to speak too loud to annoy the people sitting around them.

He looked in her eyes and saw pain. Then he patted her leg as if to say *I'm here for you.* After he conveyed his silent message, he looked forward toward Rev. Flake; he was preaching about the quality of life. Jason sat there scribbling on the tithe envelopes, and she sat there receiving her message for the week. She also realized that despite what Omar may have conjured up in his mind, Jayon was a great friend and helped her quality of life.

Church let out about 1:10, and as they exited the pew she heard Jayon ask Jason if he wanted to go to IHOP. That was the setup—ask Jason, because of course he would say yes. Once Jason was eager to go, Jordan, too, agreed. She put Jason in his booster seat, jumped in the driver's seat, and followed Jayon down Merrick Boulevard. It tickled Jordan how Jayon knew the neighborhood so well. Jayon was from the Bronx, but he had spent so much time in Queens since they'd met back in college, he knew the area like it was his own. We pulled up to IHOP and of course, like most IHOPs on a Sunday afternoon, it was crowded. She told Jayon we didn't have to wait, that Jason would be just fine, but he insisted. He claimed that he didn't want to make an empty promise to Jason, but she had a feeling he really wanted to pick her brain.

They finally got seated after half an hour, and now she was really hungry, too. They ordered their breakfasts and she and Jason sipped on chocolate milk while Jayon sipped on orange juice. Once their meals were ordered, and Jason was busy coloring, Jayon looked at Jordan and said, "You have been on my mind all weekend."

"I'm fine, Jay, really."

"No, you're not. You're trying to remain tough but this isn't court—it's OK to show emotion."

"Listen, Jay, I'm pissed, if you want to know, but I can't let it stop me."

"I'm not saying it should stop you, but take a minute to address it."

"What is there to address? That I married a big child who can't take the heat?" Jayon looked over at Jason, and she caught herself.

"See, I don't want to talk about this."

"Jordan, he is doing what he feels he needs to do," Jayon said dangerously, defending Omar.

"Exactly, and not what *we* need to do. It's always been about him, and I see that now even more."

"So what are you thinking?" he asked her.

"I'm thinking he can stay wherever he is at, because I don't need the extra stress in my life. Your husband should be a friend and someone who supports you—he hasn't been that for some time."

"He probably feels like you haven't been much of a wife, either, and I didn't help the situation."

"No, you didn't," she said, laughing.

"I'm sorry, Jordan, I really am."

"You don't have to be—you didn't do anything."

"You didn't, either. I know better than anybody you wouldn't ever have cheated on him."

"That's the problem, *he* should know better than anybody."

Jayon didn't have a reply, and Jordan didn't want to say too much more in front of Jason. So they ate their food and left it alone. What remained to be seen is what Omar was going to do. She couldn't make any decisions until she knew what was on his mind. Like she told Jayon, at this point all she could think about was how pissed she was, and she prayed that God gave her enough strength to cleanse her heart.

50

1-800-Caught

Chrasey called it "having a rejuvenation weekend." Cleaning, catching up with her to-do list, paying bills, etc. It had been a month since Keith had been gone, and she was just about done with the adjustment phase. She wasn't content with the situation, but it wasn't as hard as it had been. The guilt had subsided some, and she was dealing with life as it came her way.

She had lost a lot of weight, and she was looking damn good. She didn't know if it was the stress or if it was wanting to make sure the next time Keith saw her, he would like what he saw. She had been really focused on her diet, and had been working out like two or three times a week. She was feeling good about herself and she was actually feeling confident that Keith would be home. She had spoken to his mother, who told her that she spoke to him and he said he would be coming home.

She sat down and started writing checks to pay the bills for the month. The phone bill was unusually high, but it had been a while since she paid it, so she wasn't sure—Keith usually paid it. So she decided to look it over to see why it seemed high. After looking at it for a few moments, she noticed there was this one number listed on the bill quite frequently. She didn't know the number, so she was curious as to who this was. She called the number and the answering machine picked up. On the voice mail it said, "Hello you just reached Lourdes— please leave a message and I'll get back to you as soon as possible."

Chrasey didn't know of anyone by the name of Lourdes. She looked at the phone bill and it said Brooklyn, NY. She couldn't think of anybody in Brooklyn that she or Keith would know of.

She started to look back at previous months' bills, and every bill she could find had the same number planted all over it. Outgoing calls at all times of the night, all days of the week. There were some calls at 3:45 in the morning that lasted an hour. Chrasey knew at that point. She didn't even have to put two and two together to figure this one out—just two by itself was enough.

There was also a mobile number that was on there frequently as well. She called that one too. It was the same outgoing message. She was tempted to leave a message but she decided against it and hung up. She needed time to think before she made a hasty move. She wanted to call Keith up and ask him, but she wanted to talk to this woman first so he would be caught off guard.

She called up Jordan and Chrasey and told them. They asked how she could know it's not her husband that he is calling.

Chrasey's response was, "First of all, unless he is gay, why would he be talking to a man at 4:00 in the morning all that time? Secondly, her voice mail would have had her husband included on the outgoing message."

They eventually gave up their devil's advocate role and just admitted that this didn't look right.

"The nerve of him to have a fit over Trevor, and he was doing his thing all along," Chrasey said.

"Well, Chrasey, this explains a lot. You did know it in your heart—that's why you started dealing with Trevor to begin with," Dakota said.

"Yeah, you just lost sight of that with your guilt. Now you find out the truth. He just found out before you did," Jordan said.

"Yeah, well, I just want to see what he has to say for himself," Chrasey replied.

For some reason Chrasey wasn't as emotional as usual. She didn't know if it was because she knew it all along or because she had been doing the same thing. Her thoughts were just spinning at a rapid pace. Her curiosity started to take over—she had a hundred questions. Who was she? How long? What has it been like? So that's where he has been this past month.

While she spoke to Chrasey and Jordan on three-way, she heard a beep on her phone. She looked in the phone and it said "Lourdes McDougal" in the Caller ID.

"Guys, that's her!" Chrasey said frantically.

"Who?" Jordan and Dakota asked.

"The girl, Lourdes. She is calling me back."

"You gonna get it?" Jordan asked.

"Yeah, hold on," Chrasey said. She took a deep breath and clicked over. "Hello," she said.

"Hello, did somebody call Lourdes from this number?"

"Yes, I found your number on my phone bill and I was trying to find out who the number belonged to."

"Who is this?" she asked.

"My name is Chrasey."

She paused. "I don't know a Chrasey," she replied.

"Do you know a Keith?" she asked.

She fell silent. Chrasey also didn't say a word. "Yeah, we used to work together."

"Oh, OK. That's my husband. Can you tell me what the nature of your relationship with him is?"

All of a sudden, she asked Chrasey to hold on. Chrasey knew that she wasn't coming back to the phone, or she was calling Keith.

51

Up-Close and Personal

She never came back to the phone, just as Chrasey thought. She hung up after a few minutes and tried Keith herself—there was no answer. She called three times, then called his mother's house and still didn't get him. She even called Lourdes back later in the evening, and she didn't answer. Chrasey barely slept that night, wondering if he was staying with her. She was sure Lourdes would tell him Chrasey called, and she was upset that he hadn't called to defend himself.

It was Monday morning and Chrasey had already made up her mind that since he wasn't taking her calls, she would be stopping by his job. She dropped the kids off at school as usual and headed in to the city. She got to his job, parked in a parking garage, and went to the visitor's desk and signed in. Once she reached his floor, she walked past all the offices and secretaries that were on the way to his office. It was still early in the morning, and she could tell people questioned who she was or what she was doing there. A co-worker or two whom she had met recognized her and their faces lit up with shock. She didn't even say hello, she just kept walking. She reached his office on the back wall, and he was sitting in there with someone. She stood there and gave him a look, giving him fair warning to clear his office before he got embarrassed. He asked his guest to excuse him.

As soon as the guest passed by her, she walked up closer to Keith's desk and said to him, "You don't return your phone calls?"

"My cell phone is broken—I have to take it to get fixed," he said as he got up to close the door. He knew this had potential to be ugly.

"Really. Did you call Lourdes to let her know that so she could get in touch with you? "

"Chrasey . . ." he said in a tone that sounded like he was about to make excuses or minimize his involvement with her. She didn't even want to hear it. She didn't come all the way up here to be foolish—she knew what was what. She went into her bag and pulled out the phone bills she had gotten her number off of and threw them toward him. They weren't heavy enough to hit him, so they just fluttered throughout his office. Papers going every which way, pages with Lourdes's name and phone number everywhere, on her god damn house phone bill. Why couldn't he use his cell phone—did he have to be so sloppy? Did he have to be so sloppy not to even care? She could have picked up the house phone just like he did that night with Trevor.

Afraid her voice would carry through his door, he said "Chrasey, can we address this at home later, not here at my job?"

"Why not? They must know all about it. She said she knows you from here. Maybe I should ask one of them since neither you or her wants to tell me."

"Chrasey, she is just a friend of mine. I guess something like Trevor."

"Don't even try it. She is the reason I befriended Trevor. These bills go back over a year, and I know if I have the phone company send me copies from before that, it was even longer. This was why you were acting like that, treating me like that, and you wonder where Trevor came from."

Her eyes had begun to tear up. She felt a knot in her throat, feeling a real emotional scene coming on. She tried to regain her composure. She didn't come here to be weak and emotional—she came to let his ass know he wasn't fooling anybody with his lies.

"Don't even try to blame me for your infidelity," he said.

"Keith, I don't have to blame you. You know in your heart what you were doing to me. Lourdes must have been getting all the attention from my husband." He didn't say anything, he just looked at her. She could tell in his eyes he didn't want her to know. Even with what she did, she could tell he knew in his heart that he was the cause for the turmoil in their marriage.

"Can you at least have the decency to tell me the truth?" Chrasey said. He looked at her, and when he couldn't look her in the eyes anymore, he dropped his head. When he looked back at her, she knew that he was going to tell her, and she wasn't going to like it. He started his sentence, and then put his head back down so he didn't have to look at her.

"Lourdes was a co-worker of mine—we worked on a lot of projects together. After a few late nights together, some things just led to other things. It wasn't planned, I swear."

She just stood there, listening. She was numb inside, and although she knew this, it was still shocking to her that she was hearing what she was hearing.

"It happened, like, two or three times, and we said that we weren't going to continue. She had just got divorced, and I didn't want to risk our marriage. "

"But what?"

"It only happened, like, two or three times."

"*What* happened?"

He looked at her, to see if she was really unaware of what he was speaking of or she just wanted to hear him say it.

"We slept together two or three times."

"Keith, you know how many times you fucked her."

"I think it was three times—I can't remember for sure."

"So . . ."

"So we said we wouldn't deal with each other any longer, but it was too late."

"Why was it too late?" she said, pissed off.

All she could think was he was about to tell her he fell in love with this woman. They couldn't be apart, and he wants a divorce so he could be with her.

"Because she was pregnant . . . she will be one year old next month," he said.

52

Do Not Break Glass

Jordan hadn't seen or heard from Omar in over two weeks. She called him several times, but he wouldn't return her calls. She had many nights where she was just flat-out pissed off that he would treat her this way, but other nights she was weak and all she wanted was her life back.

The one time he took her call over two weeks ago, they had a brief conversation and it didn't seem like he had come to his senses yet.

When she called, she tried to tell him that this was rough on her and Jason, and she really wanted him to come back home. She had put her pride aside to try to talk sense into him, up until his cocky attitude pissed her off.

"You will be just fine. You have your clients and your friends."

She just giggled, a sarcastic, I-can't-believe-this-shit giggle.

"You know what, Omar? I will be. They've been all I've had for quite some time anyway. So you go ahead and do what you have to do . . . but you know what? You're a coward. You're leaving your home, your wife, and your son over some bullshit. If you're trying to get attention, this is childish. We are a family."

He could hear that she was fed up. She was frustrated, she was hurt, she was annoyed, and she was helpless. It didn't make a difference, though.

"Don't use that family line—your clients and your friends are your family. Jason and I are just part of your perfect picture. You don't need us—you just need us for your image."

Somewhere around that point, she hung up on him.

So there she was, sitting in her office wondering how she had gotten through the past two weeks. She was kind of daydreaming, just letting her mind review the events of the past few months. She still didn't think it had sunk in yet—the reality of what this could mean.

She happened to look out her office door and Jayon was standing there talking with one of his clients. It seemed that he was getting something from her assistant, so he was standing pretty much right in her direct view. He was fully engaged in the conversation, so he didn't notice her. As she just watched him talking and his mannerisms, she found herself slightly smiling to herself. He was just so handsome. His smile could light up the darkest room. The twinkle in his eye was simply mesmerizing. When she saw him laugh, he made her soul smile with him. She started to think about just how much Jayon meant to her. The person he was inside and outside always had a way of making her feel happy. She was proud to say he was her best friend, because if he was anything less, she'd feel like she was missing out on something. He was that person she wished she could be everything to—his boss, his mechanic, his mother, his barber, his bank teller, his girl, just so she could be in his presence all the time. She knew it sounded a little extreme, but Jayon was a great guy. If she wasn't married, he would surely be her ideal husband.

She tried to get back to work—she had spent enough time thinking and daydreaming. A few minutes had passed, and Jayon was still standing outside her door. Whenever she glanced to see if he had walked away, she would stop and stare for a few extra seconds. She couldn't help it, until she finally noticed what she was doing. *Shame on you, Jordan,* she thought to herself. He was standing there, looking all fine. He was wearing black suit pants with a black-and-gray button-down, and his black Prada shoes she got him for his birthday. She tried to ask herself, *What are you doing? That's Jayon—and you are married.*

She had to get it together. She couldn't understand why she was even entertaining such thoughts. Then, a few seconds later, she was wondering how she'd lasted this long being platonic friends with him. Then Jayon happened to look her way and caught her looking at him. She immediately tried to turn away. Next thing she knew, he walked up to her door and said, "What you looking at?" in a playful tone.

"Nothing special," she replied.

"Mmm-hmm—you know you were checking out my sexy body," he said.

"*Please,*" she said, trying to laugh it off.

Jayon knew that she found him attractive. Hell, she knew he found *her* attractive. They just always tried not to acknowledge it because they weren't on those terms. Still, from time to time they would have fun with each other about it.

"Lies. I saw it in your eyes."

"Shut up, Jay, and get out of here," she replied.

"You just want to watch my butt as I walk out."

"No, I want to see the back of your head."

They both laughed and he turned to walk away.

When he walked away, she was still laughing. Jordan actually enjoyed having a guy as a best friend, especially a guy like Jayon. Someone she could actually see herself with, in a different circumstance. All these years, it was a real challenge. It also proved to her that she could be faithful, even in the most tempting situations. She knew this because there were times when Jayon was looking that damn fine, and she was in the middle of hating the hell out of Omar—and even in those weakest moments, she never would've slept with Jayon. It was safe around him—somebody she wouldn't have slept with versus somebody else that she might have done something with out of spite. So, in those times he was a good guy to have around. There were times he was more her husband than Omar. She was able to share more with him than she could with Omar sometimes. She could talk to him like her diary. With him, he didn't judge her, and she didn't have to worry. She was able to have a relationship with him without having to play games or worry about arguing and all that dumb relationship crap. He was the relief in her storm sometimes. He was like a brother to her in that sense. However, even though he was like a brother to her, she wasn't blind.

53

Fantasy World

"How is this an open relationship, when you're constantly lying to me? How am I supposed to trust you, when I constantly catch you in lie after lie?" Dakota was in the process of arguing with Tony once again. "You have to know that I don't believe that shit deep down."

Last night Tony had gone to a charity event, where he was being given an award for his role in the community. Tony was born and raised in Brooklyn, so his status as an ex-pro football player was a big deal at home. So although he was becoming a mogul in the music business, Tony still had to attend different athletic events. Also just as weird, even though he now owned houses in the suburbs and was living the good life and barely went to Brooklyn, the borough was always showing him affection. This event was to honor how kids in Brooklyn looked up to him, and to announce the start of a scholarship in his name for Brooklyn students.

A few of his old NFL teammates were supposed to attend as well as some executives from the league, other teams, and local companies. Dakota wanted to go with Tony when she first heard about it. Tony's excuse for not taking her was that he would be the center of attention and didn't want her to feel neglected. Dakota had been out several times at events with Tony, and he *was* the center of attention, so she wasn't buying that. He said since he had to sit at the table on the stage, it made no sense for her to sit at a table by herself. Dakota didn't feel like arguing, and definitely didn't want to feel like she was begging to go, so she left it alone.

In her mind, Dakota thought it was because he might be bringing his daughter's mother and didn't want to tell her. She decided not to make a big deal out of it and wait to see what happened when she saw the press coverage. She was all prepared for an argument over that, but not this. A friend of Dakota's told her that she saw Tony leave the event with two girls, one on each arm. Dakota was just appalled that Tony was still out there behaving that way. He tried to deny that was what it was for; he said they were just associates and that they were all going out to dinner.

"Dakota, why you are you tripping like that?" Tony asked.

"Because you are constantly embarrassing me," she answered.

"We are not a couple. We are not one-on-one—why would that embarrass you?"

"Because I bring you places with me, and people that see us together will laugh at me, or I'll look like I'm just one of your groupies because they are constantly seeing you out messing with other girls."

"Dakota, obviously if I'm out with you at events, they should know you're more than that."

"So I should feel special because you come places with me?" she asked.

"Don't put words in my mouth—all I'm saying is it's not that serious. I don't have any rings on my finger, but yet you be bugging like I'm cheating on you."

"So should I just not expect any commitment from you whatsoever? I mean, damn," Dakota said, getting frustrated.

"You should expect me to behave like a man that doesn't have a commitment to you."

Dakota didn't say anything. What could she say? She knew the truth. He was right—she had no strings attached to him. She had just thought they'd gotten to a place where she could begin to expect stuff from him. It seemed like every time she thought they were closer to something more, he would just kindly, or not-so-kindly, remind her that they were not committed. It felt like he stuck a steak knife through her ego every time he had to say that. It was like his way of saying, *Don't get too excited with this here—we are just fucking.*

Dakota began to wonder that if time to time she was starting her own little fantasy by thinking they had become or would become more. Had she started to put Tony somewhere that he didn't want to be? The problem with that was, had she started to paint a picture to those around her that things weren't what they were? Then she realized that was why she was so embarrassed. It was because when she spoke about Tony, she spoke about him as if they had a more committed and respectful relationship, so she knew whenever he would be in public behaving like a single man, it would make her look like an idiot. That was obviously her own fault, but all she did was exaggerate the truth. She would just pretend he cared a little more than he did about the other guys she was dealing with, or like he was around more than he was, or like she had a sexy, successful man, which made her more of a diva than she really was.

What Dakota didn't bother to notice was that she was a diva without Tony. Dakota had got so caught up in how Tony made her look, in how impressed some of her friends and colleagues were by him. They were impressed that she was dating him, that she had him as a client—hell, they would have been impressed just because she knew him. She was supposed to be dealing with Tony for the same reason he was dealing with her; somewhere along the line, she lost focus.

She knew that Tony saw her change over time, but she figured if he really had a problem with it he would end things with her. He had to notice when they first started dealing with each other, Dakota was a smooth female who didn't resent anything he did. He could come and go as he pleased, and whenever he did come, he left pleased. They were just enjoying life and each other. There were no promises made, and at that point Dakota wasn't ready to make any, either. Over time things changed, and it was obvious every time Dakota had expectations, every time she complained, every time they argued.

Dakota figured it was an unspoken understanding. Did Tony really think that after all this time she wouldn't eventually want more than just some good pipe? It was almost impossible not to expect her to catch some feelings and want some respect. It wasn't like Tony didn't say things that implied they were more than just sexual partners; it wasn't until he wanted to be free that he would play the no-commitment card. Dakota just hated hearing it.

She let the argument die there, changing the topic to asking how the event was. That's what she discussed with him, but in her mind she was thinking about how she had to find a way to get her swagger back. She couldn't let Tony overshadow the diva that she was. She knew that was the reason why she bagged him in the first place— every man likes the secure, non-clingy girl. They like the girl that just wants to have fun, and that was Dakota before the fall. She had to climb her way back out so Tony wouldn't desire any woman but her.

54

Two Wrongs Make
Us Even

"How mad could I be?" Chrasey asked herself.

She was sitting there, trying to rationalize to herself the severity of the news she had gotten from Keith. He had cheated on her and the girl got pregnant. She had the baby almost a year ago. It was just crazy to her—she had no idea, and she was sure he had no intention of telling her any time in the near future.

He claimed he was using protection, but that was hard for her to believe. That whole excuse that the condom broke sounded too simple to Chrasey.

She had cursed him out real loud when she opened the door to leave so all of the co-workers and friends of that whore could hear her. Calling him all types of dogs, curse words, and small dicks, she stormed out, making a dramatic exit. She wasn't crying, though. She knew one of those secretaries was still friends with that bitch, and she refused to let her go back and tell her she was all up in his job crying. As soon as she got in her car, though, she broke down. She couldn't even pull out of the parking lot for half an hour. She called her mom, Jordan, Dakota, and Trevor. Trevor sounded really sorry to hear it. He told her if she wanted him to come over or she wanted to talk anytime, he would be there for her. Jordan was the one who finally coaxed her into calming down. Jordan told Chrasey she would meet her at Twenty-third and Seventh at a café so they could talk. Dakota was in a meeting for most of the morning, but she met up with them later. If it wasn't for them calming her down, she might have contemplated something really criminal.

After a few days had passed, she was looking at things a little differently. The reality was, what he did was inexcusable. However, it seemed from all his calls and voice mails that he was extremely sorry. Now that she knew, he seemed to feel a weight lifted. He had opened up more these past few days than he had in almost a year. He had left messages saying how much he loved her—he wanted to put all of their mistakes behind them and start over. They started young—maybe they both just lost sight of the big picture.

It was a hard thing to swallow. She had lived the past ten years trying to build a future with Keith, and just that fast he started one with some other woman. The cheating was one thing, but him having a child just negated everything they had together. This woman had the same thing they had. She couldn't even say that at least she still had the marriage, because they didn't have much of that these days, either.

She wanted to meet the woman, see what she looked like, see if she was at least better-looking than she or remotely worth all the drama she had caused. It finally explained his distance, and his inconsistency. He probably sat there on the couch for so many nights, not knowing what to do with himself. Keith told Chrasey on one of his phone messages that she wanted him to leave Chrasey and the kids, and he told her he wouldn't do that.

Chrasey didn't know what to believe anymore. Although he said he had spent the past month at his boy's crib, she knew he had spent several nights in Brooklyn with her and his daughter. The thought made her want to throw up. She thought of the few times they had had sex this past year. The times he would come home pretending to be the annoyed, mistreated husband, and he was leading another life.

She remembered she was, too. The whole dynamic had changed being that she had stepped outside of their marriage, too. What if he hadn't found out about Trevor? Since he had, he had Trevor as proof that she wasn't perfect. *We both made mistakes—we should just let it go,* she told herself.

Keith even said to her, *You and that boy slept together and what if you accidentally got pregnant—it's no different.* He was right. There was an instance or two where the condom was looking a little unsecured, and

Chrasey was worried. She guessed that because she knew what that fear was like, she couldn't really point the finger too much because it came true for him.

She had always felt that two wrongs didn't make a right, but it damn sure made them even. Still, she had to admit that in this instance she didn't have much firm ground to stand on. She did have every right to divorce Keith and get half of his check and move on with Trevor. She didn't know what it was, but something in her told her that they should have another chance. She didn't want to throw their marriage away without trying. In reality, they both messed up and they deserved another chance at what they started on their wedding day. She figured instead of making the decision herself, she would let time tell.

She knew Keith had been feeling it. He had told everybody about what she had done, and she made sure she told everybody what he had done. She tried to tell his mother and siblings before that he was up to no good, but he was trying to cry innocent. He was trying to paint Chrasey as the bad guy. Now that she was able to tell them the truth, they had been badgering and scolding him ever since. One of his brothers even called to apologize on his behalf and begged her to let Keith come back home.

She had made Keith suffer enough. She didn't get the feeling that he needed to feel more pain from what he did. She was sure he had been feeling that for over a year now. The secrets and the fear had to be stressful. Then finding out about Trevor, and her scene at his office. She figured it was probably a good time for her and Keith to iron out the rest of their problems. So she went ahead and put him out of his misery, and told him he could come back home.

55

Broken-Hearted

Jordan wasn't sure if this was just her way of mending her own heart, but she knew things weren't quite right. In all her years, she'd never had to be alone. Even when she was single as a teenager, she always had some form of male companionship. She had males who were close friends of hers, so even when she was in between re-lationships, she had a male friend to fill that void. A guy to bring along when the girls were hanging with their boyfriends. She was sure if she went to a psychologist they could diagnose what this meant in her life, but the fact still remained this is what she had be-come used to.

Things were feeling very strange between Jordan and Jayon. For the most part they hadn't addressed it, but it was very obvious that things were getting risky. Jayon sensed it, and he, too, wanted to steer away from it before they ended up on an emotional roller coaster. He had told her at one point since they had started to spend so much time together, that they should be very careful and take things very slow. There were nights when she was tempted to experience just one night with him—she knew that would be all it took to help get her mind off Omar and ease some of her pain. Jayon didn't want any part of that, though. He didn't want to be that much of a friend and then she and Omar would work things out and things between him and Jordan would never be the same. Even worse, she would probably confess to Omar and then he and Omar would have some serious issues between the two of them. So, although Jayon was trying to be a friend, he had become the sensible one in this.

Jordan knew he was right. So, time after time when she felt the urge she, too, would ignore it. Jordan had a tendency to be spiteful, and she knew if she took it there, she would be making Omar pay for his heartless behavior. Although the thought was nice, Jordan wasn't emotionally or mentally ready to go that far. Just being around Jayon outside of the work environment was enough. One night they were in the conference room at their office, working and eating some McDonald's. Jayon let out a sigh of frustration because of the taxes he was working on. Jordan got up from her chair and started to give him a neck massage. As she rubbed and squeezed, she could feel his body give in to the pleasure. After she felt him completely relax, she bent over and gave him a kiss on the forehead.

"If you want revenge sex, you have to get it somewhere else," Jayon said with his eyes closed.

Jordan could tell he was joking, but she also knew in these moments it crossed both of their minds. She wasn't sure if it was just spite, or if she was starting to catch feelings for Jayon. She was sure that her appreciation for him was magnified, being that with Omar acting a fool, she could use as much loving companionship as possible.

There were times Jayon would try to convince Jordan something was disrespectful to Omar, and he didn't know if it was a good idea. This would only make Jordan angry—that was part of the reason she would want to do these things. One time she wanted Jayon to go on a business trip with her for the weekend, and Jayon was doubtful at first. He eventually did go after Jordan reminded him she was a grown woman and wasn't going to live on some pretense of marriage. She had no clue what her husband was up to, or what or who he was doing. Her own thoughts of the things Omar could be doing made her want to do that much more that was wrong.

One night they were in the room at the hotel, and they were lying in Jayon's bed watching television. After half an hour or so, there was some slight rubbing and caressing. At some point their lips met and they started a gentle and nervous kiss. Jordan's hand had made its way toward Jayon's lower region, and Jayon's was on her breasts. They were moving very slow and soft, but they definitely had the same thing in mind. Moments into it, after their hormones were alert, Jayon's cell phone rang. Jordan sat up while Jayon answered the phone. Even though she was enjoying it, Jordan's first thought was that the phone call was a sign that they shouldn't be doing this.

As soon as Jayon got off the phone, he said, "Thank goodness my brother called—he just saved your marriage."

"You're more concerned about him than you are me," Jordan said, frustrated at his mention of her marriage. She had been trying to keep that off of her mind to prevent an emotional breakdown.

"Jordan, I *am* thinking of you, keeping you from having regrets. I am not your revenge sex. I want you, too, Jordan, but I love you too much to do this for all the wrong reasons."

It was those times that she knew Jayon knew her better than she knew herself, and he loved her more than she ever gave him credit for. She knew she could say the right thing to Jayon to get him to go through with it—she just wasn't ready to say those things yet. One of the things he wanted to hear or be sure of is that she was sure. That she was sure there was no turning back with Omar, and that the decision was based on her marriage and had nothing to do with him. She couldn't tell him that, though. As much as she wanted to believe she was mad enough, she knew a part of her wanted Omar to come home.

That was a couple of weeks ago, but on this night she sat on the edge on her bed, allowing her brain to scan through the past few months of events. She knew it was only a matter of time before there would be no turning back in her marriage. She had tried to talk to Omar about their current state, but he was still missing in action. Omar was a prideful and stubborn man when he wanted to be, so getting him to break was harder than her bar exam.

She decided to give it another try. Jayon was becoming a serious problem for her, and before things got too crazy she wanted to give Omar another chance to come to his senses. Maybe he would come around and save their marriage, and save her from herself before she completely gave in to her temptations with Jayon.

She picked up the phone and started to dial Omar's number, but after the fourth digit she hung up. She didn't know if she was afraid of the rejection or that he might agree to try to work things out and she wouldn't have a chance to see where things would go with Jayon.

She picked the phone back up and dialed Omar's number again.

This time it rang until it reached his voice mail. As usual, he was ignoring her call.

"*Omar, I know you're probably not going to call me back, but I wanted to let you know one more time I really think we should talk before this gets worse or it's too late to fix things . . . call me. I love you.*"

56

Sisters Soiree

Dakota and Chrasey were at Jordan's house, trying to get a break from their man trouble. Jordan made martinis, Jason was at his grandmother's, and we were having a private party. The radio was tuned into 98.7 Kiss FM and Kissing after Dark was on with Lenny Green. He was playing some R&B joints from a few years back, and Jordan and Chrasey were in the middle of the floor, getting down. Dakota was sitting down, singing along, but she knew she wanted to get up, too. Lenny Green was that radio DJ that would put any lady in the mood for the night. He had a sultry, sexy voice, and every word out of his mouth made you want to melt inside. He would light candles in the studio, and as he described what he would want to do with you if he were home with you, he would introduce another R&B classic. He was just the man they needed in the living room with them tonight. A man that would make it all better.

Jordan had spent most of the week stressed about the Omar thing, and worrying about her son and how he would be affected. She was in an emotional state, so tonight felt good. To just let go for a while, worry about it later, and enjoy the right now. They were like three college girls, having drinks, laughing at silly stuff, and having fun. They had spent the first half-hour talking about Tony's predictable routine, Omar's immature time off, and Keith's make-up attempts now that he had been back home for a couple of nights. After enough men-bashing, they had spent the past hour or so celebrating their womanhood.

Just as Jordan got tired and was about to sit down, Lenny started playing her jam "Be Without You," by Mary J. Blige. She immediately started back on her one-two step. A verse or so into it, she thought she heard her bell ring over the music. She turned it down a bit, and there it was again. She walked through the living room, through the porch, and to the door.

"Who is it," she asked.

"It's Jay."

She opened the door and Jayon was standing there with bags in his hands.

"What are you doing here?" She said, excited to see him.

"I went food shopping and picked you up some things," he said as he went to put the bags in the kitchen.

As he walked by Dakota and Chrasey and threw them both a "what's up," they both turned and looked at Jordan. She knew what they were thinking and what they were going to say the minute he was out of hearing distance. To avoid them and their smart comments, she followed Jayon in the kitchen.

"I didn't know you had company," he said.

"You didn't even know I was home."

"Where else would you be? You weren't at work, so you're home," he said.

"Are you trying to say I have no life?" she asked, humored.

"Was I right? You're at home."

"But I have my girls over."

"OK, fine—you have a little life."

Jayon used to always say Jordan was a homebody and a social bore. He didn't know what he was talking about. Just because he used to go out quite often, he would assume anybody who went out only once every month or two was lame. She'd say the people who live in the club have no life.

"What made you bring me groceries?"

"I just figured that you had to do everything these days, and since I was already at BJ's, I figured I would pick you up some things."

"That was so sweet of you, Jay," she said as she reached over and gave him a hug.

"You know I got to make sure my girl is OK."

She knew what he meant by "my girl," but it just sounded strange coming out of his mouth. She did have to wonder what would cause

Jay to drive all the way over here with some groceries, unannounced. Did he not fear what would happen if Omar had come home and she didn't get a chance to call and tell him? It kind of made her wonder. First church, then her house—she wondered if Jayon was getting too comfortable with her single status.

They walked back to the living room and joined Dakota and Chrasey.

"So, what's up, ladies?" he asked as he gave them kisses on the cheeks.

"Nothing much, just chilling," Chrasey said.

"Well, let me leave you ladies to your men-bashing party," he said as he walked toward the door.

"We aren't men-bashing—we are having a good old time just fine," Dakota said.

"You can stay, Jay," Jordan said as she saw him get closer to the porch.

"Nah, I don't want to crash," he said.

"You're not—you drove all this way, you might as well stay," she replied.

"How about I'll go check my boy in Laurelton and then when I'm done I'll call you—if you're still up, I'll come back by and we will watch a movie."

From the corner of her eye, she saw Dakota look at Chrasey as if to say, *What the hell is going on here?*

"OK, that works," Jordan said.

"See you, Chrase—see you, D," Jayon said as he walked toward the porch. They got to the door, and he turned to give her a hug good-bye.

"I'm going to be waiting up for you," she said.

"Make sure you do," he said as he kissed her on the forehead.

He stepped out the door and she watched him until he pulled off. She felt like she was in junior high school and he was her crush. She wanted to lean against the door after she closed it behind him. Once she got back in the living room, both Chrasey and Dakota were looking at her like they were waiting for an explanation. She didn't know what to tell them. There was nothing to tell. She knew what they saw and what they were thinking. She didn't know what it was herself. All she knew was that Jayon's presence had kept her going throughout this thing with Omar. It's like she knew that Jay would never let her down. Any night she was hysterically crying, he would just sit on the phone with her and listen for hours or drive over to be with her and bring her and Jason ice cream. There were some nights she felt bad for leaning on Jay's shoulder so much—she would tell him that he didn't have to feel bad if he didn't have the time to help her. She wondered if it was out of guilt, and she told him that he wasn't obligated to be there for her. He would always say that's not the case, and that he wanted to do it.

Dakota was the first one to ask, "Something you want to tell us, miss?"

"I know what you're thinking—it's no different than before. He is still my homeboy," Jordan answered.

"What's your homeboy doing popping up, and then what's he coming back for later tonight?" Chrasey said, instigating.

"He has been around a lot—you know, making sure I'm good."

"I bet—making sure you're good *how*," Dakota asked devilishly.

"Not in that way, but I will tell you—soon I'm going to need him for that, too," she said laughing.

"Omar better get it together," Chrasey said, laughing along.

Omar was still bugging her. He still hadn't called or come by, and he didn't seem to care either way. She had called him at least three times this week and he still hadn't called back. She knew that Chrasey was right—she wasn't planning for anything to happen; hell, it's the last thing that she and Jayon wanted to do. Still, she couldn't put her finger on it, but something was different between the two of them.

57

Hello There

It didn't take a gay man to see that Dakota put no effort into her appearance this Saturday afternoon. She had on saggy green Capri sweats, a baby blue tee, white sneakers with a red stripe, and last night's makeup and uncombed hair. No one said you have to be in tip-top shape at all times, but she just looked a hot mess.

She figured she was in Jordan's neighborhood, so she wouldn't know anybody and would probably never see them again. But just when you hope you don't see anyone you know, you see someone you wish you did know. He was six-three, slim yet thick, and brown-skinned, just like she liked them. You could tell through his fitted t-shirt that he was slightly muscular and his eyes . . . with just a glance she was mesmerized by his light brown eyes. He was the type of guy you only see in movies, and here he was, walking out of Pathmark on Elmont Road. Tony had nothing on him. As fine as she thought Tony was, he would be the ugly friend hanging out with this guy.

She quickly put on her sexy strut and threw him an inviting stare. He didn't really gaze back; he gave her a slight smile and turned away. Then she remembered her color coordination looked like a bag of M-M's. The way she looked, she knew he wouldn't pay her no mind. As she wanted to kick herself for not fixing herself up, he walked right by her like she wasn't even the diva that she was. *Hey, you win some and you lose some*, she thought to herself. But as she grabbed her cart and continued toward the supermarket, she decided she couldn't let him get away. She had to at least try.

"They don't come like that anymore," she mumbled to herself as she turned back around, facing the parking lot. Her eyes scanned the lot, and she spotted him putting the groceries into his trunk.

As comfortable as Dakota was with taking charge, for once she was shy, she was nervous. His good looks were actually intimidating. She started thinking he probably likes those real petite, light-skinned girls with wavy, long, real hair. As she started to discourage herself, her diva-ness said, *Girl, he is fine. You won't need Tony. You can show him off at every event you go to for the next year.* Besides, if she bagged him looking the way she did, she would know she was bad.

She quickly pushed her cart back toward the rest of them, and she walked over to him. Just as he was finishing unloading his groceries, she placed her hand on his empty shopping cart and said to him, "Do you mind?"

He said, "Sure," and began to walk away.

Speak now or forever hold your peace, she said to herself.

"So where is it?" she said.

He turned to see if she was talking to him.

"Where is what?"

"Your number—you said sure, you didn't mind."

He began to giggle. *Oh, my gosh,* Dakota thought to herself. He had dimples. Dimples that would make a grown man blush. She almost melted again, got intimidated, and backed out of it.

Until he said, "This is real cute—you are trying to pick me up."

"No, I was trying to get your number so I could call you later."

"Hmm, really? So we can talk about what?"

"Why a grown man like yourself isn't married, and if you are, why you're not wearing your ring."

"And this is your concern because . . ."

"Because a grown woman like myself should always learn about the mentality of the opposite gender."

"Oh, so you followed me to my car because you thought I'd be an interesting subject."

"*Interesting* is one way to put it."

He kneeled down, got a pen out of his car, and began writing his number down on a piece of paper. "Well, I am always for education," he said as he handed her the paper.

Dakota took the number, and made sure not to look at it so she wouldn't seem too eager or excited.

"So, will you be calling me later?" he said.

"Yes, I will," she said as she turned away. "And I didn't follow you over here—I wanted your cart" she said with a devilish smirk.

"Oh, OK. And I think education is overrated."

They shared a little laugh, and he got in his car and she walked off.

She finished picking up what she needed from the grocery store, which were just some more Bacardi Breezers, chips, nuts, and other snacks for the rest of what they had termed their kickback weekend. She and Chrasey had ended up spending the night at Jordan's because it got so late and they didn't want to have to drive home. So when they woke up this morning, they figured why not just keep it going? It was fun, just chilling, the three of them. No stress, no work, no men, just the three sisters having a good old time sharing stories and relaxing.

As soon as she got back to Jordan's house, she reevaluated herself in the mirror. She definitely was looking a mess. She decided that she was going to have to see that guy again so he could see what she was really working with. Then it dawned on her—he didn't give his name, or ask for her number or name. That was clear evidence he wasn't all that interested. He was just going along with things. Hell, he probably gave her the wrong number. She had it all set out in her mind—in case the number was real, she would call tomorrow, just so she wouldn't look too eager. The plan was never to look eager or desperate. Either way, she hoped the number was real so she could get a chance to meet up with him again. She wanted a chance to redeem herself, to let him see the real Dakota, and see she didn't always dress like rainbow brite.

She told Jordan and Chrasey about how fine he was, and what she did. They just laughed—they knew, just like Dakota did, that she was a trip. As much as she tried to preach that she didn't need no man, she was still trying to snag one. The second she got away from the all-female retreat, she went after a man. It seemed that it was about men after all, or the lack thereof.

58

Prisoner at Home

It wasn't as if Chrasey was feeling secure about her and Keith's situation prior to finding out about his cheating and his daughter, but now it just seemed as if every little thing made her overly suspicious. Every hang-up at home, every girl that drove by her house, everything just made her feel like it was some secretive code for Keith.

She had been back from her weekend with the girls, and this was only the third night since Keith had come home. They hadn't had sex yet—it would probably be a while before they felt comfortable enough for that. He was home at a decent time, and he was eating dinner at the table. He was coming up to bed early and watching television with Chrasey until he fell asleep. They weren't speaking much—most of their conversations were very generic. It had only been a few days, and Chrasey was questioning her decision to try to forgive Keith and move on. The only thing that made her confident was how happy her kids were that he was home. They really did love their dad, and it was obvious that they preferred having him around.

Most of the problems were obviously her own paranoia, probably stemming from her fear that Keith wasn't completely done dealing with Lourdes. It's not like Chrasey didn't know that trying to recover from something like this would be hard, or that it would cause severe trust issues. It's just that she didn't realize how the mind would play tricks on her. She wasn't sure if Keith felt similar to the way she did, but she knew they had a whole lot of mending to do.

Chrasey had come up with a million questions since he had been home. Like she found it kind of strange that all that time he stayed with his friend, he was supposedly upset with her. Then as soon as she found out about his dirt, he was quick to move home. Was it that he knew that it just affirmed that he caused all their marital issues, although previously he tried to pretend that he didn't know what she was talking about? Was it that he was never that upset to begin with, because he had no right to be? Was he actually happy when he found out about Trevor because he felt like at least it would lessen his own screw-up? She wasn't sure what it was that her finding out did for him, but she definitely noticed that he dropped the Trevor issue almost instantly. He wouldn't dare bring it up now, because all that would do is give her room to bring up the child he shared with his previous mistress.

She knew deep in her heart that although he claimed to be done with Lourdes, he had to have some dealings with her because he had to have some role in their child's life. She wasn't sure if she could deal with that and still pretend that everything was back to normal. She started to wonder if she should handle her suspicions and keep her sanity the way she did before, by indulging in some dirt of her own. She knew it had helped nothing, but it did lessen her fear and make her feel guarded from getting hurt.

The uneasy vibe in their house was getting worse and worse every day. She was beginning to feel like she couldn't even be comfortable in her own home. She would get home about 5:45 every night and begin preparing dinner. Keith would arrive at about 6:45 and start watching television and helping the kids with their homework. To the kids it looked like everything was back to normal, but Keith and she could feel it. He tried to sleep in the bed with her every night—she guessed it was an attempt to make things better, but it was clearly uncomfortable. They barely touched in the bed, and when they did by mistake, they would quickly readjust themselves. They wouldn't talk to each other, really; Chrasey would read a book and Keith would watch television until they were both ready for sleep.

There was a sense of precaution; it was as if everything was being monitored. Through the evening if he went upstairs too long while she was cooking, she would make an excuse to go up there. If she was on the phone, he would "accidentally" pick it up to use it. They didn't trust each other, and it showed. They hadn't discussed it or even tried—they basically pretended like it wasn't an issue. The positive part was that both of them had a trust issue—neither of them was suffering alone.

The way they were watching each other's every move and were doing things tit for tat had become a game of chess. It wasn't supposed to be a game, though, it was supposed to be a marriage—and Chrasey really desired the life that she had always envisioned for herself. That life included the term "happily married." She didn't know if that was possible anymore. She wasn't sure if there was a way for them to overcome the damage and one day be happy again, or if she should never have told him he could come home.

59

Risky Business

The clerks were looking at Jordan, and the shoppers were whispering to each other. She was standing in Bloomingdale's with a bunch of clothes in one hand, and her cell phone in the other, arguing with Omar. She knew she was embarrassing herself and probably should have left the store to handle this. However, she wasn't willing to put back the two-piece power suit on sale, and she finally got Omar on the phone and couldn't let that go, either.

So she sat there, yelling like a madwoman, in the middle of this bougee store.

"Our son asked me when Daddy was coming back home, Omar. Do you not see what you are doing to us?"

"He was just with me all weekend," Omar answered calmly.

"So what? He was with me every night," I replied.

"So, it's about time," he said.

"Omar, please. You are so petty. You have been gone all this time and you still won't even have a sit-down talk with me to try to resolve things."

"Jordan, I have told you all that I had to say."

"So are you coming back home, Omar?"

"Most likely."

"Most likely? What does that mean?"

"Most likely. I will be home soon."

"So let me get this straight. You walk out one day, after a week you come back home for a few hours, leave again. Now it has been months, and you still haven't sat down and told me why you left, why you won't take my calls. You don't call me, and you're just supposed to *most likely* come back home one day."

"I have called there and I return your calls."

"You have called a few times to speak to Jason, and you only return some of the calls when I tell you Jason wants to talk to you or to tell me you're picking him up from school to have him stay with you. Any time I try to talk to you, you say you have to go."

"Well, I've been in touch some—if you needed me, you could have gotten me."

"So, let me ask—when you come home, are things supposed to be or get better?"

"I don't know what's supposed to happen. I can't say I care right now."

"Well, you better hope the locks aren't changed by then," she said. *Click.*

She hung up. His whole nonchalant attitude was pissing her off. The lady beside her looking in the racks was listening to her whole conversation—Jordan felt like cursing her the hell out. Instead, she just gave her a dirty look and rolled her eyes. Jordan walked away from the corner and shook her head in disbelief. She couldn't believe Omar. He had really lost it. This was the craziest thing she had ever heard of. It just made her even more pissed that he was acting so cocky. It was like he didn't get the idea of better or worse, through thick and thin . . . the hell with marriage. You can't just walk out on your wife, not communicate with her, and not see how damaging that is. Maybe he did know how damaging it was but he just didn't care. Either way, she was just too through.

She made her way to the checkout line with her suit; she was no longer in the mood to continue shopping. She opened up her cell phone again to call Jayon. She had to vent, and although Chrasey and Dakota were only a phone call away, too, Jayon was more up to date with the play-by-play. It was actually amazing how, for the past two months, Jayon had stepped up while Omar acted retarded. She had discussed it with Chrasey and Dakota—they both had different views of the situation. Dakota had always liked Jayon for her, and thought that maybe she should just stick with him. After that phone call, she was really considering it.

Jayon answered the phone, but said he was in the middle of something with a client and would get right back to her.

Dakota swore up and down that if Jordan had an ounce of curiosity about what he would be like, something good would happen. Though there may have been truth to that, Chrasey knew from her own experience that a new man wasn't an answer. Deep down, she knew there was truth in both of their opinions. Although she had always known that she wouldn't deal with Jayon as a married woman, a piece of her . . . deep down inside . . . her wild side that never had an opportunity to show itself, wanted to do it. Jayon was fine, successful, had one of the best hearts, and had always made her a priority all the years they'd been friends. Jordan couldn't lie and say that if it wasn't for the fact that she was married and had morals, she might have given him some a long time ago.

In these past two months, they had spent a few nights together. Some nights it just got late, another night he was too drunk to drive so she stayed at his place. She asked him if she was messing up his love life, but he assured her it was fine. Jayon had always put her before his girlfriends and chicks he dealt with. The ones that he got serious with, he would let them know about her and their relationship, and he would let them know not to even question or try to alter it. Regardless of what his love life was looking like, he would be there for Jordan when she was in need. He had his way of making her feel special.

She was starting to get the feeling she was his priority for a different reason this time. Their time together had become less platonic and more like they were lovers. She knew that Jayon would never disrespect her, so it didn't matter to her. She knew nothing would happen unless they were both good and ready. Besides, all this time Jayon hadn't made a move on her. She knew he didn't want her to think he was taking advantage of her vulnerability.

The other night when he had been drinking, he was saying stuff that she was surprised to hear. Stuff like, if Omar didn't come to his senses soon, he was going to step in. She'd just brushed it off and laughed. A night or two after, they were watching a movie and he started to rub her thigh. She looked at him, and he just kept rubbing. After his hand had come very close to her no-no place, he stopped and moved it to her side. There was a part of her, her horny Scorpio side, that wanted to kill him, and then there was a part that wasn't sure if she could have gone through with anything that night, either. Even through the confusion, the idea was still appealing.

The next day when they talked about it, she let him know she wanted to be done with Omar, or at least get revenge for what he had done. Jay expressed that his concern was that she would get back with Omar, and have regrets. He knew her well enough to know that she just wanted to release her anger. Even though that was true, neither of them could deny that they were starting to feel differently toward each other. With conversations like the one she just had with Omar, where he was so willing to take risks, she was closer and closer to taking risks of her own.

Her phone rang—it was Jayon. He had gotten rid of the client as quickly as he could so he could find out what happened. She was just leaving the store and sitting in her car, so she told him the story as she tried to keep from crying.

60

When All Else Fails

It had been days since Dakota saw or spoke to Tony. She couldn't make sense of it herself—why she was so willing to take Tony's nonsense. Ever since they met, she knew she was settling for second-best.

She tried to figure out why she had a man like David in her corner, but she insisted on giving Tony her heart. Then any time she met a man, her only mission was to use him as a filler for those times when Tony wasn't around. She needed to try to have one man that could be there at all times, and be everything in one. Instead she was trying to compile a list of men that, combined, made one hell of a man.

She was supposed to meet up with the guy she met at the supermarket by Jordan's house that day, but something came up and he couldn't make it. His name was Jamille and he was a financial analyst. He worked at a big finance company and he lived alone. He had been divorced and had two kids from his marriage. Dakota was thinking to herself how much of a headache dealing with him would probably end up being. She was also realistic—at her age, most men were either married, divorced, or still trying to be a major player and most likely definitely had a kid somewhere. They rescheduled for the next week, and she was hoping they would get together then. She needed some new players on her roster because Tony was driving her crazy.

She had just called David a few hours ago and told him to come over and hang with her. As usual, he gave her no problem and said he would be over in a few hours. That was the beauty of plans with David, unlike Tony; she knew he would show or at least would call if something came up. So, as she chilled out and waited for him, she spent some me-time with herself.

She was lying on her couch watching *Sex in the City—How does Samantha do it?* she asked herself. *How does she never fall?* She had gotten the casual sex down pat, but she was forgetting the rule never to fall in love. All it does is leave you hurt and depressed, just having more meaningless sex but with someone else.

Deep down, she wanted that life that Jordan and Chrasey had, but she'd seen all the stuff they go through, too, and it's not worth the stress, either. These men think we owe them so much—the hell with them, what about us? She didn't have a desire for kids; she wanted to be able to go at the drop of a dime. Not to mention she didn't want any man thinking just because she had his kid, she won't go anywhere. She just knew if and when that day came for her, settling down and all of that, the man is going to have to want it just as much or more than she did. He was going to have to acknowledge her worth. As Dakota figured, sisters didn't come like her anymore. No kids, her own place, great job, nice car, good-looking and in shape. They should be lined up with rings.

Other than Tony, David was about the only good one she had left in her black book. The rest of them had something or other wrong. Either they weren't all that good-looking, or were broke, cheap, no car, lived at home with their parents, totally not smooth, or didn't know what good sex was to save their life. David was the only one that could really get her mind off Tony. He was a good catch like herself; she didn't have to feel like she was rebounding with David.

She was wearing brown-and-orange fitted sweats, with an orange halter tube top and her brown flip-flops. She was dressed casual—nothing that said "come and get me." She had her hair in a bun, no makeup on except some lip gloss, and diamond studs in her ears. David was coming over for dinner and a movie, so she was dressed for their casual night at home. It had been some time since she'd had some sexual attention, so David was going to have to tend to that as well. So underneath her casual attire she was freshened up, trimmed, and wore nothing but her orange metallic thong with no bra. She was prepared for the before and after party.

It was about 10:00 PM when the doorbell rang. She turned the television down and walked toward the door. After checking the peephole, she opened the door and there David stood. He was dressed in blue jeans, a light blue polo shirt, and sneakers. He looked like he had a fresh haircut, and she could smell his cologne the second he walked through the door.

"Hey there, beautiful," he said as he leaned over and gave her a hug.

"Hi, Dave," she replied in her "you're making me blush" voice.

He walked straight into the living room and put down the bag he was carrying. He had brought some snacks to watch the movie with— Twizzlers, popcorn, and Milky Ways. After they made small talk, they cuddled up on the couch for the movie. A feeling of security came over her once she was nestled under David's arm. It was like he made her feel like he would always be there. He knew what he was to her; he knew that there was some other man that she had in her heart. Still, no matter when she called, ninety percent of the time he was there. She knew most men would hop at the opportunity to have sex, but he came for more than that. He came for companionship and quality time. He never just came, hit her off, and had to go. He never rushed to business; he always took his time with her. From time to time that's just what she needed, even when she didn't want to admit it. She was happy that God had given her somebody like David. She was thankful our higher power even looked out for his most disobedient children.

61

Brown Sugar

Jordan knew deep in her heart that she was ready for all the risk that came with taking the next step with Jayon. He had been stuck on his idea that they should take things slow, but she was completely fed up with waiting, all for the sake of the possibility Omar may decide he wanted her back. She had decided not to rush things, but the next time it got a little out of hand with her and Jayon, she wouldn't stop what was obviously inevitable. If they kept finding themselves in this predicament, it was clear that both of them wanted it.

They had just come back from a dinner with business associates, and Jayon decided to come in for a piece of her sweet potato pie before he headed home. As soon as she walked in the door, she kicked off her three-inch, $600 "whatever they were called" pumps. The last few hours of the night, her pinky toe was screaming for freedom.

Jordan walked in the kitchen and removed the pie from the refrigerator. She got a knife from the utensil drawer and walked back over to where the pie was. Jayon had been leaning on the counter, and as she approached with the knife he reached over and took it out of her hand. He started to cut her and him a slice, and as he lowered the knife into the pie, he asked her, "How big do you like it?"

Now, why is he messing with me? she said to herself. She saw the smirk in his eye; he knew what he was doing. He was starting up, trying to see where her mind was and where he could take it.

Jayon played more games than a female, because he knew as well as she did that once she started to entertain this and took it there, he would be the first one to cry, "Let's be sure about this."

"A decent size, but not too big—it's too late for all those calories," she responded.

Pleased but disappointed with her somewhat perverted answer, he just continued to cut the pie.

Once he handed her a piece, she headed to the living room and plopped down on the couch. By the time Jayon followed behind her with his pie and a beer he had helped himself to, he had the remote in his hand, flicking through channels. Jayon sat down beside her and started to eat his pie. They both ate their slices as they watched a rerun of *Martin*. By the time the first commercial was on, she had finished her slice and placed the plate on the coffee table. He was still eating his and sipping on his beer. She lay down on the couch and rested her head on Jayon's leg.

It was late—she and Jayon had just had a fun evening together, and they were back at her house. She thought to herself, *I'm not making any moves on him. We decided to take things one step at a time and I need to just enjoy his company.* As she convinced herself to behave, she thought she felt a movement by her head. *Is that coming from Jayon's pants?* she wondered.

She sat still for a moment longer before she felt another movement. She rose from his lap and looked him in his eyes.

"What?" he asked with a smirk.

"Nothing," she replied trying to act equally clueless.

"Why did you get up? You ready for me to go?"

"No, just didn't want to be rude and fall asleep on you. It seems like you're wide awake," she said with a sly undertone.

Slightly laughing, Jayon replied, "Want to watch a movie?" He began flipping through channels before she could agree. When he arrived at HBO, *Brown Sugar* was playing, the movie that people would say Jordan and Jayon reminded them of. It was about two best friends that fall in love.

"Oh, lookie there," she said. "You want to watch it?"

"Why not?" he said as he placed the remote down.

He took his shoes off and got comfortable on the couch beside her. They squirmed around until they were in comfortable positions to watch the movie. They were lying side by side, with Jayon's arm rested around her waist.

They had only missed the first fifteen minutes of it, and they quickly fell silent, their attention on the movie. She couldn't help but get distracted every time she felt Jayon make a slight move. His body lying next to hers had her a little distracted. There was a slight part of her that wanted him so bad it was hard to stay focused. It had been a while for her, and they had been fighting off so much sexual tension between them that this was just torture.

She thought Jayon could tell that her body was calling for him to do something. It seemed like only fifteen minutes into the movie, his hand began to slowly rub her thigh. She had told Jayon previously that made her weak, to feel a slow and light rub pretty much anywhere on her body was all it took to get her hormones going. She tried to ignore it, for fear that all Jayon would do if she acknowledged it was come to his senses and talk them out of it, like he usually did.

After a few more minutes she was starting to believe that Jayon, too, was ready. Neither of them was paying much attention to the movie; they were paying much more attention to each other's body language. He continued to caress her thighs and monitor how her body responded to his touch. His hand reached lower and lower, and it was pretty clear that neither one of them was any longer watching the movie. She began to squirm some, moving her leg so he could know that she was completely receptive to what he had been doing.

Once he was sure that she liked his touch, he reached over and started to kiss her neck. She didn't know what it was about the way Jayon kissed her neck, but it took her from level 5 to level 10 in seconds. Ever since the first time they'd fooled around, he had done that neck thing, and he had given her a new hot spot. After a few moments of letting her body respond to the seduction, she reached down and placed her hand on his belt buckle. She wanted to see his reaction, and she was surprised he didn't say or do anything. She started to slowly unbuckle his belt. He didn't stop her, he didn't slow down, and he didn't say a word.

In one movement she had his belt open, and she went to unzip him. As she reached into his pants, she felt his lower body pull back for a second. She slowed down, and then she felt him slowly relax again. She reached in and massaged him through his boxers. His erect penis jumped around to show its excitement.

By now Jayon's mouth had made its way down her neck and to her breasts. She slowly got up and also began removing his pants. This was usually around the time that one of them would stop the party, but neither of them did this time. Jordan didn't really know what to do next. The next thing she knew, she felt Jayon helping her get undressed. She didn't expect this.

Her mind started to panic all of a sudden. *Is this really about to happen? Once this happens, we can't go back.* In between each thought, she could also hear her hormones having thoughts of their own. They wanted Jayon, and they wanted him bad. They had withheld temptation too long, and it had been months with no nookie, so her body was ready for some action.

Within moments, Jayon had her pants off and was kissing lower and lower. Her body was going wild. She didn't have any more thoughts of hesitation; her thoughts were just the opposite—she was eager and anticipating what was to come. He kissed lower until he reached her jewel. He slowly began to lick her there and her body jerked back on the couch. He was passionately kissing her intimate parts, and the feeling was heightened by his thick, warm tongue. She silently moaned and panted, trying to hold in her screams. The pleasurable strokes of his tongue had her close to orgasm. As he felt her grow more excited, he grew more excited. He grabbed her ass and licked between her legs even harder. It was feeling so good, but she wanted more of him. She wanted all of him. She began to tug on his shirt for him to come on top of her.

"I want you," she whispered.

She felt him slow down, and then he slowly crawled on top of her. Once he reached eye level, he looked at her and said, "You sure you ready for this?"

"I'm sure," she replied, looking him right in his eyes.

She didn't have to convince him. With one push, she felt him thrust through her tight walls. His eyes closed with satisfaction. He was inside of her, and all of her welcomed him. Before he started to pump his body in and out of her, they reveled in the moment for a split second. She felt him nestling on the inside of her, and they both took a deep breath of contentment. Then, slowly, he began stroking in and out of her. He kissed her and nibbled on her neck and ears as he made love to her. Her eyes were closed, but at one point she looked at him and his were, too. He opened them to check on her and she was looking at him, checking on him. They both seemed to be doing quite all right. He was going at a slow pace, allowing them to enjoy each and every moment of this first time.

After a few minutes, she felt his body tighten up, and he quickly pulled himself out of her. There was a mess on her couch a few seconds later.

As soon as it was done, they were breathing heavily and slightly nestled against each other. Neither of them wanted to look at the other. Then it hit her—the emotions from what had just occurred. Tears began to roll down her face. There was no turning back.

"What's wrong?" Jayon said, panicking.

"Nothing."

"Why are you crying?"

"No reason," she said, trying to wipe her tears.

He just held her as tight as he could, and whispered, "Please don't cry."

She felt bad, ruining their moment with tears. She wasn't crying because she was regretting what they had done. She cried because she knew that she and Jayon would never be the same, and even crazier, she and Omar would never be the same.

62

Eight Days Past Due

Dakota had been late before, but something felt different this time. She went through each day as if it was not on her mind, but there wasn't a day that went by that she wasn't worried about her "friends visit." After the first week of waiting, and the first day she was feeling nauseous, her paranoia went into overdrive and she made a doctor's appointment.

Dakota had had a few scares, and a few run-ins with pregnancy. She was always either in a terrible situation with the possible father or she was very young. It wasn't long before birth control became a real close friend of hers. She did get careless with Tony from time to time, allowing herself to be too comfortable. Deep down, she had thoughts of having a child with Tony to be sure to have him around. It wasn't until now, with the thought of really being pregnant, that she realized that might only run him farther away. Still, now at the age of thirty-one, single and motherless, the idea of having a child had a little more of a thrill to it.

The first thing the doctor asked was, "Do you think you could be pregnant?" That's usually the question they ask to see if you're going to say "impossible" or "maybe."

Dakota just responded, "I wouldn't think so—I'm on the pill."

Dr. Rothstein continued to run her tests and ask questions. She informed Dakota that it could just be stress delaying her period and the nausea could all be psychological. A million and ten thoughts went through 'Kota's head while she sat there waiting for the results of her test. She had come to the realization that being pregnant would not be a great thing. She knew she didn't know how Tony would react; she knew she wouldn't even know if it was Tony's—she'd had her share of fun over the past couple of months. She also knew she was at a great point in her career, and that everyone would be judging her because she wasn't married.

Sitting there cold and alone, Dakota realized that this was a wake-up call, and she had to make some serious changes in her life. If she wasn't pregnant, she would use this chance—whatever number it was—to get her life on track. She never wanted to feel this way again—she was too mature for this; she was even too embarrassed to tell Jordan and Chrasey. She sat there hoping that this was all, like the doctor said, psychological.

About fifteen minutes later she was informed that pregnancy was very much a reality. *Wow, I'm pregnant. How? How could I have let this happen? I used protection every time—well, almost every time,* Dakota thought to herself. Once with David the condom broke, and with Tony one night they didn't have one and they were both so horny they had to do without, but he didn't come in her. There were other times where he would just stick it in once or so before he put the condom on, but that was only a small percentage of the time. Well, it didn't matter at this point—it was already done.

When the doctor told her, as if she was a teenage girl whose parents were going to beat her, she cried. She knew that was tacky but she was so upset, embarrassed, ashamed, disappointed, and scared all in one that all she could do was cry. Besides, her doctor was well aware that she wasn't in the most stable relationship, and that she wasn't planning to have kids. She knew more than anybody about her sexual risks, after she paged her on a weekend for a birth-control prescription when she'd misplaced her pack one day. She also knew from their talks during her checkup. That's why she gave her a look when she walked in the room to tell her. By the expression on her face, Dakota knew what it meant. Still, she told her the news with as much happiness in her voice as possible.

When Dr. Rothstein came in to tell Dakota, a bunch of negative thoughts filled her mind, way more than positive. After the tears began to slide down her cheeks, Dr. Rothstein tried to console her. She reminded her that she had several options, and she told her to go home and discuss it with her partner. *Which partner?* Dakota asked herself.

Dakota called Jordan and Chrasey right away, a three-way call as usual. They were supportive, sympathetic, and happy. Of course, they said they would support any decision she made, although they both felt strongly about abortions and expressed the hope that she didn't do that. They were also sympathetic, because they knew she was afraid about not knowing for sure who the father was. Still, they were both happy as well. They probably just wanted to be new godparents, and have a kid to spoil like she did their kids. She let them both know she thought it was probably Tony's, and after she spoke to him she would make a decision. They, like most girlfriends, advised that she not let him control her decision. "It's your body, and you're going to have to raise the baby," Chrasey told her.

Her gut told her that it was Tony's, but she wouldn't know until the doctor told her how far along she was for sure. She knew she couldn't wait that long before she told him.

When it was time to call Tony, she couldn't remember the last time she'd felt so anxious. She practiced over and over how she would tell him, then she finally dialed the number. When she called, she got his voice mail at first and considered leaving it on his answering machine. She decided against that because as much as she feared what it would be, she wanted to see his initial reaction. She called back twice later on until she finally got him. She told him that it was extremely important that he come over right away. From the tone in her voice, it wasn't hard for him to realize that it was something serious.

She still didn't know how she was actually going to tell him. She even doubted every ten minutes if she even *should* tell him. Hell, what if it was David's, or somehow turned out to be Darryl's, the guy from the club. They say no form of protection is one hundred percent, and it's times like these when you wished you'd paid attention in sex ed when they said abstinence is the best way unless you're prepared to have a baby with the man you're lying down with.

He stood looking out the window in silence. Dakota didn't know whether to be glad he didn't react in a loud and rude manner, or sad that he said nothing at all. He had been there for all of five minutes, and she'd told him that she'd gone to the doctor that day and the doctor had told her that she was pregnant. Before he could reply, she gave him the rest of the information. She told him that she had to go back next week to determine how far along she was. He hadn't said a word yet. She knew this was a big deal—for both of them. She had such a mixture of feelings about it inside herself, she knew that he was probably really bugging out over it.

A piece of her wanted to be happy about the news, but deep inside she was more depressed than she could ever imagine. It wasn't helping that the man she wanted to spend her life with had absolutely no words to say regarding the matter. What was making her the most uncomfortable was that until she found out how far along she was, she wouldn't even know who the father was. She didn't know what was crazier—that she wanted it to be Tony's, even though he was the least likely to settle down, or that she knew better and should have been wanting it to be David's—but she wasn't. She didn't even call David, and had no intention to unless, for some reason, Tony was ruled out and it had to be David's. No point in getting him excited for nothing.

Two minutes went by without Tony replying. Two minutes felt like a long time—she knew what was on Tony's mind, even though he didn't say it yet. The silence was stirring her emotions. Her eyes began to fill with tears. Finally he turned around and sat at the table with her. He hung his head low, apparently not wanting to ask, but he said in a mellow tone, "Am I the father?"

That's all it took—the floods came. The tears began rolling down her face like a broken dam. From her response, he could tell that it probably wasn't a yes. He waited patiently for her response anyway. Not once did he put his hand on hers, or say anything to comfort her. He just sat there as she wept. After a few minutes, she pulled it together and began to wipe her tears away. She tried to gather her thoughts and calm down. She wasn't sure what he really wanted to hear. She didn't know if not being the father would upset him or be a relief.

"Honestly, I'm not sure yet. I think it's yours," she said in the lowest tone possible.

"And why does it have to be mine? Obviously you have been sleeping with other people."

"Because I was protected with them, but it's just that you never know, I guess."

"We used protection, too."

"Not every single time, though"

Tony stood up from the table. "Well, when you find out . . . you let me know," he said as he got up.

She watched him walk toward the door, seeing if he was going to say something else. She wanted to ask him why he was leaving, or how he could just walk out on her at a time like this. Instead she just watched him open the door, step through it, and close it behind him. She sat there for about ten more minutes, drenched in her own tears. She couldn't believe he was so cold, but then again she couldn't blame him. Why in the hell didn't she know who her own baby's father was? She knew that was pathetic, so she could only imagine what it made him think of her. She just sat there until she finally made her way into her bedroom. Like many nights, she lay in the bed, crying and hugging her pillow. She didn't even have the energy to call Chrasey and Jordan back. She just wanted to go to sleep and wake up and it would all be a dream.

63

Back to Business

When Jordan got to the office Monday morning, she was hoping to beat Jay in so he would have to come in to her when he got in. When she got off the elevator, she peeked down the hall and his door was still closed. She knew he was probably right behind her, because Jayon was rarely late for work. She scurried into her office, with her Starbucks white chocolate milk and vanilla-almond triscottis in one hand, and her briefcase and purse in the other. She managed to get the door open, and plopped her stuff down on the couch by the door. She had clients scheduled to be in by 9:30, so she had to get herself together.

By the time she signed on to her computer, she heard Jayon's voice saying good morning to the receptionist. She didn't do anything more for a few seconds, and she thought maybe he headed to his office. Then he popped up in her doorway. She looked up at him and instantly started blushing. He walked over to her and leaned over to give her a kiss on the lips. She obliged.

He placed a Starbucks bag on her desk.

"It looks like I wasted my time," he said.

Jordan looked in the bag; it was a white chocolate milk and vanilla-almond triscottis.

"Aww, thank you, Jay . . . but yeah, I had time to stop this morning. Give it to Jackie," she said.

"OK."

"But thanks—you're so sweet."

"No prob," he replied.

It fell silent for a few seconds. It was her fear that she and Jayon wouldn't be able to act the same way around each other. They wouldn't be able to talk to each other normally.

"I have some clients coming in soon so I have to get some work done real fast—I'll come down to your office in a few," Jordan said, trying to end the awkward moment.

"OK, I'm stepping out at 2:00 today and I won't be back in the office until later," he said as he walked toward the door.

"Where you going at 2:00?"

"I have a few appointments and some things to do."

"OK, I'll be down there about 11:00 or so," she answered.

He walked out of the office and she went back to work. She wasn't sure what the next few days or weeks would be like with her and Jayon but she had confidence it would be fine. They talked very little after they finished having sex that night—it was too awkward and she was too emotional. He stayed over, and the next morning when they woke up he told her he hoped that she didn't do anything she didn't want to, and he was sorry if he did anything wrong. She assured him that it was nothing that he did, and then he began to inquire if it had to do with Omar. She told him Omar didn't care what she was doing; she couldn't worry about what would happen if he began to care. He understood her answer and he left it at that. They had talked about absent Omar enough, and she had told him it was about her from now on. When he left that day he hugged her very tight and said that he loved her and last night meant more to him than she could know.

Jordan wondered if this was a mistake. She wondered if this was all to have control of something again, since Omar had taken so much of her control away. Omar had hurt her, and she knew that, but she wondered if her decision to sleep with Jayon somewhere in her subconscious was her way to hurt Omar back. She could have chosen any man in New York, but she chose Jayon. Sure, she loved him, and sure, he was attractive, and they had a history and she trusted him, so why not him? Still, Jordan knew that there was something more to her decision, and she just hoped she'd made the right one.

Jordan and Jayon had spoken once or twice the day before, but they were both running around and didn't get a chance to have a real conversation. So today was the first day of real interaction after

Jordan had broken the emergency glass. She was sitting there typing up some notes, and an instant message popped up on her screen. It was an icon of a man and woman in bed having sex. It was sent from Jay88, which was Jayon's instant message name.

"I don't know about you, but I had fun. I have no regrets and I'm ready for the next time," it read.

A big smile came across Jordan's face.

"LOL. No regrets, either—I also had fun and I'm looking forward to the next time," she wrote back.

"I'll be at your house later," he wrote.

Jayon is a mess, Jordan thought to herself. He knew Jordan well enough to know the initial conversation would be uncomfortable, so he made it easy on her. That's why she loved that guy—he knew just what she needed and when. He had her all figured out.

Jordan met with her clients, Jayon stopped in and gave her a kiss good-bye before he headed out at 2:00, and the rest of the day went by real fast. She left the office about 6:00 and headed home to shower and get ready for Jayon.

64

Beauty of Life

"This is something that you created—this will be your unique little person and it will belong to you," the doctor said to Tony and Dakota. She held on to Tony's hand as she listened to the doctor explain what their options were and what to keep in mind.

Dakota wasn't sure what Tony was feeling, but she knew what she was thinking. They had left things pretty much up in the air so far, with their only plan to come see the doctor together. When the doctor said *this is something you created*, Tony and Dakota looked into each other's eyes, and she felt a little tingle.

On the drive home, Dakota realized that she was becoming more confident that she wanted to keep the baby. She knew that it was risky, because she and Tony had a very unstable relationship. She also knew that she wasn't ready to be a mother and give up her freedom. However, she had already been wishfully thinking that maybe this would get Tony to decide to finally be with her. She also knew that although she wasn't ready to be a mother, she kind of liked the idea of adding some more purpose to her life.

As soon as they got back to Dakota's condo, Tony sat on the couch without turning the TV on. On the ride home, they barely talked, and all he asked her regarding the doctor's visit was, *Are you OK?* It was evident, though, that he had a lot on his mind, just like Dakota did.

"Are you OK?" Dakota asked him this time.

"I'm fine," Tony said, as Dakota expected he would.

"No, really. What's wrong?"

"I'm just thinking, that's all."

"I know—it's been an emotional day."

"Yeah, it has," he replied.

"Listen, Tone, what do you want me to do?"

"Dakota, I want you to do whatever you want to do. It's your body, and I really mean that."

Dakota believed him when he said that. For once she took his words at face value. They'd had a talk before about this as a hypothetical situation, and he'd said that he would be supportive either way. A piece of Dakota wanted to hear him say that he wanted her to keep it, but she knew he probably didn't and he wouldn't want to pressure her either way. Really she was just happy that he didn't make her feel like one of those girls on the Maury Povich talkshow, and request paternity testing. He was taking her word for it, and that was the best feeling of all.

"Well, I'm going to keep it, "she blurted out.

Tony snapped his neck toward her real fast and looked at her, very surprised.

"You are?"

"Yeah."

"When did you decide that?"

"Well, I've been considering it—I really thought hard about it on the way home and I think I've made up my mind."

Tony looked kind of shocked.

"OK, that's fine by me. I'll support whatever decision you make."

"Well, there's the decision."

"OK."

Dakota was sitting on one end of the couch, Tony on the other. There was an awkward silence. After a few seconds, as if he finally realized it was the right thing to do, he scooted over and put his arm around Dakota.

"Everything will be just fine," he said.

Dakota rested her head and his shoulder. "Thank you," she whispered. She was an emotional wreck, and had been trying to stay strong over the past few days.

"I'm sorry," he said.

"For what?" she asked.

"For not being very sensitive to the situation and for walking out the day you told me."

"It's OK—I understand why you walked out that day. It was kind of foul, but I knew it wasn't cool that I was telling you I wasn't sure who the father was."

"I hope this doesn't come off crazy, but who else did you think it was?"

Dakota couldn't believe he'd asked that. Tony wasn't supposed to ever care. It was a silent rule. She had actually wished that he did care; she just wished that this wasn't the time that he chose to do it.

"I thought it was yours, but in the past few months I slept with one other person," she said, feeling a tad awkward admitting it. She wasn't telling the whole truth—she had actually slept with two or three people, but she didn't want to tell him all of that—she would have sounded like a cheap whore.

"Mmm," he replied. "Who was this dude?" he asked.

"Just this guy that I had been seeing on and off for a couple of years, and when me and you were on the rocks."

"So, question . . . which one of us were you wishing was the father?"

Dakota was under attack and was unprepared for battle. She didn't know why he was asking these questions and what it was he wanted to hear.

"I wanted you to be the father, but I knew that he would have wanted to be the father more than you would have."

"What does that mean?"

"I knew that he would have been more excited about it than you, but I was hoping that it was yours."

"That's not the case. I am excited . . . and why is it that you wanted it to be mine then, if you thought he'd be happier about it?"

"Because I want you in my life, I care a lot about you, and if I had to raise a child, I wanted it to be with you."

Tony seemed to like her answer—at least, that's how Dakota took it. He had tightened his grip around Dakota, giving her a much-needed hug.

For the first time in a long time, Dakota felt happy with Tony. Not only because he seemed to be happy that the baby was his, but because he had opened dialogue with her in a way that he never had before. She felt a warmth that she'd yearned for when he held her in his arms. She actually did believe that everything was going to be all right.

That remained to be seen.

65

Lordy Lordy Lourdes

Chrasey was sitting in her bedroom, folding clothes and watching a Lifetime movie. The kids were in their room watching a Disney movie, and Keith was downstairs watching football. It felt like a typical evening at home, and it was close to bedtime for everyone.

About 10:15 the phone rang, and Chrasey picked it up. After a few questions back and forth, it became evident that it was Lourdes. Now the homewrecker wanted to talk.

"What do you want?" Chrasey asked.

"Can I speak to Keith, please?"

"No, you can't. What do you want with my husband?"

"Please . . . your husband? He is just as much mine as he is yours."

As curious as she was to hear what Lourdes had to say, now that she was talking, Chrasey refused to give her the satisfaction.

"Oh, now you want to give information? . . . Hold on." Chrasey hung up. She never did like the way Lourdes put her on hold that night and never came back. Payback was a mother.

A few seconds later, Lourdes called back. "I have just as much right to him as you do. Now, let me speak to him," Lourdes shouted in the phone.

That's when Chrasey blew up. "Really? How do you figure? Because you opened up your pussy and this time something came out?"

"Whatever—where is he?"

"Don't call my house again, bitch," Chrasey said and she hung up.

Of course, she called right back.

"What do you want, Lourdes?" Chrasey shouted into the phone.

"I want to speak to Keith—he was supposed to bring something by here for our daughter, and this has nothing to do with you."

"Really, you think so? EVERYTHING that Keith does has to do with me, and if you have a problem with that you might as well remember that your child is a bastard."

"Whatever, bitch—my child has a father. Your husband. He is by here all the time and my daughter knows her father."

At first, Chrasey was pissed hearing he was by there often, but then she realized she had to be lying or exaggerating because she couldn't think of but one or two nights that Keith hadn't been home.

"In your fantasy world where he is your husband, right? Well, he is downstairs with his children, at his house with his family like he is every night, so you're just going to have to figure something out."

"I'll call his cell phone."

"Obviously he isn't picking up for you, or you wouldn't have been so stupid to call my house . . . and I advise you not to call here again or you're going to come home one day and find me on your doorstep . . . I'm sorry, I mean *building lobby*, you ghetto rat."

Click. Chrasey slammed the phone down on her. She went straight downstairs to the living room where Keith was chilling with his beer, watching ESPN. The phone had rung a few seconds after Chrasey walked out of the bedroom, but she was done talking to that tramp. She stood in front of Keith and said in an obviously unhappy tone, "You need to control your hos."

"What are you talking about?" he said, sounding a little nervous.

"Lourdes just called here for you, and if you don't check that right away, you will be living in Brooklyn with her. I don't want her calling my house."

"I'm sorry about that, Chrasey . . . what did she want?"

"I don't know—she said you were supposed to go out there tonight. Is that true?"

"No, I've been here all night."

"Well, she seems to be waiting on you . . . and is it true that you're out there all the time?"

"Chrasey, when? I'm here all the time unless I'm at work—she is just trying to make you angry because she lost."

"What do you mean, lost?"

"Chrasey, she has been threatening me all this time that if I didn't spend time with her or leave you she would call here and tell you all about the baby. I didn't want you to find out that way but I was scared to tell you, so I would try to appease her. But now that you know and we are working out our marriage, she is pissed. She wanted me to leave you for her."

"And you told her you would?"

"No, I just tried to appease her. But now I don't have to anymore and she has lost the little power that she had . . . but I'm sorry to put you in the middle of this."

"How did you appease her?"

"I stayed with her some nights while me and you were split up, and I did make some promises to her, but they were empty promises, just to buy me time until I could find a way to tell you."

"You were never going to tell me, Keith."

"I was—I just needed time."

Chrasey was pissed off. No wonder this woman was talking about him being her husband, too—Keith had been filling her head with nonsense. She didn't even know if she could believe Keith. Who was to say he wasn't still lying and giving her empty promises, too.

"Well, I will assume that since you no longer have to appease her, you won't be over there anymore."

"No, I won't be."

"Well, call your other wife and let her know to stop calling my house."

Chrasey walked upstairs. She didn't even want to continue the conversation because it was useless—she didn't even know if she believed the things he said.

66

Too Late

Jordan hadn't called Omar since the day she hung up on him in Bloomingdale's, and he didn't call her, either. This had been the longest length of time that she hadn't reached out to him—it had been three weeks. Jason told her he stopped by his school one day for lunch. That was sweet, but it made Jordan sick how much he had tried to avoid her. Ever since she and Jayon had first slept together, her mind wasn't on what Omar was doing anymore.

Jordan was at home playing cards with Jayon when the phone rang. Jason jumped up to answer it, and because she was in the middle of kicking Jayon's butt, she let him. She heard Jason say, "Hi, Daddy."

Jordan felt her stomach drop. *Oh shucks*, she thought to herself. The good thing was if Jason was who he wanted to speak with, that's who he got, and she didn't have to endure that awkward opening conversation. The bad thing was if Jordan was who he wanted, Jayon was there with her, and she didn't want to be rude to Jayon, either.

"I'm fine," Jordan could hear Jason saying. Jayon also heard that it was Omar, and he just looked at Jordan. He gave her a smile, letting her know he was cool. Jayon and she had never discussed in depth what would happen if she worked things out with Omar, but she had said several times that she wasn't going to. Omar's behavior was irreparable, as far as she was concerned. She couldn't continue to be in a marriage with a man who would just walk out on her at will with no regard for her feelings.

She heard Jason rambling on about school and some of his friends that were mad at him, and his latest score in Madden 05. He talked for about five minutes about all the excitement in a six-year-old's life. Jordan and Jayon just continued their card game, paying close attention to Jason's conversation. Then, right after Jason finished his football story, she heard him say, "You want Mommy? OK, she is right here with Mr. Jay."

Jordan froze and looked over at Jayon. Jay looked at her.

Then Jason said, "Oh, OK. I'll talk to you later—love you." Jason hung up the phone.

"What happened?" Jordan asked Jason.

"Daddy wanted to talk to you, but then he said he would call back later."

Damn, just my luck, she thought. She knew Omar was pissed for more reasons than one. He finally called to speak with Jordan, and she was there with Jayon, not moping around like she was sure he thought and hoped she was. She knew he wasn't too happy that Jayon was around his son—Omar was the type to make a bigger deal out of that than it was. She would, too, but Jayon was not just some man— Jason had known Jay since he was born. Jay was like an uncle to him, so he wouldn't think anything of his presence.

Jordan could only imagine what was going through Omar's head at that very moment. A piece of her felt bad, because she knew he was mad. Then another piece of her, a bigger piece, was thinking, *the nerve of him*! Was she just supposed to sit around twiddling her thumbs until he thought enough of her one day to call her back?

This had been an emotional few months for Jordan, but she had been better lately, and now something like this had to happen. She had decided a week or so ago, that she just wanted her and Omar to be friends. She didn't know if they had to be officially divorced right away or what, but she knew that she couldn't see herself with him again. She knew that their marriage was in deep trouble, but she would never have expected this. She was still amazed at the way Omar handled things. To disappear like that was the most disrespectful thing he could have done. She would have preferred that he cheated on her, but to just walk away and completely close their lines of communication was terrible and torturous. In a sense, it was typical of him but never for that long. Besides, she had explained to him numerous times that that was the worst thing you could do in a relationship, but Omar kept doing it, and now she was handling it her way.

"You OK?" Jay asked her.

"I'm fine, just caught a little off guard."

"I know—you haven't spoken to him since that day in the store, right?"

"Nope, that was weeks ago. I didn't expect to hear from him."

"What do you think he wants?"

"I have no idea."

"I do."

"What?"

"It's make-up time," he said teasingly.

"Yeah, OK. That's not going to happen."

"OK, watch. I bet that's why he is calling."

"Well, it's too late for that," she answered.

"All right," Jay said, like he didn't believe her.

"How would you feel if I did get back with him?" she asked.

"I'd be upset—I would probably need some time to get cool with it, but I would understand and we would still be cool."

"So, just like that, we would go back to the way we were before?"

"No, not just like that. It would be hard, but I would understand. It's not a simple situation and I don't want to add any more stress than you are already under."

"Thanks, Jay," she said, "but I doubt that's going to happen. I'm cool with the way things are now."

He reached out and took her hand. "You're a strong cookie."

"No, I'm not. Omar has pushed me here, and I'm not trying to go back now," she replied. "Now let's finish this game so I can beat you again," she said, taking her hand from his and putting down a card.

In Jordan's opinion, Omar had had more than enough time to save their marriage. Instead he let his pride get in the way, and he didn't bother to work things out with her when he still could. She knew from some of their conversations that he could tell that what he had done had caused major damage to them, but not once did he apologize for or change his actions. Even though Omar didn't deserve it, and as strongly as she felt about Jayon, she still would probably have given him another chance if he'd made the right attempt. Unfortunately,

Omar was too prideful to admit what he had done, and say he was sorry. Instead he wanted to be tough, and all he did was push her toward Jayon. *So he can tell Jason he will talk to me later all he wants—he doesn't realize the time he has wasted is why it's too late,* Jordan thought to herself.

67

Divas' Downfall

Since the new year began, Jordan, Chrasey, and Dakota had major turns in their lives, and they were all trying to maintain or get their grooves back. Chrasey found out the hard way that two wrongs don't make a right, Dakota was pregnant and was no longer feeling like the sexy diva she had been, and Jordan's marriage was practically over and she didn't know whether she was coming or going with Jayon.

It had been a few weeks since Dakota had found out that she was pregnant. She still couldn't believe that she was in her third month. Looking back, there were days when she felt really sick, but she didn't think for a second that it was possible she could be pregnant. She had gotten her period all three months, and couldn't think of any major signs that would have made her worry. She asked the doctor if the baby would be at risk, since she had consumed liquor and been around smoke in the past three months. The doctor said it was unlikely, and to just be careful for the next six months.

In the past week or so, Dakota had started to feel better about her situation. She was beginning to look at the positive side of being a mother. She would finally have somebody that would be there with her regardless—she would never be lonely again. She would have a little person to spoil and love unconditionally, and bring her a happiness that no man could take away from her. Like the doctor said, this baby was something that she had created, and it would be all hers. She hadn't really told anybody at work yet, and she still hadn't told

David. She spoke to him once or twice, but she wasn't ready to tell him just yet. She told one co-worker of hers, her closest friend at work, who she could trust with a secret. She knew once everybody found out, there would be a ton of questions she wasn't ready for. She was in publicity and marketing—she knew that it would be on the local news the minute she told the first person, so she was keeping it on the low for a while.

Chrasey was wondering whether she could ever trust anything Keith told her anymore. There were many nights when she lay there, staring at Keith, wondering what was going through his mind. It was as if she thought that if she stared hard enough, she would be able to read his mind. Things had been even harder than she thought they would be. She was trying to hang in there and keep their family together, but each day was a challenge. She had family members judging her, and saying she was stupid for taking Keith back. She went to church a couple of Sundays, and Keith wouldn't come with her, and he needed it more than she did. Still, she came home from work every night and cooked and got the kids ready for bed as if things were normal. Most nights things were just fine, and then there were nights that Chrasey just came home mad. Mad at life, mad at her ruined marriage, and mad that until that child was 18 years old, Lourdes had a role in their life. She hated Keith for giving her that power, she hated Keith for forcing her to deal with it. Her only option was either to stick it out or leave him and be alone with the kids, which was equally miserable. She felt like she was in between the biggest rock and the biggest hard place.

They hadn't had sex in weeks, although Keith had hinted at it a few times. Chrasey wasn't ready for that—she knew the minute she was intimate with Keith, her mind would start to remember all the pain and anger she felt about his infidelity. She wondered if by doing this she would push him away, and possibly back toward Lourdes. She decided to do things at her pace, because when she did cater to his every need, it didn't matter anyway. He still cheated. There were times when she wondered if he would leave her, if Lourdes would win the fight after all. Maybe she was the better woman, maybe she looked better and was better in bed. Maybe life with her and one kid was a lot easier than life with Chrasey and two kids. She couldn't worry about that, though—Keith would do what he wanted to do. Chrasey had to do what she wanted to do. Keith didn't work late as much, but there was a night or two, and that felt like too much for Chrasey. He had no room for error—his freedom had been revoked. If he wanted her to forgive him, he had a lot of rebuilding to do.

Even though they were back together, Chrasey still felt lonely. She and Keith needed so much repairing. She wondered at times if it was too far gone, if there was no pot of the gold at the end of their rainbow. All she knew was she was still as she had been for the past couple of years—unhappy. She cried at least every other night, thinking about those nights that Keith was with Lourdes, and how he was there for their daughter's birth. How he could experience that again, without her, just broke her heart, and she knew she could never love Keith the same. Still, she was going to stay married to him for all the right reasons: for their kids, their vows, and for the business side of it. She also knew that she was ready to call Trevor, because deep down, her soul was empty and she needed him.

Jordan had finally spoken to Omar; she called him back later that same night when he had called. He said he had called to say hello and see how she was doing, but when he heard that her "best friend" was there, he didn't want to interrupt. He was clearly back on the defensive. Jordan couldn't understand why he was so determined to be so difficult—why didn't he see that he was losing her right before his eyes? She tried to give him a hint so that at least he would know the truth, but he wasn't getting it. She told him that things had changed between her and Jayon, and he said that didn't surprise him. She also asked him how he would feel if she started seeing Jayon; he said he would be happy it was him and not somebody else. When they got off the phone that day, Jordan was shocked that Omar had acted so calm about the Jayon news. She was also hurt that he cared so little.

Jordan knew something was strange about Omar's calm response. The very next day Omar called back. He was flipping, yelling and saying how disrespectful it was. How could she even consider seeing Jayon? It was just what he had been saying all along. Jordan's only response was that it wasn't anything like that—things were just different. She also asked him what he'd expected. He'd left her all alone for months, and told her she was free to do what she wanted. She asked why it would be wrong if she chose the person closest to her. She told him that what was wrong and disrespectful was what he did;

whatever she did out of necessity or as a reaction to what he did, he couldn't argue with. Omar wasn't even trying to hear her—his only message was if she got with Jayon, he would cut her off completely.

Jordan had told Jay all that Omar said, and he said that he understood. Jay said of course he was upset. He tried to explain that even though Omar had been acting tough and like he didn't care, he still cared about her. The last thing Omar wanted to hear was that she was dealing with Jayon. Little did he know—he was a day late and a dollar short. The good thing was, as long as he let his pride keep him from getting her back, the more justified Jordan was.

Jordan, Dakota, and Chrasey had all been through enough in their lives that they knew that they would also overcome these obstacles. They were small, in theory. Chrasey was married fairly young and had years of financial struggle and stress, and she overcame that. Dakota had dealt with abusive relationships, abortions, and unfaithful men, and she overcame it all. Jordan juggled law school, being a mother and wife, and working full-time, and she overcame that. They may have been at the bottom of their games, but they knew soon they would rise above it all, and before they knew it they would be back in all their diva glory.

68

Two to Tango

Dakota woke up and headed straight for the bathroom! The morning sickness had been kicking her butt all week, and the novelty of her pregnancy was starting to wear off. She had become real attached to the little belly on her body now, and the whole idea of motherhood had become the highlight of her life these days. However, every time she felt the icky feeling that caused her to throw up, she wished it was a few months earlier and she could do it all over again. After she washed out her mouth and cleaned her face, she dragged herself to the bed.

She lay on the side of the bed, a little depressed once again. Tony hadn't slept over in four nights, and it was mornings like these that she wished she'd done it the right way. She wished he was there to rub her stomach or console her through these sick mornings. But the reality was she had no claims on him, and she had no idea where he was. She spoke to him at night, but for all she knew, he was out there with his new victim. Lately he had been excited about the baby, it seemed, but not excited enough to propose or suggest moving in. So there she lay, feeling completely unsexy, nauseous and alone, and the only comfort she felt was knowing the little baby in her stomach would love her like no other.

She had finally told David that she was pregnant—she didn't know how he would take it, but she got tired of making excuses as to why he couldn't come see her. When she told him, he was very quiet for a few moments, and, of course, the first question he asked was who the father was. She tried to explain who Tony had been in her life, and since David had a vague awareness of her and Tony's relationship, he took her answer for what it was. David was no dummy, either; he knew Tony was a retired professional athlete, and the kind of life that they lead. He was probably asking himself why she would have a baby with him. There were days when even Dakota didn't know.

She thought it was very unfair that she and Tony had made this baby, but he was still free to go out and didn't even have to acknowledge the baby. She would call him at times, and wasn't able to get him. He would stop by, bring some food, and leave. It was like the pregnancy hadn't changed much for him, but it changed everything for her. She started to doubt that the baby would make any difference between them; Tony probably still wouldn't commit to her, nor would he stop living the fast life. Being pregnant made their relationship more depressing, because she couldn't get with other men or go out on those nights when she knew Tony was with some other woman. It took both of them to make the baby—Dakota didn't like one bit how it felt like she was in it all alone.

Dakota was beginning to wonder if she had been wrong about what she imagined things would be like between the two of them now. She realized she must have been bugging to think it would change him. It only made it worse, because she actually needed him more now, but yet he was still pulling his m.i.a. tricks. She felt a little bit stupid, like those girls who she always thought were dumb for trying to trap their men. Although Dakota knew she didn't get pregnant intentionally, she, like them, did hope that the baby would change things. She lay in the bed and watched some television. She was nauseous—she had vomited twice in the past twenty-four hours, and she was craving some Oreos. She called Tony, and there was no answer. Maybe it was the hormones, maybe it was because she wanted something that was unrealistic, but when she got his voice mail she slammed the phone down with the little energy that she had.

"To hell with him," she said out loud.

69

Love You for Life

"Why is there a Jodeci CD in the stereo in the conference room?" Elizabeth stepped into Jordan's office and asked her with the CD in her hand. It was the best of Jodeci CD, and Jayon and her had themselves a special evening in their conference room a couple of nights ago.

Jordan's facial expression probably said it all. It went from an *I'm caught* look of shock to a *you got me* smirk.

"No reason a girl can't mellow out at work," Jordan said playfully.

"Yeah, mmm-hmm," she said, handing me the CD.

"Give that here," she said

Elizabeth, who was the other practicing attorney on their floor and her friend from college, was in and out of the office so much, the staff probably knew more than she did about Jayon and she—and she was her partner.

"Elizabeth . . . nothing. You're just a little late, that's all."

"Late with what? I know you and Omar separated. You are seeing someone new?"

After a slight hesitation, she said, "You could say that."

"What does that mean?"

"I am seeing someone, but he is not new."

Jordan gave her that look that said, *you'll never believe it.*

"What???" Elizabeth yelped. "You and Jayon? Are you two . . . like doing it now or something?"

Jordan couldn't help but laugh. "Uhh, something like that."

"Something like that?"

"Well, yeah, we slept together."

Elizabeth damn near screamed at the top of her lungs. Jordan tried to quiet her down so no one heard her—she didn't know where Jay was on the floor. Elizabeth was around when Jordan and Jay had first met—she had seen their whole friendship develop. Back in undergrad she used to think that something was up with them, but over time, like everybody else, she managed to believe it was just a close friendship. So Jordan understood why this seemed crazy to her, that after all these years they'd finally done something.

"Omar and I are through, and Jayon has been there a lot for me, helping me at home, trying to keep me happy, and things just started to happen."

"How did things just start to happen?"

"Well, we were spending time together, he was coming over a lot, and we slept in the same bed together for the first time in years. Then we just started to increase our comfort zones."

"Are you sure that was smart, Jordan?"

"Elizabeth, I don't know. Things have been pretty good, though. I haven't cried over Omar since, so even if that's all it was for, it was worth it. I was tired of being upset and angry. Jayon gave me a reason to look forward to every day again."

"I understand, girl—well, I'm happy for you two."

"Thanks for understanding."

"Please, don't you owe me, like, twenty dollars?"

"For what?"

"I'm sure I bet you years ago this would happen," she said, laughing.

"Shut up—I owe a few people some money, then, and so does Jayon."

When Elizabeth walked out of her office, Jordan started to think about how many people would think that what she and Jayon were now admitting to had been a secret for some time. She wondered if Omar would think she had been cheating on him with Jayon from before, and was just now deciding to come out with it. That would be the last thing she would want him, or anybody, to think. At the same time, of course, people would think that. How could she convince them otherwise? All these years they were friends, and then she and Omar separate, and then she and Jayon get together. She would hope that at least Omar would know better than that. She knew he complained about stuff, but she prayed that deep down he knew his wife well enough to know that she would never have cheated on him. She hoped he didn't assume the worst if and when he did find out that she and Jayon had started an actual relationship.

70

If Only

Chrasey was sitting at her desk typing up some reports. Her boss was calling a meeting with all the directors in a couple of hours, and she wanted her report to be in tip top-shape.

Serrette, her assistant, stepped in her office doorway and called her name to get her attention.

"Trevor on line 1," she said.

"Take a mess . . ." She paused. "I'll get it, thanks," Chrasey replied.

"Hello, Chrasey speaking."

"Hi there, stranger."

"Who is calling?"

"It's me, Trevor."

"Oh, hello there," she said.

Chrasey was trying so hard to be casual and almost professional. She didn't want her eagerness to show—she didn't want him to know how happy she was to hear from him. She was so vulnerable, and she was hoping that if she kept it brief and pretended, he wouldn't be able to tell. She had wanted to call him for weeks, but she knew that it was the wrong thing to do. Deep down, she was hoping he would call because she would feel better about it, less guilty. She didn't initiate the wrongdoing, so it would be better. Now that he was on the phone, she didn't even know what to say.

"So, how have things been?" he asked.

"Great, things are great. How about you?"

"Oh, I'm good. My daughter's birthday is this weekend and I'm taking her to Sesame Place," he said.

"That's nice—she will love it. I took my kids there before."

"Yeah, I would love it if you came along."

"Actually, I can't. I will be taking my kids to a movie," Chrasey replied.

"Oh, well, could I see you at another time?"

"Umm . . . I doubt it, to tell you the truth. I'm not sure if it's wise."

"Can I ask you a question?" Trevor said, as if he'd been waiting to ask.

"Yes."

"Do you still find yourself waiting outside of your job after work?" There was a moment of silence.

"What are you trying to say?" Chrasey asked defensively.

"I'm asking does he still keep you waiting after work?"

"Trevor . . . it's very rare that I don't have my car. Of the few times I needed him for a ride . . . maybe once or twice . . . but what's that have to do with anything. There's traffic and . . ."

"Don't make excuses, Chrase. The point is, what has really changed? Why are you in denial? Let's be serious and honest with each other—what has really changed since before?"

Chrasey wanted to just pour her heart out and tell him all that she was going through. She wanted to tell him about Lourdes calling, about the abstinence, about the lonely nights, about the fear that it wasn't going to work out, and how badly she had been wanting to call him. Chrasey knew if she did that, and started depending on Trevor the way she had before, she would end up with more stress and trouble than she was able to handle. She and Keith were trying to mend their marriage, and although it wasn't working quite yet, she wanted at least to try this time around.

"Trevor, honestly, not much has changed but we are working at it."

"All right, Chrasey . . . look, I wish you two the best—I really do. I just don't want you to be in a situation where you're unhappy. You deserve better than that, Chrase—I have told you that 100 times."

"And you're the *better* that I need, right, Trevor?"

"No, it doesn't have to be me. Maybe it's Keith, as long as there is change. I just want you to be happy."

"Thanks, Trev—I appreciate the concern. I want to be happy, too."

"OK—well, if you need me, you know where to reach me," he said.

"I miss you," Chrasey slipped in.

"Huh?" Trevor said, caught off guard.

"I said, I miss you. I just want to make an attempt to save our marriage—I at least want to try," Chrasey admitted.

"I respect that, and I support you. I'm here either way."

"Thanks, Trev—I'll talk to you later."

Just as Chrasey went to hang up, she heard Trevor call her name. "Chrase . . ." he said.

"Yes?" she said, putting the phone back to her ear.

"I miss you, too," he said.

She gave a light laugh. "I'm happy to hear you still think about me. I will talk to you soon."

They hung up. Chrasey sat at her desk feeling confused. She didn't get why a woman always seemed to need multiple men to equal one good one. If Keith could only have Trevor's compassion and concern for her happiness. If only Tony could have David's sense of responsibility and desire to settle down, and if only Omar had Jayon's temperament. If a man could be everything a woman needed, there would be a lot fewer women cheating. Every woman wants to settle with just one man, but it seemed impossible these days to be happy with one because they were only giving half of themselves. So a woman has to go out and find another half to get complete satisfaction. Damn, if only.

71

She Surfaces

"Is this Dakota?" the unfamiliar voice asked.

"Who is this?" Dakota asked.

"Is this Dakota?"

"Who is this?"

"My name is Jonelle—is this Dakota?"

"Yes, Jonelle from where?"

"I am Tony's fiancée, and I just wanted to ask you a few questions."

"Fiancée?"

"Yes."

"What are your questions, Jonelle?"

"Well, I just wanted to find out about the relationship you have with Tony?"

Dakota laughed. "The relationship I have with Tony?"

"Yes, and what is so funny?"

"It's funny that you ask me that."

"And why is that?"

"Because you should be asking your fiancé."

"Listen, Dakota. I wasn't calling to start any trouble, and I had much hesitation about doing so, but I hoped that you would be the type of female to understand this situation."

"Well, you had wishful thinking, because I'm not."

"OK, Dakota. I'm sorry I bothered you then. If this is how you want to be about this, that's fine if you want to be second in line that's fine with me."

"Of course it's fine with you, because you have no choice, and I don't know anything about you. Why should I understand why I have some strange female calling my phone asking me questions about my relationship with my child's father."

"What? Child?"

"Yes, child. You heard me. Since you are so fine with me having your 'leftovers', let me know how mine tastes?"

"You have a child by Tony—is that what you're trying to say?"

"Yes, I'm pregnant; Tony and I are having a baby. So all that 'his fiancée' stuff you calling me with isn't really saying much to me, so like I said, you need to talk to him."

Click. Jonelle hung up.

Dakota sat there, livid. *This is not what I want to deal with during my pregnancy. Why now? Why after I am in my second trimester, do I have to find out that Tony is engaged to this chick?* Dakota said to herself.

She immediately dialed Tony, knowing she would be beeping in on his argument with Jonelle. She knew Jonelle had called him directly after as well, to give him hell. Still, after the fourth call to his cell phone, he didn't answer his phone.

Of course, she called Chrasey and Jordan to tell them what happened. Jordan didn't pick up the first time, but Dakota told Chrasey to dial her again, because she didn't want to have to tell the story twice. Chrasey tried again, and Jordan picked up. Dakota dived into the story about how this girl called her. She told them close to verbatim what Jonelle said to her and what she said back. Dakota was upset and sounding really stressed-out, and neither Chrasey nor Jordan wanted to add to that. However, neither of them was surprised. They knew Tony was a lot more serious with his baby's mother than he admitted. They knew he had been playing Dakota a lot more than she knew, or that she admitted. They weren't going to tell her that, though, not right then. So instead they acted just as shocked and upset as she was. Chrasey told her to call him and hear his side—maybe Jonelle was just lying to piss Dakota off. That worked—Dakota thought that was probably what it was. She knew she would do the same thing, just to make the other girl mad. Besides, Dakota said she doesn't ever remember seeing a ring in the picture she had seen of Jonelle. She knew it was the girl from the picture in *People* magazine—she just knew in her gut. Tony was a player, but he wasn't a mack like that, to have two baby mothers and a separate fiancée. Besides she had heard rumors, and she always knew deep down some of them were true.

While she was in the middle of talking to her girls, her phone beeped and the Caller ID read Tony's cell number. She told them who it was and that she would call them both back.

"Hello," she said with an attitude.

"Dakota, what the hell is going on?"

"You tell me."

"Jonelle just called me, breaking because . . ."

"Oh, *Jonelle* . . . now she has a name."

"Dakota, knock it off . . . what did you tell her?"

"Are you fucking kidding me? What about what she told me?"

"You told her you were pregnant with my baby?"

"Aren't I?"

"Yeah, from what you tell me."

"What the hell did you say?"

"I'm just saying . . . you *say* that you are."

"Are you trying to say now that you don't believe this baby is yours?"

"I didn't say that."

"That's what you're trying to say, though. Fuck you, Tony. You don't have to have shit to do with my baby. I don't need a dime from your ass, and you and your fiancée can kiss my ass."

She burst out in tears the second she hung up. Her heart was crying—the pain was unbearable. She had given so much of herself up for Tony and she was tired of letting him play her. She had tried to be accepting of his treatment by pretending she agreed with it. She pretended like she, too, didn't want more, when she and everyone close to her knew that she did, including him. He didn't care, though, he never did, and she was just another chick he was dealing with. She was on his roster, not the other way around.

Five seconds after she hung up, he called right back.

"What?" she yelled when she answered the phone.

"Dakota, why are you flipping? I didn't mean it that way—I'm just saying, why did you have to tell her?"

"Tell who? Your fiancée?"

"Dakota, what did you tell her?"

"She shared with me you that guys were getting married and I shared with her that we were having a baby."

He didn't say anything.

"Is that a problem?" she said.

"No, Dakota. I just didn't want her to know."

"Why? Are you guys really engaged?"

He hesitated for a second.

"I can't believe you have been lying to me like this all of this time."

"We aren't getting married. I gave her a ring a while back to quiet her up. To keep her happy. I'm not marrying her, though, especially not anytime soon."

"But if you were to get married, it would be with her?"

"I'm not getting married, so this is an irrelevant conversation."

"If I would have known this, I would have had an abortion."

"How could you say that?"

"Do you see how stupid I look? I'm having a baby with an engaged man. I would look better if it was a married man."

"Dakota, I'm not marrying her, OK? Can you just let it go?"

"Whatever, Tone. Well, we will talk later—I need to get some rest."

"OK, sorry about the phone call. You get a good night's rest."

"Yeah, and let her know not to call me anymore."

They hung up the phone, and Dakota sat there trying to decipher what she did and didn't believe. Most of the time she didn't know what was truth and what was a lie—she knew she barely believed what he told her, though. For all she knew, their wedding date was a few months away, and if she saw pictures of the wedding in some magazine, he would say that was just to shut her up, too.

72

Just Checking

Jordan didn't know what it was this morning, but she woke up feeling overwhelmingly guilty. Omar was her husband, and regardless of what he did to deserve it, she had broken her wedding vows and committed adultery. She had managed to justify it in her mind; all that had happened was that she'd let spite overcome her.

She was so deep in the middle of this mess, she didn't know which way to go anymore. She had definitely started to feel some strong feelings for Jayon and she really imagined spending her life with him. On the other hand, she had a marriage that she started some years ago, and just because things were at their worst, she vowed to stick through for better or for worse. She had to put her pride and ego aside and do what was right in God's eyes, and what was best for Jason. She had spent the whole day thinking about this, so as soon as she finished putting Jason to bed she called Omar. She wanted to talk to him and try again to see if and what she could do to get him to come back home.

"Hey, Omar—it's me, Jordan."

"Hey."

"You busy?"

"Not really—whassup?"

"Nothing much, just chilling at home. Jason is at Chrasey's having a play date with her kids."

"That's cool. My mother is having something next weekend—she wants him to come so I'm gonna pick him up next weekend."

"OK, that's cool."

There were a few moments of silence before she built up her courage.

"Omar, listen—I have been thinking about some things and I thought we should talk."

"About what?

"About me and you, our situation."

"What about it? What is there to talk about?"

"Well, our separation. Where are we going with this? I just thought we should meet somewhere and talk things out."

"There is nothing to talk about, Jordan. I told you how I felt and you told me how you felt."

"So, that's it? We are just going to walk away from our marriage just that easy."

"This isn't all of a sudden—like you said yourself, we have had issues for some time and I'm tired of trying to deal with it. I told you I'm done trying—there are no hard feelings, but I don't want this anymore."

She felt her heart cringing at his words. "I want you home. We are married and we need to fix this one way or the other."

"Oh, did you ask your boyfriend if I can come over?"

"Omar! What is wrong with you? We have to grow up and put our egos aside. We have a marriage to mend—let's call everything even and start over."

"Even? Even Jordan? How are we even?"

"Forget that . . . Omar do you want our marriage to work?"

"Listen, Jordan, you are doing what you are doing, and I'm doing what I'm doing. Things are fine just the way they are."

She couldn't tell if Omar was just trying to get her to grovel or if he really meant what he was saying. "Omar, are you sure? This is it? You want us to just walk away?"

"Basically."

She was speechless. Omar has lost his mind.

"Listen, Jordan. I love you, but your career and your choice of friends is a problem for me, and I'm a lot happier not having to deal with all of that and I'm sure you're a lot happier not having to worry about me."

"So, you don't think it's even worth talking about, Omar?"

"Jordan, do you? There's nothing to talk about."

"Fine, Omar."

"We will be there for Jason and we will still be cool, but there is nothing to talk about."

"Fine, Omar. I was just checking."

Omar didn't catch on, but her *just checking* meant this was his last chance. This was it—she was giving him one last opportunity to step up and be with his wife. He didn't see that, or he didn't care. Either way, she had done all that she could. She was done—he wasn't getting any more out of her. No more guilt, no more confusion. From now on, Omar was her ex-husband.

73

Oops

It was Valentine's Day, and all over the building Chrasey was seeing people receive flowers and teddy bears from their spouses. She remembered a time when Keith used to do romantic things all the time, and Valentine's Day—forget it. He would send stuff; write poems, cards, flowers, and the works. Those days were long gone. She doubted he was doing romantic stuff for Lourdes or anything like that—she thought that Keith changed that part of who he was.

She was just getting back from lunch, and she saw the bouquet of flowers on her assistant's desk. She thought to herself, *I hate this holiday—it's just a reminder of how unloved a person is.* When she walked by her desk, she asked who sent her the flowers, and she said they were for Chrasey. *For me?* Chrasey thought to herself. She didn't expect Keith to do this. She hoped he was smart enough to use Valentine's as an opportunity to get them back on good terms, but it had gotten so late, she thought he probably didn't think of it. She picked the flowers up off of the desk and brought them into her office. There were a dozen multicolored roses, with a little bear sitting on top. She took the card off and read it. *I just want things to be the way they were . . .*

That was so sweet, and just the right sentiments that expressed how she felt. Chrasey reminisced all the time about the days that she and Keith were happy, and they did things together, and played games at home and went out on dates. They were one of the cutest and happiest couples at one point. She was happy that he remembered those times, and also wanted to work toward getting things back where they were.

She sat down at her desk and called Keith. When he came to the phone, he sounded like he was busy.

"Hey, Chrasey—Happy Valentine's Day, baby," he said.

"Happy Valentine's day, baby—thanks for the flowers."

Keith paused. "Flowers?"

"Yeah . . . didn't you send me flowers?" As the words left her lips, she asked herself, *Who said they were from Keith?* The card wasn't signed by Keith.

"No, I didn't. I had plans for us later tonight. The question is, who did send you flowers?"

She knew she had messed up, but she tried to cover it anyway.

"I don't know—that's why I assumed you sent them."

"What did the card say?"

She was hesitant to answer that question; she was just going to come up with a lie, until he said, "And don't lie and say there isn't a card or there wasn't a message on it."

"It just said, *Wish things were the way they were,*" Chrasey admitted.

"No, well, that wasn't me. It was probably from your boyfriend— call *him* and thank him."

"Keith . . ." Chrasey said, trying to fix the mess but not knowing exactly how.

"I have to get back to my meeting, but Happy Valentine's Day and I wish things were the way they were, too," Keith said, obviously trying to maximize her guilt. As soon as he finished his sarcastic comment he hung up, not giving Chrasey a chance to respond.

She sat there, mad at herself for making that call. What was she thinking? She didn't even stop to ask herself why the card wasn't signed. Was she that hopeful that Keith would send her something, that she imagined it all? If she had only stopped to think about it, she could have figured that it was from Trevor. Now it felt awkward to call and thank him after that. Still, she had to, because he was probably expecting her to call when she received it. She picked her phone back up and dialed the number. When he answered, she thanked him and told him that if it wasn't for him, she would have felt like nobody cared about her. Then she told him what happened with Keith. At first he laughed, then he caught himself and apologized. He said he didn't mean to cause any problems, and that he just wanted to express his feelings on Valentine's Day because it felt like it was an appropriate time. He said he could see why she thought they were from her husband; Keith could and should feel the same way. He said he didn't sign the card, because he didn't want to make her co-workers ask a bunch of questions, but he thought she would know who they were from. He did point out the humor with her calling Keith to say thank you, bringing attention to the fact that Keith hadn't actually sent flowers. Chrasey did have to admit it was kind of funny, and she realized he couldn't get mad, because his ass should have sent some damn flowers.

74

XOXOXO

It was Valentine's night and it was pouring rain. Jordan had just come home from work and was rushing to get ready to be on time for the dinner reservations that Jayon made. She hopped out of the shower, and started lotioning up with cocoa butter as she listened to the India Arie album. She put her special scents in her special areas and then put on her favorite bra and thong set, black lace with pink ribbon from Victoria's Secret. She went into her walk-in closet and located the outfit she had set out the night before. She slipped on her black sweater dress from BCBG, and checked in the mirror to make sure it looked OK.

Damn, I am hot . . . brains and beauty . . . I am no joke, Jordan told herself as she did the front and back mirror check.

Jayon called and said he was just getting off the bridge, so he would be there in less than fifteen minutes. She quickly darkened her eyebrows with her off-black eye-liner, put on her Mac Ooh-Baby lip gloss, and finished up with her black eye liner and dark brown lip liner by Bobbi Brown. She combed down her wrap and spritzed her Razac oil mist to make it shine. She pulled her black, open-toe Dolce and Gabbana pumps from the shoe rack and slipped her foot into them. Her toes, just like her nails, were freshly done with a French manicure. She was set from head to toe, and now she was ready to go.

Less than five minutes later, Jayon rang her doorbell. She grabbed the bag with his gift in it and went to the door; he was there with an umbrella waiting to escort her to his car. He was looking damn fine himself, with a black-and-gray Prada sweater, black slacks, and his black-and-gray Prada loafers. He had a fresh haircut, facial hair perfectly trimmed, and he was wearing her favorite cologne, Jean-Paul Gaultier—she could smell it from the door. He gave her a kiss hello, took her by her arm, and walked her to the car. He opened the passenger door and waited for her to get inside, then closed the door behind her. When she sat down, she reached over and opened his door for him, and when he stepped inside, she took the umbrella from him and placed it in the back seat.

Seeping from his speakers was Jodeci's *Love You for Life*. Once he got settled inside the car, he reached in the back seat and handed her a card and a cream-colored jewelry box. She handed him the big bag with his gift in it. They both agreed they would open their gifts then, before dinner. They were both excited about exchanging gifts. They had given each other trinkets and cards in the past for Valentine's Day, but this time it was different. It was the first real holiday that they were some sort of item. He opened his gift; she had gotten him a rust-colored leather jacket with some rust-colored shoes. He loved them. Jayon was a clothes man, so she knew that he would. Jordan opened her box, and inside were some beautiful platinum earrings. They were heart-shaped with two letter J's intertwined in the center. She looked at him, and he smiled.

"The double J's are one for each of us, but together." She leaned over and gave him a kiss. "This is one of the nicest gifts I have ever seen. Thank you, baby."

The earrings were so nice and unique she thought she would cry. They read their cards and then got ready to go. Her card to him thanked him for being everything she needed for the past fourteen years and even more than she needed the past several months. It told him how much she loved him and that she hoped this was the beginning of something special. His card was a little simpler but it said that he loved her, their relationship felt like a fairy tale, he didn't deserve her, and that he wanted this to be their first Valentine's Day together with many more to come.

They hadn't even gotten to the restaurant and she was already feeling all mushy inside. She just felt at one with Jay, like this was how things were supposed to be. She remembered in the movie *Brown Sugar*, where Sanaa Lathan said, *I don't know why your heart won't do what your mind tells it*—she now understood that so much better. She realized that we really can't control who we love. At times she may have thought that it was wrong of her to deal with Jayon, but her heart said that it was all right. Besides, Omar didn't even call her today—he wasn't even thinking about her. So why was she wrong to want to be happy on Valentine's Day, and every other day for that matter, she asked herself.

When they got to the restaurant, it was beautiful. He hadn't told her where they were going; he said it was a surprise. They had passed this restaurant a few times coming from work and she had always made mention of how pretty it looked from a distance. He remembered and decided to surprise her. It was called the Water Club; it was in Manhattan, right off the water. The valet staff parked the car, and Jay escorted her in with the umbrella. They got inside and sat down; they had a beautiful view of the ocean at a candlelit table.

She felt like a teenager all over again. It was like everything Jayon did felt like the sweetest thing. She had been with Omar so long, she'd forgotten what chivalry was, and Jayon was full of it all night. The dinner was great, the ambience so romantic, and they had great conversation. It was definitely one of the best nights of her life. By the end of the night she knew that she had made the right decision. If she couldn't be with her husband, there was no better option than to be with Jayon. It may have seemed like the wrong thing because he was a small issue in her and Omar's marriage, but she couldn't help it that things turned out this way with her and Jay. She had to wonder if she and Jayon were actually meant to be, and all of this was inevitable. All she knew was that he managed to make this night feel like it was straight from a fairy tale, and she was in la-la land. She could tell Jayon was equally happy. She didn't think it was what he was trying to do all along; she just figured he was also happy with the way things were turning out. She couldn't wait to get back home with him to give him the rest of his gift.

75

Gold Digger

Dakota didn't know where she found the courage, or really why she even wanted him to, but she had just told Tony that she wanted him to move in with her. She was getting tired of being alone. This pregnancy had made her even more emotional, and every night lying in the bed by herself felt twice as lonely. After spending Valentine's night alone last night, she didn't know if she could take it anymore. Before she could do things to remind herself she wasn't lonely, like invite someone else over or make a nice, cold drink and kick back and watch some television or read a book. She was able to spend Dakota time, but now that she couldn't call anybody over and she couldn't drink, she felt like she was having too much Dakota time. Besides, she was having a baby—she wanted somebody there to tend to her, and take care of her. She didn't want to have a depressing pregnancy. Every woman wants the father of her child around during these months; it was most of the fun of pregnancy.

He was staying over this night, but this was the first time in a while, and she felt like expressing her true feelings. Tony didn't seem to be responding very positively to Dakota's suggestion.

"Why do you think I should move in?" he asked.

"Because I need you here with me and you're not around."

"Dakota, what do you need me for? You're only five months—you can still do things for yourself."

"I need you emotionally," she replied.

"Babe, I can't move in with you. I'm not ready for all of that."

"Then I can move in with you, at least through the pregnancy," she suggested.

"D, I'm not ready for that, either."

She didn't know if it was the hormones, but she started to get angry. "Why not, Tony? Why can't I get the same respect you give Jonelle? Why do I have to be here by myself all the time? When you gonna do something to shut *me* up and make *me* happy?"

"Dakota, you're bugging me right now . . . first of all, this baby isn't going to change our level of commitment. Second, stop worrying about what I do with Jonelle. You're not her and we have had this talk a million times—I'm not having it anymore."

"What are you saying? Jonelle is more important than me?" Dakota asked.

"I'm not saying anything. Dakota, I care about you, I'm going to be here for you and our child. I promise you that, but I can't promise you much more than that. As for Jonelle, I told you she was down with me for years—I just can't make y'all equal overnight."

"Yes, day one has to be before you had potential, before you were a prospect, that's day one. That bitch knew you were going pro when she met you—that doesn't count."

"Dakota, you need to stop. You're really emotional right now, and I don't want to fight with you."

He turned over in the bed on his side as if he was getting ready to go to sleep. Dakota wasn't done.

"I'm not fighting with you—I just don't understand why I get so little. At least I am independent—you don't have to take care of me. I do Dakota; Jonelle just lies around at home mooching off of you."

"Don't worry about all of that—me and you do our thing and me and Jonelle do ours."

"Fine, Tony. I'm not going to just take what you give me."

"What's that mean?" he asked.

"You are going to have to start to consider my feelings or this isn't going to be pretty."

"Are you threatening me?"

"It's not a threat," she assured him.

"All I know, Dakota, is if you ever take me to court for child support, I'm done with you."

"Why would I have to?"

"I'm just saying that we aren't a committed couple or something . . ." he answered.

She interrupted, "Don't flatter yourself—I'm not hung up on you being my man like that."

"Well, then, why you stressing what I do with Jonelle, and talking about her being with me because I'm pro? It feels like that's why you're trying to be with me."

Dakota sat up in the bed mighty fast. "Nigga, you ain't pro—you don't play ball no more. Your weak-ass football career is over."

He sat up slightly as well. She was pissed and now he was pissed. "I may not be pro no more, but I ain't over, and I ain't that weak because you have been sweating to be with me . . ." he said, clearly trying to say words that hurt.

"I can get ten times better than you—you have got the wrong one."

"They don't come ten times better than me."

"Get the hell out," she said.

"What? You kicking me out?"

"Yup, get the hell out."

She had stood up beside the bed and put her hand on her hip.

"I know you never been kicked out before—you probably not used to messing with women with their own shit."

"One of my women owns your building."

"Well, go stay with one of them tonight," she said.

Tony had gotten out of the bed and started to get dressed. They were both still mumbling shit to each other until he was putting his Timberlands on. He walked to the door and out of it, and Dakota closed the door very loudly behind him.

76

Broken Vows

Jordan finally woke up one day and realized she had come to terms with the fact that life was different. Omar had moved into his own place out in Queens and he had picked up pretty much all of his things one day when she was at work. She stopped wearing her wedding ring, and she removed his name from her bank account.

She felt like they were getting divorced, even though they hadn't gotten to that stage yet. She knew it that was only a matter of time, but she wasn't mentally ready for that and neither was he, she assumed, because he hadn't brought it up yet.

Things were going great with Jordan and Jayon, but the mourning for her marriage made it hard to enjoy their relationship one hundred percent. Jayon was understanding, though—he tried to make it as easy as he could. He never complained when she would vent about what Omar had done, he let her express her pain, and not once did he say he was tired of hearing it. Even though Jayon had become her lover, he was still her friend first and that made things so much easier.

Jason spent a lot of weekends with Omar, and those were the weekends she used to get caught up on work she didn't get to during the week since she had to be home earlier to be with Jason. There were times that she thought Omar did this to force her to be home, and be with Jason. She knew Omar wasn't that selfless, though; this wasn't about Jason's welfare. If it was, he wouldn't be breaking up his family structure. With those spare weekends, she also spent time on herself.

She went shopping, she went to the spa, and she and Jayon went away a couple of times, and those were the weekends that she healed herself.

Jason, like most kids, would tell her things that Omar said from time to time. Stuff like he wanted Jason to come live with him, or he wished he was at home with him and Mommy. She didn't know what to take for face value, so she tried never to read into it. She also was very careful what she said around Jason or what Jayon said around him, because she was sure Jason would run and tell Omar as well. It also seemed like Jason was starting to question Jayon's constant presence. He always knew Jayon to be Mommy's best friend and colleague, and he wasn't used to seeing him too often except for special occasions. Now he was around all the time, and Jason asked one day why Mr. Jay was over a lot. Jordan told him, because he is making sure that she was OK while Daddy is away. It was a downplay of the truth.

She was almost hundred percent adjusted to her new life. It was strange the nights that she slept in her bed alone, and she still cried a lot. This wasn't the life she would have chosen for herself. She wanted a successful marriage just as badly as she wanted a successful career. She just didn't have what it took to manage both well. It hurt her that she failed at her marriage, but it hurt more that she had an unsupportive husband who would leave her the way he did. Jayon helped that aspect of things. Some people thought it was too soon for her to be intimate with somebody else, but that was what she needed. To have no intimacy would just make it harder. Besides, that was a display of her strength—she had to bounce back. She couldn't let Omar take everything away from her that easily.

Jordan was an attorney—filing their divorce papers would be simple, but for some reason it was the hardest thing for her to do. She was fine with the separation and going their separate ways, but the divorce part felt so final. She had always said she would never get a divorce. Her parents didn't, even when they were separated, and they were separated for many years. They never got divorced, and after many years they moved back in together and spent their older years together, still married. It was her thing, but she knew that she and Omar couldn't live like this forever. She didn't know where things would go with her and Jayon but she was sure that being technically married would be a hindrance to any serious plans.

She knew it was probably necessary—she just wasn't in a rush.

Jayon hadn't mentioned it much and neither did Omar. She wasn't going to be the one to bring it up. She just didn't want Jayon to think she wasn't ready to move on. He had expressed to her that he would like to get married and have some kids, and he always thought she would be the perfect wife for him. Jordan knew that Jayon would be an ideal man to spend the rest of her years with as well; she just wasn't ready to take any major steps. She didn't know what Omar was doing in his love life or why he hadn't brought it up, but she also wasn't ready to serve him with divorce papers and she wasn't sure if she ever would be.

77

Heart to Heart

It was long overdue, and Chrasey was at her breaking point. When Keith moved back in, it was under the pretense that they would be working on their marriage. For some reason it didn't feel like they were doing anything of the sort. Things felt worse than they were before he left.

The phone call from Lourdes, the flowers from Trevor—their infidelities were the constant center of attention in their house. Even the silence between them reminded them of everything that was wrong. Thankfully, their kids were young enough to be unaware of what was going on around them. In a few more years, though, if they didn't fix this, they would notice the lack of love and affection between her and their father. They would hear her crying at night, they would wonder where Daddy was the nights he came home late, they would hear and understand their arguments, and they would feel the effects of having unloving parents. She didn't want to do that to them. Having your parents together isn't everything—it's worse to witness the pain they put each other through. She knew that she and Keith had options, but affecting their children wasn't one of them. He could go live with Lourdes and his bastard daughter before she would tolerate that.

So, they were heading out to Fresh Meadows, where he proposed. They were supposed to be having a talk about everything, and trying to make a plan on how to make things better. While they were driving, Keith had his station on CD 101.9. Keith loved his jazz, and listening to it with him lit her up inside. It made her remember the days they would go out to jazz clubs and she would go over to see him and he would have a dinner cooked for them and his jazz playing. That was when she was falling deeper and deeper in love with Keith. He wasn't like most men—he was mature and classy. He wasn't a man of the streets; he was a family man who preferred to stay home than run the streets. She loved the things that made him happy—he was a rare kind of man and she was proud that he chose her.

They were a few exits away from the park, and she reached in the backseat to get her purse and noticed a small, colorful thing on the floor. She looked at it a little closer—it was obviously a child's toy. She picked it up with her purse and held it in her hand in the front seat. It made noise, and Keith looked to see what she had in her hand. When he saw it, he looked at her to see her facial expression. She just looked back at him.

"I had to take them to the doctor," he said in a scared but honest tone.

"When was this?" she asked very calmly.

"Yesterday."

She just put her head down and shook it. He said nothing. She looked back up and started to stare out the window.

"Sorry I didn't tell you," he said.

"That's the thing, Keith—I don't even expect you to."

"What's that mean?"

"It's like you're leading a double life."

"Chrase, I know this is all my fault, but there are certain things that I have to do. It's not about her, it's about the baby."

"You don't have to explain that to me. You don't have to play family man, you don't have to go to the doctor with them as long as she gets seen," she said.

"She didn't have a way," he explained.

"Let her find a way—you're not her husband."

He just fell silent.

Their talk was already ruined. They were a few minutes from the park, and Chrasey already wanted to go back home. When they got to the park, Keith put the car in drive and sat back. They didn't say anything for a couple of minutes. Then Keith finally spoke.

"Listen, Chrasey, a lot has gone wrong in our marriage the last couple of years, and I take the blame for my part. I know what I did will be an issue for us for the rest of our lives—I am only hoping that we can love each other enough to get through it."

She took a few seconds to reply. "Keith, I want us to get through it, too. I didn't marry you and have two kids with you for us not to end up together. What you did was more than cause an issue—you broke our trust, and you brought another child into this world. I will never be able to erase the pain from that. I take the blame for my part, too. Maybe I should have tried harder to fix things, maybe I didn't do enough at home. Who knows? I just know that unless we rebuild our trust and communication, we don't stand a chance."

"I am willing to do my part, and if you are willing to be understanding about my situation, I am willing to be understanding about yours."

It sounded good, but in the back of Chrasey's mind she wondered how long it would last. He had apologized before, he had said he would change before; still, they were sitting in the car at the park where they got engaged, trying to get some of their positive energy back. She prayed more than anything that they had what it took. She wanted to believe that Keith wasn't still dealing with or sleeping with Lourdes. She prayed that he was really willing to understand—even more, she prayed that she could understand. Why would God bless her when she had anger and hate toward an innocent baby, she wondered. She was ashamed to admit it, but she hated her for being born just as much she hated Lourdes for being a whore and lying down with her husband.

78

Off the Market

Jamille, the guy from the grocery store by Jordan's house, had called Dakota today. She felt nauseous that morning so she stayed home. She was making some business calls when her phone beeped. It was him—he reminded her who he was, and she pretended to need a memory refresher. She was well aware who he was and was happy he called. She was happy until he asked her to meet up with him and she had to remember that she was fat as a pig, and that going on a date with a pregnant woman probably wasn't what he had in mind. She knew she probably should have told him but she didn't want to. She didn't want to run all her men away just yet—she needed their sporadic calls. They gave her a sense of hope that she still had it, and she wasn't stuck having to deal with Tony's secondhand love forever.

Hearing from him actually made her mad. She was pissed at herself that she got pregnant by that asshole Tony. She was happy about the child inside of her; she was just upset that Tony had become even more of a jerk since he heard the news. She couldn't tell if he was feeling cocky because he now knew she wasn't going anywhere or if he was upset that now she wasn't going anywhere.

Things had changed so much between them. It was like they started out enjoying each other. He loved the freak she was in bed, and she enjoyed the good sex. She didn't know how they ended up with so much more at stake. She could admit she started to catch feelings for him, and she was open off of his good looks and status. It just seemed that he was becoming open off of her, too. She was a great catch, and she would have thought that she was worthy of a man like him. She never thought that all she could be was his jump-off. It seemed, though, that maybe that was all he wanted her to be. Maybe he just said other things to keep her happy so she would keep giving him that good head. In reality, she was probably one of many pit stops on his way home to Jonelle. She just thought she was smart enough to notice something like that. She was a player herself—it wasn't in her nature to get played.

Jamille really seemed like a good catch. He gave her a sense of hope. She didn't have to settle for Tony. There were other men out there who were good-looking and not losers that would be interested in her. Now it was too late to believe this—she was already knocked up by Tony, with his doggish self. She just wished that she could be having her child with a man who loved and respected her.

She was still pissed that he called her a gold digger, and that he deals with women better than her. How do you say that to the mother of your child while she's pregnant? Dakota just wasn't cool with that at all. Tony had called a couple of times but she didn't answer her phone—she had to let him know that she wasn't some chicken-head girl. Her actions may have said that to him over the past year, but she had more self-respect than she may have been showing. So he wasn't just going to call her up and everything be OK, and then come get some ass. Not this time around. He left messages saying that he was sorry, and he was just upset, he didn't mean all of that, and he cared about her more than she knew. He even said he was excited and very happy that they were having a baby. As mad as she was, that message was what she had wanted to hear from Tony for quite some time. She was going to call him back when she heard that message, but she figured she would let him call her again, and when he did she would answer the phone. It was a shame she had to play these games but as long as they were going to be parenting a child together, she knew she had to always be ready to make her next move. At least until she popped the baby out, and she could take Jamille up on his offer, with his fine self.

79

Better Never Than Late

Eight missed calls. All from Omar. *What is this about,* Jordan thought to herself. A small piece of her was actually excited to see his name in her phone. He hadn't spoken to her in weeks since that day he called and Jayon was over. What has him calling now? And so urgently? Jordan's assistant told her he called twice, but eight missed calls on her cell phone, too? This was something for sure.

She called him immediately. After the third ring he picked up. "Hello, Jordan?" he said, as if he had been waiting for her call all day.

"Yeah. Hi, Omar. Everything OK?" she asked.

"Yeah, where are you?"

"I'm at the office," she said, sounding confused.

"I wanted to see if we can talk . . . like now," he said.

"I have a 2:00 o'clock, but I can talk for a bit now if you'd like."

"No, I want to talk face-to-face . . . where will you be at around 4:00?"

"Probably still at the office," she said, still sounding very confused.

"I'll be there then to pick you up, and we can go to Ronnie's Place to get some food and talk," he replied.

Jordan wasn't even sure she was up for this, but Omar never took rejection well. Regardless of the reason she would give, whether it was good and valid or not, it would only hurt his feelings. Especially since he was even taking this step to try to talk.

"OK, I'll meet you there," she said, trying not to show her hesitation. He seemed happy that she accepted, and they hung up. She sat there in her black leather office chair with her face in both of her hands, just trying to figure out what the hell was going on with her life. She was going on a date with her husband. The husband who she had been considering filing for a divorce from. Her partner for the past fourteen years, who now seemed more like a stranger.

She picked up the phone and called Jayon directly after she finished taking in the situation.

"Hey, baby," he said as soon as he answered.

He still made her blush with something just as simple as that.

"Hey sweetie . . . listen, what are you doing?" she replied.

"I'm leaving Time Warner now. Had to go over some things with the director for their HR meeting . . . Why, what are you doing?" he said.

"I'm actually about to head into a meeting in a few minutes. But at 4:00 P.M. I also have a meeting of some sort. I just wanted you to know so you won't look for me when you get back to the office."

"What meeting do you have at 4:00 P.M.?

"Actually . . . Omar. He wants to meet and talk," she replied.

"About what?"

"I don't know, he didn't say."

"O—K" Jayon said, sounding confused.

"Are you cool with that?"

"Baby. Please. Of course I'm cool with it. You both have some things you need to clear up and discuss anyway. It's actually about time."

"You sure?" she asked.

"Babe . . . go. Don't worry about me. Just be strong. If you need me, I'm #8 on your speed dial."

Jordan started to laugh. That's one of the things she loved about him. Jayon was always putting her first. Especially in this trying time— not once did he act like the jealous boyfriend. He had been her friend first and allowed her to do what she had to do to get through this. With all the guilt she had been dealing with, it seemed he was the one person who didn't think of her as a heartless witch.

It was about 4:45 when she walked into Ronnie's Place and saw Omar talking to Rita, Ronnie's wife. Ronnie's Place was a small soul food restaurant owned by Ronnie, and it was where Omar got his start in the cooking industry. They went there a lot when they were dating, and there were many late nights that she had talks with Rita, while she was waiting for Omar to get off work. They always looked at Ronnie's like a home away from home.

As soon as Omar noticed her he nodded in her direction to let Rita know she had arrived. Rita immediately scurried over to Jordan with open arms to greet her. It had been at least two years since they had seen one another, and Jordan was happy to see her. Omar knew what he was doing, having the talk there; he knew this place always took Jordan back to their early days. This had been where they'd made up several times, but this was different. So although it was great seeing Rita, and Jordan's stomach got excited at the smell of their soul food, she knew she and Omar had to get this wrapped up.

Jordan's mind was made up—Omar had had his chance. So as soon as they sat down at the table, she looked up at Omar and said, "What did you want to talk about?"

On the way there she had thought about when she had suggested to Omar that they talk and he said there was nothing to talk about, how mean and heartless he was, and she realized she was being nice just to show up. She knew this was her opportunity for revenge—she realized that when she first spoke to him earlier and he suggested talking. However, it was past playing games for her. She was way past revenge and spite—she had really let go. She tried to get Omar to see that months ago, but he didn't want to listen. Now here it was, going on ten months after he first left, and he finally wanted to talk.

"Jordan, I have been thinking long and hard and I realize how badly I messed up. I know there were some issues that you and I needed to resolve, but I handled it completely wrong."

"Omar, it took you a year to realize this?" she asked.

"I've noticed it for a while now, but I was too afraid to talk to you about it. I didn't know what to say or what you'd say," he answered.

"Omar, I don't know what you want me to say."

"Say you will give us another chance. Say we can have one more shot—you know we are meant to be together. We have fifteen years to-gether—we owe each other another chance."

"I tried to explain that to you before, but you said years wasn't everything."

"I was wrong, Jordan—can't you forgive me for my mistakes?"

"I can't tell you that, Omar—things are different now."

"I'm willing to take the time that it will take to get things back the way they were."

"Omar, this is so sudden. You have to understand that I'm in a different situation," she said.

"What could possibly be that serious that you can't even give us a chance?"

"Omar, my heart. I could never trust you with it again . . . and I have already started to move on," she answered.

"What does that mean?"

Jordan didn't know how to say it—it was like she wanted him to guess. She couldn't bring her lips to say what she knew would be the last thing he wanted to hear.

"Omar, I haven't been just waiting around for this day—to be honest, I didn't think it would ever come," she said.

"Are you seeing someone?"

"I wouldn't say all of that, but there is someone who has been keeping my spirits up, and I can't just go tell him thanks but I'm done."

Omar just sat there for a few seconds. Then he asked, "Who is this someone?"

"Jayon, Omar. Jayon . . . he has been there for me through all of this, and you can't just think you're gonna come back into my life complaining about my relationship with him."

"Jayon?"

"Yes, Omar, and I don't need you passing judgment right now. You have no right."

"I have no right? So the man that broke our marriage up to begin with, you're going to let him prevent us from getting back together?"

Jordan was too through. Omar just didn't get it and he probably never would. "I'm sitting with the man who broke our marriage up, and yes, he is the same one who will prevent us from getting back together." As she finished her statement she signaled to the waitress for the check.

"Jordan, you can't be willing to throw us away like that," Omar said.

"Why not? You were?" she said as her voice began to crack.

She didn't want to hurt Omar—it was actually more painful for her than it was for him. It was the last thing that she wanted to do, but Omar really didn't see what he had done to her, and she refused to take it easy on him because he didn't take it easy on her. So once the check came, she paid it and she was ready to go. She hoped that

Omar didn't think she was being rude, but he wouldn't understand where she was coming from. It could have been anyone who was "that someone." What Omar had to realize is that he caused this. She just knew that he probably wouldn't, and no matter what she said or did, he was going to be upset with her. Just like most men—he didn't miss a good thing until it was gone.

80

No Place Like Home

It had been different for the past week or so. Keith would call Chrasey once or twice during the day to say hello, or to ask if she needed him to bring anything home. He would pick up the kids for her some days; when he came home he would give them all hugs and kisses. She definitely did see the difference. It was a little odd knowing that it wasn't all natural, but it was a good start. What Chrasey enjoyed the most was when they would sit down to eat dinner, they would all talk—her, him, and the kids. They would talk about school and work, and different places and things they wanted to do together. She felt like they were a family again.

She was starting to get over all the thoughts of what he was like when he was with Lourdes—that would only damper her mood. She started to just focus on what they were doing, and try to trust that he really wasn't with Lourdes anymore. Trust is a hard thing to regain, you never know where the line is that separates trust from just being stupid. It's like trust is that one thing that is the most vulnerable between two people as it is, so when it's tainted in any way, it's almost impossible to regain it fully, because it was never quite full to begin with. She did know that trust was what you made of it. Trust came with faith more so than trust in the one you're with. Faith to leave it in God's hands, to live your life and hope for the best.

Chrasey was well aware that this was probably not the end for her and Keith; they had a lot more turmoil and stress to come, and they were just at a temporary standstill. Lourdes would soon stir up more trouble, and there would come a time when her kids and Lourdes's daughter may have to meet. Her and Keith's future was going to be filled with reminders of this time in their marriage and there was no use trying to escape it. The best they could do was try to move past it.

It had been forever since she and Keith had had sex, but they finally even crossed that bridge. The other night they were lying in bed, and they both seemed to feel more comfortable next to each other. Their legs had touched and they didn't move them. Then, before she knew it, he had scooted to her side of the bed. Her first impulse was disgust—she still felt a lot of anger toward him, and she didn't want him to touch her in that way. When he put his arm around her, though, she closed her eyes and tried to remember when she'd yearned for him to cuddle with her in the bed. She tried to remember that he was trying to change. She hadn't been with Trevor in months, and she could have used the maintenance, anyway. So when she felt him going for it, she let him go. It was more like making love—he took his time with everything. It had been a while, so it felt like something new and she enjoyed every minute of it. She worked very hard to keep all the negative and angry thoughts out of her head so that she could get through it. She was seriously considering making him wear a condom, but she knew that would ruin the whole mood. It wasn't to be mean, but she didn't know what really went down between him and Lourdes, and she knew she'd used protection with Trevor. Still, she figured if he didn't try to make her feel dirty for her affair by putting one on, she shouldn't make a big deal and make him do it, so she let it go. By the time it was over, she really did think it helped them break down a barrier between them. They had been husband and wife and had sex only three times all year—it was crazy to be able to count. She didn't have an orgasm, but that would have been too much to ask for the first time around—one step at a time. It felt nice to go to sleep afterward without feeling guilty, the way she used to sometimes when she slept with Trevor. The next morning he was as sweet as pie. She didn't know if it was because he was backed up and last night did him wonders, or he was just trying really hard to get them back on track. Either way, she went along with it; she did her part to keep their house cheerful. He had cooked breakfast and brought it to Chrasey in bed—then he crawled in next to her and started watching television with her. He asked her what she wanted to see—he didn't just turn to his sports stuff. She really started to like what life was like at home. They had been at odds for so long, she forgot about how cute and mushy a marriage could be. She didn't know how long it would last, but it finally felt good to be home.

81

Don't Wait Up

Dakota didn't know what had changed his mind, or what made him decide to finally shut her up and make her happy. Tony had come by with a few bags and said that he was going to spend a lot more time at Dakota's place. He said he wasn't moving in, but he would spend a lot more nights with her.

He got to her place at about 8:00 with three shopping bags of clothes and placed them by the door. She sat on the couch and he sat right beside her. He explained to her what his intentions were and that he wanted to be around more during her pregnancy. It felt like a practical joke, because it was too good to be true. He said he would leave some things in the closet so he could spend some nights there and leave from there in the morning. He said he wasn't ready to move in, and he owned too much property of his own to be living with somebody else. He also mentioned that maybe one day she could sell her condo and come move into one of his places, but that was *maybe one day.*

She didn't know what had gotten into him, and he really didn't explain. This was one of those things she didn't want to mess up, so she didn't ask many questions. She did thank him though, for trying, and she let him know that he was welcome there any night of the week. She had already told Tony early on that she wasn't going to be dealing with any other men while she was pregnant. She just thought that was the tackiest thing a woman could do, be pregnant and be out there fooling around with different men. So he was already aware that he wouldn't be messing up her groove—it was too late for that. Besides, she thought it was obvious to Tony that if he was ever willing to settle down, she would have no problem retiring her player card as well. Now that she had a child on the way, it was probably going to get revoked anyway.

She was tempted to ask, what about Jonelle? Is she OK with this, are you trying to piss her off? Is she going to be pissed if and when she finds out? She decided to just mind her business and not say anything to ruin this. Honestly, she really didn't care how Jonelle felt about it. As long as Dakota was getting hers, Jonelle could have hers. She wasn't hating. She just didn't want to have to be bothered with Jonelle calling her house or starting that jealous girlfriend stuff, especially now that she was aware of Dakota.

After they finished talking, they went into the bedroom to put his things away. He brought a toothbrush, a du rag, three pairs of sweatpants, some wifebeaters and white t-shirts, two button-ups, two pairs of slacks, and a few pairs of jeans. He brought socks and boxers; his Timberlands, Gucci loafers, and a pair of sneakers. It looked like Tony was really serious. Dakota knew that even the nights he didn't stay, just having his things there would make her feel like he would be coming home and she wouldn't feel so lonely.

He had promised to spend at least a few nights a week with her, and though it wasn't permanent, Dakota was happy with what she could get. Besides, in Dakota's mind she had to take things one step at a time. It started as fucking buddies, then they started dating. Things got a little more serious, there were some public appearances, and then they ended up planning for a baby. Now they were semi-living together; Dakota felt at this rate, their future looked mighty bright.

Tony stayed that same night and they had a good time. They watched a movie, managed to have some good sex with her big belly in the way, talked a bit, and then fell asleep in each other's arms. Dakota felt like Christopher Williams' old song was playing, "Don't wake me, I'm dreaming." Even if only for the night, it was a dream come true. She knew some women dream of marriage, and of the living happily ever after part, and here she was, full of joy over just one night. She didn't care if it was a pathetic dream—*We don't all have to shoot for the stars*, she thought.

82

Sincerely, Ms. Moore

*D*ear Omar,

This is the third time this week that I cried myself to sleep. I toss and turn almost every night, and then there are nights like tonight when I just cry. I guess it's guilt, but from what, I don't know. You left me. And I tried—I tried for weeks to get you just to take my phone calls. You wouldn't take my calls, you wouldn't call me back. What was I supposed to do?

I was hurt and scared—and alone. I was used to being with you. I didn't know what to do with myself after a while. Every day that went by I was more and more confused. Jason was all I had, and looking at him reminded me of my fear of doing this all alone.

Jayon has been my friend since I can remember—he was just doing what he has done for years, being a friend. I know you don't want to hear that or believe that, but this time it just so happened you pushed me so far away, you pushed me to him. I didn't expect to fall in love with him. I didn't—I knew it was wrong that I found solace in him. I wasn't expecting my life to change overnight, because trust me, had I known, I would've slowed down for a moment. Just a moment. To get my thoughts together, to prepare myself for the emotional roller coaster that I can't seem to get off of.

I know it doesn't make it easier for you to deal with, but I'm happy with him. I know you don't want to hear that, and it actually hurts to tell you. I know it's the novelty of it all. I know you're thinking with all our history, how could I give him credit for this past year? Some of the time I feel like I have been with him all this time. I know—that makes you hate me, and us, more. But in an innocent way, we had shared a relationship too. He was my friend—most of the time when you weren't able to be. Now here we are separated, and it just feels natural to be with him.

I was happily married in my own world. But in reality, I wasn't happy. I settled and was too afraid to let go, even when the times were bad. It wasn't right that when things weren't going well, I'd run to him. I was supposed to have that feeling with you.

I am almost ashamed of what has happened. I was supposed to be a faithful, happily married woman. I took pride in being the best damn wife in the world. Admitting that another man has my heart feels unacceptable. That's why I cry. I cry because this is against everything I know. Everything I believe. I feel like I'm just as bad as every woman I've always looked down upon.

At the same time, should I get back with you just to be unhappy? Now that I've tasted happiness again, going back seems impossible. Besides, you did it. If you'd never left me, I would never have explored. I would never have realized that I didn't deserve the way you treated me. You couldn't just appreciate that I was loyal to you and trying to do my best. You are the one who pushed me away. You pushed me to him. I know, you never thought I'd stray. Me, either—I am just as shocked. But it is the reality. I am gone. I am with Jayon, and I refuse to cry any more, for I did nothing wrong. These tears are for those days I was in pain because of something you did or didn't do to me. Tears for when you left me. I shouldn't be crying now that I am finally happy again.

I will always love you.

Sincerely,
Jordan Moore

She knew that when she signed her maiden name it would hurt his eyes to see. However, she needed to be clear that in her mind, she was a single woman. She didn't use Jayon's last name—that would have been something the spiteful Jordan would do, but she wasn't being spiteful. In fact, Jordan felt no pleasure whatsoever in having Omar ask her to come back. She was actually displeased. She had spent all of her adult life with him; she never wanted to hurt him, but he had pushed her to this point and there was nothing she could do but follow her heart.

83

Back to Reality

It was good while it lasted. Chrasey could feel her and Keith's attempts starting to fade. It was feeling more and more forced every day, and they were barely going through the motions. It was like he didn't feel like putting on a front anymore, and she didn't mind, 'cause she was getting tired of playing along. Love and affection isn't something you can force, and when you do, you can feel the difference from the real stuff. She knew she and Keith still loved each other, but neither of them felt mushy and emotional about their marriage. The fact that they were trying to stick together despite their issues wasn't romantic and sweet, it was comfort and convenience. It was a lot easier to stick with what they had than try to go rearranging stuff. Chrasey didn't feel that they were so badly off that it was worth affecting their children's lives. She knew that was her main reason for sticking it out, and Keith probably knew it was true what they say—*it's cheaper to keep her.*

He was still coming home at a decent time most nights, and they were still eating together and sleeping in their bed. It was just that those nights didn't feel genuine. She would tell him he could go downstairs and watch television alone, because she knew that's what he really wanted to do. She didn't want them not to be able to be themselves. She appreciated his effort, but she was losing the feeling that she actually didn't mind. She didn't want him to have to eat with them or sleep with her, either, but she knew it was only a matter of time before he started that back on his own. Most of those nights became fewer and fewer over time. It went from seven nights a week to six, and six to five, and four to three. Now it was about three or four times a week when Keith was the ideal husband. That was more than enough for her—she was used to no nights, and that was just a few months ago.

It had become nerve-wracking trying to keep an eye on Keith. One night he came home and she swore he was on the phone with Lourdes. He was talking very softly, and she noticed he was being very short with the person. He wasn't saying too much, and he looked a little nervous. She walked in and out of the living room a few times just to see what he would do; he tried to remain natural, but it still looked like he was made uncomfortable by her presence. She was in the kitchen cooking but she was paying more attention to him than the food. He realized that after a while, but she figured he didn't want to be obvious and hang up. She was trying to hear the conversation and she couldn't, and it was getting her even more frustrated. She didn't want to go in there breaking, making him hang up, because then she would never be able to get any information. That was until she got tired of struggling, and she went in the living room and sat down right beside him. He still didn't hang up. He gave a few yeah's and uh-huh's, but he didn't say much else. Chrasey shot him a few dirty looks, but she waited it out because she knew eventually he would break.

After a few more minutes he looked over at her, and he said, "Yeah, she is sitting right here." She almost saw red. She thought to herself, *Is he that bold? Would he really acknowledge her and think she would acknowledge Lourdes as if their phone call was acceptable?* Just as she was giving him a look of fury and confusion, he handed her the phone and said, "My mother wants to talk to you." It was a bit of relief, but also anger from what she had concocted in her head. She spoke to his mother and heard a speech she assumed was similar to the one she was giving Keith. Basically saying what they had to do to keep their marriage together. No wonder Keith was being short—he didn't want to hear her lecture; *she* barely did. She was able to imagine a whole conversation and misinterpret his every facial expression and word, and until she was proven wrong, she was convinced he was up to no good. How does a man beat that? Women are so eager to be detectives—they will make a crime scene out of anything.

So after she put her Nancy Drew clue book away that night, she tried to make herself give Keith a little credit. She knew he wasn't trying as hard to please her, and he wasn't up under her trying to make her feel comfortable that he wasn't still talking to that woman, but how long could she have really expected that to last, she wondered. Just because he wasn't trying to get a husband-of-the-year award anymore didn't mean he didn't deserve some credit for choosing his family. Some men would never have come back, some would have let Lourdes take them away from their wives; at least Keith was willing to give their marriage a try. For that he deserved credit and at least some trust. She should feel a little more confident than she had been. *He did choose me*, she told herself.

84

Playing House

Tony had been over almost every night this week. He didn't come over on Tuesday night or Friday night, but he was there every other. Dakota wasn't sure if he was just putting his night life and other female companions on hold, but he seemed to be really committed to being there for her. She was almost sure the nights he wasn't there he was at Jonelle's, because on those nights she had a hard time getting hold of him. He wouldn't answer, then he would call her back an hour or so later. It had only been two weeks, but she was surprised that things had gone so smoothly.

They hadn't had any fights; he had been very respectful of her feelings and her sporadic emotional outbursts. He knew it was hormonal, and he really tried to refrain from getting upset with Dakota. He went out and got stuff for her when she had cravings, and he would get her food from the kitchen all day. She had severe cravings for Twix candy bars, and Tony would buy them for her like six at a time. He was really being the ideal father-to-be, and she no longer had any regrets about having a child with him.

Some nights when they would go to bed, he would lay his head on her big, round stomach and rub it while he listened. It seemed like he was really happy to have a baby on the way. Dakota had found out a few weeks earlier that it was a boy, and she assumed that's what got him psyched. He had a girl, and having a boy is every man's dream. She was so happy that she wasn't having another girl—that would only make her child second to Jonelle's daughter. Now that she was having a boy, Tony would love her child just as much if not more than hers, and she didn't have to worry about Jonelle and her child being treated second-best. She wondered if that had to do with him actually semi-moving in, that he felt a new excitement about the baby. She didn't care about the reason—she was just happy that he was genuinely thrilled, and she was, too.

She saw little behavioral patterns with Tony that made it obvious he had some things to hide. He kept his phone on silent—she barely ever heard it ring. Then when he did answer it or make a call, he wouldn't be around her—he would use the phone in the next room. Sometimes his runs were a lot longer than they should have been, and he would come back with a different car than he'd left with. He was definitely juggling some stuff, but she tried to act oblivious to it all. She tried to understand that he was a man, and the average man couldn't avoid temptations; of course, a man of Tony's status would have an even harder time. Females are scandalous—some of them would do anything to have one night with Tony. Plus, Dakota figured most of what he was hiding involved Jonelle, anyway, so she tried to give him some room with it. Hopefully this was just while he adjusted, and soon he wouldn't have to be so secretive. At least he was trying to step up to the plate and handle his responsibility.

In the back of Dakota's mind she was hoping that she would be the survivor. That she would be the one that got Tony all to herself. She was hoping to make Jonelle the baby mother, and she would become the special one. She knew having his son would help, but she had a ways more to go before that was obtainable. She felt bad sometimes, being so trifling toward this girl; she was being that bitch that every girlfriend and wife hated. She didn't feel too bad, though—Jonelle was not her girlfriend, and Dakota figured Jonelle's man troubles were not her problem. Besides, Dakota would beat her ass if she even thought about coming to her with her problems. It's fair game now— she was having his baby. She needed him just as much as Jonelle did. She and Dakota were in the same shoes—they both had a child of his now. So even if she had been the HBIC before, as far as she was concerned, may the best woman win. Dakota thought maybe it was foolish of her to think that way, maybe it was ghetto and childish, but until she had this baby and she could get some of the old Dakota back, foolish she was just going to have to be.

85

Reality

It had been weeks, and Omar still hadn't replied to Jordan's letter. She called him once or twice to ask if he wanted to come see Jason, or wanted to discuss the letter, but he never answered her calls or returned them. On two different occasions, Jason would come home and tell her that his daddy came to see him at school. Other than that, there had been no trace of Omar. She was too embarrassed to call his mother to try to catch him, or pop up at his job and possibly cause a scene.

His best friend Elton told her that he had been getting settled in his new apartment. She was tempted to get the address and just drop by—She thought about it once or twice. She never did ask Elton for it, but she knew he would give it to her, because he, more than anybody, wanted her and Omar to reconnect. He had been their Cupid ever since they started having problems, and although in the past his arrow worked wonders, he couldn't quite fathom that this time he was shooting duds. So anything he could do to get them going in the right direction, he would, even if it meant getting Omar angry with him. He knew how stubborn Omar could be, and sometimes you have to show him what he needs. So even though she knew she could get it, she didn't ask. She wasn't ready to take any extreme measures, wasn't ready for what might happen, and she knew if she backed him in a corner he would lash out at her. She had to wait until he was ready.

She thought what bothered her the most was that he was hurting on the inside. Omar didn't have any siblings, and although he had other family and friends, at the end of the day, she and Jason were all he really had. Although she knew he would be fine, her guilt kept beating her up for taking them away from him. As she sat on the edge of her empty bed that she was used to sharing with Omar, thinking about these things, tears just started to roll down her face.

How did she get herself in this situation? All these years she had tried to be a faithful and decent wife, and here she was, doing what she'd tried to be the opposite of. Everyone can justify their actions, and why they leave their spouses—how was she any better. She began to sob, and she didn't want Jason to hear her and come in her room asking questions, so she quickly headed for the bathroom.

She turned on the faucet to splash cold water on her face, but instead she sat on the toilet and sobbed some more. She had to let it out. It was a pain deep down inside of her; it felt like a pit way down in her soul, and she could actually feel it. There was nothing like a feeling of guilt, or at least nothing she had ever experienced. She was convinced that guilt and regret were the two worst feelings a human can ever experience, because all you have is yourself to beat up and blame.

On one hand, she was thankful that she was able to have Jayon in her life. Thankful that she was able to find happiness again, that there would be life after Omar. On the other hand, she knew that Omar had been her life, all of her adult life. She didn't understand why her heart was so made up and her mind was so confused. When she tried to even imagine being with Omar again, it didn't feel right. It was like her heart had given up on him. She still cared about him, and she still loved him, but she didn't want to belong to him anymore. Her heart had truly jumped a new beat for Jayon. She woke up and went to bed thinking about Jayon—she wanted to be with him every minute of the day, and she was so happy with all of the possibilities that lay ahead for her and him. Her mind was clear, though—it knew very distinctly what she was doing was wrong. It knew that these were just untamed temptations and she needed to get a grip, but she couldn't. She had fallen in love again, and how do you tame that? It was a crazy feeling to feel guilty about being happy.

She was sitting on the toilet seat leaning over holding her stomach. She was trying to embrace herself, in hopes of comforting herself because nobody else could. Nobody could tell her what they thought, and nobody could hold her and make her feel better. Not even Jayon, because although she believed he was sincere, she knew his perspective was biased. Everybody she knew had an opinion about this, so they had chosen either to tell her how disgraceful she was or pretend they were on her side and understood. Even those who really did understand and thought she was right, they knew she was being hypocritical; it was still everything she'd said she would never do. So no matter how she sliced it, she was alone with this.

Just the thought of Omar sitting at home in his apartment without her hurt her. The thought of him missing her, or even weeping a tear, hurt her. She felt selfish—she was putting herself first, and she didn't want to be that way. Still, she knew if she worked it out with Omar, that wouldn't be right, either, because she wouldn't be able to give her all or even what she had given before. Too much had changed. There would be too many broken hearts and unforgivable behavior. Even being torn between the two, she had no desire to be without either of them. If she could have it her way, she would have had Jayon as her man and Omar as her best friend, but she knew that Omar would never be willing to switch places with Jay. He would kill her or him before he did that.

As the sobs began to slow down, she finally made her way to the cold water that had been running. She took a handful and wiped her face with it. The chill from the cold water made her lose her breath for a second and calm down. She used a handful or two more until she had completely soothed herself. She looked in her bathroom mirror—she looked a hot mess. Her eyes were bloodshot red and her face was slightly puffy.

She made her way back to her bedroom and plopped herself down on the bed. She curled up with the pillow that she pulled from Omar's side of the bed, and she just let her brain wander, assessing her situation. She wanted to come to a final decision about whether she was doing the right thing and cling to it regardless of what anyone said. The only way she could do that is if the decision was best for her. Not Omar, not Jayon, not her family, not Jason, not her friends, but her.

86

Guilt Trip

Chrasey looked at Jordan and said, "You know you're being a hypocrite."

Jordan let the steam from her tea tickle her nose before she took a tiny sip from her cup. Jordan and Chrasey had had a rough day at the office and met up for lunch for drinks and a bite to eat. They were in a small café on Twenty-third Street called The Diner. The name was as simple as the décor. The waitstaff wore jeans and white t-shirts with name tags, and they seemed to be understaffed. Although not Jordan's normal preference, the food was delicious and made up for the lack of customer service.

"This isn't the same. Omar left me—I didn't leave or cheat on him, and I never have," she defended.

"You were still married," Chrasey replied.

"Separated . . . and as far as I knew, divorce papers were headed my way. I hadn't heard from him in months. Me not being with him has nothing to do with Jayon—it's Omar's fault we are not together."

"What happened to, in a marriage you work things out?"

"Exactly, but he doesn't get that concept. I tried to tell him that—I left him that on his voice mail. I tried that, but you can't work things out on your own. He left me without even explaining what the issue was, and let months go by. What he did was unacceptable, and even if I hadn't ended up with Jayon I wouldn't have wanted to get back together with him anyway," Jordan said.

"You sure?" Chrasey said.

Jordan paused. No one had ever asked her that—they never asked if she was positive that she wouldn't have forgiven Omar despite Jayon being in the picture. After deep thought, she replied, "I would probably have worked things out, actually. I would have settled. I would have just let it go and moved on for the sake of Jason, for the sake of our history, and out of fear of not knowing if I had a better option."

Chrasey just sipped her coffee and didn't reply, allowing what Jordan had said to resonate. She took a glance around the diner. They were one of the six filled tables. Three tables had what looked like couples seated at them; another table had two men seated, possibly gay, and there was a table with what looked like two business associates meeting, and another had two old women. Life was funny. Looking at some of their facial expressions and body language, Jordan wondered what they were thinking, and what life was like for them. Were those couples in love with each other and elated to be spending those moments together? Or were they just settling because it was another person willing to spend that time with them? Were they just together out of convenience? Had they been in love at one point and were holding on to what little was left of their passion for one another? The cycle of love is a crazy and funny one. Almost every person in life experiences it, and yet there are no experts who can truly tell us how to beat it. Even Dr. Phil and Dr. Ruth struggle with the challenge.

It was 1:10 on a Tuesday afternoon—Dakota couldn't meet them for lunch because she was busy at work, and that was fine by Jordan because she needed the understanding and viewpoint of a married woman. You want to believe that the vows you make on that day will last forever. Your dreams of growing old together don't feel unrealistic. The romance and affection feels like it will be endless. When you stand there at the altar, looking into your lover's eyes, you want life together to last forever. Before God and your friends and family, you affirm your commitment to this person, with great hope that you two will stand the test of time. Talk of divorce rate and infidelity don't matter to you, because what you have with this person is special, and those others who failed just didn't have what you two have. You're the most naive woman in the world on that day, and for most women, several months after. The day you wake up and realize that you, too, are on the verge of becoming a statistic is a rude, very rude, awakening.

"But too bad for him—I realized that I did have a better option. I didn't have to be treated like a cheating wife when I wasn't. I was just trying to be successful for my son and for me and him. Some husbands are proud of their wives and their success. I was torn between Omar and my career for years. He made me feel like a terrible wife and mother. He could have been supportive of my career," Jordan blurted out of nowhere.

Chrasey didn't say anything. She just looked at her, not knowing what Jordan wanted her to say.

"I was supportive of *his* career. That damn restaurant of his kept him away from home more than I ever was. He almost missed seeing me give birth—I was always there for what mattered. He knew when I was in law school that I had goals; he obviously just hoped I didn't reach them, and when I did he was too damn selfish to be happy for me," Jordan continued.

Before Chrasey could offer a rebuttal, Jordan added, "And I also realized I didn't have to put up with a relationship where we fight every day. I didn't have to accept him disappearing every time he had a freaking issue with me. He needed time then—well, dammit, he's got it now."

All of that flew right off her tongue. It was frustration from being turned into the bad guy in this. It was her defense mode turned on towards a topic she had to defend to herself repeatedly.

"You sure you have no regrets?" Chrasey said. "You seem very emotional over this. It's like you're trying to convince yourself more than me."

Jordan hated when people psychoanalyzed her, especially when they were right. She hated it because they forced her to think about things that she was either in denial about or knew were true but wanted to ignore. She felt like asking Chrasey, *Who are you, Dr. Phil now?* Instead she realized Chrasey was just being an honest friend and she should be thankful for that.

"Chrasey, I'm not going to lie. This has been hard for me. The worst part is I feel guilty because I'm happy. How does someone get a taste of happiness and then give it up to be unhappy, all for the sake of someone else? When I used to hear spouses say or do things like that, I thought it was so selfish, and although in a way I still feel that is, now I understand. Sometimes you have to put yourself first," Jordan said.

"I was one of those people you thought were selfish. I tried to explain to you that Trevor gave me a sense of myself back, and I needed that. Keith had taken so much of my identity and my spirit, that when Trevor came along it wasn't about just getting revenge on Keith, it was about getting from Trevor what Keith refused to give me. Trevor made me feel happy again, or as close to happy as I had felt in a long time," Chrasey said.

"I know, Chrasey, and I apologize for that. All I could think of was your kids and your marriage—not once did I say think of you. Although I don't condone infidelity, I can understand how Keith's actions forced you to take those measures. These men have to understand that they can't just take our love for granted," Jordan said.

"Thanks, Jordan, for understanding, even though it's too late now," Chrasey said with a little laugh.

"Yeah, I know my timing is always perfect with these things. Just like I want to fall for Jayon only months after Omar and I split. No, it couldn't wait a year or two so the world wouldn't think I was having an affair with Jayon all along, I had to fall right away," Jordan said, managing to find her humorous side in the midst of it all.

"Well, Jordan, I know the relationship you and Jayon have has been magnetic from the day you guys met. He loves you and you love him—maybe that's who God had in store for you all along. You and Omar have been arguing for fourteen years—it's very possible that he wasn't your soul mate and Jayon was. God does everything for a reason."

Just the thought of her and Jayon made Jordan blush. "Chrasey, he is so sweet. He is so calm and caring. He does the cutest things for me. When I come into the office in the morning, I have a fresh cup of coffee or my white chocolate milk on my desk with a croissant. He will leave me little notes on my screen or instant messages just saying sweet stuff. Yet with all of the attention, he knows how to balance it—he is not overbearing. He stays in his office for the most part to give me my space, then he goes about his day. I used to think it was to make sure it wasn't obvious to our colleagues and staff, but they know already. He just wants to give me plenty of room. He comes by at night and we just watch movies and TV, play games, talk, do work, pretty much everything. He is just the best of both worlds—he is really my friend and my lover. But he has made it very clear to me if I wanted to get back with Omar, he would understand," Jordan said, sounding embarrassed, like a teenager with a crush.

"Do you take offense at that?" Chrasey asked.

"No, because I truly feel that is the part of him that truly loves me. That's my best friend in him. He just wants me to do what makes me happiest."

"And what is that, Jordan? Can you live with yourself if you choose Jayon?"

Not prepared for all the scrutiny, Jordan answered fast without really thinking about it, almost defensively. "Yes, I can. Jason will still have a relationship with Omar. Jason adores Jayon and always has, so he is not uncomfortable with him," Jordan said.

Jordan then took a second to think. "Besides, Omar hurt me so bad with what he did, I could never let him that close to me again. So, the only logical option is to follow my heart. I can't go with my mind and conscience this time around—they will lead me to worry about everyone but me, and I can safely say that I want to see where things go with Jayon," she continued.

"Safely say? . . . Truly feel that is the part of him that truly loves me?" Chrasey asked, laughing. "Jayon must be putting it on you."

Jordan burst out laughing. They used to always say when one of them was open they would start talking that "sprung talk." It had been too long for her to remember. "Good girls never tell," she said, laughing.

87

Birds of a Feather
Flock Together

Chrasey couldn't talk about Jordan or anybody else, for that matter. She was supposed to be working things out with her husband, but there were still remnants of her affair haunting her.

One night she walked out of her job and she started to walk toward her car, which was parked up the street at a metered parking spot. She had been putting quarters in every two hours for the whole day, and she was running a little late, so she was hurrying so she wouldn't get a ticket. Cops sometimes just scope the neighborhood for expired meters, and after all her efforts all day she would be pissed if she got one now. As she rushed toward the block her car was on, she noticed a black BMW parked right outside of her workplace. It was too far away to see who was in it, but it was the same model and make as an old friend of hers.

Once she saw it and thought it could be him, she instantly became nervous. Butterflies were in her stomach, her breathing patterns changed, and she could feel herself getting sweaty. She anticipated him getting out of the car and walking up behind her or calling her name. She wanted to think he wasn't still an issue, but he was. To see Trevor would probably make Chrasey weak again.

He hadn't really been in touch much. He called once or twice, but for the most part, what they shared had died. He was respectful of her request, but he made it clear that he was giving her some time to think. She imagined him popping up at her job, just because he was that kind of sweet guy that would relive the first time they met over and over. She just hadn't imagined it today. So as she continued to walk to her car, she kept glancing over her shoulder. The car was just sitting there and no one was getting out. She started to wonder if it wasn't Trevor, but what a coincidence that would be.

By the time she got to her car, there was still no activity from the BMW. Then she realized what a fool she was, because she was hoping that was Trevor and it wasn't. She had to laugh at herself. Here she was, trying to get prepared for his attempt to see her, and he was somewhere probably not even thinking about her. She had been trying to fool herself. She wanted to see Trevor just as much as she thought Trevor wanted to see her.

She just couldn't pull off without seeing if that was Trevor. She figured maybe he didn't get out of the car because he got scared or maybe he just wanted to see her but he wasn't trying to bother her. That would be considered some form of stalking, but flattering nonetheless. She had wanted Trevor to call or show up. For a second she didn't want to check so that if it wasn't him, at least she could have walked away with the thought that it possibly was. Instead she drove by anyway, and as she reached the side of the car she glanced in. There was a woman sitting there on her cell phone. Maybe she was waiting on someone or was lost, whatever—Chrasey didn't care. It wasn't Trevor.

88

Wires Crossed

Dakota and Tony had just come back from dinner, and she was ready to just pass out in the bed. Her stomach was stuffed, and not from the baby, from the food. They'd gone to the Shark Bar and had eaten steak and potatoes, macaroni and cheese, yams, all that good soul food. Tony just felt like some soul food, and Dakota wasn't up for cooking. Once he knew not to ask her twice, he decided they would make a date of it and go out to eat. That was one of the beautiful things about living in the city—all the best places were all around her house. They didn't have to travel far to go somewhere nice.

When they got back, she lay flat on her back on the bed. Her stomach was too big to lie on it anymore. She was lying there, feeling restless, when Tony walked in the room. He was full, too, and it was late—they were both going to be asleep before long. They had a case of Niggeritous. He turned on the television and started watching football as he started to change out of his clothes to get in the shower. He took his pants and shirt off and put them on the chair and went in the bathroom with his boxers on.

She lay there, too lazy to move. She did change the channel, though, turning to the TBS station to watch *Sex in the City*. She was lying there watching Samantha paint the town in her yellow minidress when she heard a slight noise from Tony's pants pockets. She figured it was his cell phone and was going to mind her own business. She heard it some more, and still ignored it, continuing to watch the show. Carrie was having some big argument with Big and it was getting good. Then, about two minutes later, she heard it vibrating some more. Once again, she ignored it, although her curiousity was starting to surface. Then she heard another noise, and this time it was coming from the dresser. She looked up and Tony had put his cell phone, wallet, and keys on the dresser. So what was shaking in his pocket then? That was when she decided against minding her own business.

She got up and waddled over to his pants pocket. At first she started not to check—she knew how invasive and insecure it was to go through his things. But then she went in his pocket anyway; she also knew how foolish it was to act blind to the obvious. She felt around and pulled out a blue cell phone. It was a different phone from the one she was used to seeing—the one she knew of was silver. She was confused for a second, but after a few moments it didn't take much for her to figure it out. The ultimate player had two cell phones. One for the girls only, one that wifey doesn't know about. She was no dummy—she was a player, too. Besides, she knew of several other players and high-profile clients of hers that did this same thing. To verify her suspicion, she proceeded to check the contacts in the blue phone. From A-Z, there was an array of female names. From Ashley, Briana, Claudette, Diandra, to Nicole, Meka, all the way to Quinece and Zane. Every single entry, excluding like six, were females. She then looked in the photos of the phone—she wasn't sure what made her check that out, but she guessed she wanted as much information as possible. When she looked at the phone photos, all the pictures were of girls. Some girls in the club, some in his limos, some even in hotel rooms. Most of them were scantily dressed and looked like they had just stepped off of a video shoot. Some were just the average scalawag that he probably met at a club. They all were assigned to a phone number—she guessed so he could remember who was who when they called or he called them.

She was disgusted—he must have really been out there doing his thing. She knew he had some sort of black book, but this was at a totally different level. Then she had to ask herself, *Was I just one of those girls gone wrong?* She wasn't supposed to be anything more than a chick in his second phone, and now he was trapped because of her big belly. She checked and her number was in the phone, and it was assigned a speed dial number. Oh whee for her—she was top ten of the 113 entries. She was so pissed that he would dare have her in there, she was ready to barge into the bathroom. First she needed to calm down and get her facts straight. She then took the silver phone off the dresser and checked it. The contacts had family and friends' numbers, and a bunch of names she didn't recognize. She was in that phone as well. *Did I graduate to this phone, or was I always in both?* she wondered to herself. She looked in the pictures of the phone on the dresser and it had just a picture or two of his daughter.

Just before she was figuring out what she would say to Tony when he came out of the bathroom, something told her to check the call history. She looked in his silver phone, and the missed call that had just come in was from Jonelle. Then she looked in his ho phone, and surprisingly, the missed call was from the same number. Jonelle knew about the phone? That didn't make sense. If she knew about the phone, what was the secret? It couldn't just be for Dakota. Was he telling the truth that he and Jonelle weren't that serious? She heard the shower turn off, so real quickly, just for any future investigation, she dialed her cell phone with the ho phone so she would have the number in her caller ID. Then she jotted down Jonelle's number and put both the ho phone and the silver phone on the dresser. She purposely didn't put the blue phone back in his pocket. She wanted him to see it. She was ready for war.

He came out of the shower with his boxers on and the towel around his neck. At first she let him walk around the bedroom for a bit before she said anything.

"Jonelle called you on both your phones," she said as she lay calmly in the bed with the remote in her hand, flicking channels.

She saw him look at the dresser as he said, "What?"

Both phones were sitting on the dresser, and she could tell he was disconcerted.

He picked up both phones and looked in them. She couldn't tell what he was thinking because he hadn't said anything to her yet. It looked like he was checking the call histories on the phone, and he seemed a little stressed after he finished looking in the ho phone. He was probably verifying that Jonelle called both phones. He sat on the edge of the bed and it looked like he was checking his voice mail on the ho phone. She turned the television down some so she could try to hear; usually his volume was up high enough that you could hear through the earpiece. After he pushed a few buttons, she heard the voice of a female who didn't sound very happy. Tony's body language showed that he was clearly not his cool self.

He hung up the phone and looked at her. "Why were you in my pockets?" he asked with an attitude.

"The phone was vibrating—I didn't know what it was," she answered with an attitude right back.

"So?" he said.

She felt herself losing her calm. He had no room for argument, he was in her house, sleeping in her bed, with his penis inside of her almost every night, and was upset because she caught him trying to be a player.

"So, I went to see what it was. I didn't expect to find your ho phone," she said.

"This is my business line," he said.

"Tony, I looked through it. That is your ho phone."

"Why you going all through my shit?"

"Why you lying, is a *better* question."

He was obviously flustered, and it turned out he had double the stress to deal with. His phone was ringing, and when she caught her quick glance it was Jonelle calling the ho phone back. He didn't answer, and she sat in silence to see what he was going to do next. The other phone rang.

He went into the bathroom, and answered it. He didn't know that she already saw the Caller ID and knew exactly who it was. She had hawk eyes, and a superhero's smell and hearing these days. He tried to start off the conversation real nonchalant; then she heard him saying, "What phone? . . . That was my business line, I don't really use it anymore."

She must not have been buying it, either. What kind of luck was that? Both of us were finding out about the phone on the same night. He was getting it from both sides. She heard him trying to convince Jonelle that the phone was for people he didn't want to give his real number to and that he did business with. Business, all right—no-good business. She felt like starting up in the background, but she knew that when he was done copping pleas to her, she would have her turn. It sounded like it didn't work, whatever he was saying, because he seemed on edge through the whole conversation.

As soon as he hung up and came back into the bedroom, she looked at him and said, "Don't even try to sell me that bullshit."

"Dakota, please—not now," he said with his back turned to her.

"Not now? Then when? I don't care if your other woman just broke on you, too—that's what you get for not keeping your dick in your pants."

"No, you being pregnant is what I get for that."

Dakota stopped in her tracks. She couldn't believe he would say something like that. He glanced at her and caught a glimpse of her expression. Before Dakota could reply, Tony realized just how hurtful that was. He turned toward her and said, "I'm sorry, D . . . I didn't mean that."

She wanted to break, wanted to curse him the hell out—that hit her where it hurt. She was speechless. All she could do was shake her head and turn over.

"D, really, I didn't mean that."

She was tired of fighting, tired of needing, tired of lying to herself. She could have been the tough diva and cursed him out and kicked him out, or given the whole 'Kota-don't-play-that speech. What was the point, though? He knew like she did that it would only be a matter of time before she would move past it, just like she did every other time he disrespected her. Why did she even complain about the phone? Jonelle got the real lies—Dakota wasn't a priority to be saved from the hurt. Hell, he was on the phone with Jonelle in her place— who was she fooling? She used to feel the fact that she was more aware of what was going on, and he was more up front and honest with her made her more important. She told herself he cared more about her. Truth was, you lie to the ones you love to save them from the pain. The chicks that you don't care what they think, or if they get mad and walk, those are the ones you are honest with. What has this relationship come to, when she was lying in her bed wishing she was the special girl that could be lied to and kept in the dark?

89

Memories

Chrasey had started her car and checked her side mirror to make sure she could pull out. Her car was filthy dirty—she needed to go to the car wash. Instead, she was on her way to the supermarket, to pick up some things for dinner.

The kids were at home with Keith, and she drove down Farmers Boulevard and pulled up in front of the Bravo Super Market. She parked the car and went inside. She was still dressed from work—she didn't bother to change, other than to take off her heels and put on her sneakers. Her hair could have used a brush, and her already-scarce makeup was pretty much completely rubbed off. She didn't look a hot mess, but it was obvious that she just gone through the beating of a day's work.

She'd already loaded her cart with bread, fruit packs, and a value-pack of chips for the kids' lunches for the rest of the week and was headed toward the frozen aisle. She rolled her cart through the store, trying to maneuver her way through the other customers. It was near to closing time and everyone was trying to get their last purchases for dinner or tomorrow's breakfast. She made it to the frozen aisle and was reaching inside the refrigerator, getting frozen broccoli to make with tonight's dinner, when she felt a bump against the refrigerator door. She tried to glance through to give the person a dirty look, but she couldn't see through the foggy glass. She finished getting the broccoli and as she closed the door back, Trevor was standing on the other side.

"Trevor?" she said.

"Chrasey . . ." he said with a big smile.

She looked down and saw he was with his daughter. She was absolutely gorgeous, with the prettiest eyes.

"This must be your little princess," she said.

"Hi," she said in the shyest little-girl voice. She had reached for her daddy's hand, and he took her hand back. They looked at each other for a couple of seconds before either one of them said anything. It seemed that they were both happy to see each other, but it was also obvious that they were uneasy as well.

"You all rude, bumping into me and stuff," she said, trying to be natural.

"My bad," he said, somewhat laughing.

He looked down at his daughter to see how much attention she was paying to them. He probably wanted to say something but wanted to see if it was safe. Of course, it wasn't—she was looking straight into both of their faces.

"Let me let you get back to your shopping . . . I'll talk to you soon," she said as she put her broccoli in her cart and tried to give him sincere eye contact.

He gave her a sincere look back, and said, "Yeah, I'll give you a call later."

They walked their separate ways. She wondered if he could see it in her eyes, if her look conveyed her thoughts. It wasn't until seeing him at that very moment, that she saw it so clearly; she just wondered if he caught a glimpse of it. She missed him. She missed the days when he was the solution to her problems. Where, when things were really bad, she could go out with him somewhere. She guessed what she missed was the control—the control over her own happiness. He allowed her to have that, because she knew when she wanted, she had someone to "make it better." Now she was back in a life where she relied on Keith. Keith's mood, Keith's words, Keith's actions. If Keith felt like coming home and trying to make her happy, then she'd have a good night, but if he wasn't in the mood, she just had to wait and see what the next night brought. The even sadder part was that even Keith didn't have total control. Her love for him wasn't genuine enough anymore. That's why she missed Trevor, and the ability to control her life.

She had walked to the register after she picked up some juice, cooking oil, and packs of chicken. She looked over at the Entenmann's section, and man, did she want some, but her thing was not to have it in her house so she wouldn't crave it. She went to line 5 and waited behind a man and a lady in front of him. The other lines had at least three to four people and there were only two other lines open. She stood there glancing at the tabloids in the magazine rack when she heard a little girl's voice say, "Excuse me." She looked down and she was squeezing by her and the man in front of her. As she passed, Chrasey noticed it was Trevor's daughter. She stopped and stood by the woman who was ringing up. Then, just as it was registering, Chrasey looked up and Trevor was walking around to the other end of the line to wait. She looked at him and he looked at her, but they said nothing and made no facial expressions. They pretended for a moment that they didn't know each other. She looked at him, she looked at his daughter, and then she looked at the woman his daughter was standing with. She made sure that Trevor saw her eyes make these moves, so he would silently get that she was telling him that she got it. Luckily, his daughter didn't see her—she squirmed by them without looking up.

She couldn't get a real good look at the lady until she went to walk off. After she paid, she took some of the bags and their daughter's hand and walked a little farther from the cashier. Trevor moved from where he had been standing and grabbed the remaining bags and walked away behind her. She was a pretty woman—not hard to imagine, with the flawless looks of their daughter. She was about Chrasey's size, a little smaller, but a full-framed figure nonetheless. She was light-skinned, had long black hair with red streaks, and it looked like she had hazel eyes. They could have been contacts, but she was pulling them off real nice. Her nails and makeup game looked on point, along with her clothes. She was dressed fairly well, but just from her demeanor it was obvious she was a well-kept woman.

For about two seconds, Chrasey got jealous. She knew what type of man Trevor was, and she wished she had that attentive and caring man walking out of the Bravo Supermarket with her and her daughter. She waited for the man in front of her to finish ringing his stuff up as she watched Trevor leave. Then it was her turn to get her items rung up, and she looked down for a second to make sure everything was on the conveyer belt. As she looked back up, she saw Trevor looking back her way. He gave her a look at the last second before he was out of sight. She interpreted the look to say *sorry, wish this wasn't how we saw each other for the first time in a while. I wish it could be different.*

Chrasey got back home and went straight to the kitchen, put the couple of bags down, and went to check on the kids. She walked by Keith, who was sitting in the living room, and went up to the kids' bedroom.

"You guys finished your homework?" she asked. "You better be, since you in here playing."

They simultaneously answered "Yes," and went on playing.

"Well, before dinner I want to see it, and if anything is incomplete you're going to get it," she said as she went back downstairs.

She went back into the kitchen and started cooking dinner. She couldn't get Trevor off her mind. Seeing him, the memories of them, life with Keith now, everything Trevor knew from before, and everything he didn't know now. He left the door open for her to call when she was ready, but how would she just try to start things back up? Just call him now that she'd seen him in the store and pick up where they'd left off? It didn't matter, anyway, because she wasn't even supposed to be thinking about Trevor. She was working things out with Keith, and Trevor was going to make that hard to do.

She had finished prepping the food, and everything was frying, boiling, and baking when she sat down for a quick second. She picked up her cell phone to call Dakota and found she had a missed call in her phone. She hit VIEW to see who it was, and it was Trevor. He had called twenty minutes ago. She felt a skip in her heartbeat. Without even thinking, she hit CALL and started ringing his phone back. She felt herself getting nervous as the rings felt shorter and shorter. He picked up the phone.

"Hey, babe," he answered.

Just hearing him call her "babe" sent a chill through her. It was sincere pet-name calling, like from his heart. The rare times that Keith did it, she could tell it was phony and forced.

"Hey, Trev."

"Listen, Chrase . . ." he started. She heard in his tone that he was about to apologize for the supermarket.

"You don't have to say anything,"

"No, I do. That was crazy for me. I left there and dropped them off at home. I called to see if you could come out for a few moments and we could talk, but now I'm almost home."

"Oh, I had to start dinner anyway." For a moment she wondered, what if he had caught her when he called twenty minutes ago? Would she have tried to sneak away for a little bit? She knew she would have wanted to. She was happy that he didn't get her.

"I figured, but still, that was Trianna's mom. I was just taking her to get some things for the house," Trevor explained.

"I figured. Trianna is gorgeous," she said.

"Thanks."

"First of all, who am I to complain anyway?" Chrasey said.

"You're my future hopefully."

"Trev? Future?"

"Well, a part of it, I hope. I miss you, Chrasey."

"You say that now, until you start seeing somebody."

"I'm seeing someone now."

"What? You are?"

"Yeah, she is cool."

"So why you care about me?" she said with a slightly obvious attitude. She didn't want to be so obvious but a little 'tude appeared.

"It's not serious like that—it could be one day, but right now we are just chilling."

She tried to get her cool back; besides, she had to wrap up the phone call. She didn't want to push it and have Keith come walking in the kitchen and they have part two.

"Well, that's good to hear—don't want you giving up my seat," she said.

"Never," he replied.

"Well, listen, Trev, I gotta go. Food is gonna burn. I'll give you a call soon."

"OK," he said. "Don't be a stranger."

"You neither," she said.

They laughed a bit and then they hung up.

She went over to the stove to check on the food. She stirred, flipped, and poked some stuff and then went to get the seasoning salt. As she walked toward the spices, her cell phone rang again. It was Trevor. She answered the phone.

"Hello?"

"Chrasey, I meant it when I said I miss you."

"I miss you, too, Trevor . . . I really do," she said back. "But I really have to go."

He seemed happy to hear her say it back—he was happy that she didn't lie about it. She just hoped he knew how much she really meant it. Trevor lifted her spirits, he lifted her self-esteem. She felt ten years younger with Trevor—they'd gone out and had fun and she felt like she was enjoying life. There was no baggage with Trevor, no ugly memories, no deep feelings of hate and distrust. With Trevor, romance was possible, and she liked the idea of possibility.

90

Emotional High

Despite all the chaos that had been caused by Jayon and Jordan, it had been nice. She felt like she was on cloud nine. Everything just felt so right.

She never would have seen this side of him if she weren't separated from Omar. Never would have explored his qualities in that way. In a way, she should thank Omar. She had always done what would make everybody else happy in her life. She'd behave a certain way so her brother could be proud to say she was his little sister when they were growing up; she always tried to make her mom and dad proud of her, never cheated on her boyfriends so they wouldn't think of her as deceitful. It was the way she had been for so long. She couldn't recall a time when she said, *I don't care what anyone thinks.* When Omar would do things when they were in college that would really piss her off, her friends would try to understand why she was so faithful to him. Especially Dakota: *You are young—you only get these years one time around; save all of that grown-up stuff for when you're married,* she would say.

She had always put others before herself, because it allowed her to have a clear conscience. This was one of the only times she could think of that she had decided to let people think less of her, so that she could do what made her happy. Jayon was like a treat in her life. They would go on dates to places that he knew she had never gone. He would open the door for her when he picked her up. They went away for weekends and went on little dinner cruises around New

York City. Some of the time they spent together was doing some of the simplest things, but yet it felt so magical. It was like her own fairy tale.

When she was with Omar, by the time they got married they had been through their newlywed phase. They dated so long before he proposed, they had fought a million times and barely made it down the aisle. From day one of their marriage, she and Omar were just in a routine—they had lost their magic years before they got married. The last time she had felt undeniable happiness with Omar was about four years before their wedding. She had every intention on spending the rest of her life with Omar. Jayon and everyone who knew her knew that. They had their issues, and Omar had his share of slip-ups and lies. She worked through them all, but she hadn't quite regained the sparkle in her eye for him. So just the new feeling of dating again felt exciting. It had been years since she'd felt the feeling of floating on air with Omar.

Jordan and Jayon would just chill and watch movies, take Jason to the park and get on the rides, too; they would have picnics and play board games—she felt like a teenager again, except better. There were a lot of nights when they did absolutely nothing. They would just be in the same room but in their own worlds. She would be briefing a case or reviewing a contract, and he would be on the other side of the room with a calculator and paperwork. Although they weren't inter-acting, just having his presence in the room was all she needed.

Ever since she and Jayon had become more than friends, they'd gone out on a few double dates here and there with close friends of theirs and family. It was actually a little funny, because sometimes people would still make comments and treat them as if they were still just friends and colleagues. Some people would, understandably, forget that they had made the switch from time to time and bring up un-comfortable topics. One time one of Jayon's associates tried to hit on Jordan right in front of him—it was weird but she and Jay found it kind of humorous. So Jayon played along, saying things like, *Yeah, she is hot—right,* and *She just got back on the market.* Jordan could have killed him; instead she just laughed it off and declined the offer. She should have fixed his butt and taken the number and set a date, all while he stood and watched—then see how many more jokes he would have had. They had become used to that kind of stuff, though, people asking her about Omar right in front of Jayon, people bringing up old memories and girls that Jay wanted to bang, right in front of her. Jay's friends were the funniest—they had been used to her being just Jay's homie for so long, it took a little adjusting for them to treat her as his girlfriend now. Really, it seemed to be quite weird for a few of them. There was Linston, and Jalil, and then there was his friend Horatio, who she just loved. He was so cool and funny, and he was always the one to have a joke about her and Jayon's supposed friendship. He would say that they had been sneaking around on the low all of these years. It was funny how some of them hesitated to bring up hot girls on TV or chicks they dealt with without giving Jordan a look. She wanted them to behave just as they had around her for years—she was still Jay's homie at the end of the day.

She remembered the day that she realized what had her so stuck where she was. She remembered realizing for the first time that this relationship with Jayon was a breath of fresh air. They were sitting at Seafood City in City Island, and the sun was beaming down upon them. It was a beautiful day, and the first day in a long time that Jordan had found the time to put everything to the side and relax. It was she, Jayon, his brother Ramar, and his fiancée Veronica. The four of them hadn't hung out together in quite some time, and had planned to do this for weeks. When they were out with Ramar and Veronica, it felt like this was the way things were meant to be all along. The four of them talked about good times, love, relationships, and just the lighter side to life. They always had good conversations when they went out. It was normal for Veronica and Jordan to be on one side, Jayon and Ramar on the other. They had been doing this for years, and it was just that much funnier now that Jay and Jordan were an item.

"I never said that a guy can't be friends with a girl—I'm just saying to guys, ass is ass," Veronica defended.

They were in the middle of a friendly debate. Veronica and Ramar had a short friendship before they hooked up, so we were commenting on where the line was.

"You were checking for me first," Ramar responded.

"Whatever," she replied. "You guys just wait for us to get weak so you can pounce."

"That's not true. I was friends with this crazy chick for over a decade—she was always having some kind of emotional breakdown, and I never pounced on her," Jayon interjected.

"Shut up," Jordan said, slapping him on his leg.

"It's true, though. If I was waiting, I would have given up," he added.

"Well, maybe not literally waiting, but a female friend is not off limits in your mind," she said.

"Well, not in y'all's minds, either, 'cause y'all are right along with us when it goes down," Ramar added.

"That's when we are vulnerable, and we are usually blinded by all your evil plotting—we fall for the charm," Jordan added with a laugh.

"Please, don't even go there, because you wanted me since freshman year of college," Jayon said to her.

Everyone started laughing. "Whatever," she said, pushing him. "I was not . . . I was taken, and you took out your lawn chair and tent and started waiting in line ever since."

"Yeah, OK," he replied.

"From the day you came into the school bookstore to buy those aspirins, and I was working there and you sparked that long conversation with me—you were on a mission."

"OK. If that's the story that makes you sleep better at night," he said, laughing.

They sat outside for hours, drinking and talking. Jordan was on her third pina colada, Veronica on her fourth Miami Vice. Jayon and Ramar were on their fourth Strawberry Yaquiri, a strawberry daiquiri made with Hennessy, which was a new concoction they came up with that they thought was the best thing since sliced bread. There was this man playing his radio real loud by the bar, entertaining the Seafood City patrons with Latin music. The sun was setting and the view looking out onto the water was absolutely beautiful. Jordan just sat there, looking out at the beautiful scenery, and she thought to herself, *This is what life is about.* She had spent the past few years trying to be all that she could be, and hadn't stopped to smell the roses. She rarely spent days like this where she was able to stop and watch the sun set. The rare days she put work aside, she was trying to make up at home to her husband and son. Time for herself felt selfish. She was thankful to Jayon for reminding her of the true meaning of life. At that moment she felt guilty that she couldn't have had that with Omar—that's all he really wanted from her. With him, he became another aspect of her busy schedule; he was another responsibility, so it was hard to see it with him. With her son staying with Omar, and spending her time with Jayon, it was the first time she was really able to see. She liked what she saw.

91

Wake Up . . .
DREAM OVER

Things hadn't been the same since that night that Tony said that. He apologized a few times, and Dakota pretended to be cool. There was no erasing what he said, and maybe it was her raging hormones, but she was convinced he'd said that from the heart.

Tony didn't want to have to be a part of her life any more than she wanted to have to give up her shape and her freedom. He was going along, trying to do the right thing, but this baby was not something he wanted. She knew that early on, but she allowed his recent behavioral changes to cloud her vision. She guessed she really believed her having a boy was enough to make their dysfunctional relationship whole. Boy, was she wrong.

They spent the next week and a half going through the motions. Tony still stayed over three nights that week, but it wasn't the same. It was obvious his mind was somewhere else, and it was also pretty damn clear that Dakota had a slight attitude. She wasn't intentionally holding a grudge—it was just hard for her to forget about that night. The two phones, calling Jonelle, and then that comment. It was like the straw that broke the camel's back, except she internalized it. She hadn't yelled or cursed Tony out yet. She just made a mental note that made her heart that much less accessible to him—not that he was trying to get in. She knew that their set up wouldn't last. That the good times were over, her fantasy of what they could be, was now a harsh reality of what they actually were. Chances were when this baby was born, if they made it to then, they wouldn't deal with each other anymore. It would be just about the baby. She was fine with that, too, because she was just about fed up with Tony.

Dakota was lying in her bed and hadn't heard from Tony all day— she figured this was one of the nights he wouldn't be staying over. Lately she was actually happy to be alone. She was able to just lie out, look a hot mess, even be a little funky if she wanted to. She would just lay her oversized butt all over the bed—she didn't have to worry about lying in a position where her rolls weren't showing, or her legs didn't look too big. She was free to be her, all 180 pounds of her.

Lying down watching some old reruns of *Martin*, it just so happened that one of her favorite episodes was on. She was sitting up with her back against the cushion headboard, sipping hot cocoa. She did have a few calls that she needed to make to some clients, but she was feeling too lazy and decided to get to them later. She was right in the middle of a hearty laugh at this scene where Pam was hypnotized and she was imitating old Marty Mar, when her house phone rang. She was still mid-laugh when she answered without checking the Caller ID.

"Hello," she answered.

"Hello," the voice on the other end said.

Her smile immediately faded. It was a female voice, and she wasn't sure who it was, but she knew she didn't recognize the voice as a friendly one.

"Yeah, who is this?" she asked.

"This is Jonelle . . . listen, I'm not calling to argue. I just want to know if Tony is there."

Dakota hesitated for a few seconds, debating whether to be the evil bitch she could be and say yes just to piss her off, or be a real sister and let her know, no, girlfriend, tonight he is probably with chick number three. Instead she just replied, "No, Jonelle, he is not here."

"Is he supposed to be coming there?"

Now she was pushing it. Dakota was trying to be nice, but she could only be so nice. Still, she thought to herself, *once this baby is born, this woman and I are probably going to have so much in common we will be the best of friends. Let me be the bigger person.*

"I don't think so, not that I know of," she answered.

Jonelle paused for a second, then responded, "Are you telling the truth?"

OK, that was it. Did this chick not see that Dakota didn't owe her anything? She could have hung up on her or hurt her damn feelings, but she didn't. Then she is going to ask Dakota if she's lying.

"Jonelle, I don't have to lie to you . . . I don't even have to answer you. I'm trying to be nice, and you gonna imply I'm lying?"

"Nice? Nice? What is *nice* about you fucking my man?"

Oh, souky-souky now. No, she didn't go there. See, this is why we black sisters can't stick together.

"If he is your man, then why the hell you calling me, asking for him?"

"'Cause you trifling, money-hungry hoes can't just stay in your lane . . ."

"What?—First of all, I got my own got damn money, don't get me twisted with these other skanks your man been screwing around on you with! Secondly, what you fail to realize is you worried about the ho's he is with and ain't worried about him. We can't stay in our lane if he lets us drive where we want to go."

She was about to take this bitch to school.

"Whatever, but if you know he has a woman, why y'all dealing with him?"

"First of all, it ain't no 'y'all.' *I* deal with him because he is damn good in bed; secondly, I don't know he has a woman. He has a baby mother . . . and now there's two of us," Dakota asserted.

She knew she'd pissed Jonelle off with that, and that was her intention. *Don't be calling my house with this nonsense and think that it's going to go in your favor. Now, when I start playing myself making phone calls to people, then that's different, she thought to herself. Until then, I am still D.D., as they used to call me in college—Dakota Diva, and that won't change.*

"You're his baby mama, I'm his fiancée."

"Well, you need to get him a damn ring for his finger, because otherwise no one can tell, 'cause he damn sure don't admit to it."

Dakota could tell she was breaking her down. The good girl can't win in this situation. Dakota couldn't be hurt because she knew her place; Jonelle was fighting a losing battle. She was the one that had to find stuff out from Dakota; she was the one who was supposed to have him, but yet Dakota was having his child. At least she was able to know Tony for what he was. Jonelle was the one being deceived—well, a lot more than Dakota was. Then, at least for the moment, she was happy she wasn't the lied-to one, the one in the dark. It didn't seem so special now.

"Whatever, bitch . . . you know that he is engaged and you're just sloppy seconds."

"Well, now that I know, I'll let him know for you as well, so he can act accordingly—but I have to go now because I'm watching television. But I'll be sure to let your man know you're looking for him."

That was that.

She sat there feeling real good about herself for a minute. Like she was an outfielder for the Red Sox, and had just hit a home run against the Yankees, she was feeling herself. She went to call Jordan and Chrasey but neither answered her phone so she left them messages. She was tickled for a while after the hang-up, until she started to think about some of what Jonelle said. 'Sloppy seconds,' 'you're his baby mama—I'm his fiancée.' She didn't want to acknowledge it, but to an extent she had lowered herself to expect very little. The diva in her was supposed to demand enough respect that she would be married or at least engaged to the man she was pregnant by.

Dakota used to drop men like hot potatoes—they did one thing against regulation, and she was terminating their butts. She was just so fly, and she knew it, that she wasn't accepting less than best. Men knew that the opportunity to be with her was one of a lifetime, and if it wasn't treasured, then there was a problem. Cheating? Forget about it. Never would she tolerate such a thing. She wanted to be wined and dined, romanced and financed; she was a diva, dammit. That was cute in college and post-college, but after a while, as she got older, that D.D. thing wasn't working out the same. Men weren't wanting to hear all of that all of the time, and over time she didn't expect them to. She lowered her standards and started to accept more. She didn't plan it, it just started to happen. There came a time when she started to realize she was getting older, and if she ever wanted a shot at growing old with someone, she'd better act like she knew. She guessed she had come to that point unconsciously and unwillingly, but she was there.

Either way, if only a little bit, the old Dakota Diva still lived on, 'cause she made damn sure Jonelle regretted calling with that bullshit tonight.

92

Guilty Conscience

It was his birthday, September 6, and he was turning 34 years old today. This was the first September 6 that Jordan hadn't spent with him in fourteen years. She felt empty, guilty. Omar hadn't called her in months, and none of her calls mattered because he ignored them. She heard from his best friend, who told her that Omar was hurt and really pissed that she would choose another man over their marriage. He said that in his mind, she was dead to him. She didn't know what hurt more, the fact that he wanted her dead or knowing he had killed her himself.

She called anyway. To no surprise, he didn't answer. She left a quick, simple message: "Happy birthday Omar. I just wanted you to know that I am thinking about you on your birthday. I hope your day is happy—you deserve it."

She hung up the phone and hung her head low. She had been reduced to generic birthday calls with the man she was supposed to have spent the rest of her life with. Her life had become one big, emotional roller coaster. It had become almost impossible for her to be completely happy with Jayon when their relationship was riddled with guilt.

Everybody who knew them both seemed to wonder if Jayon and Jordan were having an affair all along. Family of Omar's just thought she was a complete whore bag, and even some of her friends felt that she gave Omar a bad deal. Then there were those who thought she and Jayon were like a fairy tale come true, and Omar was to blame for the marriage's demise and that she had every right to be happy. She didn't know what she felt anymore. Some days she felt like Omar should never have treated her so terribly and things would never have been able to change between her and Jayon. She couldn't help what her heart felt. Yes, she loved Omar with all her heart, but the pain and misery caused her to ward her feelings off to be able to get through what he was doing to her. It wasn't her fault that he waited until it was too late to come to his senses. As for Jayon, he was just being the friend he had always been. She believed in her heart that Jayon would never have disrespected her relationship with Omar, and that day last year when he was drunk at the office he truly did regret. Jayon was an honorable man and he, too, felt terrible about Omar. He had even told her once or twice that she should give Omar another chance, and he would understand and would have no hard feelings. It seemed like a kind offer, but it wasn't just about hurting Jayon. She didn't love Omar anymore in that way. He'd hurt her for the last time, and she was truly happy with Jayon. She wasn't putting her happiness second to Omar's on this one. She might forever regret it if she did.

93

Pot Calling the Kettle Black

Chrasey was waiting on a call from her supervisor—he was supposed to be giving her the outline for a meeting he'd called. So, as she prepared herself and the kids for the next day, she kept an ear out for the phone.

She had ironed the kids' clothes for tomorrow, made their lunches, given them their baths, and gotten them ready for bed. When she was done with them, she went ahead and looked for something for her to wear. She had to put a little more effort into it since they were having a meeting—she hated meetings because she always felt like she had nothing to wear. It didn't help that she gained some of her weight back—everything she put on, she felt fat in.

When she had just about finished, it was about 9:45, and still no call from her supervisor. She figured before she called him to see if he remembered, she'd check the Caller ID. She picked up the cordless and started to press the CALL HISTORY numbers. There was Dakota, Keith's mother, Jordan, bill collectors, her parents' house, but no supervisor. Just as she was getting past the calls of the last few hours and was about to go ahead and just call him, she pushed it one more time and the name Lourdes Vincent came up. She had called at 7:20 P.M., and Chrasey tried to think about it but, couldn't remember what Keith was doing at 7:20.

She could have handled it calmly and not said anything, but she wasn't in that kind of mood. Besides, she and Keith hadn't said but two things to each other since dinner. They were back in their old routine of being in two separate worlds. So just for the purpose of having something to say to him, she had some questions.

She walked downstairs into the living room where he was sitting as usual and sat down beside him with the phone in her hand. He looked over at her, unsuspecting of what she was doing there with him. Just as he went to turn back to the television, she started up.

"Did you speak to Lourdes today?"

She could tell the mention of her name startled him some. He was never prepared for her to bring it up.

"No," he said, "why?"

"Her number was in the Caller ID and I was wondering if you spoke with her."

"No, I didn't even know she called."

"Did you tell her I said not to be calling my house?"

"She knows that—she just . . . I don't know."

"Where were you at 7:20?"

"Right here, Chrasey—why?"

She could tell by the tone of his voice and the expression on his face, he wasn't feeling her line of questioning. He was trying to scare her off with the "you're frustrating me" look. The days that mattered were over—he shouldn't have cheated.

"That's the time she called, so I wanted to know what you were doing, since you say you missed the call."

"Oh, you thought I was lying then basically?"

"Just asked a question," she said.

"Don't worry—I'm not as careless as you, on the phone with some other man while my husband is right downstairs."

Chrasey guessed it was too good to be true. She had spent almost a year cheating on her husband and had gotten off totally scot-free because she found out about something much worse. What he had done had been so drastic that she got a "get out of jail free" card. Her first reaction to his comment was to stop so he couldn't try to give her a guilt trip. Until she thought about the facts: he had a baby outside of their marriage, and he was talking about careless.

"WHAT? You have to be joking . . . *you're* not careless? Not only were you careless enough to be on the phone while I was here, you were careless enough to leave months of proof on the bills, AND you were careless enough to get her knocked up."

"I didn't *leave* anything. I was using the phone in MY house, and just because you wanted to snoop through the bills . . ."

"YOUR house? This is OUR house and those were OUR bills! Your ass shouldn't have been on the phone with your mistress in OUR house."

"Well, you have some nerve, scrutinizing me like your shit don't stink."

"Well, your shit was smelling first, AND you went out and had a baby."

He paused for a second, and then he took a deep breath. She saw his shoulders rise and fall back down.

"Whatever, are you done? I'm trying to watch television," he said finally. She sucked her teeth as hard as she could and stood up. "I'm done because there is nothing else to discuss anyway—you're just going to lie."

"Yeah, Mrs. Honesty."

"Don't forget to call your baby mama back," she said as she walked up the stairs.

Damn, she was fuming, but she knew from prior arguments that when Keith got in that mode, he would be so ignorant and stubborn he would end up pissing her off even more.

When she reached her bedroom, she wanted to vent. She wondered why she ever thought this would work. Here they were, arguing over who was sloppier with their affairs. What had they come to? she wondered. And really, didn't they see how crazy they sounded. She didn't want that for them. No matter what they tried to do to fix it, their situations were going to follow them around forever. There was almost no sense even trying to make a happy home out of this. They needed to face the reality that they had lost a part of themselves, and now they were just married with kids. No affection, no trust, no love, no desire, no attraction—just married with kids.

94

Hide and Seek

Dakota hadn't been on Jamaica Avenue in years—the last time was to accompany Tony to do an autograph signing in one of the stores. The Coliseum used to be the place to be when you were in high school, there and Gertz Mall. Jamaica Avenue referred to a certain area of a main street in Queens. They sold sneakers, fitted hats, knock-off designer bags, hair weaves, name it; it was a one-stop shop. Her godsister Ebony told Dakota to come with her there because they had some really good sales on baby stuff at Children's World. Blankets, lamps, night lights, ceiling decorations, the stuff for the room décor. She wanted her to come choose some stuff that she liked so she could get it now, and then she would have her baby shower gift. At first Dakota thought that was tacky, but Ebony knew how picky she was and she said she would have to cut her if she didn't use her gift, so this was to save both of them some trouble.

They had parked their car on top of the Coliseum—it was far from their destination, but there's never a parking spot on the Avenue. They were headed down 165th Street, about to turn on Jamaica Avenue, when Dakota heard some girl call her name. She turned around and it was an old friend from high school, Nadia. She looked kind of different, but her face was exactly the same. She came up to Dakota and gave her a hug, and she introduced her to Ebony. It was kind of awkward because it had been so long, she didn't know what to say to this girl.

"So how's life been?" she asked.

"Pretty good—yourself?"

"Well, I'm a nurse trying to change careers. What are you doing?"

"I'm in PR."

"That sounds cool," she said as she reached her hand out to touch Dakota's stomach. "I see you're expecting a little one," she said.

She hated when people touched her stomach—some days she didn't mind, but mostly it felt so invasive.

"Yeah, I'm having a boy."

"How many months are you?"

"Six and a half."

"Wow, who's the father? Are you married?"

Why did she have to ask me that, am I married? she thought. *Did she see a ring on my finger?* She was so tired of people asking her who the father was or if she was marrying him, or other nosy questions. She felt sometimes that's just what they wanted, to make you feel bad.

"Tony Martin is the father, and no, we are not married."

She figured if she had to take the ho card for not being married, she'd have to name-drop. Tacky, but it was the only defense she had.

"*The* Tony Martin?" Nadia asked.

"Yeah," she said, kind of laughing. "We been on and off for a while."

"Wow—well, you go, girl."

After Nadia finished congratulating her on getting knocked up by big-time Tony Martin, they exchanged numbers and went on their way. She told Ebony when she walked off, if Nadia only knew the half, she wouldn't be congratulating her.

They finally made their way down to Children's World. The store was crowded with half of South Jamaica, Queens, pulling and grabbing at stuff. Dakota almost turned right back around at the sight of the chaos in the store, but she had come too far. Everything was scattered about, nothing was in order, clothes were mixed with toys, and the baby bedroom stuff was mixed with gift baskets. They were tearing the store up, and the staff was trying to keep up behind them to fix up.

She went ahead and chose some things for Ebony to get, and they waited on line. They were waiting there when a fight broke out between two women over a car seat. The dispute seemed to be that one woman had the car seat first, and when she put it down for a second, another lady picked it up. They went from talking loudly to scream-ing, and it was real close to blows before one of the ladies' friends stepped in. Dakota couldn't tell who was getting away with the seat, but she lost interest when she saw she wasn't going to see a catfight.

They finished with their purchase and headed back out into busy Jamaica Avenue. They were walking back toward 165th, and coming toward them, she got a glimpse of a familiar face. There, from behind a crowd of people walking toward them, was David. She immediately wished that she could have hidden or disappeared. She didn't want him to see her like this, with her belly sticking out the way it was. She hadn't spoken to David in about a month or so, and she didn't know what he was up to.

He approached her with a warm smile, almost like he was watching his child graduate from high school. She wasn't sure how to interpret the look he was giving her, but before she knew it, he was right in front of her. He reached down and gave her a hug and a kiss on the cheek.

"Hey there, mother-to-be," he said.

"Hey, Dave," she said, laughing off his greeting.

She introduced him to Ebony, asked him what he was doing on Jamaica Avenue, and what he was up to. He said he had to pay his phone bill, and he knew someone in the Sprint store who let him cut the line. Otherwise he said he had been working and doing the same old thing. She didn't get the feeling from him that her pregnancy bothered him. She started to wonder if she had created in her mind that David cared a lot more about her than he did. It was like she was thinking that the sight of seeing her pregnant would break his heart. She didn't know why she thought that, because David was standing there, just talking and laughing as if he was just fine. He made refer-ence to how cute she looked pregnant, and that he missed talking to her, but he seemed far from distraught. After a few minutes, they fi-nally said their good-bye's and went their separate ways. He promised that he would call sometime soon, and she was really hoping he would.

When they walked away, Ebony asked her, "Was that another Dakota doing? He is cute."

"Yeah, I've done the butt-naked dance with him quite a few times. There are still times I wish he was the baby's father."

They both laughed, but deep down she meant that. David was a good man, and she messed up with him for her no-good Tony. Some women just don't learn—they can have all of their priorities mixed up. It was a Saturday—if she didn't hear from David by tomorrow evening, she was calling him. She needed to get her starting players warmed up—in three months the season would be back in.

95

Man's Job

Was he out of his mind? Jordan thought to herself. Omar had called her and told her that he wanted custody of Jason.

"My child that I squeezed out of me in nine hours of labor, you want to take and keep at your apartment with you?" she asked.

"Yes, he is my child as well. Besides, he needs his father in his life."

"I worked hard so he could live in a nice house and have a good life, and you want him to come live with you?"

"You worked for him to have a nice house, but a good life would have come with a family environment, so save that shit you talking for your acceptance speech at the next law convention. I know better."

"You know what, Omar? I'm not arguing about this. My son has a great life, and I'm not willing to subject him to all of this change."

"Change—having you as his parent is the change. He is used to me. He doesn't care about that damn house. He is seven. He needs to be with me, the man in his life. If you think I'm gonna allow you and your punk-ass boyfriend to play family with my son, you must have forgotten who your husband is," he said, sounding a bit angry.

"Omar, no one is playing family. Jason is my son."

"Well he is not his, he is mine. Sorry you can't change that, too, but it is what it is. So, why don't you just stop thinking of yourself for a second, and think of Jason. He would rather live with his father than his mother and her new boyfriend."

"He doesn't live here—he is barely over here for that reason."

"Well, look at the bright side—you can have more time for you and your man. I'll give you a little time to think about it, but let's not make this any uglier, Jordan," he said, and he hung up.

Damn. She finally spoke to Omar, and that was all he had to say to her: *Give me my child.* He was through with her; now all he wanted was what meant the most to him. What he was asking her was crazy, and she didn't know what to think. Was she being selfish? Was it time to end this little charade and work things out before her child was put in the middle of this? Then again, who was he to just think he was calling shots? All of this had become such a battle between both sides of Jordan, it was confusing. Half of her felt like, of course you get back with Omar and work this out—really, how far along do you expect this to go with Jayon? The other half felt like she was representing all the women who had been done wrong. Men always think women won't get fed up and leave them, like they have to just deal with everything. She was proud that she was standing up for herself, and that she was choosing herself. Even if she didn't stay with Jayon, did she really want to subject herself to being with Omar, never knowing if she could be happy with him? He claimed he would change, but he has said that before. Not to mention that he couldn't just walk out and change his mind when he wanted to like he did. So, even if it meant making the biggest mistake of her life, she had to take her chances.

Jordan hoped that maybe one day she and Omar would work things out, maybe years from now when they were at a different place in their lives. She just couldn't do it right now, couldn't imagine life with Omar again. However, now that he was asking her to send him Jason, it was reminding her just how serious this whole thing was. Soon, they would have to address their shared property and stuff. She was thankful that they'd had enough of a decent relationship that they hadn't already started all that ugly stuff. However, now that Jason was an issue, she was sure it wasn't going to be long before the divorce papers would have to be drafted.

96

Too Much

She didn't know what it was today, but Chrasey came home with such a chip on her shoulder. It could have been PMS, since her period was coming, but she couldn't call it and it really didn't matter. All she knew was that she was not feeling the arrangement that she and Keith had made. She had committed to a life sentence of suffering. He tried to act like it didn't have to affect them, working their marriage out, but how was that? Every day that went by, she thought about it to some degree. She couldn't get it off her mind—it didn't help that anytime she saw a baby, she thought of it. Every time she heard of someone cheating, she thought of it; hell, every time she heard about Brooklyn, she thought of it.

Chrasey didn't quite get what made Keith stay—that only made it worse. She never felt like he was there because he wanted to be—she always felt like he thought it was more convenient. Possibly to save face with his family—maybe there was something about Lourdes that she didn't know, and most likely because he couldn't afford to be out on his own. You know what they say—it's cheaper to keep her. He already had three mouths to feed—not including his wife, because Chrasey could handle herself. If he had to pay for two households, he would be stressed out completely, because he couldn't even do one by himself. So, she wasn't sure if Keith had taken all of that into account and that was why he was staying home. Either way, he didn't act like he wanted to bet there.

She came in the door from a long day's work, and decided that she wasn't cooking dinner. She was going to make the kids some sandwiches, and Keith would have to handle it himself. She wasn't up for waiting on him hand and foot. If he didn't like it too bad—he should have gone out to dinner with Lourdes. That was another thing—she found herself trying to be this perfect wife at home, so she could feel like he had no room to complain. As a woman, she didn't want to feel she was the reason he'd left. Half the time it's nothing the woman did—these men just don't know how to behave. The sad part is, most of the time it's for a woman that doesn't even compare to the woman they have.

When the kids finished eating their sandwiches, Chrasey went upstairs for a bit to relax. She figured she would get up and get the kids ready for bed shortly, but for the moment she was just letting them play in the bedroom. While she was sitting on the bed, watching television, Keith came home. He came up to the bedroom and asked about dinner. She wanted to laugh at him, or tell him where he could go. Instead, she went to the deeper issue.

"Keith, I don't think I can do this . . ."

"What?" he asked.

"I don't think I can do this, Keith . . . this . . . our marriage... I really don't know if it's possible to repair what we have broken."

She could see in Keith's face that this isn't what he wanted to hear. Not in an *I'm not in the mood* way, but in a *please don't say this* way.

"Chrasey, we haven't even been trying that long—it's going to take time."

"How much time, Keith? Time to heal the pain? Time to learn how to not think about it every day? What kind of time you talking?"

"Chrasey, we both have to deal with some things. If we just stick together, we can do it."

"Keith, those marriage-counselor lines don't work for everyone. Forgiving and forgetting are two different things, and trust will never live here again."

Keith sat down on the bed behind her. Their backs were facing each other, so he couldn't see her and she couldn't see him.

"And I'm not sure I want to live like that," she said.

Keith got up, came to where she was on the bed, and pulled her into him and held her.

"I will do whatever it takes, Chrasey. I will let Lourdes know that I will not be in their lives . . . I will send some money in the mail and that's it. I will erase them from my life."

"Keith, that's the thing—that's impossible."

"No, it's not. You'll never find a toy in my backseat, you'll never see her number in the Caller ID, we will change the house number . . . we will move on."

"Keith, why? Why do you want to work this out?"

He looked at her, surprised that she asked, it seemed. He held her face and looked her right in the eyes, and said, "Because I love you."

She moved her face so she didn't have to look into his eyes anymore. He let go of her face.

"There is no other reason, Chrasey, I promise you. I just want to grow old together like we planned, and I'm willing to do what I can to fix it."

"I need time to think about it all. Can we talk about it later?"

He looked like he wanted to say something else, but instead he just shook his head and went toward the door.

Chrasey didn't know what to do. She didn't feel ready to alter her entire life any more than it had been, and leave her husband. She also wasn't ready to settle for the life she was leading. She thought about what Keith offered to do with Lourdes and the baby. It didn't sound like a bad idea, but then again, that was probably kind of evil. For her to request such a thing would probably be wrong. At the end of the day, it wasn't the kid's fault, and that would affect her more than anyone else. It may upset Lourdes because she wanted to try to create a false reality with Keith, but it would really hurt the girl. Chrasey wasn't sure if she could live with herself if she demanded that he do that. She wished he would have just left his dick in his pants.

97

Trying to Tell Me
Something

The doctor had told Dakota to take it easy—her iron was low, and they didn't want any complications. These past few weeks had been emotionally draining enough without adding something else. All the fighting with Tony was stressful, and she didn't go on maternity leave for another two months. Tony had offered to pay all the bills at one point so she could stay home and relax, but Dakota couldn't afford to lose her job and not have one after the baby was born. Tony probably just made that offer because of his ego, to flaunt his status. Any baller doesn't like to have his woman or baby mother working.

Today when Dakota woke up, she was having a very emotional day. All her confidence had been lowered, all of her security erased. Deep down, she knew that a good black woman was hard to find, but that consisted of more than a good job and nice body. She knew she had her claim to a few one-night stands, and not-so-good-girl situations. She remembered all her dirt that she had done, and it all began to make her feel like she wasn't any prize to begin with. She kept thinking that any man would rather have a good girl with high morals that he could bring home to his mother and be proud. After she thought about it all, she definitely didn't like the feeling of vulnerability. After about a half an hour of sulking, she figured, why stress out over things you can't control? She started to make herself feel better by thinking how men would die for the freak in her. She knew that women couldn't buy what she had naturally, her sex appeal.

She also had her share of emotional nights, and she looked forward to this baby coming so she could get her life back, or what was left of it. She couldn't imagine how her love life would be if Tony wasn't a major factor in it. She also thought how that's why the fight for Tony wasn't worth it—he was like her last hope. She usually didn't call him to tell him to come over. Tonight she did, though.

"What are you doing?" she asked.

"At Ron's—what's up? You OK?"

"Yeah, I'm fine."

"Cool, what's up?"

"Can I have you tonight?"

Tony started to laugh. "Yeah, I'll be by there in about two hours."

"OK, come over with some energy."

He laughed again. "What your pregnant behind going to do?"

"You don't worry about that—under all circumstances, I'm always on point," she said.

"All right," he said. "I'll be there."

Laughing, she added, "And this little boy can't stop my head game."

Laughing even more, he said, "Scratch that—I'll be there in half an hour."

"No, take your time—I'll be here," she said.

After she hung up, she put the Best of Aretha Franklin in her CD player, and went into the bathroom. She took a nice, silky bath with her Bath & Body Sweet Pea Shower Gel, and relaxed some, thinking about all the new things she wanted to try on Tony. When she got out the bath, she started to lotion up and spray her good smells on. Then she put on her "Vicky Secrets" pink-and-black teddy that she never wore, and lay out on her bed and waited for Tony to come home.

Upon the sight of her sitting in her bed with her bulging belly, she couldn't help but laugh at herself. Still, even with her belly, she looked hot. She watched some television while she waited. She wasn't sure if he would be early or late, and she said she wouldn't call unless he was extremely late. She doubted that he would be late—he hadn't done that in a while. That was one thing she was happy about—it had been a while since she had waited in her bed for hours for Tony.

About fifteen minutes went by and Dakota's phone rang. She looked in the Caller ID—it was David. She hadn't spoken to him since she saw him on Jamaica Avenue that day. He never did call, and she never found the nerve to call him because she didn't know what to say.

"Hello," she answered.

"Hey," he said.

"For what do I deserve this?" she asked.

"I meant to call you the other day, but I have just been so crazy with work and I wanted to give you my undivided attention."

"Awww . . . well, that's fine. So what's going on?"

"It was good seeing you."

"You, too"

"I wish we could get together one night—I'm not sure what your situation is."

She felt like saying, *I don't have one. That's why I'm lying here in bed, trying to be a personal prostitute so he can see my worth and give me a situation.*

"Well, you know I'm having a baby—that's a situation. Other than that, I'm not married, engaged, or barely seeing anyone. I don't know if it's a good idea to get together, though."

"Why not?" he asked.

"David, I'm pregnant."

"If you don't mind, I don't mind."

She couldn't believe he was saying it didn't bother him that she was bearing a child that wasn't his.

"I don't mind—I just wasn't sure if it would be appropriate."

"Listen, 'Kota, I've known you too long for that. That could just as easily have been my child. If the father doesn't mind you seeing me, then I would like to see you."

She was lying down in a teddy waiting on one man, and had another trying to see her. Now, this was the Dakota she had missed, and she was thankful to David for giving her the opportunity to feel like her old self again. She told him they could get together real soon, and suggested they shoot for the weekend. He agreed and they hung up.

No more than ten minutes later, Tony showed up. She wasn't as enthused to give him all she had, mainly because she realized she didn't have to. Also maybe because she was reminded that he didn't deserve it.

98

Man Up

All of Jason's stuff was packed up and in Jordan's trunk, and she was in the car waiting for him to buckle up before she pulled out of the driveway.

"Mommy, why do your eyes look like that? Were you crying, Mommy?" he asked her.

"No, I'm just tired, baby," she replied.

"Are you going to be OK by yourself until I get back home from Daddy's?"

"Yes, I will be just fine. You will be back home in a couple of days, actually. You will still be coming home quite often, OK?"

"OK."

"Are you happy to be spending more time at Daddy's house?" she asked.

"Yeah, I missed Daddy."

A tear fell from her eye. She was driving down the Southern State Expressway, on her way to drop her child off at his father's. She was a disgrace to mothers everywhere. Here she had the opportunity to keep her family together and not put her child through this torment, and she chose not to. Jason deserved both of his parents under one roof. Here she was, taking away his chances at having an American picket-fence upbringing. Was it about time she started seeing this for what it was and stopped blaming Omar? But he was the one who walked away. He was the one who exposed Jason to dysfunction by disappearing for those months; he was the one who always put himself first. He taught her. Still, at the end of the day, it was her decision that led to this. To Jason being manipulated into believing he was going to stay with his father because Mommy had several business trips and didn't want him going back and forth.

She had been over this a million times in her head, and it never seemed to be clear. She was torn over this more than she should have been. The outcome always led to her sticking with her initial decision. She just felt like she was being broken down every time she had to face the situation head-on. She was on her way, and it was probably the hardest thing she ever had to do. As hard it was, she had to agree with Omar that there were some things that a woman just couldn't teach a man. To get through it, she remembered that this was best for Jason, and there was no guarantee it was permanent. Maybe she would forgive Omar and fall back in love with him, and then they would all learn a valuable lesson and live happily ever after. If not, then she would adjust as they went along.

She looked in her rearview mirror, and glanced at Jason. He was sitting in the backseat, looking like an angel, staring out of the window, just watching the streets go by. He was happy. Happy to be alive, happy to be young and free, happy to have two parents who loved him so. For that she was happy, too. Omar could have not wanted Jason— it could have been just the opposite. There was a bright side to it all— she and Omar may have been failing at their marriage but they hadn't failed yet at parenthood. She just hoped she wasn't by agreeing to let him have Jason.

99

Long Overdue

Chrasey stepped into her car, and dropped all of her bags in the passenger seat. She was so beat from work. Things had been really tough these days—she was definitely earning her money. She sat in the seat for an extra minute or so just to catch her breath and relax. Keith was picking up the kids today, so at least she was able to go straight home. She reached in her purse to see if Keith had called, hoping he didn't because she didn't want to hear about any problems.

When she looked in her phone, she had three missed calls, one from Dakota and two from Trevor. She and Trevor hadn't spoken since the last time he called—she wondered what he wanted. She also noticed she had two messages, so she went ahead and checked those. The first two messages were old; then she heard a message from Dakota telling her to call so that she can tell me about Tony and David. Then the next message was from Trevor.

"Hey Chrase . . . it's me. I was thinking about you ever since I saw you in the store that day. I know what you're doing, and although I commend it, I just think we shouldn't throw away what we had, either. There are times that I wish that we'd met ten years earlier so I could have been the one. I swear I would have valued the honor . . . either way, I hope you can consider picking things up where we left off. I would try my best to make every day better than the last. Think about it, and give me a call."

Chrasey missed those sweet sayings, and promises for the future.

She also hadn't had any in quite some time, and just the slight memory of what Trevor was like in bed was enough to get her going. She dialed his number back without knowing what she was going to say. He answered, they chatted for a while. Before she knew it, she had plans to meet him at the hotel on Parsons and Kew Gardens Road.

It was all happening so fast, but before long she was pulling up in the driveway of the KewG Hotel. She had parked the car, and was waiting for Trevor to arrive. In less than ten minutes, Trevor pulled into the parking lot as well. She heard his music from her car, and had to think to herself, what was she doing? Trevor was very mature for his age, but every now and then she would be reminded that he was still practically a kid. Having his 50 Cent CD blasting from the car was just one example. Because of his age, she would question dealing with him—until they were in bed.

When she saw him, she got out of her car. They walked up to each other and hugged, figuring they would save the kisses for later. They went inside the lobby, Trevor paid for the room, and they got their room number and key. In the elevator, Trevor noticed Chrasey's discomfort and asked her if she was sure she wanted to be there. Chrasey assured him that she was, and asked him not to ask her again or she might change her mind.

They got into the hotel room, and Chrasey put her purse down on the chair by the desk. She sat on the bed and looked around. Before she could look back to see what Trevor was doing, he had knelt down between her legs. She looked startled and started to smile. He smiled back and started kissing her lips and caressing her breasts. After they had gotten well acquainted again with each other's tongue, Trevor started lifting Chrasey's skirt. Once he'd exposed enough of her lower area, he placed his face between her legs and started to kiss and lick around her inner thighs. Just the tender touch of his lips between her legs was driving her crazy and he hadn't even licked her spot yet. When he did, she dropped her body backwards on the bed. It was clear that Chrasey hadn't had some good stuff in a while, and once Trevor noticed that, he was more than happy to give her a taste.

He drove her wild with circular motions with his tongue for ten minutes straight—he wasn't stopping until he heard her orgasm. Her body lay limp on the bed, grasping the sheets for mercy. Through faint breaths, she begged him not to stop. She was eager to feel him inside of her, but she couldn't get enough of his foreplay. She squirmed and moaned as Trevor changed the motions he was making with his tongue and added a slight sucking to it; before he could pick up a rhythm with it, he heard Chrasey moan loudly as her body spasmed four consecutive times. He didn't stop immediately, just slowed down as her body relaxed itself.

Trevor wasn't done with her. He slowly climbed on top of her and immediately inserted himself. The first stroke, he pushed as far back as he could, and back out. He continued in this motion until he watched Chrasey's face reflect her pleasure. He wasn't trying to come yet—he wanted at least one more orgasm out of her before he had his. He pumped and stroked until he watched her face changing expressions, felt her nails scratching his back and her body pushing hard up against his. She wanted him, all of him. She didn't put herself back in this situation not to enjoy every inch of him. He leaned his body slightly to one side, putting all of his weight on his left side, and started to enter her at an angle. Chrasey's back arched as she answered each stroke with a pump of her own. After about five more minutes of Trevor's switching up, Chrasey had another orgasm. Now Trevor was happy, and he was ready for part three.

He told her to turn around, as he moved up on his knees. He wanted to enter her from behind and get some back shots—it was well deserved and Chrasey obliged.

After his performance they lay there for a few minutes, sweaty and tired.

"I miss that," Chrasey said.

"Mmmm . . . he misses that, too."

They both laughed. Chrasey wanted to suggest that they pick up where they'd left off. That she was going to stay with her husband, but she needed Trevor in her life. She just wasn't ready yet, she wasn't ready to decide what she wanted to do with her marriage. She did know that this wouldn't be the last she saw of Trevor, or he of her.

100

Change of Plans

"Jordan, I'm at the hospital with Dakota—she had a miscarriage." Jordan was sitting at her desk when she received the call. She took no time running out of her office, getting in her car, and driving to Bellevue Hospital. The only information she took the time to get was which hospital, where they were, and if Dakota was all right. As she drove east on the LIE, tears began to stream down her face. She knew the pain Dakota felt—she had become so attached to that child growing inside of her.

They had all just gone to Pottery Barn Kids this past weekend to sign up for their registry for her baby shower that was coming up next month. Jordan tried to imagine what she would say to Dakota, how she could remain strong for her friend. Jordan was the emotional wreck of the bunch. She was the one who couldn't hold a tear to save her life; they still didn't know how she managed to be a top attorney. The reason was, Jordan loved a good debate, a good argument—she loved analyzing facts and breaking down what made sense and what didn't. So when it came to her career, she was, no joke, made of stone; but when it came to life-and-death issues, Jordan was a bowl of mush.

Once inside Bellevue, Jordan asked the receptionist for her visitor's pass. She waited at the elevator and resolved to be strong. "I'm not going to cry," she told herself over and over. Once she got off at the seventh floor, she looked for room 714. She walked slowly, trying to hold on to each extra moment she had before she had to face Dakota and the gloom that was in her room.

She stepped into 714, and there was Tony, Chrasey, and Dakota's brother, Daniel. Faces of forced normalcy was all she saw. She walked by everyone, giving silent hellos, and went straight to Dakotas's bedside. Dakota had her back to the door, lying on her side in a crunched position, and she hadn't seen Jordan walk in. She walked around the bed and stood in front of Dakota. As soon as their gaze met their eyes filled with tears. It was one of those emotional moments when all it took was the slightest human contact to trigger tears. Jordan bent over and hugged Dakota, and within moments she could feel her shake with hurt.

It was evident that everyone was trying to remain natural in an uncomfortable situation. As they saw the emotional meeting between Jordan and Dakota, a few others sniffled, Chrasey mainly. She went into the bathroom to regain her composure. It was hard to tell what Tony was feeling, but it was obvious that he was saddened by it. Maybe his mind had scanned over the positive aspects of this, but it looked like he was just as distraught as Dakota.

The doctor said that they weren't sure why it happened. It could have been stress, her previous abortions, or her low iron. She had been going to all of her prenatal doctor appointments, and other than the slight iron problem, there was nothing that indicated this would happen. Eventually, Jordan went to the bathroom as well, got herself together, and came back out with some tissue for Dakota. Then everyone was just sitting back around again.

Dakota had to stay in the hospital overnight because the baby was so far along, there were a lot of medical issues they had to tend to. She was just lying there, seeming numb to everything. She wasn't speaking or making much eye contact with anyone in the room. A few times Tony went over to her bedside and rubbed her forehead or leg, showing some type of affection. She noticed, she appreciated it, but it just wasn't enough. She needed a lot more than affection at this point, and not one person in that room could give her what she wanted—only God could give it back.

101

Lean on Me

Jordan was spending most of her time with Dakota, and she hadn't gone to work in days. She was feeling weird at home without her son, and to make matters worse she and Jayon were starting to plateau. Their honeymoon phase was over—they had made their way back to the "friend zone." They were still involved, but the cutesy couple they had become started to settle for that comfortable complacency that comes with time. Since they had been friends fo so long, they had gotten to it a lot quicker than most.

They had just had a dispute, and although it was a minor disagreement, Jordan was wondering if it was an example of what was happening to them. She was at his place because she couldn't bear being alone at her house since Dakota's miscarriage. Prior to her arrival, he had made plans with some of his boys, so when she got there he was getting dressed. He was getting ready to head out, and she was working on some case briefings in the bedroom. As he got ready to leave, he asked her not to answer his phone. She thought she was dreaming—she couldn't believe he had the nerve to tell her that. She wasn't sure if she should lash out, remain calm and just get her shit and bounce right after he left, or try not to get upset at all. The latter wasn't an option—she was too damn offended.

"What do you mean, *don't answer your phone?*"

He noticed from her tone alone that she wasn't pleased with his request, let alone dropping her pen and what she was working on to give him a direct stare.

"No, J, I'm just saying let the voice mail get it so I don't miss any calls."

"Don't give me that, Jayon. I am a grown woman and I know how to take messages—that's not why you said that. If you feel uncomfortable with me being here while you're gone, I'll go."

"Jordan, you can stay here."

"If you have to ask me not to answer your phone, then I'm misunderstanding some things and I'd rather just go," she said as she started to gather her things.

"Jordan, let's not make a big deal out of this. You are welcome to stay here—I will be back in a few hours and we can make love all night," he said, trying to repair the damage with humor.

It was too late, though. Her mind was made up. She knew why he said that—she'd had a slight feeling that Jayon still had some lingering "friends" that he hadn't gotten rid of yet. One time she'd been out with his sister, and while she was drunk she mentioned some other females that Jayon still had as acquaintances. So Jordan already had some suspicions, but she didn't want to become a jealous girlfriend. She had been a married woman for fourteen years; hell, she still was, and to go back several steps to jealous girlfriend status was not where she wanted to be. Still, she wasn't going to be the stupid, getting-played girlfriend, either.

Jayon tried to stop her, but to no avail. She was leaving, she needed to. Being in Jayon's apartment wasn't the answer, either. Maybe that was her problem—maybe she needed to be alone and just feared it more than anything else. If she could have just dealt with spending a year alone, without Omar, maybe when he came around they could have saved their marriage. Maybe she wouldn't have been so torn about making a decision.

She was out the door before Jayon could leave. He tried to get her to change her mind, but she was too emotional to have to sit there and have the one person she thought was on her side treat her like an outsider.

"J, please don't go, sweetie. I didn't mean it like that."

"It's fine, Jayon—go out. Maybe I'll come back over when you're home."

She walked out of his door, down to her X5, and sat in her Jeep and regrouped. Surprisingly, she didn't cry. After she took a deep breath, she just started her car and pulled off.

As she drove down the street, she realized she wasn't prepared for this. She wasn't prepared for the bad times between her and Jayon. She was used to him being her comforter and friend—she had no idea what it felt like to have him as the person causing her pain. There it was again—she had to wonder if she had made a mistake. She had thought things with Jayon were going to be so much better than life with her husband. She had a few reasons to question it before but had ignored them. For example, Jayon could be very irresponsible. He would go out at times with his friends and drink way more than he should have, and then drive home. He would usually wait a while or until he felt that he was up for it, but it still made her very upset that he was so careless. She remembered when they were friends she used to say that she couldn't date him because he risked his life too much with his drinking fun. It didn't make much of a difference, though, because even as his friend it worried her sick. The thought of something happening to him was hard for her even to contemplate. But now that they were together, it was that much scarier. What if she got remarried one day to Jay, and they had kids, and lost him to something so reckless she would be sad and mad at him at the same time?

Jordan was just beginning to realize that things she thought she could overlook became harder to deal with. Jayon still went out a lot, even though he should have outgrown that phase. He wasn't very communicative about deep issues. He was always so cool and calm that it was hard to really have adult conversation. He was the quiet guy at the dinner table all the time. There were times when they didn't have much to talk about, and she had to do most of the talking.

At first she thought she liked the fact that Jayon was calm and kept his cool. When she used to compare him to Omar, she thought she loved the serenity between her and Jay. Now that time had gone by, she sometimes missed Omar's spunk. It made their relationship more exciting. He was quicker to argue or voice his opinion, and let someone know what was on his mind. Jayon was always passive and calm, even with her. She had become concerned that his demeanor might become boring to her.

With Omar, when things were good, he talked. He asked questions. They cared about the same things, same favorite sports teams, same favorite boxers, and same favorite television shows. It was funny, now that they weren't together, she finally became aware of his qualities.

That's how it always goes, though—that's why they say you don't miss a good thing until it's gone. Not that she missed Omar—that wasn't it. She'd just learned that you have to love the one you're with. No one is perfect.

As these thoughts passed through her mind, she began to realize that it also applied to Jayon as well. She had to love him and everything about him, good or bad. The thing was that she did—she loved Jayon even deeper than a normal love because of their friendship. she knew him in every dimension, so their foundation was perfect. She just needed to know that Jayon was serious about their future together, and from time to time he didn't show it.

Her worst nightmare would be things not working out between her and her best friend. Nights like tonight, it seemed that much more a possibility.

102

Rock-A-Bye Baby

It had been three weeks since the miscarriage, and Dakota was just starting to get back to herself. She decided to go back to work and spent fewer of her nights curled up in a ball, crying, and more of them lying out, watching television. At first she planned on taking a month of her maternity leave, anyway, just so she could take some time to cope with her loss. She changed her mind when the days were getting longer, and she realized that she needed to stay busy.

After the miscarriage, Dakota had spent the first week and a half in the bed unable to eat, sleep, and barely wash. It was definitely a state of depression, but it was the kind that made everyone that cared worry about her safety. She wouldn't answer her calls half the time, and she was very particular about who visited her and when. Everyone close to her understood—she had been so excited about the life that had been growing inside of her; she finally was going to have her own little someone. The miscarriage was so sudden—it was like a huge brick had just crushed the life out of her. It wasn't as if she was having a high-risk pregnancy, it just happened. It happened and Dakota was definitely not prepared to handle it. Her depression came from guilt, too; although the doctor wasn't sure, she said it was possibly due to her previously terminated pregnancies. This only added to her emotional stress.

With a few more days to cry her heart out and have her friends help her get through, she was feeling a little better. Every now and then she still had moments when she felt upset. She still hadn't put away all the baby books and the items she had already purchased. She was coping better, and was able to actually be at home alone and feel fine. The first week or so, when she was really depressed, Chrasey and Jordan had spent more time at her house than ever before. Taking turns practically spending the night, making sure she was barely left alone. Tony had been by a few times, but it was obvious he didn't know what to say or do. He wanted to try to console her, but he didn't know how. His presence just depressed Dakota most of the time, because he was a reminder of what she'd lost. She also knew that without the baby, it would only be a matter of time before he would start back his old ways. So as his visits got shorter and farther in between, she welcomed his behavior. She preferred it to be what it was rather than what it was going to be.

Dakota wasn't only suffering the loss of the baby, she was coping with the loss of Tony. She had mixed feelings about losing him, though, because she knew she never really had him to begin with. When she first came home after losing the baby, Tony was there for her. Her first night back from the hospital, they both cried together—that was probably the most emotional night they'd ever experienced. It was cool until the first night that he didn't come over, when Dakota started to build resentment. Inside, she blamed Tony for the miscarriage as well because she knew that dealing with him caused unnecessary stress, and she was becoming more and more distant toward him.

Last Saturday night Jordan and Chrasey had come over to Dakota's house. They brought martini mixes and games. They sat up in Dakota's living room, having a revival. Drinking, laughing, watching movies, and playing games. The neighbors had to think there was a huge party going on with all the noise and laughter, but it was just the three of them having themselves a good old time. They were cranking ex-boyfriends and old college friends that they no longer talked to. They were just acting like they did in their younger days. It had been years since they were able to just let loose and act like wild college kids again, and it felt great, even if just for the moment. So as they got drunk with their frozen fruity drinks, they got silly and they got happy. It was meant to be therapy for Dakota, but it was a resurrection for all three of them. They needed each other, and when it was hard to verbalize what exactly they needed, actions always spoke louder than words. They just needed each other—no men, no children, no jobs, no responsibilities, and no drama. Just each other, like they were back in college. They sat there until about four in the morning, having their own little private party, and it was just what Dakota needed. It was just what all of them needed.

103

Pain and Pleasure

Keith tried to console Chrasey as she went through her own slight depression over Dakotas's loss. Chrasey came home from work and went right back out to Dakota's house. There were a few nights when Jordan told her to stay with her family—and that she'd do it. Those nights, Chrasey spent with her kids, thankful that she had them in her life. You don't remember what a blessing your children are until you meet somebody who loses theirs, or someone who can't have them.

Chrasey had spoken to Trevor twice since the last time they met up—he had called a few times, but she was usually with Dakota and she didn't want to take the calls. She did want to continue to see Trevor, but she just wasn't ready to lead that life again.

She had discussed with Jordan, now that Jordan could understand, her dilemma with Trevor. She didn't want to bother Dakota with it; she mentioned it on their girls' night out but not much because that was Dakota's time. Jordan's opinion was still that Chrasey should work things out with Keith. She said she shouldn't give up on the marriage while they were still trying to work it out. She said she'd given up when he *wasn't* trying to work it out, but Jordan said that Chrasey still had hope this time around. However, Jordan did say if Trevor was the one giving her good loving and making her days brighter, to keep him in the picture. That was what Chrasey had in mind, anyway—she just wanted to scale it down. She wasn't trying to be going out on dates and talking to him daily like before. She just didn't know how to tell Trevor she wanted him only when she needed some, and for an occasional talk.

Trevor had explained to Chrasey that he was dating someone, but that's all it was. He said even though Chrasey was married, if he could have what they had before, he would be cool with that. He said he knew that Keith wasn't going to be able to keep her happy and he wanted to be there, next in line, for when those days came. As sweet as that was to Chrasey, a piece of her hoped that Trevor would give up on her so she wouldn't have the temptation.

She also hoped that things with Keith could be better so she wouldn't give in to temptation. Things at home with Keith were cool—they had their good days and their bad days, but the typical days with minimal conversation were the majority. Chrasey didn't want to just settle for minimal; she was still young and had her whole life ahead of her. When she got married, she envisioned a life of fun days and nights at home, family vacations, kinky, spontaneous sex, visiting friends, etc. She was aware that the sex fades and the fun fades and all of that, but not this soon. They were only in their early thirties and had lost so much of their spunk, it was a shame.

She was aware that their outside distractions didn't help, but their lifestyle was still at an abnormal low. They weren't doing anything together—they weren't going anywhere, and Chrasey didn't know what Keith was doing for sexual pleasure. Plus, they barely talked to one another. The most they did was play a game together here and there, and that was their effort at making it work. She'd tried everything in the past—now it was Keith's turn. She felt that after what he did, it was his turn to fix things. She was tired of trying. He didn't have much time, though, because before long she would be regularly giving in to temptations.

104

One Day

Checking her answering machine messages, it wasn't hard for Jordan to figure out who left this one particular message. When she was back in college, one of her favorite CDs was Deborah Cox's debut album. Many of her close friends in college knew it, but only Omar would've done this. On her answering machine, she heard the words to one of the album cuts called "You Don't Miss Me Now." As she listened to the message, she heard the words, *One day you'll be walking down the street, and you'll see someone and she will look a lot like me, and you'll think about someone you left behind and it will make you cry. One day you'll wonder why you ever said good-bye, you will wish you were still right here by my side, but I won't be around . . . you don't miss me now, but one day you will.*

As she sat on the edge of her bed, listening to each and every word of the selected part of the song, tears began to roll down her face. Before she knew it, she was crying uncontrollably. She had no time to prepare for this emotional message, and she didn't even know for sure if it was Omar. She knew that it had to be, though, and even if it wasn't, he was who she thought of. Not only because who else would leave the words to that song, but when they'd first started dating, they would leave lyrics on each other's answering machines, especially when they were fighting. Lyrics that expressed the way they felt at the time or about each other. They hadn't done this in years, many years, but it had been one of their things, so she knew it was him.

She wiped her tears enough to see the phone, and dialed Omar's number. After the fourth ring, his answering machine picked up. She listened to his outgoing message—it had been a while since she'd heard his voice, and it was emotional hearing it. Once the recording was done, it took a few seconds before it beeped.

"I miss you now," she said. She paused and then hung up.

She lay back on her bed with tears rolling down her face, wondering what she had done. It had been great with Jayon—it truly had—but it seemed like not a day went by that she didn't worry about her other life that she'd left behind. It definitely didn't help when Jayon would say something or behave in a way to make her wonder if she could look forward to a future with him. She had to think—she'd had all of this. A relationship with a future, a perfect home and life, but she just couldn't make it work. She was just as wrong as she'd felt Omar had been.

Then she wondered if she really meant it when she'd said on Omar's answering machine that she missed him now, if she really meant it. She did miss him. She missed their in-depth knowledge of each other. She missed their life taking care of Jason, and all the memories they had. She even missed his masculine ways, the ones that used to drive her crazy. The way, at the drop of a hat, he would jump to her or his defense if anybody disrespected one of them. The way he would just tell it like it is; he used to call himself "the truth," because he was always keeping it real, as he put it. There were a lot of his great qualities that she'd taken for granted, too. Like, she never realized how he knew just how how to keep her appeased. He was always taking them out to dinner or a movie, or some carnival or arcade that was in town. He would bring home movies or a new game, he would just do the simple stuff that he knew she liked. It was simple for him, and meant a lot to her. She didn't realize it then, but now she saw those were the things that had kept them together for so long. He was never done courting her, even after all those years. She did miss him, and it wasn't until she heard that song, though, that she realized how much.

Jordan wanted to call Jayon and talk to him—she just needed to talk to someone who would understand, and he knew every detail of everything. However, she realized that there were just some things she was better off discussing with Jay when she wasn't emotional. She didn't want to make him feel like he wasn't doing a good job of keeping her happy, because he was. Enough of a good job to get her in this predicament. The amazing part about Jayon was that he always understood this wouldn't be easy, so he understood that she would have these doubts and fears.

After that night at Jayon's apartment when he asked her not to answer his phone, they hadn't been one hundred percent the same. They had just lost their innocence and were starting to experience the downside of being more than friends. They'd had some incidents here and there, but nothing really serious.

Instead, she called Chrasey.

"Chrasey, I don't know what to do," she whined.

"What's wrong now, drama queen?" she asked.

Jordan told her about the message, what the song was, and that she thought Omar left it, and why.

"Girl, of course that was Omar, and he's probably trying to let you know something," Chrasey replied.

"I know, but I'm just starting to have second thoughts and it's scary."

"About leaving Omar? Or about starting things with Jayon?"

"Both," she answered. "I feel so low about myself sometimes, and other days I feel on top of the world. Then I'm afraid when Jayon and I start having problems, I will realize that Omar deserved another chance."

"Jordan, you gave Omar more than enough chances. Since college, you gave Omar chances. He almost lost you before you were engaged, he almost lost you when he got caught in all those lies, and he almost lost you all those times he wanted to play games and take those stupid breaks. This time he lost you. He never learned. He still, after six years of marriage, was pulling that taking a break without talking about it. He took it too far, which was his fault."

"I know, but he was my husband. Even though I know he was dead wrong, and even though I know that Jayon has been just what I needed and I wanted these past months, I am just starting to wonder if I gave up too soon."

"Maybe you did, Jordan, but don't go having regrets now. You were under pressure from work *and* home, and Omar didn't take one minute to think about you and what you had to deal with."

"But you know what, Chrasey? I'm realizing he was right. I should have put more time into my home.

Chrasey heard the cracking in her voice, and she knew that Jordan was emotional and meant every word of what she was saying. Jordan could tell she didn't know what to say, because like her, she and Dakota always thought her decision was a little life-altering, and they all hoped it would work out for the best. There was fear, though, fear that it could all turn out wrong. It wasn't as if Omar was a bad guy— he was faithful, to her knowledge—and he was a good father and husband. Since he was a young adult, he had wanted the family he never had, and Jordan guessed she had ruined his picture-perfect vision of what it was supposed to be like. Omar just lacked sensitivity. He wasn't able to be soft when it was needed, but he was always hard, the way he grew up thinking a man should be. He was all man, she could say that. It's what turned her on to him. She loved his machismo, and his ability to stand strong in the roughest situations. He made her stronger, even strong enough to finally leave him. She had been spending life, happy and strong enough to know she deserved it, but like the message said, she hadn't missed him then but one day she probably would.

105

Too Late

Keith and Chrasey had been working at their marriage for quite some time now. It just seemed like they couldn't get it together. Things were just as they were before they decided to reconcile. She didn't know what Keith was doing outside of the house, whether he was still seeing Lourdes or not. She just knew that they weren't happy at home, either. There was too much on the table at this point. Betrayal, anger, pain, a little bit of everything that goes wrong in a relationship. They discussed counseling, but Keith pulled the "he didn't believe in some person telling us what to do" card. If there was one thing she knew, that was if both parties don't go willingly, it won't work. She wasn't wasting her time and money—all Keith would do is try to make the point that it wasn't working. So they just left things as they were.

It just seemed that they had exhausted their relationship. She was to the point where she didn't care for Keith the same way. Through all of that turmoil with him, finding out about the baby and stuff, her focus was on her family and trying to work things out. However, just the fact that she drifted back into bed with Trevor was proof to her that Keith had lost her. He may not have lost her physically, but he surely had lost her mentally and emotionally.

Chrasey was kind of thankful that Trevor was still around. The flowers, and the calls, and all the sweet messages. It was always just a matter of time before she would need that again. It kind of hurt that her husband couldn't compete with Trevor. He didn't even attempt to do half the things that Trevor did. She was sure he wondered if Trevor was still around, just as she wondered about Lourdes, but Keith didn't even try to find out. He didn't attempt to keep her away. It was like he just let Trevor creep right back into the picture. To Chrasey, it didn't even feel like he would have cared if he *did* know.

It didn't matter to her, either. She was back in the tangled web she had woven. She just knew this time around she had to handle it better. She knew in her heart that if she didn't have somebody on the side, she would have been even more miserable. Suffering from her own thoughts, her own suspicions, and her own fears. Chrasey knew she deserved better, so she was going to have to give herself something better, rather Trevor was going to have to.

106

Rise and Shine

The sunlight from the window had done enough dancing on Jordan's face. She could no longer attempt to sleep some of the day away. She opened her eyes slowly, and tried to focus on Jayon's room. His television was turned to the ESPN channel, and the cable box said 11:31.

He wasn't lying beside her, but she could hear noise in the next room, so she knew he hadn't left her alone in his apartment.

She stretched and yawned, and got herself together to get out of the bed. Ever since she was a little girl and Mommy would wake her up for school, she hated the morning time. So once her sleep and dream ended, the first moments after were usually miserable. Once she pulled the covers back, she realized she had no underwear, the result of last night's fun with Jayon. She pulled her body from under the covers and out of the bed, and walked over to his boxer drawer to get a pair to throw on to cover her behind; she still had a wifebeater on, so her top was covered. She slowly pulled a pair of his blue-and-white boxers on and made her way to the door.

She walked down the hall and she could hear Jayon was in the kitchen. She stood in the doorway, and as soon as she was in sight, all eyes were on her. Sitting at the table was Jayon along with his mother and father. She was flushed with embarrassment—if she'd been white, she would have turned red for sure.

Mrs. Mitchell said, "Hi, Jordan. How are you, sweetie?"

"I'm fine," she said as she walked in the kitchen to give her and Mr. Mitchell a kiss.

She wanted to reach over and choke Jayon. Why couldn't he come in the bedroom and tell her they were there so she wouldn't walk into this awkward moment?

"Hey, baby," Jayon said as she walked back past him without giving him a kiss or any acknowledgment.

"Hey—why didn't you tell me your parents were coming? I would have made breakfast."

"They just stopped by—they were in the area, so I warmed up some croissants and . . ."

"Yeah, we are fine," Mrs. Mitchell interrupted.

Everyone seemed to try to ignore the fact that Jordan was very inappropriately dressed. Her wife beater didn't hide the fact that she was wearing no bra, and Jayon's boxers were not exactly what she would want to be seen in, especially not by Jayon's parents. She wanted to just disappear. So, she did.

"I will be right back," she said as she walked out of the kitchen.

Jayon could read her embarrassment all over her face, and followed behind her. By the time she reached the bedroom, he was there.

"I'm sorry, baby."

"Sorry. I practically came in there with my butt hanging out."

"I know—I didn't think. They weren't here long. I didn't get a chance to come tell you. Besides, I wasn't sure when the sleeping beauty would awaken."

"Don't be funny, Jay. You know what they're thinking."

"J. They already know we are seeing each other now, and since we are both adults, they may assume you sleep in my bed sometimes, and that maybe every now and then you don't make it to the morning time with all the same articles of clothing on."

"Don't be funny, Jay—this is so embarrassing for me."

"I know, and I'm sorry, sweetie," Jayon said as he sat beside her and hugged her.

"Look at the bright side—all of your body parts were covered. It could have been worse, because that's not how I left you."

"Ha, ha, ha . . ." she said sarcastically. "Go back out there before they think you came to get a quickie."

"Can I?" Jay said.

"Get out of here, " she said, pushing him toward the door.

As he laughed his way out, she sat there trying to shake off the embarrassment. She had loved Jayon's parents since they were in college. From the first time she met his mom, she had always made her feel like she approved of her and Jayon. Whatever relationship they did or would ever have. She always treated Jordan like family, and she fell in love with her early on. She was just one of the nicest women she knew. His dad was the same—real cool and caring, too. They were the cutest couple. They had been happily married for thirty years, and they were great role models for young couples.

Jayon knew she'd always loved and respected his parents, so he probably did know how much them seeing her like that would bother Jordan. It was even more uncomfortable because they had known her as a good friend of Jayon's, not as a romantic partner. So, she knew that scene in the kitchen took everyone aback.

She also knew she had to get back out there at some point. She scanned the room for her underwear and clothing and finally saw her orange-and-pink spotted thong by the head of the bed. She grabbed them, her bra from the floor, and her clothes from the chair and went into the bathroom.

When she came out, she was dressed the way she had been when she'd come over last night. Her hair and makeup were not quite the same, but her clothes were no longer indecent. She wore a brown jogging suit and sneakers, her usual comfortable weekend outfit.

She walked back into the kitchen and made it clear that she was about to head out by dangling her keys in her hand.

"Baby, where are you going?" Jayon said immediately when he saw her dressed with her purse and keys in hand.

"I have to head out. I have some errands to run and things like that. I will be back by later."

"Are we still going over to Jamel's house?"

"Yeah, I will be back by then. If he is still having his party, we can go."

Jordan had already begun giving kisses to his parents and saying good-bye by the time she walked up to him and said, "Just call me."

"OK, let me walk you out," he said, obviously wanting a moment more to pick her brain.

She said good-bye once again and walked toward the door. Once they hit the hallway, he pulled her arm.

"What's wrong with you?" he asked.

"Nothing—I have to run, really."

"You know damn well you wouldn't be running out of here so early any other morning."

"I won't lie—I'm not up for sitting around feeling embarrassed, but I'm not upset."

"My parents don't care. They have known you for years, and they have seen you in bathing suits and pajamas several times when we were even younger. Do you really think, as two grown people, you being slightly undressed in MY apartment, they are going to judge you?"

"Jay, you look at everything that way. It's just a respect thing, OK? I'm supposed to be a married woman and a friend of yours. So I'm just a little embarrassed for them to see us like this," she said.

"You're making too much of it."

"I'm not. I really just want to end the whole moment and go take care of some of my errands. Now get back in there before they think you're getting another quickie," she said with a laugh.

As he laughed her joke off, he said, "Listen, please don't go into one of your feeling-guilty-about-everything phases. It's nothing. My parents are actually happy we are seeing each other. They don't know all the details about you and Omar, but I don't think they care," he said.

"Can you just give me a little bit? I'll be cool."

He walked from in front of her, and opened the door. She leaned in, gave him a kiss, and walked out the door.

As she walked down the hallway to the elevator, she started thinking, *Of course they care about Omar*. He was her husband for six years—everyone wonders what's going on. No matter what the situation is, they're thinking, now she's with Jayon, and she and Omar didn't even finalize the divorce papers yet.

When she sat down in her car, she picked up her phone and called Omar. The phone rang three times, and, as usual, it went to voice mail.

107

Worth a Shot

Dakota decided to just go ahead and have a talk with Tony. It was about time to figure out where things were going with them. She was tired of playing the guessing game.

Jonelle had called earlier in the day and was all hyped up, telling Dakota that she and Tony had set a wedding date and she wanted Dakota to leave him alone. Dakota entertained her for a while, but as Jonelle became more upset, Dakota decided to end the conversation.

"You need to be talking to your fiancé, not me," Dakota told her. Dakota had only been with Tony three times in the last two weeks, but she wasn't gonna tell Jonelle that. She also didn't have it in her to argue and fight. As much as she wanted to say, *Forget it, you won, you can have him—now, you and his sorry ass leave me alone,* she couldn't bring herself to lose. She had been battling too long, to be willing to lose yet another fight. So as far as Jonelle was concerned, Dakota wasn't going anywhere.

She couldn't even tell from her conversation with Jonelle if she knew about the loss of the baby yet. Knowing her, if she did, she would have thrown it in her face. So, chances were Tony hadn't gotten around to telling her yet, or although very unlikely, even Jonelle knew that was a low blow. She ended the conversation with Jonelle quickly—she didn't want to have to think of lies to make her mad and there wasn't much truth to tell. She only saw Tony once in the past week, and spoke to him maybe two or three times. The even crazier part was, Dakota didn't mind. She had been talking to David a lot more these days, and he even took her to lunch one day just to get her mind off things.

Dakota still wanted to talk to Tony—she wasn't willing to deal with Jonelle for the rest of her life, and just over some good sex. Sex that she hadn't had with Tony but once since the miscarriage. Dakota felt it was obvious that Jonelle just had it in for her, because of all the ladies that were in his phone, and all the other women she was sure Jonelle knew about. She was threatened the most by Dakota, but neither Jonelle nor Dakota knew to what extent Tony had other relationships.

"What does this mean for us?" Dakota asked Tony.

He had made his way to Dakota's house, and they were sitting in the living room in front of the television.

"What do you mean?"

"Now that there is no baby—should we just leave each other alone? Take this as an opportunity to start fresh?" Dakota asked, getting straight to the point.

"The baby wasn't why we were together," Tony said, clearly surprised where she was taking things.

"It wasn't why we got together, but it kept us together these past few months."

"I don't agree—I'm fine with things the way they are."

"That's the problem—you can probably be fine with this forever . . . even after you and Jonelle are married."

Tony didn't respond. For the first time, he didn't deny or defend it. He was silently admitting that it was true, that he was supposed to marry Jonelle.

"So, if we have two different long-term goals, maybe we should think about what we are doing," she continued.

"Dakota, I know we have had some problems here and there, but I care a lot about you and I would like us to continue seeing each other."

Dakota realized that Tony was probably not going to let her go that easy. He didn't care enough about her to make her wifey, but he still wanted her on the roster. The thing was, Dakota was tired of playing games.

108

For Life

It was about 8:00 P.M., and Jordan was just getting home from work. Jayon and Elizabeth were both out of the office that day, and she'd had a pretty busy day there alone. As she was driving up to her house, she realized that some of her lights were on. She didn't know for sure, but she figured she'd left some lights on when she'd left the house earlier. She parked her Jeep, got her stuff out of the backseat, and walked up to her door.

When she walked in her house, the living room lights were on, and the rest of them were off. She couldn't tell if the motion sensor had turned the light on in the kitchen or if it was already on. She left them all on, figuring she would be going back downstairs when she was done changing. She walked upstairs to her bedroom and kicked her beige Jimmy Choo shoes off and put her beige Hermès bag on the chair. She removed the clip from her hair, letting her hair fall. She started to scratch her head vigorously—it felt so good to loosen her hair after it had been tied up so tight all day. Then she started to remove her jewelry when she heard a noise. When she turned around, Omar was standing there. He was just standing dead smack in the middle of her doorway. From the look on his face, he wasn't very happy.

She looked at him, and instantly she knew something wasn't right.

"Omar, what are you doing here? And where is Jason?"

"You don't care where Jason is," he said.

"Are you OK, Omar?" she asked.

"Am I OK? Are *you* OK?"

"I'm fine—just a little surprised to see you here."

She was trying to remain calm because she could tell that Omar was not there for a friendly visit. She never changed the locks on the door because she never felt there was a need to. She never thought Omar even wanted to come over, let alone pop up unexpectedly.

"Where's your boyfriend?"

"Omar . . . where is Jason?"

"He is with my mother—where's your boyfriend?"

She didn't want to answer that question, so she just continued to remove her jewelry. Her heart was beating a hundred times per minutes—she didn't know what was going on. She was supposed to be happy to see Omar—she hadn't seen him in months. He always had someone drop Jason off and he was never home when she came to get him. She had been wanting to have a grown-up conversation or see Omar and just give him a hug for a long time, but now that the opportunity was here, it didn't seem like the time.

"Are you having sex with him?" Omar asked out of nowhere.

"Excuse me?" she asked.

"Don't fucking play deaf! ARE YOU HAVING SEX WITH HIM?"

Omar was not himself, and he seemed to be pissed off about something. Unfortunately, it was a surprise to her because she didn't know what.

"No, I'm not," she said, not looking at him.

"You're a lying bitch, you know that . . ."

From his response, she could tell that this wasn't going anywhere good. Omar was probably drunk and angry. She tried to calm him down, but he was just yelling and being really crazy and upset.

"Did you let another man inside of you Jordan?"

"No."

"Don't lie to me."

"Why are you doing this, Omar? Since when do you care?"

"Don't play stupid with me—we have been together fourteen years! Don't give me that, *I didn't think you cared* shit . . . did you sleep with him?"

"You and I weren't together," she said.

"Not together? Not together? You see this right here?" Omar struggled to get his wedding ring off his finger.

"'Til death do us part, remember?" he said, and he threw the ring at her. She was already on the verge of tears when he first started asking her, but when he threw the ring, she crumbled into sobs.

"Answer me, Jordan—did you let some man go inside my wife?"

She just cried—she couldn't get words out of her mouth.

He knew the truth. He knew deep down, and he was reacting from the truth that he already knew and really couldn't bear to hear.

He let out a loud noise and punched the wall. "I don't believe this shit! You're gonna answer my damn question," he said as he approached her quickly.

"Lie down," he said.

"What?"

"You heard me, lie down!"

"Omar, no. Please—just go," she said with tears running down her face.

"Jordan—lay your ass down!"

He gave her a look she had never seen in Omar's eyes before. In all the years she'd known this man, this wasn't the Omar she knew. She felt fear. Omar was at a point of rage she had never seen in him before, and she didn't know what he would do. She laid down to keep from infuriating him any further.

He began to remove her pants and it felt like a dream, or rather, a nightmare. In her mind she thought she was doubting that he could possibly be doing what it seemed he was doing—until she felt him remove her panties. Her body was tense, and she had curled her legs up, trying to make it harder for him, but it just made him rougher. She cried and asked him to stop. He said he wanted to see if someone else had had sex with her. He began to probe inside of her as he asked, "Did you let someone else in here? Tell me the truth, Jordan! I just want to know the damn truth!" he said, sounding like a crazed madman.

"Omar, stop! Please stop," she begged as tears rolled down her face.

"Not until you tell me the truth," he replied.

Finally, her weak body and broken spirit said, "Yes! . . . Yes, I did."

"Yes?" he said, surprised, as he paused.

"Yes," she repeated through her sobs.

"You slept with him?" he asked as if he needed to verify what she had said.

"Yes, I slept with him."

She felt his body tense up, as he reached and put his arm around her neck and started to choke her. "You let another man inside of you, Jordan?"

She tried to remove his arms from around her neck. He just continued yelling, "How could you, you fucking whore? After all these years, you do this to me—you sleep with your so-called fucking best friend."

As he loosened up on her neck slightly, just enough for her to wheeze some air, he started to pull his self out of his pants. It almost felt like it was all not really happening, someone was going to pinch her at any moment and wake her up. She could smell the liquor on his breath, but didn't recognize the look in his eyes.

He had removed his hands from around her neck, and he started having sex with her. She said nothing. Her spirit was broken and she was afraid.

"I am your husband. You were supposed to have sex with me, no other man. But you had to run out and be a whore—you just couldn't be alone—right, Jordan?"

He asked her this as he repeatedly thrust his manhood inside her worn-down body. She had stopped trying. She just lay there, waiting for this torture to be over.

Her cell phone rang, and it was attached to her pants buckle that he had just removed and still had on the bed. Omar grabbed it, and looked in the Caller ID. It was Jayon.

"What the fuck do you want with my wife, Jayon?" he said as he answered the phone.

"Omar?"

"Yeah, Omar. What do you want? I'm in the middle of making love to my wife—she can't talk right now."

Then he hung up.

She probably should have screamed, yelled for help, but she didn't have it in her. She didn't want to piss Omar off any more, and she didn't want to involve Jayon. This was her mess—nobody else should have to deal with the consequences.

Omar continued on as if that awkward phone call didn't even occur. He was getting his revenge on her and Jayon. Making her feel like a slut, and trying to show Jayon that he had control.

She just lay there, waiting for it to be over and to be able to run to Jayon so he could console her and make it all better. She didn't know how he would feel, knowing Omar had been back inside of her. She just cried. What had she done?

"Whose is this?" Omar asked her.

When he saw she wasn't replying, he pulled her hair real hard and then put his hand back around her throat and repeated the question.

"Whose is this?"

"Yours," she said. "All yours."

A few strokes later, he ejaculated. He didn't even pull out—he came inside of her with no regard.

"That's right, mine. And don't you ever forget it," he said as he got up from the bed and fixed his pants.

She didn't get up until she heard him walk down the stairs and out of the door.

109

About That Time

No one could believe it, and Jordan couldn't quite tell it.
The night it happened she called only Jayon and her mother.
Jayon came right over, and her mother wanted to as well. Jordan told
her Jayon was with her, and she didn't want her to let her dad know,
so she should stay home. She put the bolt lock on the door, reset the
password, and put the alarm on. She wasn't scared of the Omar she
knew, but she was of the Omar who had just left her house.

Jayon was very upset, and although she was sure he had a million
thoughts and questions, he just lay with her in the bed, letting her cry.
It was hard for him, because at the end of the day, Omar was her husband. It was almost understandable what he was going through. She
believed that it was the liquor. She knew Omar was going to wake up
the next day pretending to be oblivious to what he did, and just say he
was sorry.

Which he did, the very next day at about noon. When he called,
she didn't answer—she was home with Jayon. They had both taken
the day off. Omar left a message apologizing.

*"I can't even believe what I am remembering about last night. I'm hoping
some of it is not real. If even any of it really happened last night—PLEASE
call me. I AM so sorry, J. I would've never wanted to hurt you, physically or
emotionally. I want to come over there but I know you don't want to see me.
Please call me!"*

She was angry and hurt. She felt invaded and disrespected—he made her feel like a slut. It felt crazy to be feeling this way, when Omar was still her husband. Technically, this *was* still his. He just handled everything so terribly, and although she knew he was under the influence, it was no excuse.

She knew she could send Omar to jail over this, but she didn't want to. Chrasey and Dakota were pissed off, but they understood why she didn't want to take it there. Her mother told her to call the cops, get his black behind put in jail. She had to explain to her and Jayon that he is the father of her child—why would she want to do that to her son? These were her and his father's problems—they would have to resolve them without hurting Jason. He would never forgive her. Besides, a piece of her knew that was Omar's pain surfacing. She knew, because hers surfaced periodically, and she knew how it felt to just want to do something, or to change things. Last night was just Omar trying to feel in control again. He had called three times today—this was the man who wouldn't take her calls, so it was clear he knew he had messed up. He was probably worried she was going to press charges, and she was sure he really felt bad about what he did.

Dakota was telling her how thankful she should be that she was on the pill. The last thing Jordan wanted was to get pregnant and not know who the daddy was. That was before she told her she wasn't on the pill. She had been on and off of them, trying to find the right one for her, and this month she was off. Dakota didn't even have a response to that information. They wanted to call Jordan silly and stupid for taking those risks. She explained to them that she and Jayon were careful and barely sleeping together; she wasn't expecting to be raped.

She didn't bother to call Omar back until late that next day; he was home and answered her call immediately. First, he let her talk to Jason, as if that would remind her of their big picture. She missed her baby, and it was great to hear his voice. She didn't want to have an emotional breakdown on the phone with him, so she hurried and asked to speak to Omar. She didn't even argue or yell or anything— she remained very calm. He asked her some questions, and she answered calmly. He apologized over and over, and explained he had come over to talk, and when he was there, he saw pictures of Jayon and he got upset. He had already been drinking, but while he waited he had a drink or two from their bar. He said he never intended to get that drunk, and never intended to argue with her or hurt her.

Omar was never violent like that—not toward her at least. She believed he didn't mean to do what he did. Still, it was done, and this buried them even more. As much as he didn't mean it, would he understand what it felt like to be ungently finger-fucked or forced to have sex while you're hysterically crying? He wouldn't, and every time she remembered it, it would be his face and his liquored breath she would remember. Not something that was going to be forgotten. So she just told him not to worry, she wasn't pressing charges, and she made sure he knew it had a lot to do with Jason. She also told him that the divorce papers would be in the mail the next day. He asked her once not to do that, and repeated that he was sorry. She told him one more time to look out for the papers, sign them, and send them back. Then she ended the phone call.

More than anything she just wanted to put last night behind her and out of her memory.

110

Second Chance

Dakota didn't want to be so pessimistic.

She wasn't sure if the reason David was looking so good to her was because she was just trying to find someone to fill the void. She didn't want to be the woman who always needed someone in her bed to feel whole. She just found herself more intrigued by him than she had been for the three years she had known him.

He was on his way over to make dinner, and she was reluctant to have him over because she wasn't sure if she was ready for anything intimate. He had assured her, that he just wanted to come over and make her a meal and to make her feel better. It didn't really matter, because she wasn't ready. Her vagina hadn't been tended to in over a month, but as much as she wanted some attention, her emotions wouldn't allow her to get involved. She was still a little disturbed from the miscarriage, and was still trying to deal with the decision to leave Tony's sorry ass the hell alone.

It hadn't been an easy couple of months. Luckily, she had her girls to make it all better; they had been by almost every day, making sure she didn't slip into depression. They cooked dinner for her, brought her favorite desserts, shared movie nights. It was these past couple of months that reminded Dakota why they were truly the sisters she never had. Even Jordan, with her crazy, busy life, found time to come by regularly to do whatever she could. She loved those girls. Chrasey and Jordan were the best, and she didn't know what she would have done without them. Tony surely wasn't any help—the little he did wasn't enough. He tried to come over, do some sweet things, bring food and stuff like that. The thing was, he couldn't be with her all the time; he couldn't be there the way she needed him. The fact was, whether he would deny it or not, he had Jonelle at home and there weren't but so many unspoken-for hours in his day. He tried to make Dakota feel like a priority, but at this point, reality was harsher than ever. She knew the truth and it hurt, so just hearing the lies wasn't enough anymore. He didn't realize that, but it was becoming real obvious to her.

David never left her side through it all. She knew, even when things were good with Tony, that David would always be there. He dealt with other girls, too, but she always knew that he would be there when she needed him. He had been trying to become more than what he was to her for quite some time, but she was too silly to value that. At one point it used to annoy her, his sweet-talking and his persistency, trying to get her to settle down with him. Now she realized what she had been missing the whole time. David cared about her for her, and she didn't know how to appreciate that. She was too busy chasing Tony to realize what she had right within her reach. A good, handsome, responsible man with a good job and he wanted to settle down. David must have known it was only a matter of time before she would appreciate him, because he stuck around long enough to give her the chance to.

It was 8:37 when she heard the knock at her door. She muted her television, scooted off the bed, glanced in the mirror, and walked toward the door. For some reason, she had butterflies in her stomach. She didn't know if it was fear or curiosity, she just knew that for some reason she was not comfortable with this visit quite yet. Once she opened the door, David was standing there with a picnic basket and a flower. That was his thing—he always seemed to bring her a single rose whenever he was coming over. It became his signature, and for the first time she really noticed it. He handed her the rose as he said, "Hello, Dakota."

"Hey, David," she said as she cleared the doorway for him to walk inside. As he passed by her, he gave her a kiss on the cheek and continued toward the kitchen. She closed the door behind him, and followed him.

"So how are you feeling?" he asked while he walked by.

"I'm pretty good. Thanks for asking."

As they reached the kitchen, he placed the basket down, turned to her and scooped her in his arms.

"You don't have to thank me for asking. I truly want to know."

"I know, David. I just appreciate that you really want to know," she said as she started to feel uncomfortable.

David was too real, too genuine, and too good. She didn't know how to deal with his type of man—she was used to the phony liars who didn't take the time to cater to their women. David was truly the opposite—he made her feel like he would take care of her every emotional need.

"Well, what's for dinner?" she asked, trying to break the awkward silence.

"I brought some filet mignon, baked potatoes, yellow rice, and broccoli," he said as he backed away from her and started unpacking the basket.

"Damn, that sounds good," she said.

"Yeah, and for dessert I brought some of your favorite banana pudding from Sarah Brown Catering."

"Oh my gosh, you didn't go all the way over there, did you? Just for dessert?"

"It wasn't that far out of the way."

"You're too much, Dave. Thanks, sweetie—where is it at?"

"Nope, you can't have any until later."

She put on her baby pout face and backed away from the basket. He reached out to hold her again.

"Go lie down, get comfortable. Let me prepare dinner and you meet me on the couch. We will watch a movie and eat dinner and then we will enjoy dessert. How does that sound?"

"That sounds nice," she said. She felt the mushy feeling again, but this time she wasn't uncomfortable. She actually realized this was something she could get used to.

111

Playtime

It wasn't like before—Chrasey didn't just want to drop off her kids with her parents and go see Trevor at his house, or go catch a movie. It was a different ball game now—they had to be more discreet about things. He was coming around her way to get his daughter, so Chrasey told him to meet her at the neighborhood McDonald's Playland.

The kids were playing together nicely, with fifteen or so others. She and Trevor were sitting on the side, eating their meals, talking about their lives as usual. He was sharing the latest about his daughter's mother, and, of course, she was sharing the latest with Keith. Trevor still couldn't believe that Keith had gotten some woman pregnant, and he told her he was proud of her for sticking it out. He said she was a real woman, like Hillary Clinton, standing by her man. She didn't know about all of that, but she appreciated the acknowledgement. Keith damn sure didn't appreciate it.

She and Trevor had an understanding about what things would be like between the two of them. She explained that she did want to go on dealing with him. She also explained that her family was her first priority. He respected that, and he was willing to be respectful of her situation. He also explained that the only reason he was still around was because he really cared about her. He said from the day he met her, he knew she was a beautiful person; he also knew from day one that her husband didn't appreciate her. He made it very clear that he wasn't going to stop his life, either; he was going to date and see other people, but until the day came that he met that special someone he wanted to marry, he would be there for her whenever she needed him.

They'd been sitting there for about forty-five minutes so far. She had told Keith where she was going, because it made no sense lying—the kids could tell him, anyway. She tried to make plans that she didn't have to lie about, but could just leave information out of. For example, she was really at McDonald's—she just didn't have to mention she was meeting someone there. She told Keith she would be home in a bit, and to go ahead and fix himself something to eat. So as she was sitting there with Trevor, she wasn't thinking about Keith. She was relaxed, just taking a break from her demanding life. Keith was the last person she was expecting, but as she looked over her shoulder for a split second, she caught a glimpse of his face. She looked back and it was Keith, walking towards them. Trevor could see in her face that something had happened, but he was playing it smart and safe—he didn't look over his shoulder. He just remained natural—he could see she was keeping her eyes on someone. They weren't sitting that close to one another, and there were other parents sitting around them as well. It wasn't as if they were in some private area of McDonald's, so she knew how she had to handle this.

Within seconds, Keith walked up to her and said hello. Although there was absolutely nothing visibly strange about her sitting next to this guy, she could tell Keith was a little suspicious of her male company. Still, she showed no trace of guilt—she was about to handle it like a professional.

"Hey, baby," she said, just as normal.

He said hello back, and glanced at Trevor. Then she looked at Trevor and said to him, "This is my husband."

She looked back at Keith and said, "We were just talking about how hard it is to pull your kids out of these places. His daughter has been in there for an hour already."

They all gave a phony laugh. She couldn't tell if Keith bought it, but it was her story. Trevor caught on to what she was doing. He was just some man who was in McDonald's with his kid, not the man that she got butt naked with and had about an hour of sex with about every two weeks or so.

"What are you doing here?" she asked Keith.

"I was hungry, figured I would come hang out with you guys."

"Oh, that's nice. We were about to go in a few, though."

Trevor took that as a cue, she guessed.

"Speaking of going, let me do the mission impossible and finally get this girl out of here," Trevor said as he got up and walked toward his daughter inside the big air castle. When he stepped away, he said a phony good-bye still pretending like he was just the friendly guy waiting in McDonald's. She gave a friendly and thankful good-bye, back.

Of all days for Keith to want to come play family—just her luck. From the look in Keith's eyes, he didn't know what to think. He seemed to be behaving normally, but she couldn't tell if, in the back of his mind, he wondered if he had just caught her in McDonald's with her mystery man, or was she just being paranoid? Under normal circumstances, what he saw didn't have to be that peculiar. However, neither of them trusted the other, and deep down he figured that she had to be getting something from somewhere else. He just wouldn't have thought at McDonald's.

Trevor got his daughter out, she said good-bye to Kelsey and Quinton, and then they walked out. She and Keith sat there a little longer before they headed out. Chrasey felt awkward as Trevor left— she knew he was watching her and Keith together through the glass as he walked out. He'd never seen them together, and she wondered if he was curious now. Maybe he wondered if Keith actually was a caring husband, and he was just being a homewrecker. She was sure seeing Keith just come to hang with us made it look like she'd been lying about him not paying her and the kids any attention. Still, even a blind man could see the distance between her and Keith. They couldn't hide that, and she was sure Trevor saw it. She just hoped that he wouldn't change his mind about being her Prince Charming.

112

Confessions

Jayon had spent the night at Jordan's house. They watched a movie, and just spent the day chilling. When they were out in the backyard having a drink and playing cards, she noticed that Jay's phone was lighting up but wasn't ringing or vibrating. She reached toward his pocket clip and picked up the phone. She saw "Michelle" in the Caller ID.

"Who is Michelle?" she asked.

"A friend of mine—why you checking my Caller ID," he asked as he took his phone back.

"A friend from where? And why is your phone on SILENT?"

"Why are you grilling me like this?"

"Because I want to know."

"She is a friend . . . actually you met her—I brought her by the of-fice once," Jayon replied with obvious aggravation.

"Why is your phone silenced, and why is she calling you?"

"Just was, no reason, and I don't know why she is calling. Maybe to say hello . . . Why don't you call her and ask her since you have so many questions?"

She didn't have time for these games. After all of these years of being friends, a year into a relationship she was finally seeing the ugly side of Jayon. It's unbelievable, when you know somebody so well, and they still never cease to amaze you.

"You know what, I'm not up for games tonight. You want to keep se-crets, fine."

"What secrets?"

"Don't tell me that she is just your friend—I know she is not. That day in the office I knew that. You keep wanting to lie to me about stuff, fine."

"She is my friend—we slept together before, but she is my friend," he decided to admit.

"So, you weren't going to tell me about that?"

"For what? We weren't together when she and I first slept together."

"Well, she is still calling you—you don't think you could have shared that with me?"

"I'm not going through this. If you have a problem with it, I don't know what to tell you."

"You don't know what to tell me? After all these years, when I'm getting a divorce because of you—you don't know what to tell me? You know what, Jayon? Fuck you!!"

She said that in a much louder tone than her previous comment, and she stood up and went inside. She said it, and although she meant it from her heart, it wasn't that simple. She was pissed off. She really wanted to curse him out. Tell him, how dare he embarrass her like that. How dare he wait until she was this involved with him to start telling her shit like, *if you have a problem with it, I don't know what to tell you.*

"That asshole," she mumbled to herself. The timing had to be crazy, but not too long after she and Omar signed their divorce papers, she was starting to feel that all she had done just wasn't worth it. If she was meant to be with Jayon, the day would come—it just didn't seem that now was the time.

Jayon followed her inside the house and slowly pinned her up against the living room wall and said, "I met Michelle a few years after I met you—I'm sure I mentioned her to you but it was nothing. We were cool for a while—we slept together one night, and I really thought I mentioned it to you. It was years ago . . ." Jayon said.

His tone was fairly low and it sounded like he was trying to make her feel better about the situation—he wanted to make sure she knew everything. He continued, "We kept in touch on and off, and it was the biggest mistake of my life, but I slept with her twice this past year, and now she won't stop calling me."

She couldn't have been hearing him right. This past year he was with her. "This past year?" she asked.

He held her tight in his arms, and she knew that was his *yes.* She jerked him off of her and walked away.

"Please get out of my house, Jay."

"Jordan, at least hear what I have to say."

"Jayon, get the fuck out of my house—now!"

He stood there, not moving an inch. He was thinking of what he could say to get her to calm down. It was too late for that—there was nothing he could say. She couldn't even put her mind on her heart, but subconsciously she felt the sharp pain right through it. It was no time to dwell on it. First she had to get him out of her house, and then she would tend to her wound.

"It didn't mean anything to me, I swear. I want to be with you—she means nothing to me," he said.

She started to walk toward her front door—it didn't seem he understood how serious she was. He followed behind her.

"J, I didn't know if you were ever going to get your divorce, so I didn't know if we really had a future. I didn't want to stress you about it, either. I know it's not right—I was wrong—that's why I'm admitting it. I want to start fresh."

She looked at him, and handed him the key to his apartment.

"Jayon, please get out."

After standing there for a few seconds, he started to walk toward the door. He tried to give her a kiss on the forehead, but she moved back, and as soon as he stepped through the door she closed it behind him.

Call her naive or blind. Say by now women should know we can't put anything past a man, but she still believed there were just some things you didn't expect from certain people . . . and this she did not expect from Jayon. Deep down inside, she felt so disappointed. She felt hoodwinked. How could someone you feel you know so well, actually be so different?

In all reality, as much she hated to say it, he was just like all men, and here she really thought she would be happier with Jayon. During that honeymoon phase that things felt so good. That was her fear, that things weren't what they seemed. She just didn't think her life could be that jinxed, that this could turn out this bad.

She'd been with Omar all those years, and to think she gave it up, thinking it would be so much better with Jayon. He would be a friend and a lover all in one. That's what she'd wanted. Who could've known that once he became her lover, he would no longer be her friend?

She knew in her heart that this was it. She could never even begin to forgive him for what he'd done. She never thought Jayon, her best friend, would lie to her. Never. So she knew this wasn't going to blow over. Just the thought of him sleeping with some other woman was enough; then to think how he had to be deceitful the nights he was with her, and how he probably was kissing or having sex with her the same or next day. Just to think of it brought her to tears. She never went through this in her marriage, but she was dealing with it now. Talk about punishment for your actions.

She'd seen signs before tonight—it wasn't like this was their only issue. She just knew that with him she had to put great effort into it, because she had altered so much of her life to be with him. She hadn't prepared herself for it not working out. There were things with Jayon that she dealt with because she wanted them to work out, but she noticed that he wasn't as caring toward her as she thought he'd be.

Jayon's lack of emotion toward everything sometimes made it seem like he didn't care. All these years she thought it was his cool swagger, and early on she found it attractive. However, Jordan found it hard to be in an adult relationship when he didn't communicate. He could talk for hours on the phone with his boys, but if Jordan wanted to talk about an issue, he was damn near speechless. It drove her up a wall.

Then to make matters worse Jayon stopped wanting to have sex. Early on they were like two rabbits, having sex like every other night at least. These days it was once a week if she was lucky. He could go days without it. It was like she hooked up with an old man. That was another reason why hearing he had slept with somebody else made her absolutely furious.

She just had to deal with it the hard way: they were no *Brown Sugar*, they were no *When Harry Met Sally*, and they were no *Shark Tale*. They were just two people in lust who settled for what was easy. She just couldn't believe that a year into this relationship, she was finding this out. She felt so hoodwinked and bamboozled. It was like Omar's perfect revenge. She broke his heart, and less than two months after their divorce was official, Jayon had broken hers.

The last person she wanted to know about this was Omar—she knew he would gloat in all his glory. Karma was something else for real. Although, she didn't feel what she did was wrong, she could see why her guilt was killing her. She must've really done Omar wrong, because what else could she have done to deserve this? This was like some cruel trick.

She knew she had to face the world tomorrow. She was determined not to cry or mope too much—too embarrassed to do that. She'd bragged too much, had confessed her undying love. How could she go back and tell everybody she'd been a fool? She'd left her husband for a man who she didn't even really know, at the end of the day.

113

All Hers

Tony had called Dakota three times since this morning, and she'd ignored all three of his calls. "What is there to talk about? Go talk to Jonelle," she murmured to herself when she saw he was trying to call her. There was no need for them to pretend now, or to continue what they were doing before.

She loved Tony—she even missed Tony—but she loved and missed herself more. She'd spent so much time trying to keep him that she'd lost herself. The way she wanted him to love her was too much for him, but yet she'd settled for it and actually pretended like she was satisfied. She knew there had been a point in her life when she was cool with that type of open relationship with no strings attached. Good sex and no drama, no commitment or temptations. Even with a clear understanding of that logic, she'd outgrown it and was unable to admit it. She wanted more and was able now to request it. It was a bed she'd made, and she'd been forced to lie in it. Tony knew, she had started to want more. He knew she had come to a place where just the good old times wasn't enough, but he didn't try to change. He would have continued like this forever, hurting her and Jonelle. Well, she could have him. Dakota didn't want that pain anymore, and she didn't want the drama. Besides, now that she'd lost their baby, Jonelle had something with him that she didn't have, and she'd be damned if she'd try to get pregnant again to war with her. The next time she got pregnant, she hoped it would be on purpose and with a man she didn't have to talk into wanting to keep it.

"'Kota, I hope you're feeling OK. I really want to come see you. Maybe we can go out to dinner or something or to that bar you love on Thirty-ninth and Lexington. I just want to try to see you. I really miss you. Please call me back this time."

That was the second-to-last message on her voice mail.

"'Kota, I have been calling you for a couple days now, and you haven't been returning my calls. I'm not sure what the problem is, but this is crazy. Just a few months ago we were having a baby together, and now this week I can't even get ahold of you. Did I do something to you? Please call me back so we can talk."

She saved the messages and hung up. The reality was, he hadn't done a thing to her, but that was the problem. It was always what he didn't do, not what he did.

She wanted to call him back, but she didn't know how to explain to him yet how she was feeling. She just woke up one day and realized that he would never be able to give her what she wanted and he didn't want to. Besides, after speaking to Jonelle a month ago, she really realized that he was playing them both, but at least Jonelle had enough self-respect to have a problem with it. Here Dakota was, knowingly going along with his bullshit, and looking like an idiot.

She had spent the last few months pretending, and now she was finally ready to get real again. Tony was a fraudulent part of her life. She liked the way he made her look—he made her life look so cool. A rich, handsome, well-known man, and he was all hers; what girl doesn't like how that looks? The problem was, he was far from all hers. She had all the other hallmarks of an independent woman—good job, nice car, and comfortable home. The only thing she lacked was her man, so he'd been her way of having it all. She was able to show off and let everyone admire her life. They couldn't see the times she lay in her bed waiting on him, or crying herself to sleep because she knew that he was out with some other girl. All they needed to know was that this was the man in her perfect life.

She didn't know how to explain all of this to Tony. He would just tell her that she was overreacting, and maybe the miscarriage was still getting to her. He always tried to make her think she was the problem. The thing is, she knew that he knew he was playing her—he just wanted her to remain a cooperative player. She didn't know why, though—he could have had any girl he wanted, so why didn't he just leave her the hell alone when he realized she wanted more than he did. The sex was damn good, but still. He couldn't just hope things would be like this forever.

She wondered what he was doing with Jonelle. She knew deep in her heart that she was sitting pretty in one of his plush homes, being treated like a queen. Especially after all the things she'd told Jonelle on the phone. He probably bought her all types of expensive jewelry to get out of the doghouse. He probably said all kinds of negative stuff about Dakota to make her feel like Dakota was just some groupie slut trying to break them up. He had to have told her that, in order for her not to have called Dakota back. He had to have, because she couldn't have just fallen for a simple lie. It had to be embellished, laced with material items to make her think that it was even better than just an embellished lie. Any woman dating or married to a star or rich man learns those principles quickly. When their man cheats, messes up, or disrespects them, they forgive faster because they know a broke man gives the same drama but with way less perks. It's almost every day we hear about a regular guy that's not famous dogging his girl out, and all he can do is say he's sorry. In the relationship all he brings to the table is the same, if not less, than the female does. So what's the gain? You went through that bullshit and will again for a man who can't do shit for you? With a man with money, you say to yourself at least this man can pay all the bills, got me pushing a Benz, can afford anything I ask for, and I get to live lavish and not have to work for it. It seems almost silly not to find it in your heart to forgive him. The forgiving heart of a kept woman makes so much more sense than the forgiving heart of a woman with a no-good, worthless man.

Well, let Jonelle have him—she couldn't blame her. She wouldn't, though. She refused to be in his lineup anymore, especially since she knew he wasn't going to change. He would be using the factors that made him a great catch to lower her standards forever. Who knew how many more of them there were Dakota figured, but she was retiring from her second-place position. From now on, if she couldn't be number one, and the one and only, she didn't want to run the race.

114

It Was Fun

"What happened to us?" she said to Jayon.
They were parked in his new, all-black 2006 Audi A4 in front
of her house. It was like things had changed before they'd begun, and
she didn't even see it coming.

"Jordan, I never wanted to hurt you. I would do anything to take it
back."

"So then why did you do it?"

"I don't know," he said.

She couldn't believe this was all he had to say to her, that he didn't
know. He couldn't give her any more of that shit. She'd left her husband for him, and he couldn't even tell her more than *he didn't know.*
She tried her best to remain calm.

"Jayon—*you don't know?* That's all you can say to explain how things
have turned out?"

"Jordan, I love you. Always have and always will, but I don't know if
I can make you happy."

"What?" she said, clearly pissed at his comment.

"I don't know what you want from me anymore—it was cool in the
beginning, and I enjoyed every second of it, but . . ."

"Don't even give a *but* to that . . . did you not realize during that beginning that me and you were starting something that we were supposed to work at? Did you realize I was leaving my husband to make
this work?"

"Don't put that on me, Jordan. You said you didn't leave your husband because of me—you didn't want to be with him anymore anyway. I just happened to make it easier, you said. So don't put it on me."

That was it for her. She was almost speechless, not including the complete curse-out she wanted to do. She said to herself, it *isn't worth it to let him see me sweat.* This was something she had to deal with inside, on her own, and then just get the pain and tears out later when she was in her house alone. Then she realized he'd had it too easy, and she decided to tell him what was on her mind.

"You have a lot of fucking nerve. *Don't put it on you?* . . . How could you even fix your lips to say that?"

"I'm just saying, don't say how you left Omar because of me. I didn't ask you to do that, and we made it quite clear I wasn't the cause of that breakup."

"You know what, Jayon? You're a real asshole . . . and you're right—you weren't the reason I left Omar, and therefore there is nothing more to discuss," she said as she started to gather her stuff.

"I want this to work, Jordan—I still feel that we are meant to be. If you can just find it in your heart to forgive me."

"I don't have it in my heart, Jayon. We have had our fun—thank you for making my divorce easier, and you take care of yourself. I'll talk to you later," she said as she opened the car door and started to get out.

"Jordan, we can do this. We have been friends too long not to make this work."

"I don't need anyone or anything to make me happy, and you can go fuck yourself," she said, and slammed his car door. She was hoping to break the hinges off. He thought he was all fly in his new car—the shit wasn't no Bentley or nothing, it was still just an Audi. Her 2006 X5 was better than his car, and he had the nerve to act like he was doing shit for her life. Yeah, he was some good sex when she'd needed it, and when he was the best friend she fell in love with, he was a great companion. But ever since he started to act like this new Jayon guy, he couldn't do nothing for her that she couldn't do for herself. She just couldn't believe that he'd changed like that. It was like his good and evil side, right in front of her eyes, and he had the nerve to act like she shouldn't be upset.

Once she had put her belongings down on her couch inside the house, she heard the ring tone of "Lovers and Friends" coming from her phone. It was Jayon calling—she just wanted to toss the phone across the room. She damn sure didn't want to hear that song right now.

"I've been knowing you for a long while, but sexing never crossed my mind, but tonight I see something in ya, that makes me want to get with ya . . ."

She silenced her ringer and walked upstairs.

She remembered when that was one of her favorite songs. She immediately thought of her and Jayon's fairy tale story when she heard it. Now it was like torture, reminding her of the mistake she'd made. It made it so much worse because it was Jayon, her friend since her sophomore year of college. She wished it was some guy she'd met out one night—then she wouldn't feel so torn apart right now. She was not only breaking up with her boyfriend, she was breaking up with her best friend. She definitely wasn't ready for the pain that was to come from this. She would probably bury herself back in her work, and hopefully by the time she looked up, it would be all over.

115

It Takes Two

Until death do us part. Chrasey had been through way too much with this man to just walk away. He owed her his life, and she was going to take it. They were going to remain married, and raise their kids, and make the best of it.

Keith had his daughter to take care of, and she just learned to deal with that. She wasn't going to be angry, she was going to accept the cards she'd been dealt. Her husband cheated on her, and he was stupid enough to get the woman pregnant. Maybe Chrasey was stupid for staying, but if it wasn't for their kids together, she'd go. Why should she let him go so Lourdes could have him to raise their daughter together? She took enough from her—she wasn't giving up that easy.

Just because Chrasey was staying didn't mean she was going to submit to suffering. She knew the marriage was pretty much hopeless. They had nothing left between them but history, and that wasn't enough to make them look forward to coming home. In theory, God puts people in your life for a reason. Trevor was her gift. Even if it was only for a season, he helped her get through. When she came home at night, and Keith was just sitting on the couch not talking to her, she felt a comfort knowing that Trevor wanted to talk to her. Even the nights that they didn't talk, she knew that he would be on the other end if she wanted him to be. She also knew that when she needed some affection or good loving, he would meet her at the closest motel and put in some work.

Keith didn't seem to notice or care that their marriage was right back where it had been. It was actually worse, because now there were trust issues that they couldn't erase, and words exchanged that they wouldn't forget. The baby hardly came up—it was out of sight but not out of mind for her.

They probably never would have the healthiest marriage, but they were honoring our vows, for better or worse. Working things out with Keith kept her hopes and promise alive. Trevor kept her alive.

116

Anything's Possible

Who would've thought a girl like her, fast-tailed Dakota Watkins, would be able to have a settled-down relationship with one man? She guessed they were wrong, that you can't turn a ho into a house-wife, 'cause she was doing a pretty good job at it. She wasn't his wife, but she might as well be. She and David had something really good going. They lived together, and picked out her engagement ring last week.

They decided to stay at her place instead of his, because her condo was bigger and his was farther away from both of their jobs. She'd met all of David's friends, and he introduced her as wifey. Whenever he did go out, which was not often, he called to check on her regularly until he got home. She cooks dinner for him almost every night; he often comes home to find her in her lingerie with a mood-set room. He loves when she does that.

All she knew was she was going to make sure her daughter, when she was fortunate enough to have one, learned to carry herself like a lady. She'd always thought because she was a diva that she was a lady. She realized now that being a lady is respecting your body. It didn't just mean the nicest clothes, expensive jewelry, nice cars, and being able to get the finest men. It was what you did with all of that, and how you obtained those things. She'd used her body to get way too much of what she had, and as she got older, she felt less like a diva and more like a doormat. She wanted to make sure her daughter experienced life, but knew when to respect herself. Her mother never knew how to do that, but that's what she will have her godmothers, Aunt Chrasey and Aunt Jordan, for. They were good with it.

She never thought she'd be looking at wedding magazines, but she picked up two this week. She thought he was going to ask at his family's Thanksgiving dinner—he'd told her in so many words. So, with a wedding in her near future, she knew for a fact that anything's possible.

Tony still called from time to time, hoping that she would fall. He told her one time that he really wished he'd realized how thankful he should have been to have her. All these other women were just about the money. He was tired of Jonelle mooching, he said; at least with Dakota, she had her own, and he knew she wasn't with him for money. She'd tried to tell him that before. Too bad he'd realized it after the fact, like most men usually do. He never did marry Jonelle to her knowledge, and she was probably still waiting on the day. At least with her man, Dakota knew he was proposing to her because he wanted to. Not just to shut her up and make her happy.

117

Karma

They say what goes around comes around—got damn, they weren't lying. Jordan put her pride aside and told Omar she'd made the biggest mistake of her life. She told it all. She told him how Jayon cheated on her, and had the nerve to tell her that he still wanted them to still be friends. She knew he would get a thrill out of it, but she deserved it.

She was all prepared for the "I told you so" and the rubbing in her face. But she was not ready for the news. She couldn't forget the way he'd broken it to her.

"I'm not going to say, good for you. I'm not going to ask why you are telling me. I'm just going to make it very clear, you made your bed, you lie in it. I am engaged to somebody else, so I am definitely not an option for you."

I am engaged to somebody else, so I am definitely not an option for you . . . I am engaged to somebody else, so I am definitely not an option for you . . . I am engaged to somebody else, so I am definitely not an option for you . . . That must have echoed about three or four times before her brain even began to compute it. She was standing in his living room while he sat on his couch, watching television. He'd barely given her eye contact whenever she'd come to pick Jason up, but when he said that, he had looked her right in her eyes. She could tell he wanted to make sure she got that message.

"Wow . . . really?" she said, trying to hide overwhelming shock.

"Yeah—really, Jordan," he replied with a tone that included the *that's right, and you can't say two damn things to me about it.*

"The girl you have been seeing for a few months?"

"Yeah, the one you heard about a few months ago. I have known her a lot longer than a few months."

"Oh—well, that's nice, Omar. Congratulations." She tried to keep up the act as the knots began to form in her stomach.

As much as she tried to hide it, she could tell he saw it. He saw right through her fake nonchalance and was staring right at the pain written all over her face. She could tell he initially got a kick out of telling her. It was his chance to finally regain the pride that he always felt she took when he groveled to no avail. He had his opportunity to say, *see, I rise.* She was happy to see him rise, she truly was. It was just the worst time to find this out, especially because she wanted her family back. She'd given it away and had no right to ask for it back. When they say Karma is a motherfucker, they aren't exaggerating.

Omar had her son and a new woman in his life. What more could he ask for? Damn, sure not her. Who wanted her after what she had done to him? He had every right to treat her the way he has, she thought. She'd not only broken his heart, she'd embarrassed him in front of everyone who knew them. Although she had spent the past year justifying her actions, and she felt that he'd brought it on himself, the fact remained that what she did hurt him, and she knew it. Hurt turns to hate quicker than anything else with men. The irony is, with all the lines she gave him as justification for her behavior, he could use them right back on her if she had even one disagreement about his engagement, and he knew that. That's why he said it so firmly.

However, she could tell he didn't feel as good about gloating when he saw the pain she was hiding. Deep down, as much as he hated her, he probably pitied her. He had a big enough drop of love left for her to know that she was suffering enough, and he didn't need to make it worse. He may have even felt bad, as did she when the shoe was on the other foot. She knew how that felt, to have to feel bad for making a decision that makes you happy and hurts someone else, and she didn't want to make it any harder. So with no words of guilt, no tears for him to see, and no begging, she just started to walk away. Jason was waiting out in the car for her; she had picked him up to take him to a movie. Omar didn't move from where he was, didn't get up to walk her to the door. As she reached for the doorknob to walk out, she turned back around and said, "Omar, I'm not just saying this because of you getting engaged or the fact that I played myself. But I need you to know, because I've never had the chance to say it before, I'm sorry. I truly am sorry, and I know deep down I deserve all of this."

At first, he said nothing and didn't even look her way. Then he looked up at her, and said "We cool, Jordan—I don't resent you. It just is what it is." That was Omar's way of telling her, *I don't have any issues. Do you, because I'm doing me.* She got the hint and as she went to step through the door, he added, "And Jayon is a fool just like I was."

She wanted to die inside. His comment made her feel a little better, but it made two points. One was that he was a big enough man to still say something nice under the circumstances and not make it worse than it had to be, but more importantly, Jayon was no better, and she should have stuck with what she had.

"Thanks," she said as she walked out. Jason was in the car playing with his new PSP game his father bought him. She sat down in the car; just seeing him playing innocently, she realized Jason was all she had. This time, when Omar told her to "do you," she realized this is what she should have been doing last time he said that as well. Jason *was* her. He should have been her strength, not Jayon. If she had realized this then, she wouldn't be in this situation.

The pain won't go away tomorrow, but one day she would wake up and happiness would be shining on her face again. A true diva picks herself up. She knew being alone may be a good thing for her. She could learn to love herself again, and one day possibly love another as she did Omar and Jayon.

Hey, you win some, you lose some—she lived this lesson for a living, and she knew it better than most. Now she also learned another lesson firsthand, and that is, what goes around comes around.

DIVA DIARIES

JANINE A. MORRIS

ABOUT THIS GUIDE

The suggested questions are intended to enhance
your group's reading of this book.

DISCUSSION QUESTIONS

1. Do you think deep down Dakota was ashamed of her promiscuous lifestyle?

2. Should Chrasey have been faithful despite the way she was being treated by her husband?

3. Was Jordan wrong to not lower her career standards to be a better wife and mother?

4. Was Dakota trifling for messing with Tony, knowing he was in a relationship with Jonelle?

5. Should Chrasey have left Keith after she found out for sure about his indiscretions?

6. Did Jordan start a new relationship too soon?

7. Who was better for Dakota? David or a changed-for-the-better Tony?

8. Was Dakota wrong for blaming Lexia and/or ruining her friendship over a man?

9. Do you think Dakota will be "happy ever after" for real?

10. Did Jordan deserve bad karma for not working it out with her husband?